W9-CDS-883

The Other Windsor Girl

Bremen Public Library
Bremen, Indiana

Bremen Public Library
Bremen, Indiana

The Other Windsor Girl

A Novel of Princess Margaret, Royal Rebel

Georgie Blalock

WM

WILLIAM MORROW

An Imprint of HarperCollins*Publishers*

This book is a work of fiction. References to real people, events, establishments, organizations, or locales are intended only to provide a sense of authenticity, and are used fictitiously. All other characters, and all incidents and dialogue, are drawn from the author's imagination and are not to be construed as real.

P.S.™ is a trademark of HarperCollins Publishers.

THE OTHER WINDSOR GIRL. Copyright © 2019 by Georgie Blalock. All rights reserved. Printed in the United States of America. No part of this book may be used or reproduced in any manner whatsoever without written permission except in the case of brief quotations embodied in critical articles and reviews. For information, address HarperCollins Publishers, 195 Broadway, New York, NY 10007.

HarperCollins books may be purchased for educational, business, or sales promotional use. For information, please email the Special Markets Department at SPsales@harpercollins.com.

FIRST EDITION

Designed by Diahann Sturge

Library of Congress Cataloging-in-Publication Data

Names: Blalock, Georgie, 1974– author.
Title: The other Windsor girl : a novel of love, royalty, whiskey, and cigarettes / Georgie Blalock.
Description: First edition. | New York, NY : William Morrow, 2019. |
  Identifiers: LCCN 2018059054 (print) | LCCN 2019000677 (ebook) | ISBN 9780062871480 (ebook) | ISBN 006287148X (ebook) | ISBN 9780062871497 (trade pbk. : alk. paper) | ISBN 0062871498 (trade pbk. : alk. paper)
Subjects: LCSH: Margaret, Princess, Countess of Snowdon, 1930-2002—Fiction. | Nobility—Great Britain—Fiction. | GSAFD: Historical fiction.
Classification: LCC PS3612.E2236 (ebook) | LCC PS3612.E2236 P75 2019 (print) | DDC 813/.6—dc23
LC record available at https://lccn.loc.gov/2018059054

ISBN 978-0-06-287149-7

19 20 21 22 23   LSC   10 9 8 7 6 5 4 3 2 1

The Other Windsor Girl

Chapter One

London, Fall 1949

The Honorable Vera Strathmore touched her naked ring finger, tracing a circle where her engagement ring had once been. At the front of the Weatherly Hall ballroom, the two-carat mine-cut diamond set in Welsh gold glistened on the slender hand of the Honorable Ursula Lawrence. She stood beside David Lowell in a new evening dress of peach satin that must have taken ages' worth of rations to save for. The young couple beamed while Lord Lowell gave the toast, his round stomach covered by a white waistcoat, his thinning hair revealing a strong forehead and a sharp nose so similar to Henry's, Vera's onetime fiancé.

Gentlemen and ladies of both distinguished years and the younger set filled the old ballroom, the family jewels decorating the ladies' wrists and necks sparkling in the low light of the crystal chandeliers. Footmen in rented red livery moved stealthily to refill champagne flutes or provide new ones to those who'd mislaid theirs, the young servers' attire a sharp contrast to the dark evening suits of the invited gentlemen. Despite the austerity crippling everyone, Lord and Lady Lowell had cobbled together enough to make an impressive showing tonight for their son's engagement party.

Vera clasped her hands together tight, struggling to drive back the anger filling her. Ursula and David had every right to bask in the flood of good wishes in the same way Vera and Henry had when they'd stood there five years earlier, Henry handsome in his British Army uniform and Vera making do with her debutante ball gown redone. Ursula clasped David's arm and fell against him with smiles and giggles, the engagement ring sparkling on her finger. It was a Lowell family heirloom dating from the reign of George I. Henry had given it to Vera, but it hadn't felt right to keep it after Henry's death.

Lord Lowell raised his champagne flute in a final toast and the guests' cheers and applause rang up to the plaster-ceiling medallions. Vera didn't clap, afraid to move for fear of losing the tight hold she had on herself. It took as much self-control to remain there in grace and poise as it had taken to stand with the dignity expected of a war mourner at Henry's funeral. People had cared about her suffering back then and had even tried to comfort her. No one gave a single thought to it tonight.

"Rather dowdy affair," her mother drawled from beside her when the cheers faded and the string quartet resumed their playing. She held a champagne flute tipped at a languid angle to her body, the wide shoulders and straight lines of her dark gray satin dress suitable for a woman of mature years. She was slender, with hazel eyes and light brown hair, the only traits she shared with Vera. She peered down her long nose at old Lady Malvern, who passed them wearing a fur stole that smelled of mothballs. "And why don't they turn up the lights? Who do they think they're fooling keeping everything so dim?"

"Maybe they want to pretend for one night that things are the way they used to be," Vera whispered, glancing around to make sure no one had overheard her mother's callous remark. After the long years of the war, and with austerity and rations still choking them, turning down the lights made it easier to believe that things hadn't changed, that titles still meant money and status and position. Full power made glaringly obvious the faded carpets, the worn furniture cushions, and the chipped paint on the chair rails and molding.

"Curse Hitler and the damn death duties." Her mother tilted the remains of the champagne into her mouth, wrinkling her nose at the questionable vintage before exchanging it with a full one from the tray of a passing footman. She didn't offer to take one for Vera, allowing the footman and his tray to fade off into the crowd. "I just heard the most surprising news from your aunt Augusta. Lady Sommeville's daughter, Matilda, is engaged, which I find incredibly difficult to believe. She's the kind of aristocratic daughter that makes one think the laws of consanguinity should have been better enforced."

"Mother, really?" Vera sighed, in no mood for her vitriol.

"Don't be silly; you know it's true."

Yes, it was, but it seemed so petty to say it aloud. Vera touched her bare ring finger again. "Who's the fiancé?"

"Some officer in the Navy. At least Princess Elizabeth has made that choice of husband fashionable." Her mother waved the half-full flute, making the champagne slosh perilously close to the edge before settling safely back in the bottom. "The wedding will be in December."

The same month Vera would have been wed if the war had ended sooner or the German's aim had been higher. Vera glanced around for the footman and his silver salver of champagne, wondering where he'd gone. She needed a drink, perhaps the whole trayful, dignity and poise be damned. "I'll be sure to send a gift with my regrets."

"It'd be better if you attended. Her fiancé must have a great many friends, and you can't afford to be picky. After all, nobody likes a bitter old spinster."

"One would think I didn't have a reason to be bitter." Her mother's compassion and understanding never ceased to amaze her. It was why she kept her dreams of writing in New York to herself; she didn't want them minced to pieces by her mother's sharp tongue.

"One would think you'd realize it's better for you to be pleasant and at least try to land a gentleman rather than standing here like some forlorn wraith. After all, you can't expect me and your father to keep you forever. Our resources aren't endless."

Vera curled her hands into fists at her sides, detesting having their usual breakfast conversation moved to the evening. What she wouldn't give to escape from it all. "I have my writing."

"Oh well, there's a comfort." Her mother finished her champagne in one gulp. "Scribbling little articles on British manners for crass Americans. How lucrative." She shoved the empty flute at Vera before threading her way into the crowd.

Vera gripped the flute tight, wanting to slam it to the floor and scatter the pieces across the polished wood planks, but she wasn't one to make a spectacle of herself. Instead, she turned and marched to the open French door leading to the portico off the back of the house. Passing by the portrait of some distant Lowell relation, she left the warmth of the ballroom for the cutting chill of the autumn night.

Vera's breath curled into a cloud above her head as she sighed in relief to find herself alone. It was too cold out here for the others, in their thin chiffon and silk gowns saved and mended from before the war, but Vera welcomed the biting air. She laid her hand on the thick railing at the far end, the stone damp beneath her fingertips, the bottom of the flute clinking against it. Weatherly Hall stood in the countryside just outside London, a stately Georgian home that had once been a royal hunting retreat. The lights of London were just visible on the horizon, and Vera shivered. The last time she'd stood here at night had been in January 1944, when she'd watched the searchlights cutting through the dark sky and the distant flashes of the German bombs pummeling the city in one last attempt to bring Britain to its knees before the Germans lost. David, little more than sixteen, had stood beside her, along with Lord and Lady Lowell. During the deadly bombardment, the four of them had prayed for the survival of London, and England, and Henry. God had answered two of their three prayers.

Below her, the manor's green lawn spread out, the flatness of it sloping to a copse weakly illuminated by a half-moon. There, just visible in the spreading thickness of the grass, rested the tan gravel path leading down to a lake beyond the trees. She and Henry used to walk there when he'd come home on leave. An old Grecian temple overlooked the water, a folly built by some ancestor with far more resources than the current economy allowed. Henry had proposed to her beneath the dome, in the shade of one of the columns supporting it. Thankfully, she couldn't see it from where she stood.

Vera's fingers tightened on the stone, the roughness of it biting into her skin. What the devil had she come here for? Self-flagellation wasn't her habit and still she'd accepted the invitation, enduring her mother, the tart champagne, and a tight girdle to make a suitable presentation on behalf of the family. After all, as her mother would say, there was no point crying over the past since there was nothing she could do to change it. It was the lack of anything arising to replace even a tenth a long breath to form a cloud between them. "I'm sure your mother has been a great comfort to you this evening."

"Isn't she always?" Vera leaned against the balustrade, the cold stone cutting through the chiffon of her light blue dress. Through the French doors, she watched the young couples shifting back in forth in time to the music. Just behind them, on the other side of the dance floor, her mother stood with Lady Sommeville, holding up Vera's younger sister Alice's left hand and showing off the diamond ring adorning it. The diamond was far more modest than the Lowells' heirloom, but Alice, barring some awful railway accident, was more likely to keep it and everything that went with it. All Vera had left was the fantasy she'd nurtured since Henry's loss of writing her great novel while working in New York, and even that was growing more distant with each passing year. With the devaluation of the pound, her hoarded money wouldn't go as far as it might have even a few months earlier. It was as if the government was conspiring with fate to keep her in England and ruin everything.

Vera straightened and pushed back her shoulders, tired of this misery. Weakness, as her mother was fond of saying, wasn't an admirable trait. It was the single thing on which they agreed. "But I had my day. It's someone else's turn now."

"That's the spirit, old girl." Rupert took another deep drag off the cigarette before tapping the ash into the shrubbery below the stone. "Now, let me tell you a little secret, something that should take the pall off of tonight for you."

Vera crossed her arms. "If it's about Lady Sommeville's daughter, you needn't bother. I've already heard."

"Oh no, this is far more interesting." He took another deep drag and then exhaled. "I have someone who wants to meet you."

"One of the men of your set with a title that still has gobs of money attached to it?" Those families were rare nowadays. Hers certainly wasn't one of them, but most of the men Rupert associated with were laudable catches. One of them coming around to their London town house would be enough to make her mother put down her highball glass and take notice, but the chance that any of them had noticed her was unthinkable. She didn't breathe the same rarified air as Rupert. "Not like you to play the matchmaker."

"I'm not playing matchmaker, and it's not my set." He leveled his smoking cigarette at her. "It's Princess Margaret's Set."

"Filled with eligible, rich, and titled men enchanted enough with royalty to want to, how shall I say it, pluck a royal flower?"

"None of her set is enchanted enough to make her garden a permanent part of his estate. She's too difficult to cultivate, and I should know." The dark circles under his eyes were deepened by the moonlight. Rupert's name was often in the papers as one of the many sons of titled men who escorted Princess Margaret to the most exclusive clubs, dancing until dawn as if life were nothing more than one long coming-out ball. "I've spent enough on drinks for her at Ciro's, for which I have received nothing more than a royal thank-you, and most times not even that."

"What were you hoping for? A walk through her garden?" She silently applauded him for aiming so high.

He cocked one knowing eyebrow at her before dropping his cigarette on the ground and stamping it out with a highly polished dress shoe. "I hate to disappoint you, but it isn't a man." He leaned in close to her, a smug smile turning up the corners of his mouth. "It's Princess Margaret."

Vera studied him, waiting for him to throw back his head in a loud laugh that would make everyone inside the French doors stop and stare, but he didn't so much as chuckle.

"You're joking." Vera smacked him on the lapel, forcing him to straighten.

"I'm quite serious." Rupert leaned against the railing, the light from the ballroom spilling over his high forehead and his dark hair slicked back with Brylcreem. The glow of it turned the white shirt and waistcoat covering his thin chest and middle a subtle orange, while the shadows made the black of his tuxedo jacket even darker.

"What interest could she possibly have in me?" That she even knew Vera existed was unbelievable and a touch flattering. Her own family barely paid her any heed, and here was Rupert suggesting she'd been noticed by royalty. Usually Vera cared as much for the doings of the Royal Family as she did the activities of her mother's bridge club, but tonight she was intrigued.

"Not you, your alter ego. Her Royal Highness is a voracious reader of your, shall we say, less well-mannered writings."

"Shhhh." Vera flapped her hand at him, glancing at the French doors to make sure he hadn't been overheard. "No one knows about that."

"I know about it."

She grabbed him by the elbow and dragged him out of sight of the doors. "Only because I needed your help with the publisher in the beginning, but you weren't supposed to tell anyone."

"Not even a princess?"

"Especially not a princess."

"I didn't tell her who you are, but when she expressed admiration for your fine Shakespearean sensibilities"—he smiled mischievously, for they both knew no one would compare the novels she secretly wrote to the bard's work—"I happened to mention that the author is a personal friend of mine and I'd be happy to make an introduction if Her Royal Highness wished it, and she does. I think you should meet her. She'll like you. The two of you have a great deal in common."

Vera rolled her eyes. "Yes, except for the family jewels, a generous living from the King, and the title, we're practically sisters."

"You know what I mean. Like her, you have a way with words, and we can do it tonight, if you'd like."

Vera crossed her arms and glared at her cousin, not sure

what irritated her more, his joke or her mother's usual insensitivity. Except Rupert wasn't joking; she could see it in his cocky expression. It was the same look he'd worn during all the times they'd teased her sister or his elder brother during Christmas gatherings at her family's estate, Parkston Hall, before the war, before they'd both experienced true loss. "Tonight?"

"There's a charity ball at the Dorchester, to which I happen to have an invitation. If we leave now, we can be there in an hour, and we're both suitably dressed for the occasion. It would do you infinitely more good to go there with me than it would to stay in this mausoleum."

"I can't leave. My mother would . . ."

"What? Be disappointed in you?"

"That's practically a standing order."

"Then why not come with me?"

Vera looked out over the lawn again and the dark line of the trees hiding the temple. No, there was no reason to stay here. Everything she'd imagined for her future was gone, and torturing herself wouldn't bring it back. But what would she get for leaving? She'd meet the Princess, exchange a few deferential words, and get a royal pat on the head for something she kept as hidden as the money she made from it. Sadly, it was a better deal than going inside, a chance to finally take a little credit for her clandestine work. It might make having dusted off her old debutante gown and doing her hair worth the effort.

"Come on, Vera, what do you say?" He held out his hand to her, their grandfather's diamond cuff links dark against the white of his shirt cuffs. "Shall we make for London?"

She'd endure a world of hurt in the morning from her parents for leaving, but the conversation would be a change from her father's oppressive silence or her mother's disappointed sighs. She slapped her hand firmly in his. "Yes, let's."

Chapter Two

"Well, what do you think?" Rupert whispered, his voice almost lost beneath the lively strings of the orchestra. "Was it worth leaving?"

"It was." Vera stood with Rupert toward the end of the receiving line in the Dorchester hotel ballroom, doing her best not to gawk. She'd attended a number of coming-out balls over the last few years, but they'd all been in old houses, in rooms like the ones at Weatherly or Parkston Hall, and with the same drab flaws. There was nothing dull at the Dorchester. All the chandeliers glittered, their light catching in the mirrors adorning the pillared walls and the gilded sconces, none of which were missing gold or were faded or dirty. Everything from the plasterwork at the tops of the columns surrounding the windows to the drapery dipping in delicate folds was new and fresh and elegant. There was nothing tired or austere here, not the orchestra playing a waltz or the white cloths covering the round tables filling the perimeter of the room. Even the mix of older fashions slipped in between the new seemed lively and less worn in the glow of the ballroom, and Vera was grateful. In the midst of this much splendor, her lack of substantial jewelry and her old dress felt dowdier and plainer than before. If it didn't mean sacrificing some of her hard-earned writing money, she'd take advantage of the loosening of the clothes rations and buy herself something chicer, but there was little point in squandering the pounds. Unless she could wheedle her way into being Rupert's date for more events like this, she wasn't likely to have a place this marvelous to wear anything new. "Shame on you for keeping all this to yourself."

"It must be a cold night in hell if you're saying you want to rub elbows with the likes of this crowd." He opened his arms to the people up and down the line around them, including the tall man behind her who rocked back on the heels of his dress shoes, smiling to himself when a woman with an elaborate diamond tiara passed. He caught Vera's eyes and winked at her, not at all ashamed or humbled at being caught finding amusement in the other guests.

"It would give me a reason to buy a new dress and my mother something else to talk about at breakfast other than my lack of a future." Vera smiled at the debonair young stranger, who nodded in reply before she turned back to Rupert.

"You don't need me to get this. I've seen that wit of yours employed when you want. Why don't you use it tonight and surprise us both?" He nodded down the receiving line to where a number of tall men in uniform stood, their medals and ribbons bright against their dark blue uniforms. Princess Margaret stood somewhere between them, but she was too short for Vera to see. Once in a while, when the line shifted forward, Vera caught the tip of a diamond tiara, the faint sparkle of a gold dress, but nothing more.

"Don't be daft, Rupert. Her Royal Highness meets a thousand people a day. I doubt one short curtsey from me will change my life, not that I want it changed." Rupert raised a disbelieving eyebrow. "Not in this way, at least; you know that."

"I do, but even in New York, a connection like this could open doors for you."

She hated to admit it, but he was right, assuming she ever got to New York. The conviction that she'd escape the oppressive suffering of England for the possibilities of America and exchange her scandalous novels for something more edifying wasn't as strong as it used to be. "If that's the case, then you can help me, can't you?"

He shook his head. "It doesn't work like that. I may introduce someone to her, but she makes the choice to accept or discard people. I can open the door. You're the one who must bolt through it."

Vera laced her gloved hands in front of her, her small purse on its gold chain dangling down over her wrist. "Tonight, I'm content to merely peek."

"If you say so."

The line ahead of them shifted forward, and they moved

with it. The gentleman behind her, who she had the distinct impression had been listening to their conversation, stepped a little closer to Vera.

"You're foolish to give up this elegance for the slums of New York." He rolled his *r*'s with his American accent, but his voice was light and friendly, like his deep brown eyes.

"Yes, it would be terrible to give up rations, coal fog, sugar shortages, and biting-cold winters for New York." Vera smiled at his friendly advice, surprised by his forwardness, although she shouldn't have been. The few Americans she'd met had never been ones to stand on formality.

He shrugged at her, his dark tuxedo emphasizing the width of his shoulders and the sturdiness of his chest. The whiteness of his tie and collar heightened the amusement decorating the sharp angles of his cheeks and chin. "The winters are pretty biting there too, and we don't have the fog, but trust me when I say you don't want to go there."

"Maybe I like slums," Vera challenged with a saucy tilt of her head that widened his already too enticing smile.

"Look sharp, old girl, it's almost our turn." Rupert nudged her, and Vera whirled around to stand beside her cousin, the strange American forgotten.

The uniformed older man with a curving mustache and his plump, silver-haired wife in front of the Princess made their curtseys and left, freeing the way for Rupert and Vera to come before Her Royal Highness and giving Vera her first proper look at the diminutive royal.

A charming smile adorned the nineteen-year-old Princess's flawless complexion, made more stunning by her dark hair. It was swept back off her face in lustrous waves that draped down to large curls pinned close to her temples and around the back. Four twisted strands of pearls encircled her neck, each creamy orb highlighting the whiteness of her skin. She was small but built like a man's dream, with a narrow waist, lithe arms, and a generous bust accentuated by a dress Vera had to force herself not to stare at for there were no straps to hold up the generous royal cleavage. The stunning style of it made Vera's gown appear even older and more outdated by comparison, except there was no comparing herself to the Princess. Whatever ideas Rupert held about her and the King's younger daughter being alike she couldn't see it. There was no matching this woman, for she'd been blessed with the privileges of royalty and the beauty essential to a fairy tale.

With enviable grace, the Princess held out one hand for Rupert to bow over, and Vera finally understood why Rupert and other gentlemen rushed to offer her drinks and dances despite little chance of ever being rewarded for their efforts. There was magic in royalty, something Vera had never experienced until that moment. During the entire ride in Rupert's red Jag, he'd instructed her on how to behave for the best advantage, and she'd teased him for sounding more like old Lady Bixton than the Honorable Rupert Everston. She wished she'd paid more attention to his advice. With the Princess in front of them and Rupert serious in his white tie and tails, it was no longer a joke.

"Your Royal Highness, may I introduce my cousin, the Honorable Vera Strathmore?" Rupert announced over the strings of the quartet.

Vera dipped a regal curtsey that would have elicited a rare titter of pride from her mother if she could have seen it. As much as Vera had scoffed at the deportment lessons foisted on her the year before her coming out, she was glad for them now, including the strange instruction on how to meet royalty. She'd never expected to use it, but the training carried her through the moment, for Vera was too awestruck to do more than react out of force of habit.

Vera rose from her curtsey, silently admiring the Princess's gold-colored gown with its shimmering gold embroidered leaves on the bodice and wide tulle skirt, struggling to keep her face passive and not reveal an ounce of envy. She'd only ever seen this new style of dress in photos of Her Royal Highness in the gossip columns but never in real life. Good breeding warned her against complimenting the Princess on the daring cut of the bodice or to speak to her before she was spoken to, except there was something about the Princess's reaction, a subtle widening of her smile, a pleased but slight tilt of her head that made the diamonds in her tiara sparkle and told Vera that the Princess wanted the compliment, craved it, even. Vera would have offered it if Princess Margaret hadn't turned from her to Rupert, leaving Vera silent.

"Is this the cousin you were telling me about, Mr. Everston?" Princess Margaret addressed him with a familiarity tinged with an acute awareness of her status and his and the numerous people flanking them and listening.

"It is, Ma'am," he answered with a reverence Vera had never witnessed in him before.

Then the Princess faced her, and Vera snapped to attention.

"Miss Strathmore, Mr. Everston tells me that you're a writer," Princess Margaret stated in her soft, lilting voice, her accent so refined it would make Vera's old tutor cry with rapture. "What do you write?"

Rupert cast Vera a sideways glance as if to say now was her chance to expound on her questionable literary achievements, the ones Rupert had assured Vera he'd brought her here to address. He wasn't one to pull her leg—that he reserved for the more sedate members of their family—but how Vera would reveal the truth with all those military men hovering around and peering past their spectacles at her, and the American standing beside her listening with a touch too much interest, she didn't know. Vera could deliver her usual line about writing articles for the royal-hungry American magazines and leave it to Rupert to inform Her Royal Highness of the truth later, but, like with the compliment Vera hadn't been able to speak, she sensed the Princess wanted honesty and, in the midst of her staid companions, a touch of amusement. Rupert had brought her here to introduce the Princess to one of her favorite authors. It was time to announce herself. "I write romance novels under the pen name Rose Lavish, Ma'am."

The eyes of the officials flanking the Princess went wide in shock, and the American stepped closer to better hear. Rupert stood beside her, his hands laced behind his back as if she'd simply announced the time.

The Princess glanced back and forth between her and Rupert before settling her regal attention on Vera. "Do you?"

The Princess's words were cool and sharp enough to make Vera want to slink out of the receiving line and back to her parents' town house. She would have if it hadn't been for the delight widening the Princess's rich, blue eyes with more admiration than astonishment. If Vera had ever doubted Rupert's story about the Princess reading Vera's novels before, she didn't now.

"Yes, Ma'am, I do. They are quite popular with housewives who want a little something more than England to think about when they lie back."

The august dignitaries flanking the Princess harrumphed their disapproval while the American turned his head to one side to cover a laugh with a cough. Princess Margaret did nothing but remain serene, her gloved hands clasped together in front of her, studying Vera with a scrutiny she couldn't read before looking to Rupert for confirmation.

"Yes, Ma'am, it's true. It's how I know the author you and I spoke about at Ciro's. I'm related to her."

One of the dignitaries leaned down to address the Princess while shooting daggers at Vera over the royal shoulder, eager to have this brazen woman banished from the royal presence. "Your Royal Highness, there are others waiting."

Manners told Vera to graciously back away and leave before she caused even more of a sensation, but she didn't move. She remained before Her Royal Highness, acknowledging that it was from her and not the others that she would take her orders to stay or go, that the Princess was the power and influence in this room, not the gentlemen or ladies surrounding her. The delay sent a ripple of shock down the line of remaining officers, titled men and ladies waiting to step forward, except for the American, who watched them with as much delight as he'd taken in observing the jewel-bedecked matrons.

"Thank you for a most interesting introduction, Miss Strathmore," Princess Margaret said at last, her tone both complimentary and dismissive.

Vera dropped a perfect curtsey and then allowed Rupert to escort her away, her boldness fading with each step they took from the blinding light of the Princess and back into the anonymity of the crowd. For a moment, she'd been a woman capable of stunning and entertaining a royal. Now, she was another unremarkable daughter of a titled man good for little more than filling a dilapidated old ballroom in need of adornment. The disappointment was strangling.

"I'd say you certainly made an impression." Rupert's mood was far more buoyant than hers, as if they'd accomplished something of real value instead of Vera making a fool out of herself.

"Is that what it was, an impression?"

"Most definitely." He reached into his pocket for his cigarette case, but remembering where they were, he tucked it back inside his pocket. "I think something is in store for you."

"I think what's in store for me is my typewriter and more tales of brooding lords in their manor houses and the maiden governesses swooning over them." She studied the guests around them, wondering what old lord with a weak heart and a little family fortune she could swoon over to save her from the pointlessness of her present situation. Rupert's words of encouragement at Weatherly Hall had given her high hopes for the encounter, and like so many of her aspirations, they were scattered about the floor like ashes.

"Don't be so down. After all . . ."

"No one likes a bitter spinster," they mimicked her mother in unison, their high and affected voices making the too-familiar saying a tad easier for Vera to bear.

"That's more like it." Rupert cuffed her under the chin. "I'll get us some drinks."

He made for the bar, leaving Vera alone to contemplate the room and the people filling it. Except there was only one person who interested her. Her Royal Highness, now freed from the rigors of the receiving line, spoke with two young ladies, one a brunette and the other a blonde who towered well above the Princess. The familiarity between the three women was unmistakable, but while the brunette was sober and sedate, the blonde threw out her arms in wide gestures while she spoke, making Her Royal Highness giggle at regular intervals. The blond woman's posture suggested a boldness one usually didn't see in English roses. If it weren't for the Princess's dazzling diamonds and the gaggle of uniformed men surrounding them, one of whom was quite smitten with the brunette and commanded more of her attention than the Princess, Vera would think the women were debutantes enjoying their first Season. Vera had no idea who either of the young ladies were, but to her surprise, she was jealous of their freedom with the King's daughter. Vera's parents and all those aunts who'd looked scornfully or pityingly at her during each family wedding since the end of the war would change their tunes if she became a member of a royal's circle. Except that wasn't possible, none of it was, and Rupert had been wrong to trick her into believing it could be. One did not simply walk up to royalty and garner confidences.

While the two women spoke, Princess Margaret slid a glance at Vera. Vera kept her head held high and met the royal look with confidence. After all, there was nothing left for Vera to lose and no reason why she should prostrate herself from this far across the room. She waited for a reprimanding frown or the flick of a gloved hand to instruct one of the uniformed men to escort Vera out of the ballroom, but there was no censure in Princess Margaret's expression. Instead, her full lips curled up a touch at the corners before she turned back to her friends.

The brunette stepped away from the Princess, escorted by

Bremen Public Library

her uniformed suitor to the dance floor, while the blonde set off into the crowd, surrendering her place of preference to a tall, lanky, dark-haired man with a rounded chin. His impressive height forced the royal head to tilt back and revealed the elegant line of her neck, making the large diamonds dangling from her ears sparkle as they brushed the royal jaw.

Rupert returned, handing Vera one of the two martinis he carried.

Vera took the drink, grateful to have something more to do than stand there on the edge of the dance floor without a dance partner, as usual. "This is as dull as my coming-out ball."

"It wasn't dull for me. Lady Bixton's niece was quite accommodating that night."

"Was she now?"

"You're surprised?"

"One does hear rumors. I didn't think they were true." She cocked her head slightly in the direction of Princess Margaret. "Are the rumors about her true?"

"Some are, and some aren't."

"Which are which?"

"I leave it up to you to decide." He smirked from around the edges of his glass.

"Fine, keep your secrets, but at least tell me who the tall man talking to her is."

"The Honorable Billy Wallace. Why, seeking another introduction?"

Bremen Public Library

"Not with a man with that weak a chin."

"That weak chin is in possession of a fine lineage and a robust bank account, not that I can hold that against him. Out of five brothers, he was the only one who survived the war." Rupert twisted the signet ring on his pinkie finger, darkness clouding his eyes before he dropped his hands and smiled again. "Not too late for me to introduce you so you can captivate him with your wit."

"No thank you." Vera took a healthy drink of her martini. "I've done enough charming for one night."

"Rupert, darling, it's magnificent to see you here." The elegant words made clipped and blunted by an American accent drifted over them, and Vera turned to find the Princess's blond friend before them. Where Her Majesty was petite, this woman was strapping, the type of girl one always imagined when anyone said American corn-fed.

"Sass, I see you're holding up in all this excitement." Rupert leaned past Vera to place kisses on each of the woman's round cheeks. "I hope this isn't the highlight of the evening."

He nodded to the thick-waisted matrons in the arms of their round-bellied husbands mixing with the young ladies dragged here by their mamas in the hope of landing a socially acceptable husband.

"Oh, heavens no." Sass waved one hand in dismissal before clasping them in conspiracy. "There are much more exciting things to come."

"I'm glad to hear it." Rupert motioned to Vera. "The Honorable Vera Strathmore, may I introduce you to Sharman Douglas, daughter of the American Ambassador?"

Vera offered her hand in greeting. "Miss Douglas, it's a pleasure to meet you."

"Call me Sass; all my friends do." She gave Vera's hand a vigorous shake. "I hope we'll be friends. I'm always looking for people to come to embassy parties and liven things up. I think you'd fit right in. I love your books, Miss Strathmore, or should I say Mrs. Lavish. I never would have guessed a lord's daughter could write romance novels."

"I'm glad you enjoyed them." Vera tried to extricate her hand, but Sass held on tight.

"Oh, I do, they're so gothic. Like half the magnificent houses in this country. Does your family have a grand old house?"

"Yes, but it's not quite as grand as it used to be." Few things were.

"But it must be full of inspiration." Across the room, Princess Margaret motioned for Sass to rejoin her. Sass turned to Rupert, in no particular hurry to leave but no longer content to linger. "Rupert, we're going to Monty's tonight. Danny and Noël will be there, and Her Royal Highness is dying to dance with you."

"Is she now?" He glanced over her head at the Princess, the faint crease between his brows deepening with his curiosity.

"She especially wants you to bring Miss Strathmore." Sass,

still clutching Vera's hand, fixed on her. "She told me she hasn't been that amused by a receiving line in ages."

"I'm glad I could do something to lighten her evening," Vera said.

"Oh, you did. You must come with us and do it again."

"I'll do my best."

"Wonderful, then we'll see you there."

Sass finally let go of Vera and with a very American wave, turned on her heel, the full skirt of her pink satin ball gown flowing out about her legs before settling down to sway with her gait while she strode back to her royal friend.

Rupert smirked at Vera in triumph. "I told you you'd made an impression."

"I stand corrected." Her instincts had been right. Well, there was a first time for everything.

"What will you do for your second act?"

"I don't know." But she was as curious as him and Her Royal Highness to see.

Chapter Three

The taxi turned down a dark and dirty side road with old stone buildings choking out the pavement on either side. Newspapers, damp with night mist, littered the gutter, but the men standing in doorways smoking, their hats pulled down low over their eyes, paid no attention to the filth surrounding them. Their interest was on the black cab coming to a stop in front of a closed tobacconist shop. Rupert had left his Jag at the Dorchester, and seeing this, Vera understood why. Vera ignored the men and peered out the window and up to the lights blazing in the room over the shop, hesitant to step out of the safety of the cab. She would look a sight in her ball gown on this dark little street in Soho.

"Where are we?" she asked while Rupert handed money over the seat to the driver.

"My dear, you are looking at none other than Monty's."

"Here?"

"Indeed." He stepped out and rounded the car, rapping the hood with his knuckles as he passed it. Vera watched him, sure at any moment the men standing in the doorway would rush out of the shadows and pound him, stealing his fine cuff links and wrinkling his tuxedo. They neither moved nor did anything besides take the cigarettes out of their mouths once in a while to knock off the ash before setting them back between their lips.

Rupert pulled open the car door and offered Vera his hand to help her out. "Come on, you'll love it once you're inside."

"Are you telling me that Princess Margaret is in there?" The quick tempo of piano music drifting through the old, thick brick walls settled like dust over the alley.

"Monty's is a very chic secret. And we do our best to keep it that way. If the press found out about this place, then every nob in London would mob the place."

Chic seemed a strange word for it, but Vera was willing to play along. This odd game had already carried her to a ball at the Dorchester. She was curious to see what was next, including the other things of interest Rupert must be keeping secret. Maybe she could wheedle a few of them out of him. It might make for good fodder for her next book.

She held on tight to Rupert as he escorted her to the door at the side of the shop and pulled it open to reveal a narrow staircase that smelled like the old upstairs water closet in their Mayfair town house. Behind them, the cab sped off, leaving them alone on the dimly lit street.

"Remember, always address her as *Ma'am* or *Your Royal Highness*," he instructed as he led her up the stairs. From somewhere above them, the music changed from the fast beat of jazz to the slower melody of a piano accompanied by a talented female singer. "She might act like one of us, but she isn't, and allowing someone to forget that is her favorite way to catch people out."

"Sounds like a charming acquaintance."

"It has its moments." They reached the landing and the faded green door at the top. Vera waited for him to throw it open and lead her in, but he paused. "Another thing: she likes gossip, so if you have any, this isn't the time to be shy with it."

"Nothing I know can compare to this."

"And you can't tell anyone about it, or whatever else you see tonight. One word to the press and you'll be out of the Set before you're even in."

"How scandalous you make it sound, Rupert."

He winked at her. "It is."

He pushed open the door, and the full force of the piano accompanied by a woman singing "People Will Say We're in Love" from *Oklahoma!*, a song Vera had become sick of ages ago when the American musical had swept London, drifted over them. Before Vera had a chance to complain about the tune, she stopped dead at the sight before her.

Princess Margaret sat with the wide skirt of her gold gown spread out around her at an old upright piano. Her long fingers, now devoid of her gloves, moved swiftly over the yellowed keys while she sang in a voice as clear as any London performer. A large group of people, some Vera vaguely knew from social events, others she recognized from newspaper clippings, surrounded the Princess, enraptured by the royal command performance.

"She's the singer?" Vera shrugged out of her coat and handed it to Rupert to drape over a chair near the door.

"She's marvelous, isn't she?" an elderly gentleman with his thinning hair slicked back off his high forehead and a red carnation in the buttonhole of his tuxedo jacket gushed from beside her. Vera didn't know what to say. Yes, the Princess was good—excellent, in fact—but the sight of a member of the Royal Family singing like a cabaret performer in a rundown club in a back alley in Soho made her want to grab her pearls in shock. Vera was no lover of convention, but some old aristocratic instinct in her said this just wasn't done.

"I told you you'd be surprised," Rupert whispered as the gathered guests applauded when Princess Margaret brought the song to end. The man who'd been beside Vera rushed up to congratulate the Princess, edging out many other well-wishers half his age.

"Who's he?" Vera asked.

"Noël Coward, and there's Danny Kaye, another of her many famous admirers." He pointed to the lanky, red-haired actor lounging with one arm propped up on the piano, as captivated by the woman on the bench below him as Mr. Coward. Vera would have recognized the actor anywhere, having seen his films and his performance at the Palladium. Attending had practically been a requirement in London, especially after the King and Queen, their daughters in tow, had graced the theatre and turned the American into a sensation. "Maybe you can work your charm on one of them and get yourself to New York quicker."

"My charm would work a great deal better with a martini, dirty and three olives."

"Careful, Vera—she has the title to be demanding; you don't." He cuffed her playfully under the chin and then made for the bar in the corner. It was an old wooden one bordered with tufted leather and manned by a round little man she assumed to be Monty, who poured drinks with the speed and all the panache of a publican.

Vera shifted along the wall away from the door, passing behind a number of people and unnoticed by anyone, even those with whom she had a passing acquaintance. Any other night it would have irked her to be ignored, but tonight it offered the chance to watch the strange spectacle of the Princess and the men flittering around her. To each, the Princess gave absolute attention when he spoke. If she was bored, she didn't show it, for the royal gaze never wandered listlessly to someone or someplace else. The men who enjoyed her favor, however briefly, basked in it as though she were showering them with honors and land. Vera couldn't help but admire her skill or wish she possessed even a tenth of the woman's ability to charm and cajole. It was impressive, but she did wonder if, without the title, diamonds, and Dior dresses, the Princess would still be so captivating. It was difficult to say.

Vera was about to join Rupert at the crowded bar when,

through a gap in the crowd, Princess Margaret caught Vera's eye. In an instant, she rose from the piano bench, left her admirers, and started for Vera. The guests parted for the Princess, acknowledging her superiority with a subtle reverence that rippled through the room like the notes of the piano now played by Mr. Coward. The surroundings might have changed from silk curtains to rough brick walls, but there was no easing of the royal posture or any acknowledgment that they were in a rundown club above a tobacconist shop and not the White Drawing Room in Buckingham Palace.

Vera stood still as the Princess approached, every one of Rupert's words of advice and warning fleeing her. She wondered what to say when the Princess addressed her, assuming the Princess didn't command her to leave. Unlike the ball, there was nothing to stop the Princess from telling Vera off for having been so bold in the receiving line. Rupert hadn't said she was vindictive, but Vera had heard enough whispers and rumors about unpredictable royal whims to make her worry.

"Miss Strathmore, how wonderful to see you again. I am so glad you could come," Princess Margaret greeted, all smiles and politeness, with no hint of anything malicious in her high voice.

Vera let out a long breath as she rose from her curtsey, determined to relax as much as one could in front of royalty. It almost made her laugh to think she was so nervous around a woman five years younger than her, but this was no ordinary woman. Her father was the King, for heaven's sake. "Thank you so much for inviting me, Ma'am. I've never been to such a unique club before."

"It certainly is unique, but it's private and far less formal than even the American embassy where we often meet." Princess Margaret withdrew an ivory cigarette holder from the small evening bag dangling from a thin strap on one lithe arm. She needn't take out a pack of cigarettes because Lord Dalkeith, without having been summoned or asked, hurried to offer her one. She tucked it in the end of the holder and, wrapping her fingers around his, drew the lighter he held out to her up to the cigarette and lit it. It was an intimate gesture, but there was no furtive raising of the royal eyes, no subtle sweeping of fingers, and she let go of him as easily as she'd clasped him. "Thank you, Johnny."

"Anything for you, Ma'am." Understanding he was being both thanked and dismissed, the red-haired son of the Duke of Buccleuch made off to join Rupert at the bar.

"Tell me, Mrs. Lavish, for I think I'll call you that from now on for it's so marvelous"—she poked her cigarette holder toward Vera, making a bit of ash fall off the end and flitter to the floor—"what do your parents think of your occupation?"

"They aren't aware of it, Ma'am. They think I write articles on English manners for American newspapers, and I do, just enough to maintain the ruse."

"I'm among the privileged, then?" She laughed and tapped more ash onto the floor. "How delightful."

"Do your"—Vera stumbled, about to say *parents* before she

caught herself, sure such familiarity with the royal wouldn't be appreciated—"Their Royal Highnesses know that you're here, Ma'am?"

"If not, then my detective will tell them. I dismissed him when we arrived, but he's sure to mention it to Papa and Mummy. They'll pretend to be cross in the morning, but nothing will come of it. Mummy believes I should have a good time since I'm young, and Papa never says no to me." She took a dainty puff from her cigarette and exhaled the most ladylike breath of smoke. "And what do you do with all the money you make from your scintillating novels?"

All my money, Vera nearly snorted, about to tell her "all" was being generous, but the innocent and expectant tilt of the Princess's head indicated there was no insult behind the question. She genuinely wished to know. "I save it, Ma'am, in the hopes it will take me to New York one day. I'd like to work for a publishing house or a magazine while I write something of more literary note than *The Duke's Secret Seduction*."

"How grand. Crawfie always used to praise my writing and said I could've been a novelist if Uncle David hadn't given up the throne and changed everything." Princess Margaret took a deep drag off the cigarette, her exhalation much less ladylike than before. "Of course, she's the author now with her beastly little book about me and my sister, our childhood laid out for everyone to read. You can't imagine what it's like to be betrayed by your own governess, and in so public a manner."

Vera had heard about the book detailing the princesses'

childhood written by Marion Crawford, their former governess. She never imagined she'd be standing before the very subject of the publication.

The Princess tugged the half-smoked cigarette out of the holder, dropped it on the floor, and crushed it with the toe of one dainty but very high heeled shoe. "I'd like to go to New York. Sass has told me all about it and the places I absolutely must see. But it isn't easy for one to get away. It was difficult enough to go to Italy and face those beastly foreign photographers crowding about when all I wanted to do was see the Blue Grotto and Pompeii like anyone else."

"I'm sure you'll get there one day, Ma'am," Vera said encouragingly, as much for herself as for the Princess. Their lives might be very different, but she recognized the frustration of being unable to live the way she wanted to, because it haunted Vera every day.

"Yes, you're right. I'm quite certain of it."

The conversation began to lag, and Vera, fearing the loss of the royal attention, and her chance to do more than discuss dreams of travel, cast about for another topic to amuse the Princess. Her sights landed on Lord Westmorland sitting with Sass and Lord Sunny Blandford, the Duke of Marlborough's heir. Sass threw Vera an enthusiastic wave before leaning over the table to say something to Lord Westmorland, giving Vera an idea. "I understand Lord Westmorland is engaged to Sir Roland Findlay's daughter, Ma'am."

Princess Margaret twisted around to peer at the Earl before

turning back to Vera, her once vivacious eyes hard. "I hadn't heard."

Vera feared she'd stepped in it for the second time that night. So much for Rupert's grand advice about gossip. "It hasn't been announced yet, Ma'am, but my great-aunt, Lady Bixton, is good friends with Lord Westmorland's grandmother. They're to be married in June."

Princess Margaret turned the ivory holder over in her hands, the look in her eyes softening with a wistfulness all too familiar to Vera. "First my sister, and now Lord Westmorland."

"My sister recently became engaged. My parents were as pleased with it being her and not me as they would be finding out I'm Rose Lavish."

"Very soon everyone will be married, and then where will we be?" She paused in her examination of the ivory, no more immune to the threat of spinsterhood than Vera. Then she looked up at Vera, the unease snuffed out like the forgotten cigarette on the floor. "But of course, you have your work."

"Yes, Ma'am." If only it were rewarding enough to replace everything she'd lost with Henry or to really alter her life, but it wasn't. It might never be.

Rupert returned, carrying two drinks, breaking the heaviness that had settled between Vera and Her Royal Highness.

"Oh Rupert, you read my mind." Princess Margaret took the fuller of the two glasses, drained it, and then held out the empty glass to a passing man. "Julian, be a dear and do something with this for me." The young man, thwarted in whatever pursuit was driving him across the room, took the glass and hurried off to do the royal bidding, saving any grumbling for when he was well out of royal earshot. "Do you have a cigarette, Rupert? I'm simply dying for one."

"I wouldn't travel without them." He pulled the silver case from his pocket and held it out to her.

With two long, delicate fingers she slid a cigarette out and tucked it into the end of her holder. Rupert removed his lighter, snapped it open, and held it out for her. The flame flickered over the smooth planes of her face as she leaned in to light the end, wrapping her slender fingers around his hand and drawing him close, again with no hint of furtive glances, no intimacy in her touch. If Vera didn't know these men, she'd think, with the way Princess Margaret treated them, they were nothing more than overdressed footmen.

Princess Margaret released his hand and straightened, tilting the ivory holder off to her side while smoke trailed from the end to circle her dark hair. The music changed to a less-rousing tune that encouraged a number of guests to get a little closer on the dance floor, such that it was. The people dropped the required curtseys and Ma'ams when they passed, but Princess Margaret acknowledged them with only a slight wave of her hand, her smoldering blue eyes rimmed by dark lashes, taking in Rupert as if he were a selection of available jewelry.

"Shall we dance, Rupert?" It was a command, not a question, and Vera wondered what the Princess was really like when stripped of her title, dresses, and diamonds. Probably just as demanding as she was in her fashionable frock.

"Of course, Ma'am." He handed his glass to Vera. "If you'll excuse us."

He escorted Her Royal Highness to the dance floor, leaving Vera alone with his drink. Vera took a taste of it and blanched. Whiskey and water. She hated it as much as she detested standing there like a potted plant. Vera slid off one shoe and raised her foot behind her to rub the ball of it, eager to be home where she could kick off her heels. It was one thing to stay up late writing in her robe in her room. It was another to stand in this smoky dive with someone, she didn't know who, banging out the latest slow tune while everyone but her danced. Rupert had told her in the cab that no one left until the royal did, not even the illustrious Mr. Kaye or Mr. Coward who, like many of the others in the club, were beginning to droop. Instead, everyone continued to smile and chat as if no one had anywhere to be the next day and their sole purpose in life was to amuse the Princess. Vera wondered if the Princess even noticed how all of this was done for her. If she did notice, did she care, or did she think she deserved it by right of birth?

A familiar male voice with an American accent carried over the tinny piano. "I wouldn't have believed it if I hadn't seen it for myself." The man from behind her in the Dorchester receiving line stood beside her, visibly more amused here than he'd been at the luxury hotel.

"Believe what? That a princess sings at a piano in a dive bar?" She was still trying to comprehend the reality of it.

"That a country girl like you does like to slum it."

"What makes you think I'm from the country?"

"Your cheeks. They're a little too rosy for you to have grown up in the city. I bet you're used to riding horses, fresh air, some large house set in the middle of parklands with a lot of old paintings and ghosts."

At one time, yes, when she'd been a young girl and Parkston Hall had still been prosperous and able to support her family, but that was a long time ago. They lived in the town house in London, and Parkston Hall was let to an American businessman who enjoyed pretending at being a lord. "You Americans are quite taken by old houses."

"We can't help ourselves. For some of us it's in the blood, albeit a few generations back, but it's there. And who do I have the pleasure of speaking with? I couldn't hear your name at the ball."

"The Honorable Vera Strathmore."

"Well, if we're using full titles. Dr. Dominic Reynolds." He held out his hand to her, and she took it, his grip firm and encompassing her entire hand. Over the stench of cigarette smoke permeating the air, Vera caught the faint scent of his crisp aftershave, a lighter one than London men usually preferred. "Would you like all the extra letters behind my name, or will the *doctor* before it suffice?"

Vera laughed and let go of him. "Doctor will suffice."

"What's your father, then, a duke, an earl?"

"The Fifth Baron Ratherdale."

"The fifth, heh?" He nodded his head in mock seriousness. "I'm the second doctor Reynolds. My father is a doctor too, one of the leading American pulmonologists specializing in tuberculosis."

"Impressive. And does he have a Texas ranch with lots of cattle and a large white hat he wears when he rides his horse?" Vera worked hard to conjure up all the images she'd seen of America at the cinema.

"He does. Except our ranch is in Arizona, and my father's hat is brown."

Sass came to stand beside Dr. Reynolds, her pink ball gown with the wide tulle skirt as out of place in here as the Princess's. "I see you've met Doc. He and I grew up together in Arizona. You'll love him; he has the best sense of humor."

Vera slid a sideways glance at the tall doctor. "So I've discovered."

"Doc, good to see you again." Lord David Fane, the Earl of Westmorland, stepped, or Vera should say staggered, a touch, into their group, not even so much as tipping the whiskey out of his highball glass while he enthusiastically shook Dr. Reynolds's hand before turning to Vera. "Vera, I thought it was you. Didn't expect to see you here."

She tilted forward to receive two whiskey-laden kisses on her cheeks. "I didn't expect to be here."

"Who does? But we do as we are told." He waved his glass in

the direction of Princess Margaret, who noted the gesture before Rupert gently turned her away in time to the music. Billy Wallace walked by, and David stopped him with a hand on his chest. "Billy, have you met Rupert's cousin, the Honorable Vera Strathmore?"

"A pleasure," he offered. "Always good to have new blood in this crowd."

Before Vera could say more, David jerked up straight as Princess Margaret bore down on them like a royal torrent, the quick click of her heels out of sync with the beat of the bass notes of the piano. Rupert followed behind, his twisted frown well out of sight of Her Royal Highness.

"David, I understand you're to be married." Princess Margaret's high, clipped words carried over the slow music, causing the player to strike the keys a bit softer in an effort to not miss a note or any of the irritated Princess's words. The others, gathered around rickety old tables or leaning against the bar, paused in their conversations and cocked their heads to listen. Even Dr. Reynolds took a step back, more in surprise than fear. Sass didn't move, her smile gone and her face clouded with concern.

"Y-yes, Ma'am," David stammered, swirling his drink and making the ice cubes in the glass clink together.

"How dare you make it so I'm the last to know. I'm the first. I'm always the first." She stomped one impressively high heel against the floor, her hands balled in tight fists at her sides. "Billy, take me home at once."

She marched off, expecting Billy to follow. Helpless to do anything else, the tall man threw them an apologetic shrug and then strode after her, hurrying to collect her white fur coat and his cape from the pile of outerwear near the door before disappearing into the hallway after his royal charge.

"I better go too. Poor girl. It hasn't been easy for her," Sass offered apologetically before following after the Princess and Billy.

The Princess's unexpected departure left the room in silence a moment before a wave of speculative whispers rushed in to fill the void, followed by no small amount of relief. People began to stub out their cigarettes and collect their jackets, the party over.

"What a charming end to the evening," Vera remarked to David, who threw back the last of his drink.

"It always is." He strode off, pausing long enough to deposit his glass on a table and collect his coat before heading out the door.

Dr. Reynolds, as eager it seemed as everyone else to leave, bent in a gracious bow over Vera and held out his hand. "It was a pleasure to meet you, the Honorable Vera Strathmore."

She laid her hand in his, about to tell him he didn't have to leave, when he raised it to his lips, pressing a soft kiss to the back of her cool skin and sending a shiver racing through her. Then he straightened and let go, standing a good foot taller than her, his dusty blond hair cut shorter than Rupert's and free of Brylcreem.

"Did I do it right?" he asked, and Vera laughed, a little of the strain from the strange royal outburst, and the trepidation that she'd played some part in it, easing.

"Yes, very well. You'll be a courtier in no time."

"God, I hope not." He backed away from her as if she were royalty before offering one last parting bow at the door, then disappearing into the darkness beyond.

The sense she shouldn't have let him go draped her like the old wool coat that Rupert placed on her shoulders. Vera almost rejected it as not hers. Like the table linens in Weatherly, it looked all right in low light, but sunlight would reveal its tired seams. It would last only another winter or two before it was so limp and worn it wouldn't be good for anything except warming her feet at night, but for the moment it would have to do. She hated to spend money on another one. In New York, with the right job at the right publishing house, she could buy a myriad of coats and dresses in a more fashionable style than her current means allowed.

"What happened with Her Royal Highness?" he asked, slipping into his overcoat and laying his white scarf around his neck.

"Before she danced with you, I told her about Lord Westmorland being engaged." Vera stuffed one arm and then another in the sleeves of her coat. "You said to give her gossip. You should've been more specific about what kind."

"I wasn't aware she didn't know about Westmorland, but it

explains a great many things about tonight. She hates to lose anyone's attention."

"I think it's more than that." Vera flipped her hair out from beneath the collar, stunned by the pity she felt for the Princess. After that infantile outburst, she didn't deserve it, but Vera couldn't help herself. "Her sister is married, and the most important member of the family, and the Princess isn't. Imagine how difficult that must be."

He slid his signet ring on and off his finger. "I don't think either of us has to imagine it."

"No, we don't."

Chapter Four

*Y*ou came in late last night, or should I say this morning," Vera's father grumbled from behind the black-and-white pages of the *Daily Mirror* when Vera entered the dining room. Behind him on the far wall, the portrait of her father's great-uncle William, one of Nelson's admirals, hung in a gilded frame, the morning sunlight bringing out the brushstrokes in the dark paint of his old-fashioned uniform.

Her mother at least put down her copy of *The Lady* to glare at her elder daughter. Alice stared at her plate, eating her eggs as if they were the most fascinating objects in the room. "You left us without even so much as a word about where you were going or when you'd return. I didn't know what to tell Lady Lowell."

"I doubt she or anyone else even noticed I was gone." Vera scraped out a spoonful of eggs from the chafing dish on the sideboard and dropped them on her plate. The smell made her stomach roll not because she'd come home soused but because of how little sleep she'd caught since Rupert had dropped her at the front door. She'd been too keyed up to do more than doze until a little past sunrise, and then it'd been up to work. She had a deadline this Friday and she hadn't finished typing up the last chapter.

"That's beside the point. Where were you?" her mother demanded.

Vera sat down across from her sister and laid a linen napkin over her lap. She took up her silverware and set her shoulders and her irritation before answering. "At a private party thrown by Princess Margaret after a charity ball at the Dorchester hotel. Rupert had an invitation and needed a date, and I was only too happy to oblige."

It wasn't quite the truth, but it was enough. Vera began eating her eggs, her fork clinking against the family china. The still hovering over the table was almost heavy enough to bring down the chandelier. Even her father deigned to lower his newspaper and peer at her.

Well, this was a change from the usual morning greeting.

"And did you meet Her Royal Highness?" her mother asked with as much disbelief as curiosity.

"I did." She took another bite of eggs, keeping her family waiting for details of what amounted to nothing more than a few snippets of royal conversation and a very unroyal temper tantrum. If Vera wasn't mistaken, there was almost a glimmer of admiration in her mother's eyes. It didn't last.

"Well, I hope you didn't say anything untoward during the course of it. You do have a way of forgetting yourself."

Vera dropped her fork to clank against the china. "I tell you I spoke with Princess Margaret and the most you can say is you hope I didn't embarrass myself?"

Her mother laid one hand on her chest, anything but contrite. "Your way with words can sometimes be very off-putting."

"I can't imagine where I inherited that particular trait from."

"She could have opened doors for you." Her father rapped the table with his knuckles, as if Vera having put the Princess off her was a solidly established fact and not her mother's mean speculation. It might very well be after the Princess's outburst last night, in which Vera had played a small hand.

She was about to inform them that it was Her Royal Highness herself who'd invited Vera to the party and hold it over them that yes, she was indeed capable of making a favorable impression on people when the shuffling of sturdy-soled shoes over the floorboards interrupted the tense mood.

"Miss Vera, this arrived for you." The day maid held out an envelope to Vera, her hand trembling. "It's from Buckingham Palace."

The air in the room shifted again, especially around Vera when the maid laid the envelope on the table with near reverence. It was the most respectful the ruddy-faced woman had been since she'd taken on the duties of both head maid and butler after the butler had left for a factory job and her parents hadn't rushed to fill the vacancy. Much like Vera's monthly allowance, the staff was shrinking, one position at a time, but her parents never mentioned it. It was too crass. She wouldn't be surprised if one day she came home to find removers tak-ing what was left of the antique furniture, and still her parents would say nothing, as they said nothing about the portraits and landscapes that disappeared with increasing regularity from the walls.

"Thank you, Mary," Vera offered in dismissal before pick-ing up the sturdy envelope with the words *Buckingham Palace* engraved on the back. The suspense in the room was palpable as Vera opened it and removed the card inside.

"Well, what does it say?" her mother demanded.

"It's from Princess Margaret. She's asked me to luncheon with her today at the Savoy." Vera tucked the card in the enve-lope and rose from the table. "See, all your fears of me being off-putting were for nothing."

She strode out of the dining room and, once out of sight, sprinted down the hall to her father's study and the black tele-phone perched on the desk inside. She had to get to it before her mother locked herself in here to call all her friends and sisters to tell them about the royal invitation, at last having some good news from Vera to brag about. What Vera needed to do was much more important, and she wished the phone were somewhere less oppressive than her father's office. Why it was in here she'd never discovered. Her father, being a gentle-man of the old school, didn't work but lived off the dwindling income from his lands. If he, like a few of his peers, had dis-covered employment, there might be fewer gaps between the paintings on the walls. She snatched up the receiver and dialed.

"Who the bloody hell is calling me at this hour?" Rupert growled into the phone, his usual smooth voice gravelly with the last of his sleep and the long night. "Whatever it is, it'd better be important."

"Princess Margaret invited me to lunch today," Vera said in a rush, flicking one stiff edge of the envelope and the card inside. When Vera had crawled into bed at four that morning, she hadn't been certain what she'd gained from her experience the night before, but she hadn't expected this. "What should I do?"

"Accept it, of course."

"Of course, but what about attire and conversation? You said an acquaintance with her could change things for me. I need the change."

"And it will, if you can swing it, and I think you can. You have a knack for guessing what she likes as much as Sass. As for your attire, I agree, it's awful."

Vera twisted the telephone cord around her finger, wanting to strangle him with it. "You sound like my mother."

"She's the reason your wardrobe is so pitiful."

"Rupert, be serious."

"I am. What time is it?"

"Nine."

"Then you have plenty of time to figure out how to make yourself presentable."

"And what about conversation? What does she like, dislike, what topics should I avoid?" Gossip had been a dismal failure at Monty's, or perhaps it hadn't. With her stomach in knots it was difficult to gauge what was what.

"Let her lead and you'll figure it out. Have faith, old girl. You'll be a smash."

VERA DRUMMED HER fingers on the flat side of her leather pocketbook, hoping the wear near the left seam didn't show when she arrived at the Savoy. She'd eschewed the underground for the quicker transport of a black cab, trying not to calculate again how this little indulgence would eat into her savings. For the second time in the last twenty-four hours she wished she hadn't been so miserly about her clothes. When clothes rationing had been eased in March, she could have done like so many girls and rushed out to buy something new; then she wouldn't have been forced to resort to this dusty rose shirtwaist dress that still smacked of utility clothes. It wasn't shabby—it was the newest frock she owned, the one she saved for all informal special occasions—but it was three years old, and the style more than the quality of the fabric showed its age. If she were simply shopping, she might appear almost chic to some ladies. Before a Princess, she was going to look like a frog.

Outside the cab, the gray London sky muted what little color existed in the stone buildings of the city, the black cars and the ashen faces of people hurrying to and from work or the shops. The sandbags that had protected buildings and the endless sea of uniformed men were gone, with only a hint of khaki to be spied here and there, but the dullness had not worn off, and some days it felt to Vera as if it never would. Gaping holes left in blocks of buildings continued to mar the roads. Some of them had been cleaned out, but too many remained filled with charred and broken timbers and mounds of rubble, a horrid reminder that not everything destroyed had been rebuilt or ever could be.

The face of the city outside the cab changed as the driver turned from St. James onto Pall Mall. The stream of people on the sidewalk lessened, the subtle difference in the tone of the street here noticeable like a clearing in the clouds over the Thames. Vera caught glimpses of the river between the buildings, the boats plying the dark and muddy water never carrying enough materials or food to ease austerity or the money needed from goods sold overseas to make the pound the currency it had once been, but these things faded when the tall building of the Savoy came into view.

Vera dug into her purse for the fare when the cab turned into the courtyard leading to the black-and-white marble-columned entrance of the grand hotel. A footman in a long coat and smart black hat approached and opened the door. Vera handed the money to the driver and stepped out of the car, peering up at the massive Savoy Hotel. For the last four years, since the end of the war, she and her family had resided in their nearby Mayfair town house, and never once had she been here. Not for tea or a ball or simply to stride through the columned and dark wood front hall to make her way to the

Thames Foyer to buy one of their famed chocolates. There'd simply never been a reason to come here, until today.

Vera, conscious of the time, hurried to the concierge desk and the thin-haired, slim man standing behind it in his black suit.

"Excuse me, sir, I'm the Honorable Vera Strathmore. Her Royal Highness, the Princess Margaret is expecting me for lunch." These were words she'd never imagined she'd utter to anyone, and they rolled across her tongue like expensive caviar. She wished she'd brought the invitation with her, but in the frantic three hours it had taken her and Alice to fuss over her dress and hair, she'd forgotten it. She shouldn't have; she might need it in case the man behind the desk didn't believe her. She barely believed it.

Without so much as a questioning curl of his thin mustache, he checked a piece of paper beside the phone in front of him. "I'm sorry, miss, we have no one listed under that name for the Royal Suite."

Vera's heart began to race as the triumph that had set the Strathmore house abuzz that morning threatened to come to an inglorious end. She would have to go home and endure her mother's cutting remarks about her having squandered a rare opportunity. Then it struck her. "Would you please check and see if it's under the name Mrs. Rose Lavish."

He checked his list again, a more deferential air coming over him. "Yes, Mrs. Lavish, right this way."

He led her across the checkered marble floor of the entrance hall to one of the elevators leading to the upper stories. Vera clutched her pocketbook tight while the elevator climbed up into the hotel and closer to Her Royal Highness. When they stopped and the elevator attendant shoved aside the metal gate, the concierge led her down the long hall toward an unremarkable door at the far end. Their muffled steps against the hallway carpet were accompanied by the muted sound of a jazz number's saxophone emanating from one of the rooms flanking the hall. The closer they drew to the room at the end, the louder the music became, until it was clear it was coming from inside. The concierge rapped on the door, and a portly man in a morning suit with a gray waistcoat and ascot opened it and the music spilled out in rapid, clear bursts of notes.

"Mrs. Rose Lavish to see Her Royal Highness," the concierge announced, passing Vera off to the butler.

"This way, Mrs. Lavish. Her Royal Highness is in the sitting room."

He led her through the gracious foyer of the suite with its view of the Thames, and past a hallway of yellow silk curtains framing the windows, the brightness of the fabric and the white walls behind them dispersing the cloudy gray from outside. At the end of the hall, Vera could see a bedroom with a pair of silk stockings tossed over a chair and a white robe crumpled on the floor.

The music increased in tempo, accompanied by girlish laughs and chatter. Vera wondered if, when they reached the sitting room, she might not find the Princess playing the saxophone herself to heaven knew which distinguished guests. Her imagination wasn't far off the mark when the butler led her into the room. At the far end of it, Sass and Princess Margaret danced together in what could only be described as a more frenetic version of the Lindy Hop.

The elegantly appointed room was painted white with elaborate molding framing an oil painting of a ship at sea. Two yellow silk sofas faced each other across an oval table. Beside them stood rosewood tables supporting blue-and-white willow-patterned lamps and half-full glasses of lemonade. In the corner, near the built-in bookcase of rosewood to match the table stood the record player, surrounded by a hearty collection of records some of which had spilled onto the floor. The room looked more like Alice's had the night of her engagement party than a royal setting for lunch.

"Mrs. Lavish, welcome." Princess Margaret rushed to her, taking her hand and pulling her into the room, as excited as Alice usually was after reading something interesting in the newspaper. "You figured out my little game, then?"

"About the name, yes, Ma'am."

"I just couldn't resist, and you're so clever, I knew you'd figure it out, didn't I, Sass?"

"You certainly did." Sass dropped down on one of the sofas and took up the pitcher of lemonade from the center table and poured herself a glass. "Lemonade, Mrs. Lavish?"

"Yes, please."

The Princess kicked off her dainty shoes and dropped onto

the sofa opposite Sass's. She removed her cigarette holder from where it balanced on the edge of a crystal ashtray, the cigarette in the end still smoking. She rested against the arm of the sofa, the holder at an angle to her so as not to drop ash on the pale pink of her full-skirted dress. The rounded arm of the sofa didn't fare so well, with a number of ashes dirtying the smooth surface.

Sass, wearing a dark green dress in a similar style to the Princess's but with less embroidery and a touch of white lace at the rounded neckline, poured a second glass of lemonade and handed it to Vera.

Vera sat down beside Sass, who pulled her feet up under her dress to make room for the newcomer. Vera set her pocketbook on the table, careful to lay it with the bad seam down, then rested her hands in her lap, her back stiff, afraid to relax too much. Despite the invitation, she wasn't one of them and might be dismissed as easily as she'd been invited. She smoothed her free hand over her skirt, painfully aware of how much limper and plainer it seemed in these rich surroundings.

If the Princess took any note of Vera's attire, she gave no sign of it, smiling with genuine delight and the same ease of manner she'd displayed at Monty's. "Dalton, you may serve lunch now."

"Shall I serve it in the dining room or the sitting room, Ma'am?" he asked with a deference none of the Parkston Hall butlers had ever demonstrated, not even to Vera's father.

"Where shall we dine, Sass?" the Princess asked.

"Let's let our guest decide." Sass rubbed the bottom of one bare foot with her finely manicured hand. Vera did her best to hide her lack of nail polish. With all the typing she did, it was too difficult to keep it from chipping. "What do you say, Mrs. Lavish—here or the dining room?"

Princess Margaret turned to Vera, waiting for an answer with surprising eagerness, and Vera hesitated, wondering which the right answer was, but the discarded shoes, the changing song on the record player, and the table littered with *Photoplay* and *Movie Life* resisted too much formality.

"The living room?" She didn't want to make it a dictate; after all, this was Her Royal Highness's suite, and Vera was simply a guest.

"The living room, of course, how splendid. Dalton, see to it."

"Yes, Ma'am." Dalton strode off to make the arrangement, leaving the three young women alone.

The Princess jumped up to change the record to one of the many from the pile on the floor. She set the needle at the beginning, and the familiar voice of Bing Crosby drifted out of the speaker. "Have you heard his new album? It's divine."

"I haven't heard it, Ma'am," but Bing Crosby wasn't a particular favorite of hers either.

"Sass gets me all the new records from America. If there's anything you want, you must let her know and she'll see what she can do. There's no rationing or shortages in America."

"I do have my connections." Sass set her glass on a side table and clapped her hands when the butler brought in the tray of food, followed by a young maid carrying a tray of desserts. "What a spread. I'm starving."

Vera moved her pocketbook out of the way while a white-capped maid set down her tray at one end of the table and hustled to collect the magazines, filled ashtray, and errant glasses so the butler could deposit his silver tray on the other end.

Vera took in the selection, doing her best not to appear surprised or overly hungry at the tantalizing delicacies laid before her. Everyone might be making do, but it didn't mean one had to fall on a bounty like a starving street dog.

Princess Margaret was the first to make her choice, taking two small sandwiches and placing them in the center of her fine china plate before sitting back. Sass followed her lead, except she filled her plate, sitting forward to eat while the Princess made no more than a cursory taste of her fare.

Vera selected a respectable number of sandwiches, forcing herself to eat slowly despite wanting to be through with them and on to the tempting desserts. With the reinstatement of the sugar rationing, it'd been a long time since she'd been allowed to indulge.

"I suppose you're wondering why you're here?" Princess Margaret set aside her barely eaten food and folded her hands in her lap, a touch of the regal coming over her. It made Vera sit up a little straighter too.

"To read aloud from one of my novels, Ma'am?" She balanced her plate on her lap while she fished a copy of her latest novel out of her handbag and held it out to the Princess.

"How marvelous, I haven't read this one. Thank you so very much, but I want something a touch more real." She laid the book on the side table beside the Chinese lamp and went to the bar trolley near the record player. She selected a bottle of whiskey and poured two fingers' worth into a glass and added a splash of Malvern Water. Vera drank her lemonade to avoid any whisper of shock appearing on her face. That was rather strong stuff for a young woman, and this early in the day. "I pride myself on . . . how do you say it, Sass? Keeping my ear to the ground? But it appears from last night, not even I am aware of everything." She slid an irritated glance toward the floor, her vivacity tempered a bit before she regained it as she settled back on the sofa, her drink in hand. "I want you to tell me everything you know about anyone else in my Set, although I don't know why everyone calls it my Set when it's really Sass's."

"Because Sass's Set doesn't sell newspapers like Princess Margaret's Set does," Sass answered, plucking three more sandwiches from the tray.

Princess Margaret pursed her lips. "Beastly press, they can't find fault with my sister, their future queen, so they find it with me. The Germans should have bombed Fleet Street."

"The press sounds like my mother, Ma'am," Vera hazarded, recalling the brief moment of solidarity at Monty's last night. "My sister, Alice, can do no wrong. I, on the other hand . . ."

"She sounds like a real peach." Sass darkened her fingertips with chocolate while taking an éclair.

"She is." Vera finished her sandwich and, trying not to

appear like Oliver Twist, set her sights on the desserts, wondering whatever she was going to tell the Princess. Other than Rupert and David, she wasn't acquainted with the grand secrets of anyone in the Margaret Set.

"So, what do you know?" the Princess pressed.

Vera chewed her éclair, the chocolate not very decadent under the weight of royal anticipation, but the pause gave her time to think. She could lie, repeat some of the things her mother regularly told her about lords and ladies, but she doubted stories of inconsequential country lords were of any interest to Princess Margaret. It was clear the young royal had been embarrassed last night because she'd been the last to learn that one of her admirers was striking out and she didn't wish to find herself in that position again. It was a goal Vera could not help her achieve. Meeting the Princess's eager eyes, she knew she couldn't lie to her. She was being kind to Vera, and Vera owed her the single thing she could offer: the truth. "I'm sorry, Ma'am, there isn't much I know that'd be of interest to you. My knowledge of Lord Westmorland's engagement was a fluke. I can tell you Rupert is leaving for America in January to start an import business. Americans love our sports cars, and he aims to give them more of what they want, but he probably already told you about that."

"Yes, he did, and thank you for being honest with me. Not many people are." She took a cigarette out of the pack on the table, tucked it into her holder, grabbed a silver box full of matches, lit one, and held it to the end. "So, I'm to lose another one, then?"

"You still have all the others the King approves of," Sass reminded, trying to cheer up her friend before tilting her head in knowing secret at Her Royal Highness. "And there's also a certain equerry."

"Who happens to be married." Princess Margaret shook out the match hard, like a terrier killing a rat, then flicked it on the table, where it smoked, leaving a little mark in the smooth polish. "But we're not, and we can enjoy ourselves until we are, whenever that may be, can't we, Mrs. Lavish?"

It wasn't a bold proclamation but a genuine question asked with a searching that touched Vera. No, neither of them was married, or likely to be anytime soon, and the world was making that fact painfully clear to them through their sisters.

"Yes, we must, Ma'am," Vera stated with conviction. "What else can we do? Cry into our pillows every night?"

"We can't have that." Princess Margaret tipped her glass to Vera, the confidence that had marked her in the receiving line in her attitude once again. No, she wouldn't give up, and neither would Vera. Things would change; they had to, because change was the only certainty. "Let's start enjoying ourselves by you telling me what gossip you have heard, even if it's about people I've never met. I always enjoy a good tale."

"I can certainly do that." Selecting another sandwich to fortify her, she began to repeat every story she'd heard at the

Lowells' or from her mother in the past few weeks. She started with Lady Sommeville's daughter becoming engaged and continued on to Lady Sommeville's supposed affair with a young underbutler, who, owing to being particularly blessed below the waist, was popular with the maids, and more than one house party guest who'd gotten wind of his special talents. Vera told her tales until she too had kicked off her shoes and sat with her feet tucked beneath her, keeping Her Royal Highness and Sass in fits of laughter, Princess Margaret devouring each whispered rumor as if it was worthy of print in *The People*.

After more than an hour, their peals of laughter were interrupted when the door to the sitting room opened and the rosy-cheeked brunette who'd been speaking with Her Royal Highness during the Dorchester ball entered the room. Behind her, a small legion of maids carrying a dress bag, hat box, and makeup case filed down the hall to the suite bedroom, taking their order from the imperious Scotswoman who commanded them. "Your Royal Highness, it's time to dress for the charity tea."

Princess Margaret let out a cloud of smoke in her exasperated exhale. "Oh, Bevies, can't you tell Mummy I have a headache?"

"I'm sorry, Ma'am, but the Queen is especially insistent that you attend. You know she prefers you and Princess Elizabeth to appear together at these events."

"Yes, heaven forbid we not be a matched set." Princess Margaret stubbed out the cigarette in the crystal ashtray. "Not having to be paraded about like an heirloom salt and pepper set will be one of the few consolations I'll enjoy when Lilibet finally ascends to her glorious throne."

The young brunette ignored the remark, continuing on with her duty. "Miss MacDonald brought the dress so that you may change here, and the hairdresser is on her way to do your hair."

"I suppose if I must, I must." Princess Margaret set down her glass and hurried up to the woman, gripping her gloved hands in her bare ones. "I hope you don't plan on leaving me for that Captain of yours anytime soon. I don't know what I'd do without you."

"Thank you, Ma'am." The young lady, who couldn't have been much older than the Princess or Sass, nodded with the manners of a courtier far beyond her years.

"Before we go, allow me to introduce you to the Honorable Vera Strathmore, or should I say Mrs. Rose Lavish. She writes those naughty romances I gave you. Vera, this is my lady-in-waiting Miss Jennifer Bevan."

"Oh, I quite enjoyed those novels and how they always work out in the end," Miss Bevan exclaimed.

"I'm glad. I think no matter how destitute or perilous a woman's situation, she deserves a happy ending."

"Yes, they do," Miss Bevan agreed, with a blush that told Vera she would leave the Princess for her Captain sooner rather than later, and the Princess didn't know it yet. Vera gave no hint of noticing or suggesting it might happen. The Princess, standing beside her friend, was happy, and Vera didn't want to be like her mother and crush it.

"Miss Strathmore is Lord Ratherdale's daughter." Apparently, the Princess had checked her copy of *Debrett's* since Vera had last seen her. "Think of it: if she can write those novels secretly, imagine what I might do on the sly."

"You mean what you haven't already done." Sass laughed.

"Not as much as I'd like. Good day, ladies."

Vera rose and curtseyed to the Princess. "Good day, Ma'am, and thank you for lunch."

Princess Margaret nodded and then escorted her lady-in-waiting down the hall. The butler, having positioned himself just outside the door, reached in and closed it on Sass and Vera.

"I suppose I should be going." Vera was reluctant to surrender this opulence for the dour furnishings of home, but she had a novel to finish. Her obligations weren't as glamorous as Her Royal Highness's, but if she didn't meet them, then there wouldn't be another few pounds to add to her growing travel fund, the one that would someday carry her out of Mayfair and England.

"Not at all. We can stay here as long as we like. Have some more to eat if you want." Sass leaned back on the sofa and tossed her arm up over the back of it, kicking her feet into the empty space where Vera had been. "My father is entertaining the Russian finance minister this afternoon, so I intend to stay for a good, long time."

"I suppose I can stay for a little while longer." Vera sat down on what had been the royal sofa and helped herself to more food. She'd be far more productive at her typewriter on a full stomach. She'd written on an empty one enough times in the past four years to know. She'd just selected a small fruit tart when Sass rose and came to sit beside her.

"I'm holding an exclusive fashion show at the embassy next week, very intimate but a great chance to see the new American designers without the press getting on their high horses about austerity. I think you should come."

So much for no one commenting on Vera's obvious lack of style.

"Thank you so much, but I can't." She didn't want to look at new dresses she couldn't afford to buy without dipping deeper into her savings than the few bob for the cabdriver.

"Of course you can come. I'll have something sent over for you so you aren't uncomfortable." Vera was uncomfortable about this obvious charity and was about to say so in very polite terms, but Sass didn't give her the chance. "I get so many things from designers, I can't hope to wear them all. It's one of the advantages of knowing me, the things I can get from America and other sources." Sass nudged her with her elbow and then turned serious. "Margo likes you, I can tell, and she needs friends, not all the bowing and kowtowing yes-people, or those blue-blooded men the King keeps picking out for her. Oh, they do a good game of flattering her and jumping at her every whim, but as you saw with David, they aren't here for the long haul. They'll have their fun and then marry someone else, and then where will Margo be?"

Wealthy, a king's daughter, still residing in the palace, Vera wanted to say, but as she'd learned from her own experiences, titles were no guarantee of security or happiness.

"She needs people who understand her, and I think you do, and you're discreet and capable of keeping a secret, what with your writing and all. That's a rare trait and a good one for Margo."

Vera gripped the side of her plate, Sass's eagerness to bring her into the Set tempting and terrifying at the same time. It was one thing to come here and pretend for an hour that she was merely chatting with friends, but they weren't friends, they were something entirely different, and Vera wasn't one for make-believe, but Sass's plea called to her. Vera longed to be noticed and to become more than a pitied spinster. But a friend of royalty? It sounded as ludicrous in Sass's straightforward American voice as it had in Rupert's Eton tone, and yet Sass shared the same opinion as her cousin. Vera didn't have the resources to enjoy this life to the full, but to be a small part of it even for a short time, to perhaps meet someone who might help her achieve her dreams or forget her disappointments, proved irresistible. Nothing still might come of it, but for a while she could enjoy herself and finally prove to her mother—

and to herself—that she was more than a disappointment, that she was someone worthy of notice. She could finally find some benefit in the freedom of being single. "I'd love to come."

"Good, then it's settled."

Vera had no idea what was settled except that she was going to do something that might, with any luck, bomb her old life to smithereens like the Luftwaffe had done to great swaths of London. She'd craved change when she'd followed Rupert to the Dorchester. She might just have it.

Chapter Five

Vera pulled the blanket closer around her neck and breathed on her fingers in an attempt to thaw them out. The Strathmores' Mayfair town house had never been a bastion of warmth and heat during the cold months, but it'd become worse in the past few years. The restrictions on heating fuel were a good reason for her parents to spend even less of their dwindling income on basic necessities than they had during the war. Not even the weak early-November sun filtering in through her bedroom window was enough to take the chill off the room. She could lug the Remington typewriter downstairs and try to work in the sitting room, but her mother hadn't left for her bridge club yet and would complain about the clicking keys giving her a headache. It was worth risking chilblains to stay upstairs and work in peace.

Vera sat up and stretched the stiffness out of her lower back. She'd tried to work after coming home from the Savoy the day before, but she'd been too keyed up by her time with Princess

Margaret and Sass to concentrate. It was costing her today, but with the novel due Friday and still one more chapter to go, she had to work. Heaven knew how she would end the story. Ever since the engagement party, tales of love and happily ever after didn't hold the same allure they once had. If she thought she could get away with it, she'd kill the hero and heroine in a carriage accident and be done with it, but Mr. Baker, her publisher, wasn't about to approve that.

She fingered the stack of typewritten pages beside the typewriter, lifting up a corner and allowing them to fall into place one by one. There was another, different story she very much wanted to write, a work of fiction with a sparkle of truth to it like Nancy Mitford's novels. It involved a country countess, Lady Penrose, and a world Vera knew a great deal better than that of Victorian dukes and the governesses they seduced. What she wouldn't give to abandon Rose Lavish to concentrate on the Lady Penrose novel, but she had a deadline, and at present, her Mrs. Lavish stories paid the bills.

She settled her fingers over the typewriter keys, ready to resurrect her characters, when a sharp knock at the door made her hands stiffen. Her mother wasn't likely to leave the warmth of the downstairs sitting room to trouble Vera, but it wasn't beyond contemplation to imagine that curiosity had finally gotten the better of her. At dinner the night before, her mother had tried to drag every last detail of Vera's trip to the Savoy out of her, but Vera had given her only the barest of details.

Rupert and even Sass had cautioned discretion, and Vera's mother was not the most discreet woman, at least not where gossip was concerned.

"Come in." Vera braced herself for a confrontation with her mother. Her shoulders relaxed when Alice slipped through the door carrying a large parcel wrapped in brown paper.

"This arrived for you." She handed the package to Vera. "It's from the American embassy. Who do you know there?"

"Sass Douglas."

"The Ambassador's daughter? She's always in the papers with Princess Margaret. What did she send you?" Alice dropped down onto the bed and clasped one bedpost, her hazel eyes wide with her eagerness for Vera to open the parcel and reveal what was inside.

Vera pulled off the brown paper and then took the lid off the rectangular box and set it on the floor. With the box balanced on her legs, she unfolded the tissue paper and removed a number of packages of nylons.

"Nylons!" Alice reached out to touch one of the packages before pulling back her hand as if they were breakable and she might shatter them. "I haven't seen a new pair in ages."

Vera selected two packages and handed them to her sister. "Have them. You deserve them, but be sure to save one for your wedding day. I don't know if I'll get something like this again."

Alice clasped the packages to her chest with a smile of delight before coming to stand over Vera. "What else is in there?"

Vera moved aside more tissue paper to reveal a deep green

wool suit. She held up the jacket, noting the matching pencil skirt folded beneath it.

"Oh my," she breathed, running her thumb and forefinger over the dark brown velvet trimming the cuffs and the collar. Not since she'd sat with her grandmother in the attic all those years ago and helped her remove her old debutante gowns from the trunk had she felt material this fine and soft.

Alice fingered one of the gold buttons on the double-breasted top. "Your new friend is very generous."

"And at least a size larger than me." The suit would have to be taken in to fit Vera correctly, but it would be worth the extra expense to have it done professionally. She didn't trust the maids to do it properly, and she couldn't afford to have it ruined. An outfit like this could help her make influential friends, none of whom she wished to meet looking as though she were wearing someone else's castoffs.

Vera carefully laid the suit jacket and matching skirt on the quilted coverlet of her bed, then moved aside more tissue paper to reveal a seafoam-green satin tea dress. It wasn't so much the mature cut of the dress or the fine fabric that caught her attention as the label sewn inside.

"She sent you a Madame Grès!" Alice squealed, her excitement matching Vera's restrained shock.

Vera took it out of the box and then set the cardboard on the bed beside the suit. The dress had the same full skirt as the ones Sass and Princess Margaret had worn at the Savoy, but with a chic scooped neck trimmed in white lace to contrast with the darker satin. For a quick moment, the amount Vera could earn by selling it flicked through her mind, but the slide of the soft fabric between her fingertips was more alluring than money. Dressed in this, she could hold her own in any room in front of any person, and she would not trade that for all the pounds in England.

"There's an evening dress too." Alice removed the last item from the box and held it up to reveal the rich champagne color with a scalloped V-neck and three-quarter-length sleeves. The waist was drawn in the middle with rushing, but the skirt flared out with a touch of netting beneath to make it even fuller. "If this didn't put my wedding dress to shame, I'd insist you wear it to the wedding."

"No, I'm not about to allow someone else's generosity to let Mother and Father get out of paying for my new bridesmaid dress." Besides, if things continued to work out with Sass and Her Royal Highness, Vera would need all the new clothes she could get her hands on. These outfits from Sass were marvelous and far more than she'd expected, but they would carry her only so far. How she'd ever repay this kindness she didn't know, but she'd think of something.

"Mother and Father should buy you something new. It's the least you deserve for putting up with them." Alice's eyes lit up with conspiracy before she dropped down onto the bed and riffled through the tissue paper to see if there were any other surprises, but the box was empty.

"Too bad there isn't a winter coat in the lot. I could use one

of those." Vera selected a hanger from the _____
up the evening dress.

Alice watched her, her lighter hair swept ba___
forehead, her nose shorter and rounded like the____
her eyes were kind and filled with a concern tha___
showed in their father's similarly shaped eyes when h_
hunting dog was sick. "These are lovely things, and you
lucky to get them, but I'm surprised to see you accepting __
ity. It isn't like you to admit you want or need anything."

Vera paused in fixing the suit on a hanger, careful not to
crush the fabric as she tucked it in between her other clothes. "I
don't have a choice. I can't make a good impression with this."
She waved her hand at the open wardrobe door and the muted
and limp dresses and skirts hanging inside the old burled
wood piece. The place where she and numerous past Strathmores had opened and closed the doors showed in the worn-
off varnish and the naked and scratched wood beneath. "I'm
not about to attend an embassy fashion show and be looked
down on by dukes' daughters who still have the money to afford nice things."

If all went well at the fashion show, perhaps Vera might
widen her current set of male acquaintances and join the ranks
of their exalted sisters. The prosperous men of Margaret's Set
would be a change from the men usually trotted before her at
places like Weatherly Hall.

"I don't blame you, and I'm glad to see you're meeting new
people and doing new things." She crinkled the tissue paper

ers. "I worry about you and what'll happen
between hing when it's just you and Mother and Father.
after spend your entire life cramped up here over your
er."

a pushed aside the window curtain to watch the quiet
et below and the single car passing by. The clouds weren't
s thick today, allowing patches of sun and blue sky to appear
occasionally over the tops of the town houses spreading down
the block and the gold and brown leaves still clinging to the
mostly bare branches of the trees in the iron-fenced square in
the center. Alice wasn't the only one worried about Vera. Ever
since Alice had become engaged, Vera had done all she could
not to think about the day Alice would leave. She glanced at
the flash of seafoam-green satin from inside the wardrobe, the
fabric so bright against the muddy ones beside it. She didn't
just want to wear it; she *needed* to wear it. "What if nothing
comes of it?"

"With everything that's happened already, I think a great
deal will come of it. Why wouldn't it?"

The yellowed and faded telegram from the War Office tucked
in the top of Vera's dresser beside the picture of Henry in his
uniform was why, but Vera didn't say it. She couldn't admit to
even Alice how much the loneliness and meaninglessness of
her life still engulfed whole days. Her sister might sympathize,
but with her time filled with future plans or the company of
her fiancé, she couldn't understand the depth of Vera's loss. No
one did. Vera picked the crumpled blanket off the back of her

"By the way, the dress looks gorgeous on you."

"You won't tell anyone, will you?" Vera didn't want to be reduced to a charity case in the middle of this group of daughters of high-ranking peers, all of whom had barely acknowledged her presence.

"I won't say a word." Sass gave her shoulder a friendly squeeze and then rose, returning to her seat beside Princess Margaret. Before reaching the Princess, she stopped to speak with two young ladies Vera vaguely recognized from the *Court Circular* as Lady Elizabeth Montagu Douglas Scott, Johnny Dalkeith's sister, and Lady Caroline Thynne. Across from them, Jennifer Bevan sat with Katharine and Laura Smith. Despite their simple last names, they were the daughters of Viscount Hambleden and had all but grown up with Princess Margaret.

Vera sat by herself, pretending not to mind that there was no one for her to ooh and aah with over the clothes. Despite her couture dress and heritage, she was still the odd woman out. If it hadn't been for the look of respect on her mother's face when she'd climbed in the taxi to come here, the quid spent to alter her dress wouldn't have been worth it.

Of course it was worth it. She couldn't expect to become fast friends with these women after a single introduction. She had to give it time, which she would have at the luncheon after the show. Until then, Vera focused on the mannequin standing in front of her, who opened her cape to reveal the brocade trim inside. Past the winglike movement of the mannequin's arms and cape, Vera noticed Sass whispering to Princess Margaret.

The royal studied a gown of light pink with sprigs of olive leaves embroidered near the waist. The Princess dismissed the mannequin with the wave of one gloved hand and stood.

The royal movement caused the mannequins' steps to stutter, and a brief pause in the vendeuse's melodious voice. Even the ladies in the audience hesitated in their examination of the clothes to watch what the royal did. With a flick of the Princess's slender fingers, everyone carried on as they had before. The vendeuse resumed her fluid speech, her voice like the plucked notes of the harp, marking the pace of Princess Margaret's stride across the room. Vera held her breath when she realized that Princess Margaret was making for her.

"Which dress is your favorite, Mrs. Lavish?" Princess Margaret lowered herself into the empty chair beside Vera, resting her elbow on the arm, her legs crossed at the heels where they curved off to one side. She was languid but not in the manner of the teenager who'd been with Vera at the Savoy.

"There's too many I adore, but if I had to pick one, it would be the navy blue tea dress with the sheer sleeves, Ma'am. Which one would you choose?"

"The strapless gown in dark red."

"A daring choice, Ma'am."

"I'd get one wear out of it before Mummy made me add straps to it like she did that beautiful Dior you saw me in the other night. As if a scrap of satin really makes a difference."

It did when there was a great deal more aristocratic acreage to hold up than what Vera possessed, but not even she was bold enough to point this out. The attention of everyone in the room was no longer on the mannequins but on the two of them. The women pretended to admire a robin's-egg-blue swing jacket with floral print inside, but they were all probably wondering who this Johnny-come-lately commanding the Princess's attention was. Vera sat up a touch straighter, remembering that for all the lack of luster her father's title might carry, it was still a title, and she, by right of birth, had as much reason to be here as they did. The only real difference between them and her was the size of their Bank of England accounts.

"I read the book you gave me." Princess Margaret never took her eyes off the mannequins or the dresses they paraded through the room. "I heartily enjoyed it."

Vera wished that was a quote she could put on the front cover. It might increase her sales and at last make her enough money in royalties to send her to New York or allow her to buy a few of these outfits. Sadly, she'd have to suffer smaller royalty checks if she wanted more invitations to events like this.

"Tell me, Mrs. Lavish, where do you get your ideas for your novels?" Princess Margaret raised one gloved finger and motioned for the model in the blue swing jacket to come closer.

Vera shrugged. "Things I hear, stories I read in the newspaper."

The mannequin stopped in front of them and turned from side to side, opening the jacket to reveal the very intricate rose pattern of the silk lining it.

"Come now, Mrs. Lavish, I've read your books, and some of

those scenes are nothing an unmarried girl could glean from the newspapers, at least not British ones. Are the more intimate scenes derived from personal knowledge?"

The mannequin's eyes met Vera's before she raised them to stare over her and Princess Margaret's heads, as if she wasn't standing in front of them and waiting to hear the answer too.

Vera swallowed hard, working to not squirm. She wasn't averse to having such a personal discussion with friends, but not with a woman third in line to the throne and in front of a mannequin who might return to her mother in the East End tonight with a whopper of a tale. How the devil was she supposed to answer the question?

Princess Margaret turned in her chair to face Vera, waiting for an answer. The last thing Vera wanted to do was make this woman wait.

"I was engaged during the war." Vera slid a glance at the mannequin in an attempt to hint that she should be sent away. Princess Margaret either didn't care that the woman was still listening or didn't take the hint, continuing to fix on Vera, waiting for her to continue. "My fiancé and I were intimate before he was sent overseas."

Given the way her life had turned out, she was glad they had been, for it didn't seem likely she'd ever be on such familiar terms with a man again.

"I see." With a curt wave, Princess Margaret finally sent the mannequin along to the next interested group of young ladies. She then sat up and leaned closer, with an intimacy Vera never in all her life would have imagined engaging in with royalty. "And how did you avoid any consequences?"

Vera blinked hard, wondering how much detail Princess Margaret expected, and in the sitting room of the American embassy of all places. Not even for her books had she dreamed up something like this, but she had to imagine there weren't too many other places for a sheltered Princess to learn a thing or two. Maybe Princess Elizabeth had enlightened her younger sister after her wedding night, but Vera doubted it. It was near impossible to picture the staid heir to the throne perching on the edge of her sister's bed and telling her everything the way Vera had told Alice all those years ago. What the King and Queen would think of Vera giving their daughter this education was even more unnerving. It was one thing to secretly write about these things under a pen name and quite another to speak to the King's daughter about it, but with the Princess eagerly waiting for an answer, she couldn't become a prude now.

"The army gave the men things." Vera's throat was so tight she could hardly get the words out. "To help prevent consequences, Ma'am."

"What things?" Princess Margaret pressed, as if inquiring after the price of a new strand of pearls to go with the ones already encircling her neck.

Good lord. How Vera would get through the rest of this conversation without dying of embarrassment she wasn't sure, but if this was the way into the royal confidence, then so be it.

"They gave him things to cover his . . ." Vera rolled her hand in the air between them, hoping she didn't need to explain everything to the Princess. Hopefully a governess or Sass, maybe even one of the men from the Set, had given her at least the basics. Even Vera's mother, who always repeated salacious stories with more innuendo than details, had possessed the wherewithal to do that. ". . . So as to prevent consequences."

Princess Margaret nodded with the same seriousness as if Vera had just explained the importance of the Magna Carta. "And where, when not in the service, does a man get these kinds of things?"

Oh, for heaven's sake. Was she going to have to draw pictures for her next? "From the chemist or a doctor."

"It's as easy as that?"

"If not, there'd be a great deal more gossip going around than there already is." She wondered what the Princess's interest in the availability of prophylactics was, but she was not about to ask. The royal inquisition went only one way.

"I suppose you're right." Princess Margaret nodded thoughtfully before the introduction of the evening collection drew her attention back to the fashion show, providing Vera with a much-needed break from teaching the royal anything more about the birds and the bees.

Princess Margaret, to Vera's surprise, remained beside her through the presentation, and Vera began to relax until the Princess's next question nearly knocked her out of her chair.

"Your gentleman didn't survive the war, did he?"

The colors of the models' silk gowns and the bright gilding on the molding faded. "No, Ma'am, he didn't."

Sympathy filled the Princess's blue eyes, and she reached over and laid a small hand on Vera's, giving it a light squeeze. "I'm very sorry for your loss."

"Thank you, Ma'am." She was truly grateful for her concern, for there'd been very little of it since the weeks after the funeral.

"I admire you for defying convention to seize your enjoyment while you could." She set her hands back in her lap, picking at the small button on her glove. "You're lucky to have the freedom to choose who you wish to be with without anyone criticizing."

"I'm not free from my parents' criticism. With my sister's wedding approaching, it's been especially frequent lately."

"Yes, but your parents aren't the King and Queen of England."

Vera studied the Princess, the curiosity in her eyes from their previous conversation replaced by disappointment. This woman had everything, but it was plain she was being denied something she truly wanted, and it was more than dresses without straps or hearing gossip first. "Even a princess can find a way to do what she wants and be with whom she wants, Ma'am, and gain her happiness."

"Do you really believe that?"

"It's what I write in all my novels."

"Then it must be true." Princess Margaret laughed and clapped her gloved hands together, drawing the attention of the room before it settled again on the mannequins. "Speaking of what I want, what do you think of this dress? It would be marvelous for the Buck Place Christmas Ball."

"You'd be the toast of the press in it." In the white organdy dress drawn to one side at the waist and decorated with matching white bows, the press would fawn over her more than they already did. She could already see knockoffs of the dress appearing at debutante balls all over London next spring.

"What would you wear if you were to go to the ball?"

Vera's heart raced, wondering if this was a prelude to an invitation or simply another game of what-if. "The hunter-green taffeta one. It's marvelous."

"Then you must get it."

"No, I can't." The cost of it would take a good chunk out of her last advance and set her that much further behind in reaching New York.

"You must." Princess Margaret waved over the mannequin.

The mannequin glided toward them, the fine taffeta, scooped neckline, and fitted bodice whispering of elegance and everything Vera could never be in the sad clothes hanging in her wardrobe.

"You should get it; I can see already how it suits you," Princess Margaret tempted from beside her.

"Yes, I should." In this, she'd be the talk of Lady Mattlemore's annual Christmas ball, and for all the right reasons for once. Her advance and New York be damned. They were in the future and this was now, and she wanted this dress and everything it and the Princess promised.

Before the show was over, Princess Margaret tempted Vera into purchasing three blouses and two skirts. Vera's eyes nearly watered at the price afterward when the ladies sat with the assistant vendeuses to finalize the orders. Under normal circumstances, Vera would have been required to pay half up front, but the pretty little representative with the glossy hair and the very red lips assured Vera that her being a close friend of the Princess was as good as credit. Vera didn't have the courage to inform the perky girl that she wasn't all that close to royalty. It risked being revealed by this working-class girl who'd improved her accent but not enough to erase every trace of the Midlands from her vowels that Vera was a bigger fraud than her when it came to refinement and elegance. She'd have to pay the balance at the final fitting, and it made her stomach hurt to think about handing over that much of her savings for new clothes, but she couldn't have the vendeuse badgering the Princess because one of her friends had skipped out on her bill.

When the orders were finished, Sass led the ladies through to the embassy dining room and the tea arranged on the large table in the center. A moment later, a number of men from the Margaret Set spilled into the room, fanning out among the women to chat and enjoy sandwiches and cakes. Dr. Reynolds was among them, and Sass gave him an exuberant hug before pointing him in Vera's direction. He needed little encouragement to make his way through the throng of dukes' and earls' daughters to reach her.

"The Honorable Vera Strathmore, it's a pleasure to see you

again." He shook her hand, his fingers firm and tight around hers. It'd been a long time since any man had made her stomach flutter like this, and it both thrilled and terrified her. "Tell me, how does your title stand up to everyone else's in here?"

"It's not as grand as some, but I can hold my own." It was her pocketbook that couldn't keep pace.

"Am I very far down the pecking order?"

"Very, but the *doctor* in front of your name places you a bit above the footmen but not quite as high as the ambassador's assistant. You're allowed to come in the front door instead of the servants' entrance and eat at the table with your host."

He laughed, a low, guttural sound that made her breath catch in her chest. "I'm truly honored, then."

"You shouldn't be. A title isn't what it used to be, but stay here in England long enough and perhaps you'll gain one. A famous medical technique or something might do the trick."

He rubbed his square chin thoughtfully with his thumb and forefinger. "It's tempting to have Sir or Lord on my letterhead, but I'm afraid I won't be here long enough to earn the honor. I go home in another month, when my teaching tenure ends."

Leave it to her to have the one man in the room who wouldn't be here past the New Year show an interest in her. "And then it's back to reality."

"For both of us, I imagine."

"Sooner for me." The moment she strode out of the embassy doors and walked to the tube station. "In the meantime, I'm enjoying a little taste of the new fashion you Yanks take for granted."

"I suppose there's no harm in that, as long as you know your limits and don't get too caught up in all this."

"I think I'm perfectly capable of knowing my limits."

He leaned in close, his words whispering across her cheek and making her skin tingle. "Yes, but temptation is a powerful force."

"It is." He stood so close that she could see the flecks of amber in his brown eyes and the deep black circle around the iris. Across the room, the light notes of Princess Margaret's laugh made her turn. Princess Margaret stood in her couture dress, her tortoiseshell cigarette holder between her slender fingers and the smoke swirling up from the end adding a haze to the already dreamlike atmosphere of the room. It wouldn't take much to lose herself in pursuit of all this and forget that she had other goals to achieve. "Thankfully, I'm too level-headed to succumb too much to it."

"I'm glad to hear it."

"Doc, tell me you're coming to the embassy Thanksgiving dinner next week." Sass slid up to them, appraising them as if they were a matched set of antique vases. "I can't bear to think of you alone during the holiday."

"I'll be there."

"You must bring Vera as your guest. I'm sure she'd love to see a good old-fashioned American holiday celebrated."

"What do you say, Miss Strathmore? Can I tempt you with some turkey and cranberry sauce?"

He could tempt her with a great deal more, including forgetting he wouldn't be around in the New Year. Who cared? He was there now and offering her a chance to wear that champagne evening gown that Sass had given her. "It sounds wonderful. How could I resist?"

He winked at her, making her heart skip a beat. "You can't."

"That's cracking, as you Brits say. You two will love the party." Sass bounced on her toes and then took Vera's arm. "Sorry to steal her away, but I've been told to introduce Vera to the other ladies. The Smith sisters are dying to meet you."

"Dying?" They hadn't been dying enough to bother to speak with her the entire time she'd been here. Vera was sure they weren't waiting on etiquette to be introduced. A number of the old customs had gone by the wayside after the war, including that one, at least with the younger sort.

"Of course. Everyone wants to meet the woman that Margo sat next to for most of the fashion show."

Vera offered Dominic an apologizing look, much preferring to stay there with him but not wishing to be rude. "It seems I must go."

His smile widened with the same amusement he'd shown at the Dorchester. "See you later, Cinderella."

Yes, the fairy tale was going to continue for a little while longer.

Chapter Six

*I*s Rupert escorting you to the embassy dinner?" Vera's mother stood behind her, watching her turn from side to side in front of the mirror to admire the wide champagne-colored skirt flowing around her legs.

At the sight of herself, Vera felt her lingering doubts about the cost of altering the dress and this evening fade. All she could imagine was Dominic seeing her in this when she came down the stairs to greet him. "No, Rupert is too busy preparing for America to carouse with the Princess like he used to."

"Don't use the word *carouse*. It makes you sound like a shopgirl," her mother chided.

Vera threw a look of exasperation at Alice, who could do little but shrug in sympathy. "My escort tonight is Dr. Reynolds, a friend of the daughter of the American Ambassador."

"An American." Her mother rolled the words in her mouth like an unripe cherry with an especially large pit. "Well, I suppose he's better than the nothing you've brought home for the last few years."

Vera tugged on her gloves in an effort to not throttle her mother. "For once you could tell me how happy you are for me and this new opportunity instead of all these insults."

"They aren't insults but suggestions for how to better yourself." Her mother clasped her hands in front of her and threw back her shoulders. "It's what mothers are supposed to do."

The clank of the front doorknocker echoing through the house spared Vera from enduring any more motherly advice.

"Let's have a look at this American doctor of yours." Her mother left the room, not waiting for either of her daughters.

Vera smoothed her hands over the front of her dress, far more nervous than she should be about seeing Dominic. His time in England was limited, and nothing more than a little fun could ever come of this flirtation. There was nothing to be nervous about. "How do I look?"

"Beautiful, but you'd better get downstairs. You don't want to leave Dr. Reynolds alone with Mother and Father for too long."

"He's a doctor. I'm sure he's dealt with worse." She gathered up her purse and faux fur wrap, another indulgence since the fashion show she still hadn't quite squared with her conscience. When she'd complained about the recent outlays to Rupert, he'd called it an investment in her future. With the faux fur soft against her neck and her scratchy old coat left behind, this was easier to believe.

With Alice close on her heels, Vera passed the empty walls

and over the creaking floorboards until she reached the stairs and the rough banister in need of a polish. She stopped at the top, took a deep breath, and then started slowly down, determined to descend with all the poise expected of the daughter of an aristocrat on her way to a high-society event. "Good evening, Dr. Reynolds."

Dominic's gaze swept the length of her, and his lips turned up in an appreciative smile that made Vera descend with a confidence she hadn't experienced in ages. He stood in the foyer in his black tuxedo, holding his top hat in his gloved hands, the height of him increased by the tailored jacket and the white scarf draped around his neck. He was striking, but in the American way that whispered of rugged men on horseback in an untamed wilderness combined with gallantness to take a girl's breath away. It made Vera wonder why Sass hadn't already snapped him up.

"Good evening, Miss Strathmore." He motioned for her hand, and she proffered it. When he leaned over it to sweep the back of her satin gloves with his lips, it made her girdle go tight beneath her dress. "Shall we be off?"

"Please." She turned to her parents, who watched them with all the excitement of a couple of wax figures. Vera pursed her lips, trying not to allow their lack of enthusiasm to dampen hers. "Don't wait up for me."

"We never wait up for you." Even in front of a guest, her mother saw no reason to pretend at maternal affection.

At least her father had the wherewithal to act like something of a host, extending his hand to Dominic. "It was a pleasure to meet you, Dr. Reynolds."

"And you, Lord Strathmore, and Lady Strathmore." Dominic gave them a little nod that made the corner of Vera's mother's mouth twitch. Whether it developed into a full smile Vera didn't see, hurrying out into the bracing night air and away from the strangling stuffiness indoors.

"How did I do?" Dominic jogged forward to open the passenger door of the white Morris Minor parked at the curb. "Was I appropriately reverential to their stations?"

"I think you impressed Father. Very little impresses Mother." She slid inside the car, the air in there barely warmer than outside. Dominic came around it and sat behind the wheel.

"I'm sorry I can't convey you to the dinner in something more regal, but I didn't bring my Cadillac with me. I borrowed this from another doctor at the hospital."

"They don't ride horses to work in Arizona?" she teased as he guided the car along Hyde Park to where it curved toward the Wellington Arch. She admired his strong profile in the dim light of the dashboard, catching sharper flashes of his face whenever they passed a streetlight or the bright lights of a theatre.

"I would if I could, but I can no longer ride. Accident when I was sixteen." He flexed his fingers over the steering wheel, his arms and shoulders going stiff before he relaxed. "There are days when I really miss the peace of heading out into the wide-open country."

"Me too, but Father sold our horses at the start of the war. They were too expensive to maintain." Vera touched her thumb to her ring finger. Riding had been another in the long list of things she'd once loved that'd been consigned to the past.

"We still have horses, and the ranch." Dominic turned the Morris Minor onto Park Lane and into the line of cars waiting to pull up to the embassy at the far end of Prince's Gate. "When my father decides to retire and turn the clinic over to me, he's going to dedicate his life to raising cattle. My guess is he'll try to cure bovine TB. He can't help himself, and neither can I."

"It's in the blood?"

"It wasn't always, but it is now."

"Good." It was nice to meet a man who was more interested in helping others than bringing a bit of polish to the family's dusty coat of arms.

It wasn't long before they inched up to the front of the embassy. One of the hired drivers took Dominic's place behind the wheel while another opened Vera's door. She stepped out, enjoying the swing of the dress around her calves as she admired the row house. The blazing lights in the windows, the crowd, and the music made it stand out from the long line of sedate houses flanking it.

Vera strode with Dominic up the front walk and into the sea

of voices and people inside. He guided her through the main foyer with its curved, iron-railing staircase and the musicians arranged on the steps playing a selection of patriotic American songs. Amid the cacophony of American accents mingling with the posh tones of Vera's countrymen surged an energy that even the Weatherly Hall party had lacked. There was nothing tired and old here except the building, but even it glittered with fresh gilding and paint and flowers and decorations that scented the air with cinnamon, apples, and wheat. The regular furniture and fixtures had been pushed aside or taken to storage and replaced with numerous round tables covered with white linens that were crisp and new. A wreath of yellow and orange leaves surrounded the seating board listing everyone's names and tables.

"Number two sounds pretty far up in the ranking," Dominic said, peering over the heads of the people clustered around the board to find their names. "Perhaps they've heard about your father's title."

"All that would get us is a place by the back door." She could imagine Princess Margaret being seated well above the salt, but they weren't important enough to merit such an honor.

They walked through the formal reception room adjacent to the main dining room. Like the front sitting room, the furniture had been replaced by arrangements of tables beneath the large chandelier. In the center of each table sat cornucopias filled with dark-kernelled Indian corncobs, squashes, miniature pumpkins, and small papier-mâché turkeys. Following the descending table numbers, they continued on into the main dining room.

Sass's robust laugh caught their attention first, and they wove through the guests toward the gaggle of young, titled men surrounding her and Princess Margaret at the head table. The Princess sat as if holding court; all she needed was a gilded throne, a canopy with a coat of arms, and a red rug in front of her to make the image complete. She was stunning in a white tulle dress with butterflies in flight embroidered on the skirt and sheer ruffled sleeves. A pale blue accent at the waist matched the color of her eyes, while her red lips, when not drawn up in a smile, were closed around the end of her cigarette holder. She was the embodiment of everything meant by English rose, a strange contradiction to the American songs filling the air along with the loud and clipped American accents.

"Friends in high places and all that, right?" Dominic asked. They were seated not at the head table but at the one beside it reserved for the Set.

"The highest of the high."

Laura and Katharine Smith and their escorts were already seated. Lady Caroline Thynne sat beside them, chatting with Billy Wallace and Lady Elizabeth Montagu Douglas Scott. Sunny Blandford stood behind them, listening with his sister, Lady Imogene Spencer-Churchill.

"Vera, you're finally here. Love the dress." Sass batted a hand at Vera from where she stood beside Princess Margaret, her

compliment ensuring that everyone at both tables acknowledged the newcomers.

"Isn't this magnificent, and what a crush," Vera gushed,
wincing at the childish awe in her voice.

Lady Imogene Spencer-Churchill turned her head, set on a
swanlike neck draped with a strand of pearls that would have
made Vera's mother salivate, and looked down on Vera as if
she'd just stepped in something foul. "Not really. We always
have this many people, especially when Uncle Winston is with
us, don't we, Sunny?"

Well, la-di-da, Vera almost mocked, before she bit it back.
The niece of Winston Churchill and the daughter of the Duke
of Marlborough wasn't one to be put in her place by the likes of
a mere baron's daughter.

"Oh, come off your high horse, Imogene, we can't all live in
Blenheim Palace," Lady Caroline Thynne scolded with a wave
of her hand.

Vera was wrong. The Marquess of Bath's daughter, who
would someday become a Duchess when she married the Duke
of Beaufort's heir, could knock the Duke of Marlborough's
daughter down a peg or two.

"I have to admit, there is something refreshing in the way
Americans jam a place full and then wander about as if everyone is simply no one," Lady Spencer-Churchill said, dipping
her chin to lose some of her imperious air, her chestnut-colored
hair fashioned into a thick curl that encircled her head as
much as the stunning diamond tiara set firmly inside it. "If

parties at Blenheim were half this relaxed, they'd be more fun."

A group of American men at the next table laughed so loud it temporarily drowned out "Yankee Doodle Dandy." Vera didn't know who the men were, but if their table was this close to the royal seating arrangement, they had to be of some importance. Americans might profess equality, but they could be status conscious when the need called for it, and an embassy dinner did.

Lady Spencer-Churchill held out her gloved hand with the large diamond on one finger to Vera. "Lady Imogene Spencer-Churchill, but you may call me Imogene."

"The Honorable Vera Strathmore." For the first time in a long time she said her name with pride. She may not have these women's wealth or lands, but she could trace her family tree back as far as theirs, and not through some royal mistress whose bastard had been ennobled.

"You can call her Mrs. Lavish," Princess Margaret commanded.

"So, you're the novelist Sass has been telling me about. I have got to get you alone tonight and pick your brain," Imogene effused, her dark, wide eyes taking on something of a Bette Davis–in–*Jezebel* air. "If I could get away with half of what your characters get away with, I could have a grand time, not that I don't already have my share of fun."

"Don't you just," Caroline teased with a smirk. She was slender with a small nose and a delicate jaw, her chestnut-colored hair brushed up into a mass of tight curls at the crown of her head. "But not as much as you, Ma'am."

"I intend to get up to a great deal more, for Mrs. Lavish is full of helpful information and stories."

"Then don't keep her to yourself," Caroline insisted.

"Oh, I won't." Princess Margaret entwined her arm with Vera's as if she had been her dearest friend for years.

Imogene, Caroline, and the others took note of the gesture, moving back a small half step to welcome Vera and Dominic into the circle.

Dominic watched with all the detached amusement of a man who had no horse in this race. She wished she could be so cavalier, but unlike him, if she wanted to get a little more out of life than a few ten-pence novels she had to play by the rules of her countrymen, especially the ones closest to the throne.

"Ma'am, Mr. Tom O'Brien, MP for Nottinghamshire, would like to speak to you about the film industry tax," Jennifer Bevan tactfully interrupted.

Margaret didn't sigh the way Vera did whenever her mother called her away from friends at parties to introduce her to some doddery old earl or the gap-toothed son of a baronet. Instead, an air of businesslike regality descended over her, replacing the naughty teenager of only a moment before. "If you'll excuse me."

The others dipped respectful curtseys to the highest-ranking person in the room and Vera did the same, expecting the Princess to let go of her and walk off with Jennifer. Instead, she turned to Vera with all the reverence for duty that Jennifer had shown her employer. "Come with me, Mrs. Lavish. I'd like the company."

"Yes, Ma'am." Vera couldn't imagine what use she'd be to the Princess during her conversation with the MP, but she'd been given an order.

"Don't worry, Vera, I'll keep an eye on Doc while you're gone," Sass offered.

Vera wondered how well Sass would take care of him, but if Sass really wanted him, then she could have had him long before he and Vera had been introduced. She could have him again when they returned to the States and Vera was a long way across the channel. Vera adjusted the shoulder of her dress, thinking she should be a little more guarded where he was concerned. Dominic wasn't here for the long haul, simply her date for tonight, and she should leave it at that. It would hurt a great deal less when he left if she did.

"You Royal Highness, may I introduce Mr. O'Brien," Jennifer said when they reached the man.

The elder MP snapped to attention with all the deference of an enlisted man being passed by an officer. "A pleasure, Your Royal Highness."

Princess Margaret let go of Vera, leaving her to wait dutifully off to one side with Miss Bevan while she stood before this member of her father's government. The Princess crossed her hands demurely in front of her with the same royal air that Vera had seen the Queen exhibit in many news reels during the war. "How may I help you?"

"The British film industry is on the verge of crisis. With Mr. Ranke threatening to end productions, what little gains we've made in the American market will vanish. We can't allow this to happen. If His Majesty would support a policy to return in taxes to the Americans the same amount every British film makes in profits in the United States, it will go a long way to ending this awful stalemate over the withholdings."

"Perhaps if we offered more tax incentives for our own productions, and created more films, then the British film industry could better compete in the American market," Princess Margaret suggested.

Vera struggled to keep her jaw from cracking against the floor in surprise, the Princess's grasp of the issue as startling to Vera as it was to the elder Member of Parliament.

"That's an excellent idea, Ma'am."

"I'll be sure to discuss it with the King, for I believe we should do all we can to promote our British-born talent instead of constantly surrendering our market to Hollywood," Princess Margaret assured the MP with a confidence Vera had seen in every picture of her christening a ship or opening a charity school. This was the Princess the public saw, the one Vera, until tonight, had yet to meet. "Good evening, Mr. O'Brien."

With a reverent bow, the MP backed away from Princess Margaret.

"Thank you, Jennifer, for the introduction."

"You're welcome, Ma'am." Understanding that she was also being dismissed, Miss Bevan waded back into the crowd, risking more requests for interviews with the Princess from other political people.

"I may never hold the scepter, but it doesn't mean I'm useless. I'm not, am I?" The façade of the confident royal slipped for a moment to reveal the insecure young woman beneath.

"No, Ma'am, not at all. You have the King's ear and a real grasp of his subjects' concerns. There's a great deal of influence in both."

"There is something of value in that, isn't there?" The Princess didn't seem so certain.

"Very much so, and you're a national asset, crucial to the British economy. Half of Fleet Street would be unemployed if it weren't for you, Ma'am," Vera teased, as she sometimes did with Alice after one of their mother's particularly cutting remarks. Except this wasn't Alice, and, if Vera's limited time with the Set had taught her anything, it was that it wasn't wise to be too unguarded with the Princess. The muscles in the back of Vera's neck went stiff, and she braced herself for a very royal and public rebuke until a sly smile softened the tight line of the Princess's lips.

Princess Margaret drew herself up at least an inch taller, as proud as she was pleased by Vera's frank comment. "I am an industry all to myself, aren't I?"

"You are, Ma'am," Vera agreed, with no small amount of relief at not having inadvertently irked the royal.

"Excuse me, Your Royal Highness, but *Tatler* would like a photo of you," interrupted a man in a tuxedo dinner jacket whom Princess Margaret must have known but who remained a mystery to Vera.

"Yes, of course."

Vera tried to step off to one side, but the Princess clasped her by the arm, forcing her to stay beside her while a man with a large camera and flash stepped forward. "Smile, please."

Vera did as she was told and was blinded by the pop of the flashbulb. "Thank you, Your Royal Highness. What is your name, miss?"

Princess Margaret answered for Vera. "The Honorable Vera Strathmore."

The man wrote down her name and then was led off by his minder to another subject for the next day's edition of *Tatler*.

"Once that picture runs, the press might become a bit of a nuisance," Princess Margaret warned. "They may ask you for details about me for slanderous articles, especially the foreign press, who are beastly and have no sense of restraint where I'm concerned. I know I can trust you not to speak to any of them about our private time together."

"You can count on my discretion, Ma'am." Vera would have preferred not to be in the picture, but she hadn't been given any choice except the one Princess Margaret had made for her.

"Good. Tomorrow, I'll messenger over instructions on how to address your correspondence and calls so they come straight through to me. It's exasperating the silly things I have to go through to simply receive letters or phone calls."

That the Princess was expecting correspondence and calls from Vera almost made her trip as the two of them returned to the tables. She was no longer on the edge of the Princess's circles but a full-fledged member of it. She was as elated as she'd been the day she'd received her first payment for an article on manners for *Ladies' Home Journal* and had finally become more than a pitied ex-fiancée; she'd become a real and true writer. Suddenly, the assurances she'd made to the Princess at the fashion show that they would have their happiness too didn't sound so hollow.

"I'll also send you an invitation to the Royal Command Film Performance, and another for the Buck Place Christmas party. You'll be sure to come."

"I'll be there, Ma'am." Nothing could have kept her away.

"Good, we'll have a marvelous time, especially at the 400 Club after the film."

The Princess took her seat at the top table, drawing around her the other ladies while the gentlemen stood in groups chatting, less interested in the upcoming Royal Command Film Performance of *The Forsyte Saga* than their dates.

"Let's find the bar. I'm parched," Sunny Blandford called

out, then rested his hand on the back of Princess Margaret's chair and leaned over it, more, Vera thought, to take a peek down the front of her dress than to take her drink order. "What would you like, Ma'am?"

"The usual." The Princess didn't even look up at him, addressing him like any other nameless waiter while she dug through her small, pearl-encrusted purse.

"Come on then, gentlemen." Sunny waved the men on. "You too, Doc. You have to make sure they mix us a proper American cocktail."

"I'll do my best," Dominic answered, then leaned in close to Vera. "Will you be all right here by yourself?"

"I can hold my own; can you?" She flicked a glance at the Eton and Harrow classmates gathering to storm some poor, unsuspecting barman.

"I'm old enough to babysit this group." With a wink, he joined the men, the lot of them disappearing into the steadily increasing crowd. Over the heads of the guests, the occasional flashbulb threw shadows on the gilded and plastered walls and a sharp laugh or two rose up to cut through the constant murmur of conversation and the jaunty American tunes.

"I absolutely adore Errol Flynn," Laura Smith said with a sigh, leaning forward on her elbows. Like almost all the women of the Set except Sass, Laura had dark hair, and her face was oval with high cheekbones. "Will we get to meet him at the film, Ma'am?"

The Princess took a tube of lipstick from her clutch and,

opening a matching gold compact, held up both and swiped the vibrant red color over her lips. Vera's mother would have had a fit if Vera had been so gauche as to fix her lipstick in public, but no one here batted an eye. Vera suspected the royal could do her hair up in curlers at the table and it would become all the rage. "I can arrange a meeting with Errol if you'd like."

"Errol, is it?" Caroline purred, her almond-shaped eyes narrowing in impish delight. "I thought it was Danny, or are red-haired men not as fiery as they say?"

"Oh, they're fiery." Princess Margaret slowly twisted her lipstick back into its tube and clicked the lid closed over it. "But you know American film stars—they always think they're so much bigger than they really are."

The other ladies, far from being scandalized, threw back their heads and laughed while Vera forced an awkward smile before catching Sass's eye. Sass shrugged as if to say this was the way of it and that's all there was to it, but Vera couldn't believe it was this simple. The Princess and the actor Danny Kaye? It wasn't possible, but given her response, it was.

"Does that pertain to all redheads, Margo?" Sass jerked a thumb toward Johnny Dalkeith, who, with his height and the red hair made a touch darker by Brylcreem, stood out in the crowd of gentlemen returning to the table with their drinks.

No one balked at the familiar nickname Sass flung at the Princess, nor was there a moment of awkward silence while everyone waited for the Princess to banish the Ambassador's daughter for being overly familiar. Instead, the Princess dropped her lipstick tube into her purse, snapped the clasp closed, and laid it on the table. "I'll leave that to you and the others to discover."

"Oh good, I do like a challenge." Katharine Smith touched the tip of one gloved finger against her lips and eyed Johnny as though he were a new diamond ring.

The table erupted in wicked laughter.

"What's so funny?" Johnny demanded, as he handed Katharine her drink.

"Nothing you'd find amusing." Caroline accepted a drink from Billy while Sunny set one down before Her Royal Highness, not receiving so much as a thank-you for his efforts. It didn't seem to trouble him as he took his place at the table along with the other men.

Dominic handed Vera a glass of champagne and sat down beside her. "I was watching you on the way back. You really fit in with this crowd."

"Is that a good thing or a bad thing?"

"I think that depends on what you make of your new acquaintance."

"Is there anything to make of it?"

He raised his cocktail glass to her. "I suppose we'll see."

She clinked her glass against his. "I suppose we will."

Chapter Seven

I thought you said I didn't have to come in through the servants' entrance." Dominic steered the Morris Minor under the wrought iron arch of the Buckingham Palace Road gate where everyone from plumbers to deliverymen came and went from the palace.

"At this time of night, I'm sure everyone has to use the service entrance."

They passed the guard lodge, and the policeman inside lazily waved them through. Vera wondered what these commoners thought of the Princess coming home in such inglorious fashion. The fact that she wasn't alone in a car at this hour with a gentleman but part of a convoy of young revelers must blunt the curt cut of their comments to their wives, but Vera still wondered. People expected a touch more decorum from their royals. What they expected of those of more title but lower birth Vera had yet to discover, but her mother was bound to give her a taste of it when she finally arrived home tomorrow, or, she should say, much later today. It was well past midnight.

They parked their cars near the tradesmen's entrance and spilled out into the cold and damp night. They made their way through a side door held open by another police officer, who bowed to the royal. No one questioned where they were going but followed the Princess as if they'd tramped these plain corridors and narrow stairs in the less-glorious part of the palace a hundred times. They probably had.

Vera tried not to stop and stare when the bare floors and unadorned ceilings of the staff passage opened up into the richly carpeted and decorated main hall. She all but squealed with excitement when they left the long corridor for the grand staircase, with its gilded and swirling banister, marble columns, and priceless artwork. Overhead, a round glass window glowed with the light from the city shining off the clouds, the faint glow catching in the gilded sconces and the white painted faces of the past monarchs hanging in their grand portraits on the walls.

Vera held on tight to the banister, afraid she might trip. If she hadn't believed her luck all the times she'd been with Princess Margaret before, it positively stupefied her now. She'd seen pictures of the inside of the palace, but she'd never imagined actually being in here, and with Princess Margaret and her friends, of all people. Their soft voices echoed off the white plasterwork and iron railings while they climbed higher and higher into the palace.

"Swell digs," Dominic said, whistling, as the two of them fell behind the others in their attempts to take it all in. "You should come here more often."

"I've never been here before."

"Never?"

"They don't exactly offer tours."

"Unless we want to get arrested by a guard and thrown in the Tower, we'd better catch up." Dominic took her hand, and together they hurried up the remaining stairs and along the hallway at the top.

He didn't let go of her hand when they fell in with the rest of the group, giving her fingers a gentle squeeze that perked her up more than the coffee she'd had after dinner. In one large group they crept up a more modest staircase to a long and much plainer hallway before the entourage at last stopped at a suite of rooms at the far end.

Vera read the handwritten card on the wall naming this room: "Maggie's Playroom."

"Philip named it that." Princess Margaret threw open the door and strode in, stopping just over the threshold to remove her coat and drop it on the floor. "He can be a beast when he wants to be, but I can't blame him for thinking up that name. That's what this room used to be before Mummy changed it for me. One can't expect the spinster sister to be given the future Queen's bedroom, or even one next to it. I might interrupt the royal heir making. But we aren't ones for bitterness, are we, Mrs. Lavish? After all, our happiness will come too, won't it?"

It was the second time Her Royal Highness had looked to Vera for reassurance, and she wondered why. Perhaps it was Vera's distance from this world that made the Princess think she could get an honest answer from her. "Yes, Ma'am, it will."

It already had for Vera. There was no reason it couldn't happen for the Princess.

"Come and sit next to me." Princess Margaret tugged her away from Dominic, who let go of her hand without protest. Vera wished she could remain with him instead of garnering the attention of the room by sitting next to Princess Margaret, but there was nothing to do but follow the royal to the sofa.

The Princess's private apartment languished in the same disarray as her room at the Savoy. Copies of *Tatler* and the *Daily Express* along with playbills and dance programs littered the top of the coffee table. The white desk near the window sported a number of empty pop bottles, crumpled red-and-white packages of Gigante cigarettes, and a few tubes of lipstick. The record player in the corner was nearly buried in the stacks of records on the table and floor in front of it and on the back of the black-lacquered baby grand piano.

The brass-and-glass bar cart near the window was the most organized item in the salmon-pink-colored room, with a generous selection of expensive spirits and mixers, and an array of crystal glasses carefully arranged on top. The chairs not occupied by the Set were draped with sweaters, scarves, and limp nylons. If the clutter bothered the Princess, she didn't show it as she picked up a scarf and flung it aside before dropping onto the thick sofa cushions and making them puff up on either side of her. Vera sat beside her and, to her surprise, Johnny sat down on Vera's other side.

The Princess slid off her dainty but very high heels to join the growing collection of shoes abandoned by the others under the coffee table. The group that had demonstrated a modicum of formality at the embassy lounged about like Vera and her cousins usually did after a particularly boring ball or hunting party. Vera, thankful for Sass's gift of new nylons, confidently took off her shoes too, not having to worry about a hole in the toe.

"Sunny, put something on the record player," Princess Margaret instructed with a languid roll of her hand, forcing the young man who'd looked relieved to finally be off his feet to stand up again.

"What would you like me to play, Ma'am?"

"I don't care. Anything." Princess Margaret rested her head against the back of the sofa and uttered a sigh of relief, revealing that she was mortal enough to feel the effects of a long night and a few stiff drinks. Then she jerked up her head and looked at Sunny, who was about to remove a record from its cardboard sleeve. "Not that one, the new one there on the top of the other pile that Sass gave me."

Sunny slipped the record back in its jacket and laid it aside before picking up the other and setting it on the turntable.

With a scratch of the needle, he started it, and very soon the crooning voice of Frank Sinatra flowed from the small speaker. Someone dimmed the lights, softening the conversation and the mood.

"I absolutely love him." Princess Margaret trilled her perfectly manicured fingers against her thigh in time to the music before she shot up straight, as if the brief rest had given her the energy to continue on for hours more. Vera rubbed the back of her neck, wondering how much longer it would be. She'd been up the last few nights working, and the lack of sleep was beginning to tell. "I need a cigarette."

Johnny leaned across Vera with an open cigarette case. He offered Vera one too, but she refused. It was Sunny who provided the requisite lighter. Princess Margaret tucked the cigarette between her lips without her holder and set the tip to the flame, leaning forward to reveal a great deal of royal cleavage to the son of the Duke of Marlborough. He admired it more here than he had at the embassy. When the paper began to burn, Princess Margaret tilted her head back and inhaled, making her neck lengthen like the models in perfume ads did when they slid glass stoppers along the hollows of their necks. Sunny nearly let his lighter burn out its liquid until she flashed him a look from the side of her eyes that made him flip the lighter closed, slide it in his pocket, and sit down beside her.

Princess Margaret wrapped her lips around the cigarette, her red lipstick stark against the white burning paper. She inhaled deeply, making the tip of the cigarette burn bright before she slowly let out the smoke. "Tell me, Vera, what do you think of him?"

What do I think of who? Sunny? She barely knew him. With the way he was devouring Princess Margaret with his eyes, she doubted he even realized Vera was in the room. It made Vera want to throw one of the discarded scarves over the Princess's chest. "Ma'am?"

"Sinatra. I think he's one of the best." It was the breathiest compliment Vera had ever heard.

Sinatra was a good singer, but he wasn't one to blow up her skirt, as Rupert had so crassly put it once. Not that it mattered what Vera thought, for the Princess wouldn't have heard her anyway. She fixed on Sunny, who remained entranced by the Princess and was not shy about showing it. Vera wondered if this was the man the Princess had spoken of at the fashion show, except there was no reason Vera could think of why they couldn't be together, but she wasn't privy to all the wrangling behind the royal scenes. Maybe the King was pushing the Princess toward Billy or Johnny. Whatever their relationship, she'd singled him out for special attention tonight, and he wasn't turning her down.

"The crease in your trousers is quite stiff." Princess Margaret brushed the curve of his knee, her fingers lingering over the crisp crease at the top of it. Vera didn't move, feeling as if she'd walked in on a private moment, except it was anything but private with everyone around them lounging on the antique Louis XVII settees and Queen Anne chairs.

Sunny rested his arm on the back of the couch, his finger dangling just over the bare royal shoulders, his jacket opening to reveal his white shirt beneath and the waistcoat wrapped tight against his trim waist. "Just the way I like it."

"Do you?"

"Very much. Shall we dance?"

"Yes."

He slid his fingers under hers, at last dislodging her hand from his thigh. Together they rose with the elegance of a practiced couple at a ball and stepped into the center of the room. He took her in his arms and pulled her close, swaying with her in time to the slow Frank Sinatra melody, his hips pressed tight against hers. She didn't push him away but rather raised her shapely arms to entwine her hands around his neck, her breasts pressed flat against his chest.

No one moved to join or acknowledge them but continued with their conversations and drink requests, the ice clinking as Billy dropped the cubes in the glasses at the bar cart. Vera wondered if Sunny and Princess Margaret sagged to the floor and began to neck if people crossing the room for a refill would simply step over them. She would rise and get a drink if panic didn't keep her rooted to the cushion, continually glancing at the door in fear the King or Queen might walk in and catch their youngest daughter in a very inappropriate stance. However, the door remained closed, and everyone carried on as if nothing were out of the ordinary.

Past the organza and tulle of the Princess's skirt, Vera

caught Dominic's eyes where he sat across the room with the Honorable Peter Ward, who talked with him in big gestures of heaven knew what. Dominic winked at Vera but made no effort to extricate himself from his current companion and come sit beside her. She would have liked his company instead of sitting there wondering what to think of everything that was happening.

When the song eased toward its end, Princess Margaret slid one hand along the straight line of Sunny's shoulder and down the length of his arm, her pink nails leaving no mark on the black wool of his tuxedo jacket. She caught his hand, tracing the lines of his palm with her finger before she slid them apart. With the lightness of a nymph, she stepped to a door on the far side of the room, her stride heightening the swing of her skirt about her legs. She opened the door and, offering Sunny one enticing look over her nearly bare shoulder, slipped into the darkness beyond. Sunny didn't hesitate, following her inside. He closed the door behind him, neither of them at all concerned about the room full of people on the other side.

If Vera had to guess, they hadn't gone off to discuss the merits of Sinatra's vocal skills. The same shock to her sensibilities that had gripped her at the sight of the Princess playing piano at Monty's hit her again. It wouldn't be just the guard outside complaining about the royal behavior when the sun came up; Vera would too.

"For a woman who writes what you do, you seem awful surprised when it's in front of you." Sass dropped into the empty place on the sofa beside Vera. Across Vera, Johnny and Sass exchanged a look that told Vera she was about to be initiated into a club she wasn't sure she wished to be a part of. Vera could carouse with this group, but she didn't need to be privy to *all* of the Princess's secrets. One did like a touch of the mythic where the Royal Family was concerned, and this was just a little too much of the real tonight for her tastes.

"Why don't I get you ladies a drink," Johnny offered.

"Thanks, Johnny, that would be great," Sass answered for both of them.

He pushed out of the deep cushion and strolled across the room, in no particular hurry to reach the bar cart.

"I suppose you're wondering about Margo and Sunny?" Sass nodded toward the closed door.

So much for not hearing it all and keeping a touch of the mythic. "I can imagine."

"With what you write, I don't doubt you can, but it isn't quite so much."

"Everything but, then?" The Princess wasn't the first girl in England to do so before a wedding ring was slipped on her finger.

"She can be reckless at times, but she isn't foolish enough to court that kind of trouble."

After Vera's discreet conversation with the Princess at the fashion show, she wasn't so certain, but she didn't contradict Sass. Clearly, Sass knew a great deal more about the Princess's life than Vera. That she was even having this frank a discussion with the daughter of the American Ambassador felt as surreal as having crept through the palace hallways after dark. If she wrote this into one of her novels, readers would accuse Vera of being too inventive.

"Margo likes Sunny well enough, and there are very few people she can really trust."

"Will he propose to her?"

Sass smothered a laugh with her hand. "Oh no, he's engaged to Susan Hornby."

"What?" Perhaps this was why the Duke of Edinburgh had named this the playroom. She hoped it was a bad coincidence, but with a palace this big, Vera imagined quite a few people would be disappearing behind different doors before the night was over. She wondered if they rang bells at sunrise here like they did at country house parties to make sure everyone got back to where they belonged before the maids walked in with the breakfast trays. "Does the Princess know?"

"No, and we don't tell her because we don't want her to go off on him like she did David. He'll tell her eventually, and if things keep going the way they have, you might even receive an invitation, but you must be discreet. As you may have noticed, this crowd does things a little differently."

"I'll say." Vera glanced at the door, thinking Princess Margaret already knew that Sunny was off the market and that's exactly why she was alone with him. After her outburst at

Monty's over Lord Westmorland's engagement, it was clear she wasn't going to be made useless by another engagement but prove to him and everyone that she could have anything she wanted, even a man promised to another. If Vera weren't busy trying to figure out how to work this into her Lady Penrose novel, she'd be absolutely horrified. "I won't tell Her Royal Highness."

"Good. I knew we could count on you. In the meantime, I think someone else wants to chat with you." Sass rose as Dominic approached carrying two very full old-fashioned glasses.

"Here you go. The specialty *à la maison*, according to Billy." He handed Vera a glass. "Would you like to get some air?"

"Please."

They stepped out onto the narrow balcony adjoining the room and into the chilly night, the grass and trees of the Buckingham Palace garden beneath them dark against the lights of the city. Vera shifted closer to Dominic and took a bracing sip of her drink, shuddering at the strength. "They like them strong here."

He wrinkled his nose at the overwhelming scent of alcohol that would take the finish off the furniture if he spilled it. "With this much booze, it's hard to tell if it's the good stuff."

"You didn't get a look at the bottles?"

"Maybe they're for show, something the servants refill with cheap stuff to make it seem like they're buying the better goods." He set the drink down on the balustrade.

"While they pocket the profits or sell the better stuff on the black market." She set her drink beside his, afraid she'd pass out if she enjoyed any more.

"How you talk about your fellow countrymen."

"I know what goes on here in London."

"Do you?" He nodded toward the sitting room and the closed bedroom door.

"I do now."

"And?"

"As Queen Elizabeth once said, *video et taceo*." It was the only Latin phrase she remembered from her education.

"See everything and say nothing," Dominic translated, raising her opinion of him even higher.

"Exactly." She leaned back against the stone, ignoring the chill of it cutting through the silk and netting of the dress. "What about you? Are you going to go home and sell this story to the press?"

"Not unless they cure TB and I find myself out of a job. Besides, Sass would have me taken care of if I spilled the beans on her friend."

"Her father is that influential?"

"No, she is."

Vera laughed, imagining it possible for Sass, who'd so easily ingratiated herself with the Princess, to wield influence among the elite circles in America too. "What kind of influence does she have over you?"

"None. She's too much like a younger sister to me to ever be anything else." He slipped off his jacket and draped it over her shoulders.

"Good." She pulled the jacket close, inhaling the crisp scent of him lingering in the wool.

He rested his hands on either side of her on the balustrade, catching her between his arms. "Tell me, have you ever kissed a man in Buckingham Palace?"

"Never." She laid her hands on his chest, marveling at the shift of his muscles beneath her palms and the heady scent of his warm skin. It'd been so long since she'd been this close to a man. Too long.

"Then there's about to be a number of firsts for both of us." He stroked her cheek with the backs of his fingers, slid them across the line of her jaw and behind her neck, and drew her to him.

Frank Sinatra's voice and the low chatter of the Set faded beneath the pressure of Dominic's lips against hers. She fell into him, encircling his waist with her hands, craving him more than the intimacy of the Set. No wonder Princess Margaret had wandered off with Sunny. To be wanted and treated as if there was no one but her was too precious to push away, even if it couldn't last.

No, she refused to think about Dominic leaving or how awful it would be when he did. She was tired of having the past drag at her while always looking forward to a future that never seemed to arrive. She wanted to live life as it was at this moment, and at present she was pressed against Dominic and dropping deeper into his kiss. He and this night were more real than almost any dream she'd ever held, and she would make the most of it for however long it lasted. Heaven only knew where it might take her next, but she couldn't wait to see where that would be.

Chapter Eight

The manuscript was due over a week ago," Mr. Baker, Vera's rotund and penny-pinching publisher, growled into the phone. "If I don't have it by Friday, it'll push back the schedule and the second half of your advance."

"I apologize, Mr. Baker. I'll have it to you by Friday." Heaven knew when she'd get it done what with the required fittings for the green dress so it would be ready in time for the Buckingham Palace Christmas Ball and the hours she'd spent at the salon getting her hair and nails done for tonight's Royal Command Film Performance. After laying out so much money on nail varnish, she was loath to chip it by clanking her nails against the typewriter keys. She'd have to find a way to type in gloves, because Mr. Baker, who'd never been effusive about her talents, especially when she asked for more money, had never been this stern with her either. Until tonight, she hadn't given him a reason to be, and he should damn well appreciate it enough to remember it. She was about to tell him what he could do with his schedule but then stopped. His paltry advances were paying for her hairdresser and manicures.

Sunny stuck his head in her father's office. "Come on, Vera. Caroline and Johnny are waiting in the car for us, and we don't want to be late."

She covered the receiver with her hand. "I'm almost done."

The call had come in moments before Sunny's arrival, as if Mr. Baker had been able to sense that she was about to have fun instead of chaining herself to the Remington typewriter for another evening of drudgery in the land of pulp love.

"You'd better have the manuscript turned in by Friday, Mrs. Lavish, or your future with the Baker Publishing House will very much be at risk—do you understand?"

"Yes, sir." She dropped the headset on the receiver, refusing to allow him to further dampen her excitement about the evening. The note from Dominic that afternoon saying he couldn't escort her because of a problem at the hospital had been bad enough. Thankfully, Sunny had been more than happy to oblige, giving her mother yet another fit of the vapors that her daughter was being escorted to a Royal Command Film Performance by the son of a duke. She didn't dare tell her mother that there was no hope of Vera becoming a duchess. There were too many other women standing in line in front of her for that honor, and Vera wasn't about to thank him for the ride with more than a polite peck on the cheek.

With Vera and Sunny looking as regal as any movie star

couple, they said their goodbyes to her gawking mother, her indifferent father, and her silently cheering sister and left the house. Vera stepped into the back of the hired saloon car parked out front where Caroline and Johnny sat laughing, half-empty collins glasses clutched in their hands. Vera gathered in the hem of her blue velvet dress, the one she'd received when she'd visited the fashion house to pay for her embassy purchases. It'd been part of a canceled order, and the head vendeuse, stuck with the outfits and having seen the picture of Vera and the Princess in *Tatler*, had rushed to gift the clothes to Vera. The fashion house couldn't pass up a chance to have an intimate of the most popular royal photographed in their creations, and Vera was more than happy to be a clotheshorse if it meant acquiring a fine wardrobe that she didn't have to pay for.

"Can I mix you something, Vera?" Johnny pressed open a compartment built into the side panel and revealed a small bar with decanters of liquor and glasses.

"Whatever you're having."

"Make mine a double." Sunny slid in beside her and the driver closed the door behind him.

Vera accepted her drink, surprised the ratio of whiskey to water didn't melt the glass. They'd all be soused if they had to wait a long time in the car before entering the theatre. Still, if there was one thing Vera had noticed during all their nights out, this crowd could hold their liquor. Their gentlemen ancestors would be proud. Vera would have to pace herself, because the last thing she wished to do was act like a tumbling drunk at a Royal Command Performance surrounded by press. That kind of picture in the newspapers would give her mother seizures.

"Colin's joining us tonight." Johnny handed Sunny his drink, the scent of alcohol from it lingering like petrol from a car.

"Colin Tennant, Lord Glenconner's son," Sunny explained to Vera. "He's been in America on business for his family's firm."

"I'm sure he was a smashing success there, like Rupert will be." Caroline swirled the ice in her drink. "Where has your handsome cousin been? We've hardly seen him."

"Preparing for his imminent departure." Vera moved her drink to one side to avoid Johnny topping it off. "He's joining us at the 400 Club after the film, and so is Dr. Reynolds."

It was the reason she'd forgiven him for standing her up tonight.

"I bet Rupert is looking forward to America. American girls love a man with a title or the prospect of one." Caroline slid Johnny a sly look. "They don't know what scoundrels you lords really are."

"Women love scoundrels, and a large manor is a benefit to a gentleman." Johnny took up the decanter and added more to Caroline's glass.

"I wouldn't say Rupert's manor is large." Caroline twisted the impressive diamond engagement ring on her finger. Like the Princess, she wasn't about to allow something like a formal understanding with the Duke of Beaufort's heir get in the way of her fun. "But he does have a great deal of lineage."

Vera nearly spit out her drink. She could have lived the rest of her life without hearing about the size of Rupert's inheritance, but the fact that Caroline had touched his family crest was interesting. Rupert had proven far more discreet about his affairs than Vera had believed him capable of being. Caroline, not so much, and she leveled a gloved finger at Vera. "You have my permission to use that in one of your novels, Mrs. Lavish."

"I'll be sure to change the names of the guilty to protect them."

"I might be guilty, but you can't say I haven't had fun."

"Haven't we all?" Johnny took Caroline's glass and refilled it.

Vera leaned forward, her chin in her hand. "Do tell."

"A gentleman never tells."

"At least not when ladies are present," Sunny added. "Now if we were at White's . . ."

"Don't give away our secrets." Johnny lobbed the round decanter stopper at Sunny, who caught it with one hand.

The ribald jokes and the free-flowing liquor continued until the car reached the Odeon Theatre in Leicester Square, creeping along in the queue of cars until it finally rolled up to the brightly lit entrance.

Vera marveled at the crush of onlookers outside the theatre. Lines of black-uniformed bobbies with their arms linked held back a crush of women and men cheering and screaming for each new arrival. The four of them waved to the onlookers as they promenaded into the flower-bedecked lobby where a line of velvet ropes fronted by a wall of greenery punctuated by white carnations and chrysanthemums held back a cavalcade of reporters and photographers. Lords and ladies and Hollywood royalty milled about, the actors and actresses speaking to the press while the titled nobility promenaded past them and into the theatre. Motion picture cameras set up on a platform filmed the entire scene while radiomen announced into their microphones each new arrival for the audiences listening at home.

Lady Riverdowne and Lady Chansford, two grand dames whom Vera recognized from the *Court Circular*, scrutinized the people filing into the theatre while their husbands discussed who knew what business. The two ladies eyed Vera and the others with stiff, Victorian disapproval, the kind of looks they'd practiced so as not to deepen the wrinkles on their ever-smooth foreheads.

Vera was about to point out the matrons to Caroline and Johnny and give them all something more to laugh about until she realized it wasn't Caroline, Johnny, or Sunny they were scowling at but her.

"In my day, we were more discerning about who our children chose as companions," Lady Riverdowne said much too loudly to Lady Chansford.

"The royals and certain dukes will allow their children to fraternize with almost anyone these days."

"Ignore them." Caroline caught Vera's arm and ushered

her forward. "They're snobs, aren't they, the Honorable Vera Strathmore?"

She said it loud enough for the two ladies to hear, the honorarium announcing that she wasn't simply some guttersnipe they'd picked up on the way here, but even this didn't raise the disapproving downturn of their lips.

"What did I ever do to twist their knickers?" Vera had as much right to consort with royalty and the children of higher nobles as anybody, and she wouldn't let anyone take that away from her, especially not two chiding biddies of her mother's moldering era.

"They're on guard against parvenus. All these old women haven't realized how much things have changed, and once in a while they need a good dressing down to remind them of it. Titles are all well and good, and I enjoy my family's as much as anyone would, but it doesn't mean we have to sneer at everyone because of it."

Given the Set's near reverence of Princess Margaret, Vera didn't think the old order had fallen as far as Caroline believed, but she was thankful for the support. It was a nice change from having to endure scowling old matrons on her own.

The air inside the theatre crackled with a more subdued excitement than in the lobby, the rippled art deco ceiling and walls of the theatre collecting all the voices and conversation. There were no studio lights or cameras in here, simply people privileged enough to warrant an invitation for tonight, including Vera.

She followed the others to where the rest of the Set sat near the front of the audience. Sass sat not with them but with her parents one row above the empty risers that served as the Odeon Theatre's royal box. She wore an off-the-shoulder blue dress and a tasteful string of pearls, appearing as dignified as her ambassador father until she threw Vera a hearty wave. Vera answered with a more restrained one, not wishing to garner any more aristocratic comments from anyone of consequence in the audience.

The royal box stood empty, awaiting the guests of honor. It was festooned with two ornate gilded chairs that appeared more like thrones than theatre seats and flanked by smaller gilded chairs to accommodate the Royal Family. In the seats surrounding the royal box sat Gregory Peck, Rosalind Russell, and a bevy of glamorous American and British film stars. Vera had a great deal of trouble not gawking at them, but she wasn't alone. Laura Smith sat beside her, and the two of them turned around every few minutes to take in a new arrival or simply admire the ones already seated. Caroline was busy talking to Johnny from where she sat by Lady Elizabeth Montagu Douglas Scott and her escort, Colin Tennant. The young man, whom Vera hadn't met before, had a youthful oval face aged by a high forehead where his hair had receded at a pitifully young age.

"Isn't Errol Flynn's fiancée lucky?" Laura swooned, taking in the petite blonde who sat beside the strapping actor.

"I'm not sure she is. He has to be at least twenty years older than her, and she looks like she's barely out of the schoolroom."

"If she isn't, he's about to offer her some very unique tutoring."

"Assuming he still has it in him to crack a book at his age."

"Mrs. Lavish, you're awful."

"You're both awful." Katharine Smith leaned forward from where she sat one row behind them. Like her sister, she had dark hair and the same strong cheekbones. "If you're going to whisper and giggle about people, at least let me in on it."

Vera was about to say more when the roar of the crowd from outside filtered into the theatre, quieting all conversation.

"It sounds like Their Royal Highnesses have arrived," Laura said.

The roar outside continued, and many minutes passed inside the theatre until everyone rose to their feet in thunderous applause at the Royal Family's appearance. The King and Queen made their way to the royal box, followed by Princess Elizabeth and her husband, the Duke of Edinburgh, and Princess Margaret, who nodded to her friends but didn't offer the effusive wave that Sass had thrown their way. The Queen was resplendent in a wide-skirted satin evening gown with a nipped-in waist and off-the-shoulder arms covered by a dark fur coat. The diamonds in her tiara and her large necklace glittered beneath the theatre's house lights, especially when she raised one gloved hand to her subjects.

The King walked beside her, dashing in his dark coat and white waistcoat, accepting his subjects' applause with all the grace and history of his position. He deserved every courtesy paid to him, having accepted the crown when his brother had tossed it away for that second-rate American tart. His Majesty had helped carry the nation through the horrors of the war, and while Vera clapped, she wondered how much longer the King would hold up under the strain of his work. Even the muted house lights couldn't hide the darkness beneath his eyes and the gaunt hollowness of his cheeks. The King was far more ill than the public had been led to believe, and it made Vera's heart catch even while she joined in the thunderous ovation. In spite of his illness, he carried on as if all were splendidly well, smiling and waving to his subjects as he and the Royal Family stood at their seats.

Princess Margaret waved with the others, watching her father more than the audience, and it made the family scene all the more poignant. This happy picture would probably end much sooner than any of them desired, and then everything would change for all of them, except Princess Margaret. Princess Elizabeth and her husband would move to the gilded thrones, and the Queen would step aside, while Princess Margaret stayed where she was, except what little influence she enjoyed through the King would be gone. For all the titles and wealth bestowed on the Princess, she was simply second best, and nothing but a tragedy of unprecedented proportions would ever change this. She was as aware of this fact as Vera, and the entire world. No wonder she behaved as she did sometimes. In such a family, she had to elbow her way to the front one way or another.

The rousing applause continued for some time until the King finally took his seat and everyone else followed the royal lead. The house lights dimmed, and the next two hours drew them back into Victorian times with the adaptation of a novel Vera vaguely remembered reading during one of her mother's haphazard attempts to bestow something resembling an education on her. If it hadn't been for the four years when she, Rupert, Alice, and Rupert's elder brother had shared a tutor, all four of them would have been as illiterate as a Dickens orphan.

When the film ended and the house lights came up, everyone remained in the theatre while the actresses and actors proceeded to the lobby to line up and be presented to the Royal Family.

Vera and the rest of the Set cracked jokes and chatted as they waited for word that they could grab a cigarette and mingle with some of the other guests in the lobby before their cars arrived to take them to the 400 Club. The Princess, having left with the Royal Family, would meet them at their usual table later.

AN ECLECTIC MIX of new money and old lineage climbed from their cars to descend the stairs into the 400 Club, the chicest cellar in all of London. A crowd of pressmen gathered near the entrance as Caroline, Vera, and Johnny stepped out of Sunny's car. The photographers took little interest in the new arrivals until the car that pulled up behind Sunny's sent them into a frenzy. The photographers rushed the black Rolls-Royce, but not before Vera caught sight of Her Royal Highness inside. She didn't shrink from the cameras pressed up against the windows but pursed her lips in irritation at their presence.

"Bloody animals. Why don't they leave her alone?" Sunny grumbled while the club doorman and Mr. Ashbrook, the Princess's private detective, pushed the photographers back far enough for Princess Margaret to step out of the car.

"Because even a bad photograph of her is better than nothing," Caroline answered. "The people just can't get enough."

"Come on, Ma'am." Johnny waved Princess Margaret into the center of their group, and with the two men behind her and Caroline and Vera in front to block her from view of the photographers, they descended the club stairs.

They were only a few feet inside and the Princess had just removed her coat for Sunny to give to the coat check when a lanky man in a brown suit carrying a large camera jumped in front of her. His flash went off, blinding the Princess and Vera and Caroline, who stood on either side of her.

"What the hell are you doing?" Mr. Ashbrook roared, wresting the camera out of the photographer's hands and ripping open the back to expose the film.

"Tryin' to make a livin'."

"Not this way, you won't." With a signal from the detective and the club management, two burly waiters grabbed the photographer by the arms and dragged him out. It was one thing to be photographed at the opening of a dockyard where Her Royal Highness could politely smile and wave, aware she was on display for the sole purpose of representing the monarchy, but not here during an evening out with friends.

"I'm so sorry, Your Royal Highness." The club manager with his pencil-thin mustache groveled before her. "I don't know how he got in here."

"They're like roaches." She fixed on the proprietor as if he were a surly palace maid. "Make sure it doesn't happen again or I and my friends will have to go elsewhere for our celebrations. We come here for privacy, not to be blinded."

"Yes, Your Royal Highness." He bent in half with his bow, but the Princess didn't notice, striding past him and into the club, the perturbed stiffness in her back easing as the familiar music and surroundings enveloped her.

The orchestra played for both the mature crowd in their respectable suits and furs from before the war and the younger guests interspersed between them. The two groups didn't mingle, except for one couple at a private table near the back of the room. There, tucked into the shadows, a young woman in a cheap satin dress and an expensive diamond bracelet sat across from the much-older Lord Foley. Vera knew that someone with lipstick that red and hair that peroxide blond wasn't likely to afford jewelry like that, although it was apparent from her partner's undignified fawning that she'd earned it.

It wasn't toward the shadows that Vera and the others headed but to the table reserved for them near the orchestra—the royal box, as it was affectionately called. It offered a good view of the room and the dancing couples but required other diners to turn and make their gawking evident if they wanted a good look at Princess Margaret. It discouraged a great deal of curiosity.

Dominic and Rupert were already seated at the table, and they stood to greet the arriving ladies. The others filled the table in a gust of voices and discussion of drinks while Dominic pulled out a chair for Vera.

"Good evening, Dr. Reynolds," Vera purred as she sat down, trying to entice a wider smile than the stiff one he greeted her with. "I missed you at the theatre."

"I'm sure there were enough of the others there to entertain you." He dropped into the chair beside her, more than one empty drink glass in front of him, his lack of enthusiasm threatening to upend her more than Mr. Baker's threat or Lady Riverdowne's snide comment. Vera's stomach tightened, and she wondered what had happened between Buckingham Palace and tonight to change his attitude toward her.

"Mrs. Lavish, wasn't the film wonderful?" Princess Margaret called across the table.

"It was, Ma'am." It was the 400 Club and Dominic that wasn't turning out to be so grand.

"Mr. Ashbrook, I think the danger has passed for tonight. You are dismissed," the Princess said to the detective who'd taken his usual place against the wall behind her chair, ready to protect her from any more nefarious forces. Vera wondered whose responsibility it was to protect her from her sometimes questionable impulses. Either it wasn't in Jennifer's job description or she didn't possess the will to risk stepping between the Princess and what she wanted. There were few who did, especially not Vera, who had her own troubles to wrestle with tonight.

"Dominic, what's wrong?" Vera reached out to touch his shoulder and then pulled back her hand, afraid to be too open with him in a place like this. She wasn't important enough for the gossip columns, but the gossip of High Street was another matter. Her aunt Augusta had a knack for hearing and passing on stories, and Vera had no desire for her to relay this. Like her friendship with the Princess, her relationship with Dominic wasn't fodder for her mother to chew on at the breakfast table, especially if it was going to come to an ignoble end before it had really begun.

"It isn't a good time to talk about it." Dominic took a hearty drink of whatever poison was in front of him. "I wouldn't want your Princess to hear bad news and have it ruin the taste of her food."

"With the King being ill, she's accustomed to doctors and bad news. We all are." She sensed she was going to hear a great deal more of it from Dominic's lips tonight. Oh well, this was the price she'd pay for living in the moment. The moment had passed. It was time to endure another less-pleasant one.

"I'm sorry." The ice in his glass fell as it melted, turning the whiskey a lighter shade of amber. "It's been a difficult day."

"Select your partners for an eightsome reel," the band leader announced.

"I love this one!" Princess Margaret exclaimed, jumping to her feet and forcing the men to theirs. "Come on, everyone, we'll dance it together."

At the royal command, the others began to choose their partners. Vera hesitated, torn between remaining beside Dominic and following the Princess.

"Go ahead," he urged as he sat down. "I don't know this dance."

"It's easy. I'll guide you through it."

He didn't move, and Vera glanced back and forth between Dominic and the Princess, who stood with a number of others of the Set waiting for the dance to begin. Vera couldn't go without a partner and she couldn't stay here.

"I'm not in the mood. Go on, your sovereign awaits."

"She isn't a sovereign."

"Isn't she?" He raised the glass to his lips and drained it before setting it back on the water-ringed tablecloth.

Vera, stunned by his callousness, stalked off to join the others on the dance floor, wondering who in heaven's name she would dance with when she got there. She couldn't bloody well sashay about the circle by herself.

"Your doctor isn't coming?" Princess Margaret asked when Vera took the empty place beside her.

"He doesn't know the steps." Even if he did, he wasn't going to jump at a royal command like the rest of them. Vera wasn't sure if she should admire or despise him for it. At least he was his own man. It was more than the rest of the Set could say, but this was the price they all paid to be a part of it, the one she'd willingly accepted a few weeks ago. She couldn't balk at it now.

"Colin, dance with Mrs. Lavish; she doesn't have a partner," the Princess commanded, and they both obeyed like a couple of well-trained terriers.

The musicians began the rousing Scottish tune, and Vera and Colin moved with the others in time to the music and the clapping audience. During a turn, Vera caught sight of Dominic hunched over a fresh cocktail. She wished she could go to him, but she was obliged to stay here and pretend that she was enjoying herself as much as Her Royal Highness. The Princess turned and stepped between the men, her gold and beaded dress glittering beneath the lights of the club. Every gentleman who partnered with her appeared entranced, as if her touch could cure their ills. Vera wished she could pull Dominic out of his seat and have him take the royal hand, but it wouldn't work. He wasn't besotted by Her Royal Highness or the Set. He wasn't about to magically become so tonight.

The orchestra brought the tune to its exuberant end, and everyone applauded the dancers and the orchestra.

"Let's have some more drinks." The Princess led the Set back to the table, garnering curtseys and compliments from the admiring public as she went. She was the center of attention here in a way she could never hope to be when out in public with her family, and she knew it.

It wasn't until her gaze fell on Dominic that her regal self-importance faltered. When he stood at her return, Princess Margaret drew herself up to what little height she possessed to try to look down on the tall American with her ice blue eyes. "Dr. Reynolds, you must be sure to dance with us next time."

Sass came out from behind the Princess and entwined her arm with Dominic's. "Go easy on Doc, Margo; he's American. You know how we are."

The conversation around them stilled while everyone waited for the royal reaction. Vera braced herself too, afraid Dominic would be banished from the Set in this little standoff. Sass enjoyed a great deal of influence with the Princess, but Vera didn't think she possessed quite enough to win this battle of wills.

Vera was wrong, for the Princess lowered her pert chin and settled her very raised hackles.

"You're forgiven, Dr. Reynolds." Princess Margaret, having bestowed the royal pardon, sat down and slipped her cigarette holder between her lips, waiting while the men dug in their pockets for cigarettes to fill the little ivory hole. If Katharine and Laura minded the Princess hoarding so much male attention, neither one of them said so or even gave so much as a perturbed look to each other to indicate it. They accepted their places as second best with all the grace of practiced courtiers.

If they were second best, heaven only knew how far down the rung Vera was. It didn't matter; at least she was still on the ladder, but at what cost?

She sat down beside Dominic and rested her hand on top of

his where it lay on his thigh beneath the table. "What happened today?"

"I was granted clemency from being beheaded."

"I don't mean *that*."

"Isn't *that* all that matters?"

She snatched back her hand. "It is when I don't have the family medical practice to fall back on to guarantee my future."

"Touché." He took a deep breath, the irritation draining from him. "One of my colleagues contracted a deadly strain of TB and isn't likely to survive the month."

Vera laced her fingers in his. "I'm sorry, Dominic."

"It's an occupational hazard, I'm afraid." He traced the rim of his drink glass with his free hand before pushing it away. "I'd better go. I don't want to be hungover when I face him and his family in the morning with the bad news."

She didn't dare remind him that one didn't leave before Her Royal Highness, feeling like a heel for worrying about royal protocol when he had this terrible thing hanging over him. Even without Sass's intervention, Princess Margaret should understand, or at least Vera hoped she did. She cringed to think the woman was so petty as to deny a doctor his rest before a difficult day. "If there's anything I can do . . ."

"There isn't." He slid his hand out from under hers and fished his coat-check ticket out of his pocket. "Shall I see you home?"

"No, I have to stay." She nodded toward Princess Margaret, who danced with Sunny, both of them standing a respectable distance apart as they did a box step. Her Royal Highness wasn't nearly as enthralled with him tonight as she had been in her rooms, but the evening was still young, especially for the Princess.

"Of course. Good night, Vera." He left with no promises of when or even if they'd see each other again. She watched him cross the room to the entrance leading into the club foyer to see if he looked back at her with any sort of regret, but he didn't.

"What's wrong with Dr. Charming?" Rupert set a martini down in front of her and dropped into Dominic's vacant chair.

"Professional difficulties." She tapped the gin off her olive skewer. Perhaps it was better this way. If for some reason he decided to remain in England, he might catch a nasty strain himself someday, and then she'd have to face it all again, the grief, the loneliness. She bit the olives off the skewer. There was no point thinking about that. After that exit, she wasn't likely to be living in the moment with him again anytime soon.

"He thinks all of this is silly, doesn't he?"

"Is he wrong?" She glanced at the peroxide blonde who smiled coyly at her older gentleman as he slid one thick hand across the table to clasp hers. "Are we all fools for chasing after whatever it is she's offering us?"

"There's nothing wrong with trying to better yourself in whatever way you can, and your good doctor should understand and applaud that. I do. As for his snarling, don't worry about it. Men like to growl, but we have short memories. I predict he'll be back to panting around you in no time."

It was a slim if crass reassurance. "Even if he is, he's leaving soon, and so are you. I wish you didn't have to go. I could use your help." He'd introduced her to this world, and now he was abandoning her to make her way through it alone. Tonight wouldn't be the first in which she'd need his advice, and she wanted it without the cost of a transatlantic telephone call or telegram. A lot of good a letter would do her two weeks after the fact.

"If there was anything left to my future title, I wouldn't leave, but I need money if I'm to be a viscount someday, and it isn't here."

"You think it's in sports cars in America?"

"I know it is; besides, you don't need my help. I saw your picture with her in *Tatler*. I expect to read great things about you in the American press. They're obsessed with her, you know."

"Who isn't?" *Dominic*. She took a deep drink of the martini, the lightness in her head more irritating than welcome.

"Just don't forget who got you here." He cuffed her under the chin and then threw a roguish smile across the table to Caroline, who batted her eyelashes at him as if she wanted another tour of his estate before he left for America. "If you'll excuse me, I have a few more goodbyes to make."

"As long as you don't make any little future viscounts while you're at it."

"Don't worry, my dear cousin, this isn't my first fox hunt." With a wink he strolled around the table, offered Caroline a gallant bow, and then escorted her to the dance floor.

Vera watched the various members of the Set dance together, glad for once to be left behind. For the last few weeks, they and Princess Margaret had become her world, to the detriment of her plans for New York. Other than the languishing Rose Lavish novel, she hadn't written anything else, and getting her more serious Lady Penrose novel down on paper hadn't felt as urgent as it once had, but she was beginning to think she should keep her horizons a bit broader than Buckingham Palace. Her time with the Set wouldn't last forever, and beyond it there wasn't much else to look forward to if she gave up on her dreams.

This is helping me achieve my dream, she thought, and all Dominic's naysaying could go to the devil. Rupert was right about the Princess opening doors for her and giving her connections. However, exactly what she'd achieve from these connections beyond new clothes and nights out at fancy clubs had yet to reveal itself.

Chapter Nine

Princess Margaret, Sass, Vera, Caroline, Laura, and Katharine giggled together as they walked from Princess Margaret's rooms to the indoor pool at the back of Buckingham Palace, their bare footsteps muffled by the hallway's thick red carpet.

Sass eyed a tall young man dressed in the Palace's red-and-black livery and carrying a tray. At their approach, he stepped off to one side, his back against the wall and ramrod straight while he waited for them to pass. "Is that a new footman, Margo? He's quite a dish."

Princess Margaret turned to admire him, forced to walk backward to keep him in sight. "Yes, he is."

The young man pretended to be part of the fixtures and just as deaf. Only a slight flush about his neck above his collar indicated that he was aware he was being ogled by the Princess and her friends.

"He isn't your type, Margo." Sass nudged the Princess, forcing her to face forward again. "He's much too young. A little horsey in the stables told me you like much older men."

"She's awful, isn't she, Mrs. Lavish?" Princess Margaret raised her nose in the air but not before glancing at Vera, Caroline, and the Smith sisters with a twitch of nervousness. "I should have her banished back to America."

"But you won't because you like me too much." Sass made a circle around the royal and then walked backward in front of them, smiling like the devil. "*The Princess and the Footman.* Wouldn't that make quite a love story, Mrs. Lavish?"

"It'd be a smashing success."

"Don't you dare," Princess Margaret warned with a half-joking laugh. "You can scribble what you like about everyone else but not me."

"I'd never write about you, Ma'am." Even if Her Royal Highness was providing more fodder for stories than Vera's thrice-divorced great-aunt ever could. If Vera was doing any writing at the moment, she might type a few of these anecdotes up as part of Lady Penrose's story, but the Remington was beginning to collect dust. She'd finished her last Rose Lavish novel in time to avoid any additional production delays and to earn the second half of her advance, but she was in no hurry to start another.

"Are we there yet, Ma'am?" Caroline asked. "I feel like I've walked a mile. Why do these palaces have to be so big?"

"Yeah, these old palaces are nothing like the comfy small-ness of Longleat," Laura teased. "How many rooms does it have, one hundred fifty or so?"

"I haven't counted them, but you can pay your two shillings

sixpence and do it yourself." Caroline's father, the Marquess of Bath, hadn't fared much better than Vera's father after the war. Death duties had almost sunk him, and to save the old estate, he'd opened it for public tours. Vera admired the Marquess's fortitude. If her parents had demonstrated half as much creativity with their assets, they might have enjoyed the same success. Vera had once suggested that her father find a job, and he'd turned red with apoplexy at the idea of doing more every day than reading his paper and smoking his cigars. There were times when Vera wondered how she could be the offspring of parents who wouldn't lift a finger to help themselves.

"Here we are, ladies." Princess Margaret pushed through the metal-and-glass doors at the end of the corridor, filling the hall with the scent of chlorine and damp.

The white-tiled brightness of the indoor pool was a blinding contrast to the dark reds and greens of the palace. The clouds of the last week had cleared, and the blue sky was sharp outside the floor-to-ceiling glass windows enclosing the pool, their uniformity enhanced by evenly spaced Greek columns. Outside, it was bitingly cold, but in here the air was so warm the mosaic tiles were inviting instead of chilly underfoot.

"Isn't this grand?" Princess Margaret allowed her robe to fall from her shoulders and onto the pool deck. The bathing costume beneath it nearly made Vera snatch up the robe and fling it back over her. The material was so pale that if someone simply glanced at her, they'd look twice to make sure she wasn't nude. One of the gardeners trimming a hedge near the window outside did just that, staring dumbfounded through the glass before his companion hauled him off to work in a different part of the garden. How this two-piece costume in flesh-colored nylon had escaped the Queen's scrutiny when the strapless Dior had been altered to protect the royal modesty Vera didn't know.

Princess Margaret left the robe in a rumpled pile on the deck and walked with the elegance of a ballet dancer to the deep end of the pool. Raising her arms over her head so that Vera wondered if the top would contain her, she dove into the water, gliding beneath it to the shallow end, where the others stood tucking their hair under swimming caps. Vera expected the Princess to come up with the top around her waist, for it didn't appear sturdy enough to withstand the dive, but, to her amazement, the top remained intact to cover the royal turrets.

"Ma'am, your hair," Katharine exclaimed when the Princess broke the surface of the water and rested her bare arms on the pool deck. Her dark hair flowed in wet and dripping tendrils down the sides of her face and over her shoulders.

"It doesn't matter. I'm having it done for the art gala tonight anyway. Come in, everyone, the water is splendid." She pushed off from the wall, kicking her dainty feet and lifting first one arm and then the other in a smooth backstroke.

Vera hesitantly removed her robe, a quick purchase she'd made during a detour to Harrods on the way here, and set it on one of the blue-and-white-striped cushioned deck chairs surrounding the pool. The single bathing suit she'd been able to get her hands on in time for this early December swim had no straps, but the one-piece with the hibiscus pattern left far more to any unsuspecting gardener's imagination than the Princess's did.

Vera dipped a toe to test the water. It was warm, and she lowered her body into it, enjoying the heat and weightlessness. When she was a girl, she'd spent summers swimming at Rupert's parents' house, but they'd been forced to drain and fill in the pool during the war, and it'd been years since Vera had last gone for a swim. She glided out toward the deep end with a breaststroke that would have made her aunt proud but was nothing compared to Princess Margaret's graceful strokes.

Laura, Katharine, and Caroline remained where the pool was shallow while Sass, not to be outdone by her royal friend, dove in, breaking the surface of the water to splash the sisters, who squealed in horror at getting wet.

"How's your doctor?" Princess Margaret swam in a circle around Vera, her lips, for once without their red lipstick, pursed in a frown. "He was very impertinent at the 400 Club."

Vera treaded water as warily as if she were being circled by a shark. The Princess might have forgiven Dominic, but she obviously hadn't forgotten what had happened. "Please forgive him, Ma'am; he'd attended a terminal case that day and was having a bad time of it."

She wasn't sure why she was defending him. She had yet to hear from him since the 400 Club, and she doubted today

would be any different. The nerve-racking and annoying un-
certainty of dating was the part of romance she'd forgotten
about.

"I see." Margaret treaded water in front of Vera, the crease
between her brow softening. "Lilibet can be like that, especially
after a meeting with Papa and his ministers. She becomes very
cross with me when I tell her about parties at the embassy or
what we saw at the theatre, as if I can help it that I don't have
her responsibilities. Will you see your doctor again?"

"I can't say, Ma'am." She swam with the Princess to the end
of the pool, the two of them throwing their arms up on the
pool deck and lazily kicking their legs out in front of them.
At the other end, Sass and Caroline chatted with the sisters,
their voices echoing off the tile and glass and covering Vera
and Princess Margaret's conversation. "My parents would prefer someone with a grander title, but I'm partial to him."

Whether he was still partial to her remained to be seen. She
shouldn't care if he was or not since he wasn't here for much
longer, but she did care, far more than she wished.

"Papa and his entire government would come down on me
if I followed my heart." Princess Margaret slapped the water
with one hand, sending up a small wave to break the pale blue
surface.

"You mean with Sunny, Ma'am?"

"Heavens no, especially not with him engaged to Susan
Hornby."

"You know, then?" Sass had made it seem as if it would be a national crisis if Princess Margaret found out.

"Of course I know. The Set isn't my only source of gossip. Mummy's ladies-in-waiting have some of the best stories." Vera didn't ask when Her Royal Highness had found out, preferring to believe it was sometime after her indiscretion with him. It made Vera think that perhaps it was better that things with Dominic had cooled. Vera had no desire to smell the Princess's perfume on his collar one night. "We're in a similar predicament when it comes to marriage prospects, aren't we, Mrs. Lavish?"

"It's an awful place to be in, Ma'am." Vera wasn't at all sure their situations were alike, for any romance of hers wasn't likely to land on the front page of world newspapers, but she appreciated the camaraderie.

"Stinking awful. But the New Year is almost upon us, and I predict a great deal of change for you, Mrs. Lavish."

"Really? What kind of change?" From where she swam it didn't seem like much had changed except for a more active and prestigious social life.

"We'll have to see, now, won't we?"

Vera didn't have the chance to ask what exactly the Princess thought they might see because the pool doors opened and a slender man of distinguished years in a dark brown suit walked in.

Captain Peter Townsend crossed the pool deck, the cuff of

his pants catching a few drops of water when Sass splashed the sisters. He didn't notice them, his whole attention on Princess Margaret. The sight of her changed the air of his somber face, and it did the same to hers.

"Captain Townsend, you should join us. The water is marvelous." Princess Margaret dropped her legs beneath the water and kicked, raising herself a touch above the surface to make her breasts float in front of her, the sight of them enhanced by her slender arms spread out on the pool deck. It was a startling contrast to Vera, who dropped down to her chin in the water, holding on to the edge of the pool with one hand. Not that it mattered. Vera could have been floating there naked and the King's Equerry wouldn't have noticed anyone but the Princess.

"I'm on duty, but you enjoy it for both of us." He didn't turn red like the footman had but dipped his head in the most annoyingly beguiling gesture for a man. It was difficult to imagine that with his delicate features he'd been hearty enough to survive the ice cold of the North Sea, where he'd crash-landed during the war. He seemed more like a don at Oxford, tucked away between books rather than a former pilot who'd made a name for himself during the Battle of Britain.

"I will but only after you tell me why you've barged in here. Is it to get a peek at us in our bathing costumes?"

Again, no hint of embarrassment or blushes. Vera guessed that after Captain Townsend's trials during the war, he could withstand the rigors of a little teasing from a teenager.

Except Princess Margaret looked not like a teenager but a well-developed woman, and there was no mistaking that they were both aware of it.

Too aware of it.

Vera felt as though she should swim to the other end and stop interrupting this exchange, but she didn't move, entranced by the possibility that this might be the man Princess Margaret had spoken of at the fashion show of wanting but not being able to have, the older gentleman the horse had told Sass about.

It can't be.

He was handsome, yes, but in the soft manner of Leslie Howard, not the rugged maleness of Errol Flynn, and from a background far too humble for a woman like her. He was also nearly old enough to be her father.

"His Majesty would like you to review the seating list for tomorrow night's charity dinner." Captain Townsend held up the paper he carried. "He's afraid you might object to the arrangement, and His Majesty wishes to send over any changes as soon as possible."

"If I must." The Princess swam to the metal ladder and, with all the grace of Ethel Merman, climbed out of the pool. Beads of water dripped from the wet tendrils of her dark hair to run down her shoulders and over her exposed stomach and legs. Captain Townsend watched every one of them fall, his fingers so tight on the paper he held that Vera could see him creasing it from where she was in the pool.

The Princess made no move for her robe but stood before

him, a puddle forming at her feet while she slowly slid the paper out from between his fingers, her head tilted, her eyes peering up at him through her thick lashes.

Vera tried not to stare, but she couldn't stop. It wasn't so much Princess Margaret turning her charm on Captain Townsend the way she did but how obvious it was to anyone who was looking that it was not a one-sided infatuation. Except no one but Vera was looking. Sass had intensified the splashing fight with Caroline and the sisters, distracting them from the show on the pool deck.

"It's too noisy in here for me to concentrate. Let's step out into the hall." Princess Margaret didn't wait for him to agree but strode past him, her hips swaying beneath the small piece of almost-nude fabric as she made for the door. She paused long enough for Captain Townsend to open it for her before leading him into the hallway. The door swung closed behind him.

"Vera, ring the butler and have him bring us some drinks and food. I'm famished," Sass instructed, snapping Vera out of her surprise. "The phone is by the door."

That was the last place Vera wished to venture, but she made for the white phone tucked into a nook beside the door and lifted the handset off the receiver. She barely heard the tinny ring at the other end as she stared through the glass at the Princess and Captain Townsend. They stood far too close together, her elbow brushing his every now and again while she examined the paper, chewing on the end of the pen he'd given her to make notes on the list.

This would all be amusing—and another anecdote to add to her growing list of fodder for a novel—if it wasn't the King's Equerry out there tickling the royal fancy. After all his years of service to the King, Captain Townsend should have known better than to betray His Majesty's trust by openly flirting with his daughter. No wonder Princess Margaret had said the world would come down on her if she pursued her heart's desire. It would, and rightly so because he was a married man with two small sons and well aware that he shouldn't be encouraging this inappropriate infatuation. He had little to lose from this game except his position, while Princess Margaret would be raked through the coals if it were ever discovered.

"Operator, how shall I direct your call?"

"The bu-butler."

The Princess stepped closer to Captain Townsend, his fingers brushing hers as she handed the list back to him, the gold band encircling his ring finger evident.

"This is the butler. How may I help you?"

"Princess Margaret would like some refreshments sent to the pool." Even if one might say she already had enough of that in the form of the Equerry.

"The usual?"

Vera wondered if this was the usual and who else besides her and Sass had seen it. "Yes."

The line went dead, and Vera lowered the receiver, fumbling around for the cradle as she continued to stare through the glass door. Princess Margaret threw her arms around Captain

Townsend's neck and leaned into him. He kept his hands out to the sides, at least having the common sense not to touch her, but he didn't push her away either. She let go of him, laughing and pointing at the two wet marks left on his chest by hers. He wagged a naughty finger at her, but she appeared anything but contrite, turning on her bare feet and striding back to the pool, offering him one last seductive glance over her shoulder before pushing through the door.

Captain Townsend watched her until the door closed, clearly smitten. He'd have to be dead not to be after that display.

"Isn't Captain Townsend marvelous?" Princess Margaret sighed, putting on her rumpled robe and sinking into the cushioned chaise beside Vera.

Vera felt as if she was standing on a rickety bridge. She wasn't the courtier to object to the Princess's flirtation, but Princess Margaret wanted more than an opinion—she wanted downright encouragement.

"He's quite dashing. It's a shame he's married." It was the only subtle check to her friend's enthusiasm that Vera could think of.

"It isn't much of a marriage. She's a dowdy housewife who doesn't understand what an honor it is for him to serve Papa or how much a man like him needs a supportive woman by his side, a woman with vitality."

"I suppose that's their issue to struggle with and no one else's," Vera cautioned, tying the sash of her robe and taking the lounge chair beside the Princess's.

"It isn't fair." Princess Margaret pouted. "I could make him happy and he already makes me so happy. Papa is awfully keen on him. I'm sure, if Captain Townsend were free, Papa would approve."

Vera wasn't so certain, but surely the King must suspect something, for the two of them weren't exactly subtle. Either His Majesty chose not to see it or not to believe it or, as Sass had said on more than one occasion, Princess Margaret could do no wrong in her father's eyes. Vera hoped for Princess Margaret's sake that someone here possessed the wherewithal to check the infatuation before the Princess decided she had as much right to a married man as she did to an engaged one. "He isn't free."

"And I'm alone, like I've been ever since Lilibet married Philip." She smacked one small fist against the striped cushion. "It used to be the two of us here to share everything, but now she has a husband, a child, and a future. What do I have?"

"Your friends."

"What good are they?" She crossed her arms in such a huff that Vera wanted to rise, offer her a curtsey, and leave. If Her Royal Highness couldn't appreciate what she and the others endured to keep her amused, then there was little reason to be here, except Vera stayed where she was. One did not walk out on a member of the Royal Family but waited until they were dismissed.

Princess Margaret unclenched her arms, her face falling as much as her spirits. "Everyone will leave me eventually to marry and have children of their own, and then where will I be? I'm nothing but the spare, and not even that anymore. Every time Papa falls ill or has an operation, everyone rallies around Lilibet, waiting for the moment when they can curtsey to her. They forget about me, as if I don't worry about Papa as much as she does, but Peter never forgets me." She touched her hand where Captain Townsend had caressed it, admiring the backs of her fingers as if he'd slipped a sparkling diamond on her hand. "If I could take the Set with me when I go to events and we could laugh at all the serious, old mustached men and their endless speeches, it wouldn't be so difficult, but only ladies-in-waiting are allowed to go, and as much as I adore Jennifer, she's so serious, not at all like you and Sass, and she's leaving me in the New Year to marry her Captain."

"I hadn't heard." Jennifer was the most private and reserved of the Set, rarely joining in the ribald jokes but always in the background, dedicated to her Princess and the duties required of her position, but not enough to sacrifice her future to them.

"She gets her Captain while I get to attend yet another wedding as a guest." The door opened, and the butler and the young footman they'd passed in the hallway entered with a tray of drinks, a bottle of vodka, and a selection of small sandwiches. "Oh, thank heavens. Portman is here with drinks."

She marched up to the butler, who barely had time to set down the tray before the Princess took up the pitcher of orange juice, filled a glass, then tipped a healthy dose of vodka into it. Unlike Captain Townsend, the butler respectfully diverted his eyes from the open robe revealing a little too much of the Princess. The footman did the same, hoping this time to avoid any royal attention and succeeding. With her mind full of Captain Townsend, Princess Margaret paid the young man no mind as she dismissed both servants. Behind them, the others climbed out of the pool, donning their robes and making for the food.

"This looks absolutely marvelous." Caroline selected a small finger sandwich, her engagement ring sparkling with every movement. "This is exactly what I'm planning to serve at my wedding breakfast."

Princess Margaret watched Caroline while she downed her vodka and orange juice, her eyes narrowing more and more after every sip. "If I were Queen, I'd ban weddings. They're bloody awful, and all they do is make everyone who isn't married miserable. Caroline's would be the first I'd ban."

Caroline paused in raising a sandwich to her mouth. "Ma'am?"

"Tell me, Caroline, is your father going to sell tickets to your wedding the way he does to Longleat so everyone can gawk at the Duke of Beaufort's son who's getting a second-rate marquess's daughter for a bride?"

Only the faint lap of the pool water against the tiles filled the tense quiet.

"Margo," Sass breathed, treading carefully for once. "We're having so much fun; let's not ruin it."

"All I'm saying is the truth, for it is the truth, isn't it, Caroline?"

"No, Ma'am, it isn't." Caroline dropped her half-eaten sandwich on the plate. "Better a second-rate daughter of a marquess than the second-rate daughter of a king."

"You bitch." Princess Margaret threw her vodka and orange juice in Caroline's face. "Get out."

Caroline staggered back, the orange juice dripping over her cheeks and down her chin. She'd taken off her bathing cap, and bits of pulp clung to her dark hair. Caroline wiped the orange juice from her face and flicked it off her hands. Drawing her shoulders back with all the weight of her lineage, she held her head high and strode around the Princess and out the door.

"The rest of you can go too. I feel a headache coming on." Princess Margaret snatched up the vodka bottle and, leaving behind the pitcher of orange juice, marched out of the pool room.

"HAS SHE EVER done that before?" Vera sat across from Sass in one of the Prince's Gate embassy's sitting rooms, the two of them enjoying afternoon tea alone together. "She missed the art gala. The press says it was because of a migraine."

Vera tapped the folded newspaper on the table beside her plate with the small article about Princess Margaret at the bottom.

"A migraine from the vodka." Sass snorted. "She overdoes it sometimes when she's down, and this isn't the first time she's missed an official engagement because of it."

This was news to Vera. She'd seen the Princess drink on occasion but, like the rest of the Set, she could usually hold her liquor. Nor did it seem right that the woman who'd taken her conversation with the MP so seriously should shirk a royal engagement simply because she'd been in a bad mood. "What do the King and Queen say about it?"

"Nothing, I'm sure. I wish my parents were as closed lip when it came to commenting on my behavior." Sass tasted her tea and then set it aside. "What I can't figure out is what set her off. Usually she's in such a good mood after she sees Captain Townsend."

"I know what it was." Like everything else about Princess Margaret, Sass was aware of this too. There was no reason not to let her in on the rest of it, and Vera related her discussion with the Princess about marriage.

"Well, that explains it." Sass lounged back in her chair, drumming her fingers on the curved arm. "Leave it to Margo to set her heart on something she can't have."

"What are we setting our hearts on that we can't have?" Vera rubbed the ache out of her fingers from having spent most of yesterday and last night hunched over her typewriter, working furiously on her next Rose Lavish novel. After the incident at the pool, she'd had second thoughts about being so flippant with her means of employment.

Sass dropped a sugar cube in her tea. "You mean a certain doctor?"

"No." As Vera had predicted, there'd been no word from Dominic when she'd returned home yesterday. She still hadn't heard from him, and the things he'd said to her at the 400 Club chafed as much as his silence. "I mean, chasing after Princess Margaret and everything she offers. You left Vassar to stay in London."

"I'm glad I did. I've learned more and met more interesting and influential people here than I ever would have there."

"But is it worth risking orange juice in our faces to have it?" Vera wasn't so sure. She'd already sacrificed so much of her time and hard-earned money to be part of the Set, and she'd seen yesterday how easily one could be cast out of it. "If Princess Margaret lashed out at Caroline like that, simply because she's getting married, she could do it to any of us."

Sass uncrossed her legs and leaned forward in a rare moment of seriousness. "If you want the good, then you have to take the bad too, like in any friendship."

Vera picked at the dried drops of tea on her saucer. Were they really friends or glorified servants? It was difficult to tell sometimes, but there were moments when Vera could say things to the Princess that she hadn't been able to say to anyone else, and Princess Margaret understood. She'd done the same for the Princess more than once, including yesterday, but not even Vera's sympathy or Sass's influence had been enough to settle her. For all the shock and second-guessing the royal outburst had caused, Vera pitied the Princess. She knew what it was like to be deeply unhappy in a situation and powerless to do anything about it. Henry's death had permanently changed her life. Princess Margaret's uncle's abdication had done the same to hers.

"Miss Douglas," the embassy butler interrupted. "Dr. Reynolds is here to see you."

"What do you say, Vera—should we see him or send him away?"

"Send him away." Dominic didn't deserve her attention, not after the way he'd behaved at the 400 Club and his silence in the days since.

"Carlton, see him in."

"Sass, no!" Vera set down her cup and saucer with a clank.

"Oh, come off it. You want to see him as much as he wants to see you; that's why I told him you'd be here."

Vera could have throttled her friend. Instead, she gripped the arm of the chair to keep from fidgeting while she watched the door, waiting for Dominic.

She might force her body to be serene, but there was nothing she could do to slow her racing heart when he entered the sitting room. He wore a dark gray suit, and his bearing was as strong and erect as she'd come to expect from a man so confident in himself and his professional status. He smiled when his eyes met hers but didn't have a chance to speak before Sass rushed over and tugged him to a seat at the table.

"Dominic, I didn't expect to see you today," Vera greeted, determined to behave as if his rebuke the other night and his silence since didn't mean anything to her and neither did he. She didn't want him to think she'd been pining for him.

"The hospital is keeping me busy. I only have a few minutes before I have to be back to oversee a procedure. They're determined to get every bit of work and knowledge they can out of me before I have to leave." He tapped his knee with his fingers, the idea of leaving making him pause and Vera's chest hurt. She should have known better than to get herself in this situation, and yet she had. It was time to show a little more caution where he was concerned.

"Then I'll leave you two alone." Sass bolted for the door, stopping to point one reprimanding finger at them. "Don't get into any trouble while I'm gone, or if you do, be quick about it. Father has a meeting with the Italian transportation minister in here at two o'clock."

Sass closed the door behind her.

Dominic perched his hat on the arm of his chair while Vera fingered the lace napkin in her lap. Footsteps on the floor overhead echoed through the room before Dominic cleared his throat and spoke. "I want to apologize for my behavior the other night. It was wrong of me to speak to you like I did. I'd had a bad day and I took it out on you and I shouldn't have. Can you forgive me?"

Vera longed to throw her arms around him and kiss him, but she kept her feet on the rug. "That depends on whether or not you're willing to escort me to the Buckingham Palace Christmas Ball."

She'd spent a good amount of her hard-earned money on the green dress, and she intended to be admired in it. At least that sounded like a good enough excuse to her.

"Are you sure you can tolerate me as your date?"

"It'll be a monumental feat, but I think I can manage."

"Perhaps lunch at the Ritz would make it a little more tolerable."

"I think it would." So much for being cautious.

"Tomorrow at noon, then?"

She slid to the front of her cushion, the skirt of her dress riding up a bit over her knees with the movement. "Tomorrow at noon."

He leaned forward and, not caring whether the Italian transportation minister or any other official walked in on them, pressed his lips to hers. She curled her toes in her shoes, resisting the desire to settle herself in his lap and enjoy a little more. After all, she had some sense of decorum.

At last, with her dizzy and devoid of all rational thought, he pulled away from her, grinning like a chap who'd shared a taxi ride with a notoriously lax debutante. "Until tomorrow."

She wiggled her fingers at him as he paused at the door to offer her one last parting glance. Whatever happened with Princess Margaret, there was still her dream of America. With Dominic soon to be in the States, it made the desire to go much more urgent. There was a future beyond the Set. It may or may not be with him, but whatever it entailed, it was up to her to not be distracted from finding it, no matter how easy it was to be distracted as of late.

Chapter Ten

"To my daughter, Elizabeth, and her husband, Philip. I'm sorry you're leaving us, but we wish you well and hope you come back soon." The King raised his glass of champagne to Princess Elizabeth and the Duke of Edinburgh. The young couple, he tall and strapping in his naval uniform and she charming in a silver silk, floor-length gown, stood in the middle of the Buckingham Palace Ballroom surrounded by a throng of regal guests. The Queen smiled with pride from beside her husband, who, despite the gauntness hollowing out the space beneath his cheeks, looked better tonight than he had at the Royal Command Film Performance. "Wherever you live in the world so wide, we wish you a nook on the sunny side, with much love and little care, a little purse with money to spare, your own little hearth when day is spent, in a little house with the heart's content. To the happy couple!"

"The happy couple," the guests echoed, raising their champagne flutes.

Princess Margaret limply lifted her glass of champagne in

toast to her sister and brother-in-law, offering little more than a tight, closed-lip smile. If anyone, including Their Majesties, noticed, they didn't say anything, leaving her to stew in her ill humor alone. Not even Vera was brave enough to try to approach her and soften the harsh set of her mouth with a joke or two.

"Where are the Princess and her husband going?" Dominic took Vera's empty glass and his and deposited them on the tray of a passing footman.

"His Grace has been stationed in Malta, and the Princess is accompanying him, like any Navy wife."

"Except she isn't any Navy wife, is she?"

"Not at all."

"Ladies and gentlemen, take your places for the eightsome reel," the orchestra leader called out, and the crowd surged to the dance floor to form up.

"Shall we?" Dominic held out his elbow to her.

"I thought you didn't know this dance."

"I've taken a few lessons with Sass since the 400 Club. I think you'll be surprised."

"I already am."

The two of them joined the nearest circle with Sunny and Colin, and Laura and Imogene. Princess Margaret didn't join them, wandering off toward the refreshments in the State Dining Room. The music began, and they whirled through the reel, clasping hands to circle and turn. Around them, the Buckingham Palace Ballroom glittered beneath the numerous teardrop chandeliers. The white walls with their cornices and gilding were bright under the sparkling lights, making the curtains trimmed with gold hanging over the small thrones on the dais at the front of the room stand out. At the back of the ballroom, matching red curtains flanked the orchestra, who played in their Royal Guard uniforms on a balcony above the crowd. Men and women, most of them acquaintances of the royals, stood in their silks, black tails, Royal Navy uniforms, and ancestral diamonds, eating and enjoying the night. In the center of the dance floor, Princess Elizabeth and her husband danced together with her circle of friends.

When the reel came to an end, they took their places in the circle to clap before the orchestra struck up a slower tune. Dominic slipped his arm around Vera's waist and took her other hand, sweeping her along into an enthusiastic if poorly executed waltz. The green silk dress she'd spent so much money on swayed back and forth with their movements, the flowing skirt, the V of the bodice that tastefully revealed the tops of her breasts, and the soft straps gracing her shoulders worth every pound. Dominic kept his hand respectfully below where the dress ended just beneath her shoulders, but his desire to slide it up farther lingered in his rich brown eyes.

"You make a girl feel like a princess." Vera moved her hand up Dominic's shoulder and stretched out one finger to caress his bare neck above his shirt collar, feeling the slight perspiration gracing his skin from the exertion of the reel moisten the tip of her glove.

"I'm sure being in a palace helps." He slid his thumb along the line of her dress, caressing her bare skin there and making her shiver.

"It does, but promise me you won't turn into a pumpkin at midnight." She wanted a great deal more from him than this innocent teasing.

"I can promise that tonight but not for much longer." The heat and fun in his eyes faded to regret. "I'm going home before Christmas."

Vera slid her hand back to where it should be on his shoulder. "So soon?"

"I wish I could stay longer, but the clinic in Arizona needs me, like your Princess and country need you." He tapped her playfully on the nose, and she batted his hand away.

"Will you come back?"

"I don't know, but I'm not gone yet."

"No, you're not." She shifted closer to him, the desire to be with him before he left, like she'd been with Henry, to seize the present in the face of an uncertain future, blotted out all thoughts of loss and reservation. "Tell me, Doc, would you like another snog in the palace?"

"I would." He glanced around them at the tight press of revelers. "But I don't want to treat any of the old ladies here for a sprain from clutching their pearls so hard at the sight of us necking on the dance floor."

"It's a big palace. I'm sure there's some corner we can find where we won't scandalize the nation."

He pressed his hand into her lower back and drew her subtly closer to his hips. "And risk having your visitor credentials revoked?"

"I wouldn't take that chance for just anyone."

"Then I hope my attentions live up to your expectations."

"I'm sure they will."

He led her off the dance floor, and together they wove through the tightly packed crowd, offering and accepting greetings to Johnny, Billy, Elizabeth, and Katharine as they went.

Near the door, Sass passed them, resting her hand on Vera's shoulder and stopping her. "The White Drawing Room is usually empty on nights like this."

With an exaggerated wink, she floated off into the crowd in her pale orange organza gown toward whatever adventure she'd concocted for herself tonight.

"The White Drawing Room it is."

They left the ballroom, not through the West Gallery and State Dining Room, where the refreshments were being served, but through the East Gallery to avoid any watchful footmen. From there they crept into the Picture Gallery, stealing past the pink wallpaper covered in priceless art as fast and quietly as they could. Since this was a family ball rather than an official state function, no guards were posted at the ends of the hallways to keep anyone from wandering too far away from the party, and Dominic and Vera soon found themselves alone with nothing but Rubenses and Vermeers and the door to the White Drawing Room.

They fell against each other, Dominic's body hard and hot against hers. The tips of her gloved fingers slid over the wool of his jacket while his found the bare skin of her back above the bodice of her dress. She hoped he didn't find the fastenings of her gown too intricate, for she would rather enjoy something more than a snog in a sitting room tonight. Reaching behind her, she grabbed the doorknob and turned it, and the two of them stumbled into the drawing room lit only by the moon and the lights of London. Dominic pushed the door closed behind him with his foot, his fingers working at the button of her dress before he froze inside the circle of her arms.

Vera turned to see Princess Margaret standing at the window overlooking the dark Buckingham Palace gardens. The lights of the city silhouetted her petite figure in her wide skirt, and the draping curtains framed her against the large glass-paned window. She didn't turn at the sound of them, too lost in her thoughts or perhaps too used to having maids and footmen coming in and out of rooms to be startled by the noise of someone behind her.

Dominic tugged Vera's hand, trying to urge her back out of the room, but she raised her other one to stop him. "I need to make sure she's all right."

A frown of disappointment replaced the excitement of a moment before, but he let go of her without any argument. This wasn't the time for a discussion. "I'll wait for you in the ballroom. I don't want to be accused of stealing a painting by lingering in the hallway."

Vera caressed the side of his face, thankful for his patience and tempted to follow him along the corridors to another room, but she couldn't leave the Princess until she was sure she was all right. The loneliness swathing her reminded Vera too much of herself on the balcony at Weatherly Hall before Rupert had joined her and changed everything.

Dominic shut the door quietly behind him, blocking out the noise of the party.

The netting supporting the skirt of Vera's green dress rustled with each step she took toward the Princess. Her Royal Highness didn't startle at the noise or Vera's presence but continued to stare at the garden, as if the resolutions to all her troubles lay out there in the dark. She clutched a crystal tumbler in one gloved hand, and it wasn't until Vera was beside her that she noticed the tears trickling down the Princess's cheeks.

Vera reached out to lay a comforting hand on Princess Margaret's arm, then stopped. It didn't seem proper to touch her. "Ma'am, what's wrong?"

"Sass's father has been recalled. She's returning to America in the spring." The Princess wiped the tears away with the back of her hand. "First Jennifer, then Lilibet, now Sass."

"I'm sorry to hear that, Ma'am." Sass was the light of the Set and the most steadying influence on Her Royal Highness. Heaven help the Princess when Sass was gone. "Dr. Reynolds is also leaving for America too, before Christmas."

"It seems we're both being deprived of our favorite Americans." She handed Vera her glass of whiskey, silently urging her to take a sip. "It's too bad. I enjoy seeing the two of you together."

"So do I." Vera winced at the oaky burning of the whiskey spreading through her chest.

"Everyone leaves while we stay. Stuck here and of no consequence to anyone." The Princess took back the whiskey and finished it without flinching, then set the glass on a table beside her. "No one understands what it's like to live this life, no one except you sometimes. You know what it's like to be lonely."

"I do, Ma'am." It touched her that the Princess had noticed and cared. Few people did.

"So does Peter."

"Peter Ward, Ma'am?" The Earl of Dudley's son, who enjoyed the camaraderie of his fellow officers of the Fleet Air Arm, wasn't a man Vera thought of as lonely.

"No, Captain Townsend. His marriage has been devoid of love for years, and his wife is cheating on him. He's going to divorce her as soon as he has enough evidence to bring it to trial, and then he'll be free."

A faint whiff of trouble hung in the air like lemon-scented wood polish. Captain Townsend would never be free, not in the way Her Royal Highness imagined, assuming what he'd told her about his marriage was true. He wouldn't be the first man to lie about being on the verge of divorce in order to cajole a young woman into forgetting herself. Vera had heard that story many times during her debutante year and had written it into enough plots of her novels to know, but she kept it to herself. She wasn't one to yank away whatever faint comfort a person might find to ease the loneliness surrounding them.

Behind them, the click of the door opening made them both turn to see the very subject of their conversation enter the room. Captain Townsend, dressed in a black tuxedo, the white of his shirt and collar broken by a dark bow tie, entered the room. He didn't startle as Vera and Dominic had done or try to slip out, apologizing for interrupting, but approached them as if his arrival wasn't a coincidence but very much expected.

"Margaret, what are you doing hiding in here instead of out dancing?"

Not *Ma'am*, not *Your Royal Highness*, but *Margaret*.

"Oh Peter, I'm so glad you're here." She rushed into his arms and rested her head on his chest, the soft tears from before falling steadily to wet the lapel of his jacket and the red-ribbon medal pinned to it. He didn't push her away or deftly step aside to avoid the royal embrace but welcomed her small body against his. "What am I going to do without Lilibet?"

"Princess Elizabeth isn't going away for good, and she'll be back before you know it."

"But it won't be the same without her. It hasn't been the same since she married Philip. She has a husband and children, and what do I have? Nothing."

"Someday you'll be married with children of your own." He rested his chin on her hair, slightly ruffling the carefully constructed coiffure that was conspicuously missing a tiara. "I promise."

"Do you?"

"I do." He rocked her back and forth, soothing her as one might a child after a nightmare, the two of them so lost in each other that they'd forgotten Vera was still here.

Vera shifted a touch, and the netting of her skirt rustled, drawing Captain Townsend's attention. He let go of Princess Margaret, took a handkerchief out of his jacket pocket, and handed it to the Princess. "Let's go back to the ball and cheer you up. This isn't a night to be sad."

"I can't face the party. I want to go somewhere where we can be alone and talk. No one will miss us in this crush."

"Do you think that's a good idea?" Captain Townsend flicked a glance at Vera.

"She won't tell anyone, will you, Vera?"

"No, Ma'am, I won't tell anyone." She'd worked too hard to become a member of the Set to chance being thrown out of it by playing the prude. Besides, it wasn't up to Vera to stop them, especially not when the man involved was old enough to know better than to sneak off with the nineteen-year-old Princess. Both of their reputations would be destroyed if someone with less discretion than Vera discovered them.

"Come, Peter." Princess Margaret took his hand and tugged him across the room.

Apparently, Captain Townsend wasn't going to be the voice of reason tonight, uttering not one word of protest when Princess Margaret led him to one of the two ebony-and-marble-topped sideboards flanking the fireplace at the far end of the room. Princess Margaret ran her hand along the side of the mirror, and with a click, it and the sideboard swung open to reveal a door hidden behind it. Princess Margaret and Captain Townsend slipped through the secret entrance, and the door swung closed behind them.

Vera stared at her dark reflection in the large mirror, certain that passage didn't lead to a room full of chaperones. Whatever Captain Townsend felt he might gain by canoodling with the Princess must far outweigh what he thought he could lose by taking such a risk. Either that or he didn't believe there was any danger in being alone with her. Perhaps his position or the Princess's might protect them. Vera hoped he was right, for the pillorying in the press they'd both receive if this ever got out was a torture Vera didn't wish on anyone, especially not the Princess.

Vera hurried out the drawing room door. The last thing she needed was someone of prominence coming in and demanding to know why she was in there alone or wondering where the Princess had gotten off to. Vera wasn't going to tattle on the Princess, but she wasn't going to stammer through a lot of bad lies and excuses in front of who knew what palace official either.

She hurried back down the Picture Gallery, eager to find Dominic, and especially Sass. Nothing about Princess Margaret ever shocked her, and she'd have a level-headed take on this absurd situation. Vera was almost to the entrance to the ballroom when Lady Rankin, one of the Queen's Women of the Bedchamber, stepped in front of her, stopping her cold.

"Miss Strathmore. The Queen requests a private audience with you."

She knows. They both do. Vera almost bolted down the hall and right out the front of Buckingham Palace before she took hold of herself. They weren't likely to ask her where Princess Margaret was. She wasn't important enough. *Then why does the Queen want to see me?*

"Would you be so kind as to follow me?"

There was only one way to discover it. "Of course."

Vera almost came out of her heels in an effort to keep pace with Lady Rankin's quick clip as she led Vera though the State Dining Room and into the long Picture Gallery. "When you first address the Queen, it is *Your Majesty*. After that it's *Ma'am*. When your interview is over you will curtsey and, without turning your back on Her Royal Highness, take three steps before leaving. I will escort you back to the ball."

"Yes, Lady Rankin." With the door to the White Drawing Room looming at the end of the gallery, Vera's palms went moist beneath her gloves. She wasn't sure she could hold it together if she had to face Her Majesty in there. To her relief, Lady Rankin stopped at the door in the middle of the hallway, the Green Drawing Room.

The Queen stood in the center of the Green Drawing Room. The descendants of former monarchs watched them from their gilded framed paintings hanging high on the pale green silk-covered walls. If Vera's conscience had plagued her in the Picture Gallery, it absolutely flogged her in here, but it was tempered by knowing a thing or two about what those royal children had got up to in their time. If nothing else, their descendent was simply carrying on a long line of tradition, the kind people didn't erect monuments to.

"Your Majesty." Vera dropped into the curtsey she'd recited so many times before her debutante season and had only ever used tonight. Her parents hadn't possessed the means to present her at court, but she was receiving her presentation now. Vera rose and waited for the royal to address her, thinking, of all things, how her dress went well with the green silk covering the chairs in the room.

"Thank you so much for coming to see me, Miss Strathmore." The Queen wore a wide-skirted pale blue gown with fluttering sleeves and a demure V neck. A blue sash hung with various gold and diamond orders draped across her shoulder and full bosom to the side of her thick waist. It was matched in sparkle by the large diamond-and-sapphire necklace and earrings she wore and the small tiara set expertly in her coiffure. For all the grandeurs of her dress and the room, it was her smile that most awed Vera, for it was warm and welcoming and instantly set her at ease. Certainly, Her Majesty wouldn't smile like that if she was going to hurl accusations and questions at Vera, or maybe she would? The woman was a force to be reckoned with, and it was said that even Hitler had feared her. Vera did too. "I've heard so much about you from Margaret. She's quite fond of you."

"She's a good friend, and I hope I've been half as good a friend to her in return, Ma'am." What other friend would face Her Majesty while knowing what Vera did about what was probably going on behind that sideboard?

"You have been, and it's why I've asked to see you this evening. Miss Bevan is leaving us in the New Year to wed her Captain. I'm so happy for her, but I'm worried about Margaret. So many of those close to her are leaving all at once, and I don't want her to be alone. She needs dependable friends to support her and help her during this difficult time."

Vera's legs shook. If Her Majesty knew who was helping and supporting Princess Margaret at that moment, she'd have Vera and Captain Townsend tossed out of the palace. "Yes, Ma'am."

"Therefore, I wish to offer you the position of second lady-in-waiting to Princess Margaret. The first will be the Honorable Iris Peake."

Vera locked her knees tight to keep from falling over. Never in all her nights out with the Set and not once when she'd worked furiously at her typewriter, wondering what the future would hold, had she imagined this. The Princess's comment about change in the New Year came rushing back to her. *Princess Margaret must have spoken to the Queen on my behalf.*

Her mother would die of shock when she told her. How Vera didn't keel over from astonishment was a miracle.

"I understand this must be quite a surprise for you and that you'll need some time to think it over," Her Majesty continued. "I do hope you will consider this honor and everything it will mean to Margaret and my family."

"I will consider it most carefully, Ma'am."

"I'm sure you will. Have a great rest of your evening at the ball." It was the most subtle and polite dismissal Vera had ever received.

Vera curtseyed and then backed up the required three steps, praying as she went that she wouldn't catch the edge of her hem with her heel and tear it or send herself tumbling butt over shoulders in front of Her Majesty. She didn't, executing the leave with admirable poise that made all those hours of deportment lessons worth the trouble.

"Your duties as second lady-in-waiting will require you to familiarize yourself with the Princess's schedule, but you will not manage it. That will fall to Miss Peake, who will oversee you and your duties. You will answer correspondence, deal with press inquiries and invitations, and assist with travel arrangements." Lady Rankin spoke as fast as she walked as she escorted Vera back to the ball. "On occasion, you will be required to travel with Her Royal Highness. You will train with Miss Bevan in the New Year and assume your duties in the early spring."

Vera floated along the carpeted hallways behind Lady Rankin, barely hearing what she said. If Vera accepted the position, she'd no longer be only a friend or a member of the

Set but someone with real purpose in the royal household, a part of the Royal Family's intimate lives. She'd be seen with the Princess at royal functions and travel with her when she visited exciting countries and places.

"Any other means of employment you currently engage in must cease. There must be no conflicts between the Princess's schedule and yours."

This yanked Vera out of her daydream.

Do they know about my being Rose Lavish? She doubted it. No amount of persuasion on Princess Margaret's part was likely to have made them overlook that little detail. However, the King and Queen's tendency to never deny the Princess anything was not above possibility.

It was what Vera was willing to deny herself to accept the position that remained to be seen. It was one thing to follow the royal whims on nights out but quite another for them to control every aspect of her life, including ending the dream she'd spent so many years pursuing, the one that had sustained her through so many difficult and lonely days. The thought of abandoning it made her hesitate, as she had the day she'd taken off Henry's engagement ring before she'd given it back.

I don't have to give it up. Just set it aside for a while. I can always write in my spare time. It was only Mrs. Lavish who'd have to be sacrificed, and Vera should have been glad to bid her adieu, but she wasn't. The pen name was as much a part of the past four years as her dreams and all the grief that had been a great deal lighter lately. It was thanks to the Princess that it was, and she couldn't ignore that.

Lady Rankin stopped at the entrance to the State Dining Room and turned to Vera, as imperious as when she'd first approached her. "I hope you'll choose to serve the Royal Family as so many have done before you."

"I will think it over very carefully, Lady Rankin."

The two curtsied to each other and then went their separate ways.

Vera searched for Dominic in the State Dining Room, eager to talk to him about the offer. He more than Sass could help her root through the myriad thoughts making her head spin and help her decide what to do. He could see things concerning the Princess so much clearer than any of them, even Vera, and she needed his insight.

She didn't see him in the State Dining Room and went through to the ballroom. Princess Elizabeth and the Duke of Edinburgh continued to dance, as did most of the Set, including Sass, who jumped back and forth in an exaggerated foxtrot with Peter Ward. At last, Vera spied Dominic standing alone across the room.

"You weren't caught by a guard, were you?" he asked when she finally reached him, the music grating on her already agitated nerves.

"No, I had an audience with the Queen."

He let out an impressed whistle. "Maybe I should have stayed with you. Did she give you a title?"

"She asked me to be Princess Margaret's second lady-in-waiting."

He jerked back in surprise. "That's quite an honor."

"Is it?"

"Isn't it?"

"I'm not sure." She took his hand and pulled him out of the ballroom and into the quiet of the hallway. When they were a good distance from the other guests but not so far away as to attract the curiosity of the attentive footmen standing beside the door, she let go of him and began to pace. "Accepting it means giving up everything else, including New York."

"Are you willing to sacrifice what you want for her?"

"In the long run, it may not be a sacrifice." Vera fingered the small gold pendant around her neck, making it rub against the chain. "Working for her could give me opportunities I never knew were possible, ones that will make New York pale in comparison or change how I eventually get there."

"But?"

"It isn't easy letting go of something I've craved for so long."

"I know." He took her small hands in his large ones to stop her fidgeting, his palms warm against her satin gloves. "When I was young, all I wanted to be was a rancher. It was the only thing I ever thought about, until a horse threw me when I was sixteen. I spent a year learning to walk again, but I can no longer ride, and some days, despite my professional success, it still hurts to think about what might have been."

"That's how it was when I lost Henry." Tears blurred the image of their intertwined hands. Vera slid her arms around his waist and hugged him tight. For years she'd endured jealousy and bitterness every time one of her friends had walked down the aisle and claimed everything that she'd been denied. During all those weddings and the lonely nights afterward, she'd worked hard to convince herself that her writing dreams were enough to sustain her, but they weren't. If they had been, she wouldn't have chased after her place in the Set with such abandon.

"Dreams change, Vera, sometimes when we want them to and sometimes when we don't." He stroked her back while she rested her head against his chest, the steady rhythm of his heartbeat in her ear. "I lost one life, but there was another waiting for me with far more meaning and rewards than I could've imagined. The same might be true for you."

"And it all depends on the whims of Her Royal Highness." She slid out of his embrace but held tight to his hands. "She turned her back on Caroline without a second thought. She could do the same to me, and then where will I be?"

"Where will you be if you turn this down?"

"Dumped back in my old life as Mrs. Lavish, except with a great wardrobe and nowhere to wear it." Princess Margaret would probably take Vera's refusal as an insult, the offer having all but made the decisions for Vera as much as the picture in *Tatler*. Something inside Vera rebelled at the thought. She'd done so much for herself the last few years that it was difficult to imagine losing that freedom.

"And if you accept the position?"

"I'd have almost everything I'd hoped to gain by writing and going to New York." She'd no longer be pitied, forgotten, looked down upon, or ignored but someone of position and consequence.

All these things were worth the loss of her freedom.

The one thing she wouldn't have is Dominic.

"Then I think you have your answer."

She tilted her head to the side and peered up at him, the low lights of the hallways making his hair darker. "I thought you didn't approve of chasing after royalty?"

"I have the family business to support me. Someone made me realize not everyone is so lucky." He gave her hands a squeeze and then raised them to his chest. "Promise me one thing, Vera."

She clasped his hands tight. "Anything."

"Promise me you won't surrender everything to her. I've made that mistake at times. Keep a little of your life for yourself."

"I promise." It was him she wished she could hold on to, but like her, he had his responsibilities, and she admired him for his commitment to them, as much as he'd gained respect for hers. "Too bad you're leaving, for in a few months I could have made that second kiss in the palace come true."

"It can still come true. I haven't left yet." He slid one finger across her palm, raising a line of goose bumps beneath the satin.

"No, you haven't." She rose up on her toes and pressed her lips to his, the kiss bittersweet. He, like 1949, would soon be gone. She'd miss his steady presence, especially when she accepted the position and her new life began. There would be letters between them and perhaps, if the Princess got her wish to visit America, she would see him again. It was the wish she silently made in his arms.

Chapter Eleven

*L*ady Carden will greet you at the door and lead you into the Whistler Room," Vera said, outlining the Princess's schedule as their Rolls-Royce carried them toward the Tate Gallery for the annual meeting of the Westminster Cultural and Historical Society, of which Princess Margaret was a patron.

"'Oh, Your Royal Highness.'" Princess Margaret mimicked the grand dame, perfectly capturing her slight lisp. "'How marvelous for you to join us today.'"

"'Our speaker is going to thrill us with his knowledge of rare paint pigments.'" Vera's impression wasn't as perfect as the Princess's, but it made Her Royal Highness laugh.

"'A most thrilling subject to be sure,'" the Princess performed with one last duchess-like flair and then rolled her eyes. "If I had a pound for every time I had to listen to one of these awful speeches, I wouldn't need an income from the Civil

List, but as Mummy always says, I have to appear as if I'm interested, even if I'm bored to tears. I should earn a BAFTA for these performances."

The Rolls-Royce slowed to a stop in front of the Tate Gallery. A flock of cameramen surrounded the car and shoved their cameras against the window, fighting for the best shot of the Princess. Princess Margaret tucked her purse under her arm and adjusted her white calot hat as if ready to do battle. "Let's see if we can give them a decent picture of me to use this time instead of all those beastly ones they usually print."

While the museum officials and her private detective cleared a way through the press for the diminutive royal, the Princess stepped out of the car. She walked past the cameramen and up to the doors of the Tate, ignoring the photographers' calls to look their way so they could capture the best shot. Once in a while one of them would yell to Vera, who nodded and smiled, enjoying this far more than Her Royal Highness. Their attention didn't rattle her like it used to do, and tomorrow she'd appear in the background of most of those pictures of the Princess, another memory to add to the already thick scrapbook on her bedroom desk.

The Royal Command Performance continued as Princess Margaret stopped to accept a small bouquet of roses from a young girl standing beside the entrance. Princess Margaret exchanged a few words with the pigtailed child and her mother, both of whom stared at the Princess as if she were an angel. Then, with all the politeness of the Queen Mother, she took her leave and, handing Vera the bouquet, entered the semi-stillness of the gallery.

"Oh, Your Royal Highness, how marvelous for you to join us today," the Marchioness of Carden effused while she dipped the required curtsey. "Dr. Reginald Taylor is going to thrill us with his knowledge of medieval calligraphy styles and methods. It'll be a fascinating lecture."

"A most thrilling subject, to be sure," Her Royal Highness responded, with no note of mockery, the kind that sometimes crept into her voice after a late night and one too many stiff drinks. Official mourning for the Princess's grandmother Queen Mary had tempered the Princess's late nights since March, making her more amenable to fulfilling her official duties. Heaven help them all, especially Vera and Iris, when mourning ended next week and the coronation festivities began.

"If you'll follow me, Ma'am. We are about to begin." Lady Carden escorted Princess Margaret into the Whistler Room. Princess Margaret was, of course, the last to arrive, making her the center of attention when she took her place of precedence with the chairman and president. Vera followed behind her, flanked by Lady Chansford and Lady Riverdowne.

"Miss Strathmore, I have a proposal I wish to present to Her Royal Highness for presentation to Her Majesty in support of my husband's efforts to secure passage of the Transportation Bill in Parliament," Lady Chansford implored.

"If you send it to me, I'll see that she reads and considers it."

Vera settled herself in the chair behind the Princess, ready to assist Her Royal Highness if necessary during the meeting.

"Thank you very much, Miss Strathmore."

Lady Chansford fell back, and Lady Riverdowne stepped up, their movement to present their inquiries to Vera seemingly coordinated in advance. "We should very much like it if Her Royal Highness could take a moment to personally thank Lady Ranfurly for selling so many tickets to this year's Museum Ball."

"I'll do my best to arrange it."

"Thank you, Miss Strathmore. Might I take those flowers from you and place them in water until after the meeting?"

"Please." Vera handed the flowers to Lady Riverdowne while smothering a smile of glee. Three years ago they'd looked down their aquiline noses at Vera. Today they practically scattered rose petals at her feet. If she'd ever held doubts about accepting this position, they were far from her mind today as she put on an appearance of interest in the upcoming speech that was as worthy of an award as the Princess's.

Princess Margaret raised one hand and motioned Vera forward, and Vera leaned over the royal shoulder.

"Yes, Ma'am?"

"What did Lady Chansford want?" Her Royal Highness whispered, never allowing her attention to wander from the speaker droning on about a treasurer's report at the front of the room.

"Your help in encouraging Her Majesty to support the Transportation Bill."

"She's always nagging me to promote her husband's interests. Hasn't she figured out yet I have no influence with Lilibet when it comes to anything important? I did with Papa, but now that he's gone, no one listens to me." Her Royal Highness swallowed hard, her false look of interest faltering before she shored it up. "Lilibet only listens to Philip and all her old mustached ministers, none of whom believe I have a brain in my head. They only think I'm fit for things like this." She waved her hand at the room in agitation all the while holding her smile so no one would think she was discussing anything more important with Vera than how excited she was to be there.

Yes, Princess Margaret should get BAFTAs for this performance, for if they knew how much the Princess longed to be anywhere but in this room, it would cause a genteel uproar.

"WHERE'S CAPTAIN TOWNSEND? He doesn't usually miss afternoon tea when he's here," Captain Oliver Dawnay, Private Secretary to the Queen Mother and Princess Margaret, mused from over the rim of his china teacup. Vera sat with him and the other senior staff in the Garden Room next to the tiny lady-in-waiting office. The two rooms had been hastily created by splitting the Garden Room in unequal halves before Princess Margaret and the Queen Mother's move to Clarence House two weeks earlier. The Garden Room, with its wide walls hung with large paintings of fowls, served as Princess Margaret's official sitting room but until the dining room was ready, the senior staff enjoyed their afternoon tea in here. This daily ritual was a welcome distraction for everyone who regularly attended, for it was the only place they could commiserate about the challenges of their employment without fear of retribution or the gossip columns. This small cabal of servants so close to royalty would sooner suffer death than repeat what was said around this table.

"Find Princess Margaret and you'll find Captain Townsend, especially with the rest of the Royal Family being at Windsor and she remaining here," Ruby MacDonald, Princess Margaret's personal dresser, observed in her soft Scottish brogue. At thirty-seven years old, Ruby wasn't as intimidating as Lady Rankin, but she possessed the elder lady's steel spine.

"She has the most convenient headaches, doesn't she?" Lady Rankin sniffed.

"At least during the day. At night when the Queen Mum isn't here it's a different matter."

"Ruby, really," Vera chided, stirring sugar into her tea.

"Come off it, you know as well as we do what's going on."

Vera did, perhaps better than anyone else in the room, but the rumors of Princess Margaret and Captain Townsend were being spoken of a little too loudly for her liking today. "At least she's finally smiling again."

"And not biting the heads off the maids, who come crying to the head housekeeper, who comes crying to me because I have *influence*." Lady Rankin sighed. "I suppose we can at least thank Captain Townsend for that."

"Mark my words, it'll be Her Royal Highness who'll be crying if this little flirtation ever develops into anything deeper," Ruby tutted. "The King, God rest his soul, isn't here to give her everything she wants anymore, and she'll have to contend with harder men like Sir Lascelles, who aren't likely to approve of a divorced man."

The Queen's Private Secretary was a man of the old guard who'd served under the last three kings. He was a stickler for formality who hadn't thought twice about opposing King Edward's desire to marry Wallis Simpson.

"But the Queen will support the Princess. Her Majesty likes Captain Townsend, and she wants her sister to be happy as much as the rest of us do." Vera had seen the Queen and Princess Margaret together on many occasions, and despite the differences in their personalities, the Queen very much loved her sister.

Vera's belief in sisterly affection was met with a disbelieving harrumph from Lady Rankin. "Her Majesty will support who and what her ministers tell her to support. The court and the country might be in an uproar over the coronation, but Her Majesty's government will not set aside their responsibilities to the crown and the church because of one of Princess Margaret's whims."

"I don't think Captain Townsend is a whim or she'd have lost interest in him long ago." Princess Margaret hadn't lost interest in Captain Townsend like she had Sunny; she had clung to him, the two of them drawing even closer after the King's unexpected death last year had irrevocably changed both of their positions. He'd been demoted from the King's Equerry at Buckingham Palace to Comptroller of the Queen Mother's household at Clarence House. Princess Margaret had lost the revered place she'd enjoyed as her father's favorite daughter in the beloved Royal Family. There was another Royal Family in Buck Place now, and they were the only ones who mattered.

"Hard for it to fade when he's always ready to offer her a shoulder to cry on," Captain Dawnay mumbled into his tea.

"Can't blame her for accepting it either, what with everyone supporting Her Majesty and the Queen Mother after His Royal Highness's passing and not giving Princess Margaret's grief a second thought," Ruby defended, having consoled the Princess as many times as Vera and Captain Townsend had over the last year.

As if his ears were itching, Captain Townsend strode in through the garden door. "Am I late for tea?"

China cups clanked against saucers accompanied by a cacophony of coughs as everyone murmured their excuses about having work to do and hurried out of the room, leaving Vera alone with Captain Townsend.

"They were talking about me, weren't they?" Captain Townsend reached for the teapot and poured himself a cup.

"You know the rules. He who misses tea becomes the subject of it."

"What are they saying about me?"

"They don't approve of your divorce," Vera lied. She and

Captain Townsend had always been cordial to each other, but she didn't think they were on such intimate terms as to admit that his relationship with Princess Margaret wasn't the secret he and the Princess believed it to be.

"I didn't expect them to approve, nor did I ask for their opinion on the matter." He snapped out a linen napkin and laid it over his dark blue trousers.

Vera drank her tea, wondering if he'd be so cavalier about the opinions of Queen Elizabeth, Her Majesty's Private Secretary, the Prime Minister, or the public if his clandestine relationship with Princess Margaret ever became more than gossip. Vera had long ago lost hope that the thirty-eight-year-old man might realize the consequences of his chivalrous attention to Her Royal Highness and put a stop to it, but he hadn't. Instead, he and the Princess appeared to delight in contriving ways to be alone. Vera had accompanied them on enough horseback rides at Royal Lodge, Windsor, in which they'd politely invited her to take another bridle path to know. Vera hoped he'd contrived a few prophylactics while he was at it; then again, either of them might use an unintended consequence to push this issue wherever it was they pictured it ending.

"I'm also the innocent party in the whole sad affair. My wife cheated on me," Captain Townsend insisted.

Innocent, my eye. Vera bit back a reminder about the Buck Place Christmas Ball all those years ago *before* his divorce, along with the numerous solitary walks and private teas with

Princess Margaret in his grace-and-favor apartment that had taken place since. No wonder his wife cheated on him. A commoner could never hope to compete with a Princess. "Well, you know how people are."

"I do, and you'd think, given my many years in royal service, I'd be used to it, but I'm not. But here's to us, who keep toughing it out for Queen and Country." He leaned across the table to clink his teacup against hers. The purple enamel Fabergé clock on the mantle chimed four o'clock. He swept the napkin off his lap, set it on the table, and rose. "If you'll excuse me, I have the Queen Mother's accounts to keep."

"And I have the Princess's schedule to review." Vera plucked the leather folio with the typewritten schedule off the floor beside her chair. Together, she and Captain Townsend left the Garden Room, passing through the Lancaster Room with its yellow walls covered with drawings of Windsor Castle during the war. They continued on into the main hallway where footmen and maids worked to unpack and arrange items to the royal liking. Clarence House was at sixes and sevens except for the royal apartments upstairs, which were in perfect order, established with all the efficiency the Buck Place footmen had been able to spare this close to the coronation. While Vera and the rest of the staff made do, not even the slightest bit of discomfort was allowed for the Queen Mother or Princess Margaret. Except for the change of address, it was as if everything from their rooms at the Palace had been transported here so they wouldn't be aware of the move, but they were. How could they not be? They'd been unceremoniously shoved aside to make way for Queen Elizabeth, the Duke of Edinburgh, and their children.

"Don't forget to have the Princess's money for the collection plate to me or Iris by Sunday morning," she reminded him. As Comptroller, he should already know to have the ten quid ready, but he'd forgotten last Sunday. Thankfully, Iris had supplied the required ten pounds for the offering and saved them all from a great deal of embarrassment.

"Don't worry, I'll make sure you have it."

Vera wasn't so confident in his ability to remember since the lack of church money wasn't the first mistake he'd made in his new position. It made her wonder what the Queen Mother saw in Captain Townsend's service. There were more capable men who could execute the duties of Comptroller far better than he could, but Vera supposed in this time of change, the Queen Mother needed the familiar about her. She wondered if the Queen Mother would keep him so close if she knew exactly how familiar he'd become with her younger daughter. Most likely she'd carry on as if nothing were the matter. For a woman who'd faced great difficulties during the war, the Queen Mother had a knack for avoiding conflict in all aspects of her life. Vera wished she could be so ignorant of problems, but anticipating and then avoiding and overcoming them was a crucial part of her lady-in-waiting duties.

"By the way, Margaret is in the garden, at the steps between the lion statues." He strolled off down the long hallway toward the dark wood staircase at the end, exchanging greetings with the maid dusting the collection of porcelain figures on a sideboard near the dining room. Vera turned and strode out the Clarence House front doors and into the long expanse of flat lawn outside.

"It's a wonderful day, isn't it, Mrs. Lavish?" Princess Margaret sat on the top stone step, the lions covered in green moss gracing either side of it silently standing guard. Her Royal Highness leaned back on her hands, her legs stretched out in front of her as if it were a sunny summer day.

"Is it, Ma'am?" It'd been foggy all morning and a pall of gray clouds still lingered over the city. Not exactly the kind of spring weather one wished to enjoy.

"It's the very best." She waved for Vera to join her on the step. "You won't believe what's happened to me. Peter proposed, and I accepted."

"He proposed?" She could have knocked Vera down those six steps with a feather.

"He did, while we were alone in the Morning Room. He told me how long he's cared for me and how well we get along and I told him I feel the same way. Then he knelt on one knee and asked me to be his wife." She rose to pace in front of the steps, tapping the nose of the left lion each time she turned, the giddiest she'd been in the fifteen months since the King's death. "I must tell Lilibet at once. She'll be thrilled."

She might be, but as Lady Rankin had said, others, such as Commander Richard Colville, the Queen's Press Secretary, wouldn't be. With the entire world watching Britain because of the coronation, this was no time for the Princess and Captain Townsend to make their already questionable relationship public. "I'm sure Her Majesty will be thrilled, but perhaps it'd be best to wait and discuss it with her later this summer when Her Majesty and her government can give the matter the concern it deserves without the pressures of the coronation hanging over them."

The Princess stopped pacing and chewed her thumbnail. Vera picked at a loose pebble in the cement, the roughness of it scratching her fingertips while she waited for the royal reaction. She hoped for once that good sense and calm prevailed and the Princess recognized how rashness could cost her what she wanted. It didn't.

"No, I won't wait. I'm tired of being treated like I'm nothing and no one, as if I and my life don't matter while everything Lilibet does is held up as almost sacred. I'll tell her this week. I'll have a husband and a family of my own, someone who loves and cherishes me, and the coronation be damned."

"Sass, he proposed to her."

"Oh hell," came Sass's crackling reply from New York. She was staying there with friends while waiting for the ship to England. As Sass was a special guest of Princess Margaret's for many of the coronation festivities, Vera had made the long-distance call on the pretext of discussing the royal itinerary, but that was the furthest thing from her mind. "Not to make things worse, but rumors of her being in love with someone inside the royal household have been burning up the gossip columns over here for some time. I've seen more articles on her and her secret flame than I have the coronation."

Vera hadn't seen any stories here, which meant the Buck Place Press Office was doing a bang-up job of keeping it quiet. "Are they naming Captain Townsend?"

"Not yet, but it won't be long before they uncover it, especially with all the foreign press descending on London. Once his name is out on your side of the pond, all hell will break loose."

"All hell is already about to break loose. She's insisting on telling the Queen immediately. I suggested she wait until things calm down, but she wouldn't listen."

"Of course not."

Vera rubbed her forehead with her fingers, the Bakelite of the phone receiver growing warm against her ear. "Thank god you'll be here. Maybe you can talk her out of being rash."

"I doubt it, but I wouldn't miss the show for the world, and I mean both of them. By the way, I'm bringing someone with me."

"Who?"

"Doc."

Vera pulled the phone cord through her fingers, her nails catching on the weave of it. "Is he bringing his wife?"

"He isn't married, and he wants to see you as much as you

want to see him. He'll have a room at the Savoy, and you'll be able to do all those things to each other you used to write about in your novels. You remember what that was like, don't you?"

"I do." Vera ran her fingers over the new electric typewriter on her desk, her last night with Dominic in his rented flat when they'd done a number of the things she'd only ever written about as Mrs. Lavish as vivid as the plastic keys beneath her fingertips. Suddenly, the Princess's impulsive engagement didn't seem so rash after all, except Vera understood the consequences of giving in to temptation better than Her Royal Highness did. "I also remember how much it hurt to see him off at the station."

She didn't wish to endure that torture again. They'd written to each other in the first few months of their separation, but as time had gone on and the demands of her position and his had increased, the letters had become fewer and fewer until they'd stopped altogether. However, she'd never forgotten him, and he'd soon be here and he wanted to see her again.

"Simply enjoy yourselves and see what happens. It doesn't have to be serious."

Sass was right. This needn't to be a grand affair but a chance to have fun and a regular date for all the upcoming balls and coronation events, a steadying influence in the whirlwind of the coronation and her present life.

Chapter Twelve

"You've become quite the dancer since you were last here." Vera followed Dominic's lead as they swayed with a host of other revelers in the Savoy Hotel's ballroom. The large room with its Wedgwood blue walls trimmed in white molding with gilded accents hummed with excitement. The Dockland Settlements Ball was the first of the social events taking place in the run-up to the coronation. Even Princess Margaret, despite the absence of Captain Townsend, danced with Billy Wallace with all the enthusiasm of a deb at her coming-out.

"With maturity comes grace." Dominic made an exaggerated step forward, and Vera followed his lead as if she were Ginger Rogers and he Fred Astaire. He was dressed like the movie star, his black tuxedo every bit as elegant. He hadn't changed at all except for the faint honey tone to his skin, the mark of a man who'd spent many days outdoors at his father's ranch, instead of the paleness of the near-sunless autumn he'd spent in Britain three years ago.

"And wisdom. What have you leaned since you were last

in England?" She obviously hadn't learned a thing from the heartache of having seen him off the last time, for there they were, as if they'd never been apart.

Dominic spun them around, making her pink satin ball gown with its fitted bodice and wide tulle skirt rustle about her legs and his. When Vera's position as lady-in-waiting had been announced, a number of designers had rushed to offer her clothes in exchange for the right to brag about a member of Princess Margaret's intimate circle wearing their designs. It was one of the many advantages of her position, and she no longer worried about paying the milliner bill.

"I've learned that my countrymen are as royalty mad as yours. When the nurses heard I was coming to London, they begged me for every kind of souvenir you can imagine. I'll need another steamer trunk to get it all home."

Vera's hand stiffened on his arm. "I'm sure they'll be quite obliging when you give them their gifts."

He tilted his head back in scrutiny. "Are you jealous?"

"Of course I am. They get to see you every day."

"Luckily, I'm not interested in any of them. I prefer someone with a little more exalted status."

He squeezed her hand and whirled her into another spin. She held on tight to him, enjoying the weight of his arms about her and the giddiness of his attention. In the back of her mind, the warning that she should better guard her heart so it wouldn't sting so much when he left again threatened to pull down her joy, but she ignored it. For the moment he was there, and she would wring out of their time together every ounce of happiness she could and leave the rest up to fate and the future. "What else have you learned?"

"That you've given up writing. Why?"

Vera's steps slowed as she thought of the Remington consigned to the bottom of her wardrobe to languish with all her unwritten stories, including Lady Penrose's. She might have told herself before she'd accepted the position that she'd keep writing, but she hadn't. There always seemed to be so many more exciting things to do instead. "Because nothing I ever wrote gave me the recognition and success I have with the Princess. Everyone knows who I am, and I can be proud of what I do in a way I could never be with Mrs. Lavish."

"Life doesn't have to be all Mrs. Lavish; there can be the Honorable Vera Strathmore."

"There is, and she's a lady-in-waiting to Her Royal Highness, Princess Margaret."

"And a beautiful one at that."

The orchestra leader brought the song to its end, forcing Vera and Dominic apart to applaud. The next song began, and Dominic rubbed the small of his back. "I think I've had all the dancing I can take for the moment. I'll get some drinks and we'll sit out this next one."

"A drink would be lovely."

"I live to serve." With an overexaggerated bow, he made for the bar while Vera returned to the table.

Almost everyone from the old Margaret Set stood around

the Princess, laughing and drinking like they used to do in the old days, all of them having returned to London for the festivities surrounding the coronation.

"My feet are killing me," Imogene complained, shifting in her shoes. "We've done nothing but parade up and down the halls of Buck Place pretending an old tablecloth is a train."

"But you wouldn't miss it for the world, would you?" Lady Anne Coke, a fellow maid of honor to Her Majesty for the coronation, nudged Imogene with a satin glove–covered elbow. The two of them had spent weeks practicing for the coronation ceremony along with the other women chosen for the honor.

"Absolutely not. I didn't move my wedding date to make sure I'm an unsullied maid as required for the august day for nothing."

"Unsullied." Princess Margaret snorted. "Should I tell the Earl Marshall the truth?"

"You do, and I'll murder you, Ma'am," Imogene shot back before her already wide eyes opened wider at having been too candid. It was one thing to joke freely with Anne and quite another to do so with the Princess.

The air around the table tensed while everyone waited for the Princess's reaction. Vera thought it a very good thing Her Royal Highness wasn't holding a drink or Imogene would be quite wet by now. To their great relief, Princess Margaret threw back her head and laughed. "If you did kill me, then Lilibet would have you beheaded and that would put a damper on your wedding, wouldn't it?"

"I'll say." Sunny laughed along with the others, his deep voice joined by the high notes of his wife's giggle from behind one ungloved hand, her large diamond engagement ring and the simple band behind it glinting in the ballroom's chandelier lights.

"Speaking of which, where is your fiancé tonight?" Johnny changed the subject, draping his arm around his wife's slender waist where she stood beside him in her teal floor-length dress and family pearls.

"Held up by some important stockbroker business. I've told him that if he misses the Savoy Coronation Ball, I'll murder him."

"But not before you marry him," Laura Smith teased.

"Heavens no. I want my freedom and a nice little inheritance."

"We all do," Princess Margaret said with a wistfulness that made Vera and Sass exchange curious looks. They were the only members of the Set privy to the Princess and Captain Townsend's secret. Despite Princess Margaret's insistence in the garden the week before, the Princess had yet to tell Her Majesty the news. It gave Vera a little hope that Her Royal Highness might finally be thinking first and acting later.

The orchestra began to play a fox-trot, and one by one the men and their wives excused themselves to join the dance. Imogene, realizing that she'd been granted clemency from the royal temper, grabbed Anne and made for the loo, leaving Sass, Vera, and the Princess alone.

"Peter and I are dining with Lilibet and Philip tomorrow night and we're going to tell her the news," Princess Margaret announced. "Given how I asked for the invitation for Peter, she and Philip must suspect something."

So much for her not being rash.

"Does the Queen Mother know?" Sass asked.

"I told her at tea today. She took the news with her usual aplomb."

"You mean she stuck her head in the sand and left it up to you, Peter, and the others to work out." Sass had lost none of her old candor or her ability to get away with it in the royal presence.

The Princess frowned into her drink. "For once I wish Mummy would intervene, but she won't. She never does, not even when it might benefit me. Lilibet would listen to her, but once again, I'm on my own."

"Captain Townsend will be there with you, Ma'am," Vera reminded her.

"Yes, he will be. He's always been there for me, and he always will be, and I'm sure everything will be well. After all, I'm not Uncle David, and with Charles and Anne ahead of me, I'm practically nowhere near the throne. Besides, Philip is always banging on about how we should modernize to keep up with the times. My marrying Peter will show everyone that we aren't a bunch of old Victorian fuddy-duddies."

Vera had a sinking feeling that Princess Margaret's thoroughly modern brother-in-law and Her Majesty were about to prove just how fuddy-duddy they really were, and at Princess Margaret's expense.

The flash of a photographer's camera blinded the women. Vera's eyes were barely clear of the glare when the Princess's private detective rushed forward, shoving people out of the way to reach Her Royal Highness, who was in no more danger than momentarily seeing spots. The orchestra continued to play, but everyone, including the band leader, craned their necks to see what all the commotion at the Princess's table was about.

"What do you think you're doing?" Mr. Ashbrook yanked the camera out of the man's hands, about to rip the film out of the back when Princess Margaret, still blinking off the flash, laid a staying hand on his arm.

"Let him have his picture; after all, we're in a season of celebration, aren't we, Mr. . . . ?" Princess Margaret entreated, in the same voice she used to set awkward young military cadets who'd been given the privilege of dancing with her at charity events at ease.

"M-Mason," the photographer stammered, as slack-jawed as Vera and Sass by the Princess's cordial reaction.

"Yes, Mr. Mason, you are exuberantly fulfilling the requirements of your position. Give him his camera so he can take a proper photo." The detective did as he was told while Princess Margaret motioned for Sass and Vera to shift closer. "Smile, ladies."

They leaned in beside the Princess while the man screwed

in a fresh bulb, then positioned his camera and took another picture.

"Be sure to send me a copy, won't you?"

"Yes, Ma'am. Thank you, Ma'am." The photographer nearly stumbled over himself in his gratitude even while Mr. Ashbrook shoved him toward the ballroom door.

Colin strolled by before the Princess stopped him. "Colin, you're the best dancer here, and it's been ages since we've done the fox-trot together."

"Yes, Ma'am." Colin escorted the Princess to the dance floor.

Sass sat back in astonishment while Colin and the Princess faded into the mass of bouncing revelers on the dance floor. "Hard to believe Margo pardoned that photographer instead of having him thrown out on his ear like all the others, but I suppose miracles will never cease."

"She's in love and happy." Vera caught Dominic's eye as he came back from the crowded bar, a drink in each hand and a beaming smile for her. "It's made her more generous and forgiving. Let's hope it lasts."

"VERA, IS THIS the right dress for tonight?" Princess Margaret stood before the full-length mirror in her bedroom, turning this way and that to study the dark blue dress with demure neckline and three-quarter-length sleeves. It was one of the most understated and modest evening dresses she owned, a far cry from the more daring ones she usually wore to Ciro's and the 400 Club.

Ruby stood off to one side, her hands patiently crossed in front of her while she waited to see if this dress would be exchanged for another. It wasn't like Her Royal Highness to question Ruby's selected outfit. She usually accepted Ruby's choice, and then went on her way as if deciding what to wear was beneath a woman of her rank, but tonight was no dinner with dignitaries or a ribbon-cutting ceremony. Tonight, Princess Margaret would announce to her sister, and by extension to all the old men who comprised her government, that she and the divorced commoner Captain Townsend wished to be married.

Heaven help them all.

Vera caught Ruby's none-too-subtle gesture to assure Her Royal Highness that this was the right dress. Vera didn't need to be encouraged to agree, for the sooner Princess Margaret and Captain Townsend were packed off to Buck Place, the sooner she could slip out the side entrance of Clarence House and join Dominic for dinner at the Savoy and dessert in his room. She'd told her parents not to expect her home tonight, lying about attending a party at Clarence House and her bunking up with Sass. It galled her that at twenty-seven years old she had to lie like a debutante about where she was at night. However, the fib was preferable to a morning row with her mother. If she could take the money from the position and let a flat, she would, but she'd never broken the habit of saving her income. It was worth enduring her parents' sour faces every day across the dining room table to keep her financial options open. "It's perfect, Ma'am. It sets the tone of how serious you and Captain Townsend are while not being too showy."

Princess Margaret ran her hands down the front of the dress, each motion jerky and unsure in a way Vera had never seen before. "You're right. Peter is wearing his uniform with his orders to remind Lilibet and Philip of his loyal years of service to the crown. I'm sure there's nothing to worry about. She likes Peter, and if she's for the marriage, then her ministers can't be against it. Can they?"

"Of course not, Ma'am," Vera reassured, ignoring the disbelieving roll of Ruby's eyes from behind the Princess.

The butler knocked on the door and entered. "Captain Townsend has arrived, Ma'am."

"Tell him I'll be down shortly." The butler slid out of the door as Princess Margaret checked herself one last time in the mirror. "Yes, this dress will have to do. Wish me luck, both of you."

"I wish you all the luck there is, Ma'am," Vera offered, while Ruby stayed silent.

With a nod, Princess Margaret swept from the room. Vera and Ruby followed a short distance behind, remaining on the stair landing when Princess Margaret rushed down the main hall and into Captain Townsend's arms. He swung her around, making her laugh with delight before setting her down to admire her.

"You look like a dream."

"And you're quite dashing." She ran her hands over the front of Captain Townsend's uniform the way Rupert's mother used to do to his father before a dinner, picking off a small leaf that had fallen on him during his short walk over from his grace-and-favor apartment.

He took her hands and clasped them to his chest, stopping their constant fluttering over his uniform. "Don't worry, Margaret, everything will be all right."

"But everything depends on this."

"When Her Majesty sees us together and how happy it makes you, she won't stand in our way." He laid a tender and reassuring kiss on her forehead, lingering close to her, his eyes and hers closed as they drew strength from each other. Whatever Captain Townsend's faults and shortcomings, he loved her, of this there was no doubt, and for the first time Vera realized how deeply Princess Margaret felt for him. He wasn't a whim or a chance to prove that she could have her way; he was someone she genuinely adored. His quiet patience and tenderness were a rarity in the Princess's life, qualities that had been missing in Vera's after Henry's death.

"What do you think, Ruby?" Vera whispered, touching her thumb to her empty ring finger. "Do they have a chance?"

Ruby sighed. "If she was walking in there on Lord Dalkeith's or Lord Blandford's arm, the Palace would turn itself inside out to make her happy, but not with him, no matter how well he served the King."

"Perhaps the Princess is right and Philip's ideas on modernization will sway them." With Princess Margaret's hand tucked lovingly in the crook of Captain Townsend's arm, Vera clung to the same hope for happiness carrying the couple out the door, the one she used to write into every one of her old stories. She'd been in their position once, during her last night with Henry, when the two of them had innocently believed that the war wouldn't consume them the way it had so many others. They'd been so terribly wrong.

"That's about as likely as a bean nighe being invited in for tea and behaving. Now off with you so we can both enjoy our evenings." Ruby trudged back upstairs, eager to be done with preparing the royal wardrobe for the night so she could go to dinner with her fiancé. She'd return in the morning to pick the blue dress off the floor and have it and the Princess's underthings laundered and returned to the wardrobe ready for the next use.

There was nothing so practical for Vera to do but collect her things from the lady-in-waiting room and catch a taxi for the Savoy and Dominic.

"Where to?" the cockney cabbie asked when Vera climbed into the back of the black cab.

Vera hesitated, tempted to tell him to take her home. For the first time in a long time she wanted to sit up with the Remington and lose herself in a world where she could make everything all right and give everyone, even the most wayward of fictional countesses, a happy ending. Every moment she spent with Dominic, she fell deeper into him. He was everything she wanted and everything she couldn't have, not without a sacrifice the likes of which she could not imagine.

Don't be silly. He hasn't known me long enough to take that kind of risk. She'd known Henry almost all her life, the two of them always dancing at coming-out balls and eating together at garden parties until the war and his imminent deployment had forced their feelings to mature so much faster. This time there wasn't death but a separation as definitive as death, and it pushed Vera to rush again when experience urged her to slow down.

"Well, where you going, luv?" the cabbie demanded.

Up the Mall, the lights of Buck Place illuminated the white stone front of the palace behind the black-and-gold gates. Princess Margaret's life may not go as she wanted, but at least she had the courage to try to seize her happiness. Vera must do the same no matter how short a time it might last.

"The Savoy."

The PHONE RANG, jarring Vera out of a deep sleep. She raised her head off Dominic's bare chest and reached past him to snatch up the handset, her breasts brushing his skin as she mumbled, "Hello?"

Dominic shifted awake under her, turning the clock on the bedside table to reveal that it was past two o'clock in the morning.

"Vera, come to Clarence House at once." The line went dead.

Vera dropped the phone onto the cradle and slid back down beside Dominic. He wrapped his arms around her, drawing her naked body close to his.

"Who was that?"

"Princess Margaret. She needs me."

"Did she break a fingernail?" She playfully swatted him, but he caught her hand and pressed it against his lips. "She isn't the only one who needs you."

Vera bit her bottom lip as he traced the inside of her arm with his fingers, enticing her to remain beneath the Savoy's fine sheets and feel the weight of him on top of her again.

"I can't. If she tracked me down here, it must be important." Vera had an inkling that Her Royal Highness's dinner with the Queen hadn't gone as swimmingly as she'd hoped. "I have to go."

"Must you?" He raised his arm so she could turn on the light, pick her brassiere off the floor, and hook it on.

"You get your midnight calls summoning you to duty, and I get mine." She pulled on her dress and then stepped off the bed, searching for her slip and panties.

"Fair enough." He placed his arms behind his head, his tan and solid chest above the white sheets as inviting as his lopsided and sleepy smile. His hair was a tousled mess, so unlike the polished doctor who'd sat across from her at dinner. "Will I see you tomorrow, or I should say, later today?"

"Most certainly." She crawled up the bed to him, straddling him as she leaned in to kiss him in a manner that would keep him up the rest of the night. "I wouldn't miss you for all the royalty in England."

"Liar."

"She's my boss."

He ran his finger along her jawline, his eyes turning serious. "She doesn't have to be."

Vera held her breath at the question lingering in his eyes. He didn't say it, and she was glad. Half-asleep and satiated by their night together was no time for this kind of discussion. She wanted such questions asked in the daylight when his head and hers were clear and she was sure he meant every word he said. She stepped off him and the bed. "But she is. Good night, Dominic."

"Good night, the Honorable Vera Strathmore."

She gathered up her heels, purse, and coat from where they'd been disregarded hours ago. She felt not honorable but wicked, and very, very happy.

VERA SLIPPED INTO Princess Margaret's bedroom, wrinkling her nose at the stench of cigarettes permeating the air. Princess Margaret sat in a pink-cushioned Thomas Sheraton armchair near the window, smoking yet another, her eyeliner smudged and streaked, the blue dress rumpled and wrinkled around her. She clutched a glass of whiskey in the other hand, and heaven only knew how many she'd had before Vera's arrival. It probably rivaled the number of cigarettes crumpled in the ashtray.

Vera took off her coat, the faint scent of Dominic's after-shave still clinging to the dress beneath. She'd done her hair as best she could in the car, risking the cabbie tsking at her beneath his breath because he'd guessed what she'd been up to before he'd been summoned. If Princess Margaret guessed, she said nothing, continuing to stare at the floor in front of her, as despondent tonight as the many times Vera had sat with her in the days following the King's death.

Vera settled on the edge of the sofa closest to the Princess. "Things didn't go well tonight, Ma'am?"

She stubbed out the cigarette, rose, and went to the bar cart, adding more whiskey to the glass and not bothering to dilute it with Malvern Water. "It went swimmingly. Lilibet and Philip were quite the charming hosts, with Philip cracking jokes and Lilibet her usual dignified self."

She threw back the whiskey and poured herself another.

"Then they didn't object, Ma'am?" Something must have happened to leave the Princess in this state.

"Not in so many words." She dropped into the chair, set down the whiskey, and slid a cigarette out of the gold Cartier holder, a gift from the King, on the table beside her and lit it. "She asked us to wait until after the coronation so she and her ministers can properly consider the matter, as if I'm some sort of bill in Parliament." She wiped the tears off her cheeks and then took a deep drag off the cigarette, the smoke failing to settle her shaking hands.

Vera didn't dare point out that the Queen's request was the

same advice Vera had given her and she'd ignored. "Then in another month, all might be well?"

"No, it won't," the Princess snapped, almost crushing the cigarette between her fingers. "I saw it in her eyes when she spoke to me, humoring me as if I was some foreign head of state she was hosting and not her own damn sister."

She flicked the cigarette away, and it landed on the carpet in front of the fireplace and singed the intricate weave. Vera picked it up and tossed it in the cold fireplace, where the orange end of it smoldered. "Ma'am, I'm sure she cares about you and wants what's best, but she must be overwhelmed with the coronation. If you wait, like she's asked—"

"I know exactly what'll happen if I wait." She slammed the glass down on the table, making a wave of whiskey spill over the edge and down the skirt of the Princess's dress. She didn't notice or care that the silk was ruined, her eyes stony points as she fixed on Vera. "Lilibet will step back and let her ministers lecture me about morals and duty and how a divorced man who they see as no better than a servant isn't an appropriate choice for a princess. She won't support us or tell all those old men in her government that her sister's happiness and future are more important to her than their dictates. I don't care what they think. I won't let them control my life the way they control Lilibet's. I'll show them it isn't their opinions that matter but mine, and the British people's."

The determination in her voice made Vera nervous. "What do you mean, Ma'am?"

"The public loves me. You've seen the way the press clamors after me. If the British people hear about my desire to wed Captain Townsend, a man they admire and respect, they'll stand behind me, and then Lilibet and her government can't stand against us."

Vera didn't dare tell her that the whole world was already involved in her love life judging by the American newspaper stories Sass had shown her. Buck Place must be aware of it too and how it wouldn't be long before the British press broke their silence, and it still hadn't stopped Her Majesty from hesitating. "Ma'am, if you force this out into the open and make them face it before they're ready, things will be worse for everyone involved."

"I don't care. One way or another, I'll make my sister and those old men give us their consent. I won't be pushed around by them, and I won't lose Peter. We will be married, and we will be happy." Princess Margaret stormed into her bedroom and slammed the door behind her.

Vera slouched in her chair, exhausted and anxious about the coming week. She didn't doubt Princess Margaret would find a way to bring her engagement to the forefront and at the worst possible time, and that the answer she'd receive because of it was bound to be one she wouldn't like. King Edward had been forced to give up his throne to marry a divorced commoner. Vera hated to imagine what the government might demand of Her Royal Highness for the same privilege.

Chapter Thirteen

A multitude of Union Jacks fluttered over the streets of London, and banners depicting the Queen's coat of arms or crowns with intertwined *ER*s hung suspended over roads and bridges. The thousands of people who'd lined the processional route from Buckingham Palace to Westminster Abbey to cheer the royals remained outside Westminster Abbey and along the procession route, braving the steadily falling rain to catch another glimpse of their monarch. A part of Vera longed to be out among those crowds. Not since she'd danced in the streets with strangers the night victory over Germany had been declared had she been so excited about her country and her monarch. She would gladly share a warm beer with a dockworker again today to show her spirit.

The Archbishop of Canterbury held St. Edward's Crown over Her Majesty's head, and a still settled over the guests inside the Abbey and the massive crowds following along on their wireless sets outside. The Queen, seated on the gilded coronation throne, appeared small in the midst of the stained-glass windows and rising stone arches of the ancient Abbey. With the bishops standing to one side of her and her maids of honor on the other, she seemed too young to be heir to the long line of men and women before her and to shoulder the hopes of so many people all over the country and the world.

When the Archbishop at last lowered the crown onto Her Majesty's head, it wasn't her that Vera watched from her seat high up in the special stands constructed in the Abbey, nor the numerous Peers and Peeresses who set their coronets on their heads while shouting, "God Save the Queen"; it was Princess Margaret. Her Royal Highness placed her coronet on her head and cheered from where she sat with the Queen Mother and young Prince Charles in the Royal Gallery behind the Queen.

During the entire service, there'd been no sly jealousy in the Princess's blue eyes or forced interest but a reverence for her sister and her position to rival the Archbishop's. Princess Margaret had risen above her current conflict with the Queen to show her respect and to dutifully play her small part in the coronation ceremony. The Princess's genuine admiration eased a good many of Vera's worries. Vera had spent the last week on edge, waiting for Princess Margaret to make good on her promise to publicly force the issue with Captain Townsend. So far, nothing had come of it, and the Princess, like everyone, had thrown herself wholeheartedly into the coronation celebrations. Vera closed her eyes as the cheers of the Peers continued to echo off the stone and prayed that Her Royal Highness would be granted the happiness of a life with Captain Townsend and that she'd continue to show a measure of maturity and wisdom when it came to choosing the best course for achieving it.

"Wow, you Brits really know how to put on a show," Sass complimented as she stood with Vera in the specially constructed annex alongside Westminster Abbey. Guests of all levels of importance and nationalities, from dukes to visiting prime ministers, stood in groups discussing the magnificence of the coronation while the royals relaxed in their private retiring room to enjoy a luncheon before the procession back down the Mall to Buckingham Palace. "Was the King's coronation this grand?"

"I don't know. I wasn't here to see it." Her memories of King George's coronation were hazy, a garden party at Rupert's parents' house, listening to the radio broadcast of the ceremonies and hearing the cheers of the crowds on the Mall as they'd called to the King to appear on the Buck Place balcony. Back then Vera never would have guessed that one day she'd be so close to royalty as to earn a place in the Abbey on such a special day. The only thing missing to make it more memorable was Dominic by her side. He hadn't merited a seat in Westminster Abbey, and not even Vera's influence had been able to secure him one. Instead, he was at a party in the Knightsbridge flat of a doctor friend, and he would join them later at the Savoy for the Coronation Night Ball, the most elaborate in the hotel's history.

"With all this excitement, I'm surprised you aren't more in demand." Sass dabbed her forehead with her handkerchief, the chill outside failing to penetrate the stuffy heat inside the annex.

"Iris has the joy of serving Her Royal Highness today. I helped them both dress this morning, but for the moment I'm free; of course, how long that lasts remains to be seen." Vera noticed Princess Margaret exiting the royal retiring room, her presence causing a bit of a stir among the newspapermen huddled together along the far side of the room.

The Princess was luminous in her coronation gown of cream satin encrusted with small pearls and crystals in the shape of roses and marguerites. The dark purple and ermine robe with its train, and the coronet that she'd worn for the service inside the Abbey, had been given to Ruby for safekeeping until it was time to don them again to ride with the Queen Mother in the Irish State Coach back to Buck Place.

The reverence that had marked Princess Margaret inside the Abbey was gone, replaced with the shared jubilation of the day. She exchanged pleasantries with many people, but her attention never settled on any of them, shifting here and there in search of someone standing among the Peers and Peeresses in their court dress and flowing coronation robes. Vera thought Her Royal Highness might be searching for her, but it wasn't like Princess Margaret to seek out people on her own. She usually delegated that task to servants or Iris. Then, Princess Margaret came to a stop, her face lighting up when she found who she was looking for, and Vera's stomach sank.

"What's wrong?" Sass followed the line of Vera's frown to where Princess Margaret approached Captain Townsend, Her Royal Highness sparkling as brightly as the small crystals sewn into her gown.

He greeted her with the same ecstatic expression, one of a lover parted from his beloved for too long. The Princess's promise to make everyone deal with the matter of her and the Captain's marriage rang in Vera's ears like the Abbey bells. So much for Vera's prayers for maturity and wisdom.

Princess Margaret and Captain Townsend stood close together, chatting, the way they'd done a hundred times in Clarence House and Buck Place and various other royal establishments. The rapport between the Equerry and the Princess was unmistakable, and neither of them took any pains to hide it. It was a sight that anyone who worked in the royal household must have seen numerous times, except they had the decency not to comment on it except in private and within the confines of the palaces, where discretion was all but assured. But the Princess and Captain Townsend weren't in a royal palace; they were in the coronation annex at Westminster Abbey, surrounded by dignitaries, Peers, and a fair number of the press, all of whom stood to profit a great deal from not keeping silent.

"What the devil is she up to?" Sass whispered.

"Keeping her promise to force the issue."

"Oh, she'll force it for sure, right over a cliff." Sass motioned to the reporters who'd lost interest in everything but the Princess. In the center of the group stood a writer for *The People*, the lowest of the already low gossip rags, captivated by the royal performance.

Princess Margaret knew they were there because she slid them a sly glance and then curled her full lips into a plotting smirk before she turned back to Captain Townsend. She raised one lithe hand covered in a long satin glove and brushed some offending speck off Captain Townsend's lapel. Her fingers lingered too long on the wool before she dropped her hand to touch his, their fingers intertwining for the briefest of seconds before they parted.

Vera groaned at the spectacle. A lesser gesture twenty years earlier had made the world aware of the Duke of Windsor's relationship with Wallis Simpson and cost him his crown. The Princess lived a sheltered life, but it wasn't sheltered enough for her to think she could get away with this without paying a similarly hefty price. "She's her own worst enemy."

"And she's about to make more." Sass motioned to where the newspapermen bent together chatting and gesturing excitedly to one another. Once in a while, one of them would look up at the Princess before bowing back down to confer with his colleagues. Vera could practically hear them salivating over the information they'd just gleaned and the glee with which they'd use it to break a story that was sure to see them all promoted and their newspaper circulations boosted. No amount of Palace Press Office strong-arming would keep what they'd just learned from reaching the public, including the British one. Vera considered approaching them and pleading to their better natures for their silence, but if she acknowledged their suspicions in any way, it would only reinforce them. Unwilling to make a bad situation worse, Vera remained where she was. Thankfully, Iris emerged from the retiring room to summon Princess Margaret back to it before the Princess got it into her head to stand on a chair and publicly announce her engagement and ensure that she hadn't been too subtle in making her interest in Captain Townsend clear.

"This isn't at all going to turn out as she expects." Vera kept her voice low, conscious of those around her.

"I suppose you tried to tell her that."

"I did, but no one can tell her anything, especially not 'no.'"

"She's going to hear a great deal of it after that performance, and from people who aren't going to change their minds because of her temper tantrums. If you've ever considered a change in career, now might be the time to act on it."

It wasn't something she'd ever considered until that moment. "I burned those bridges three years ago."

"Then build some new ones. If I know you, Mrs. Lavish, you could whip up a story in no time, one with a little royal flare and a lot of naughty scenes that'll make a killing."

"Heavens no." She flapped her hand at Sass to shush her, both flattered and horrified by Sass's suggestion. "I'm not allowed to have any other employment. I'd be sacked if I did and anyone found out."

"I'm sure you could manage it without giving away the game, like you did before. If not, then you should." Sass faced Vera, as serious as the Princess had been in the Abbey. "Listen, not even my family's money softened the shock of coming back to reality after I left London. Margo might complain about having no place, but she does, and she always will, even when this love affair of hers blows up in her face. It might never be more than representing the Queen at ship christenings or charity galas, but it's there, along with a sizable income and a permanent home. The rest of us can't say the same. I don't want it to be so hard for you the day this all ends."

"It won't end because I don't intend to leave her service." She refused to be nobody again, derided by her parents and ignored by everyone. She enjoyed influence and station, and she would bloody well keep it.

"You might not leave, but it doesn't mean that someday you won't be invited to leave. Remember what happened to Caroline. Say the wrong thing and it could very well happen to you."

Vera clutched her coronation program to her chest. This wasn't something she wanted to think about on a regular day, much less this one, but the truth in Sass's warning was too real to ignore. Vera was employed at the royal pleasure, and the royals could change their minds at any moment and she might very well be tossed back into her old life. The landing wouldn't be as hard if she had something else besides her savings to fall back on, a little of the old ambition that had carried her through so many dark hours. *The one that never got me more than an introduction to the Princess, the one I had to rely on my own wits to turn into everything I have today.* "Don't worry, Sass, I'll be all right."

"I'm sure you will be, and I promise I won't be so serious the rest of the day. Come on, let's see if we can talk Johnny into giving us a ride out of here in his carriage. Otherwise we'll never get through this crowd in time for the Coronation Ball."

THE FIREWORKS SIZZLED and exploded in the sky over London, the light rain that had marred the marvelous day abating long enough to offer everyone at the Savoy Coronation Night Ball, and those gathered on the banks of the Thames, a marvelous view of the display of the century. A light breeze wafted the smoke away from each new explosion launched from the shore and the decks of the Royal Navy ships moored in the river, leaving each sparkling firework as magnificent as the first until the last hundred exploded in quick succession over the river and lit up the city.

Dominic and Vera stood with most of the other twelve hundred guests just beyond the protection of the River Entrance canopy strung along the length of the Savoy. The hotel had been transformed into a whimsical version of an Elizabethan court, the walls hung with light gray fabric shot with stripes of pink and red and overlaid with numerous heralds of ancient families. Mirrors painted to look like a garden disappearing into the distance were arranged beyond the magnificent tent constructed to house this fantasy, and real boxwood hedges were arranged before them to continue the illusions. The Queen Mother's favorite photographer, Cecil Beaton, had led the charge on this imaginative take on English history, helped by a bevy of famous and rich assistants, from Vivien Leigh to the Savoy Hotel heiress, all of whom mingled among the foreign dignitaries, aristocracy, and government officials.

"Quite a day, isn't it, Miss Strathmore?" a tall man in tails said to Vera as she and Dominic squeezed back inside with the rest of the crowd.

"Indeed, it is, Your Excellency."

The man staggered off to join the Duchess of Rutland, adjusting his velvet Elizabethan hat, a party favor, on his balding head.

"Who was that?" Dominic kept a tight hold on Vera's hand to keep from losing her in the crush.

"The Prime Minister of Australia."

"You do get around, don't you?"

"Yes, I do." She waved at Imogene, who danced with her fiancé. They were the first members of the Set that Vera had seen in this crowd in ages. The Princess was somewhere in the hotel, but Vera had lost sight of her hours ago. It wouldn't surprise Vera if she'd slipped out to join Captain Townsend upstairs in the Royal Suite, the two of them stealing a little quiet during the coronation frenzy.

"Have you had enough of this glorious day yet?" Dominic laughed when Vera stifled a yawn with the back of her hand.

"Not at all, I could go on for hours. The revue at midnight is a must-see. Bing Crosby is going to sing."

"They're repeating the show at two a.m. if you want to wait."

"I'd better see Noël Coward's grand production the first time. He'll expect fawning compliments over his genius when he visits Clarence House this week. Heaven help me if I miss it. Besides, I have another celebration in mind for two a.m." She looped her arms around his neck, heedless of where they were or who might see them. Tonight, no one cared, especially not Vera.

"Do you, now?" He rested his hands on her waist and gently pulled her closer.

"Mrs. Lavish, are you being naughty?" Princess Margaret asked, much to Vera's surprise. She was escorted by Billy Wallace instead of Captain Townsend, but it didn't mean Captain Townsend wasn't waiting upstairs for Her Royal Highness's grace and favor.

"Not yet, Ma'am, but I hope to be very soon." She tugged Dominic's green Elizabethan cap down to a more rakish angle over his forehead.

"Good, for you two make quite the couple." Princess Margaret let go of Billy and gripped Vera's arm with tender seriousness. "You deserve to be happy, Vera."

"So do you, Ma'am."

"And we will be, won't we?"

"Yes, Ma'am, we will." With another rousing cry of "God Save the Queen" echoing off the hotel's tall ceiling, Vera believed it could be true. It was a new, grand Elizabethan age, and anything, including the happiness of a Princess and a commoner—and a lady-in-waiting and an American—was possible.

Chapter Fourteen

"Vera, come to Clarence House at once," Iris commanded in a tone she'd never used with Vera before. With Iris it was always pleasant requests and a polite "would you mind terribly," never commands. Those were left for Princess Margaret to employ.

This shook the last of the sleep out of Vera, who stood in her father's study in her robe and slippers, her long lie-in after a night at Ciro's with Her Royal Highness, Dominic, Sass, and a number of the old Set brutally interrupted by the summons. "What's wrong? Is the Princess all right?"

The fear that something had happened to Her Royal Highness, and that Vera's time in the royal household might end, made the heavy bookshelves around her more oppressive than usual. She shouldn't be so selfish, but she couldn't help it. It'd been two weeks since the coronation, but Vera, like the rest of the nation, still floated on the excitement and she didn't want an awful comedown, especially not after Sass's ominous warning. She'd be lying if she said she hadn't considered what Sass had said, far more than she would have liked, especially at night, whenever she caught sight of the old Remington in its box at the bottom of her wardrobe when she changed.

"The Princess is fine, but I don't wish to discuss it over the phone. We need you here immediately. I'm afraid it's going to be a shocker of a day."

An hour later, Vera stepped out of a black cab across the street from Clarence House, and it drove off. A throng of reporters milled outside the gate, smoking, drinking coffee, and talking. Walter, the red-uniformed morning guard, remained on alert at the guard shack, his eyes straight ahead as always, as dismissive of the mob as he was of overly irritating tourists. Vera didn't have the same detached manner as the guardsman and stood marveling at the spectacle. A few members of the press usually milled about the gate hoping for a photograph, but never this many. She considered walking around the block and going in the side entrance to avoid them when one finally noticed her.

"There's one of her ladies-in-waiting." He pointed at her, and a sea of brown hats and flapping overcoats rushed to surround her, shouting questions. Vera staggered back, never having borne the sole brunt of press attention before. There'd always been a group, guards, drivers, friends, a number of people to buffer her from this pigeon-like swarm.

"Get inside, Miss Strathmore." Walter took her by the arm and pulled her out of the center of the crowd then shoved her through the gate, slamming the black metal closed behind her.

Vera leaned against it, too shaken to do more than concentrate on standing. The green lawn, rosebushes, and trees rustling in the breeze made everything seem so calm, but it wasn't. She could hear the men outside pestering the guard about when Princess Margaret might come out.

She had no idea what had happened since last night, but she could guess.

Inside the cramped lady-in-waiting office, everyone huddled together, their faces so grim one would think Germany had decided to have another crack at taking over the world.

"Have you seen this?" Iris held up a copy of *The People*, her skin far paler than it usually was, her light brown hair drawn back into a quick bun instead of its usual careful chignon. It gave her the hurriedly put together look of someone who'd been pulled out of bed much too early, like Vera.

"No, I haven't." She'd rushed by the newsstands in her haste to get here.

"Then you'd better have a look. It's a whopper." Ruby handed Vera her copy, on the front page of which was the story in blazing headline:

"THE *PEOPLE* SPEAKS OUT"

Ever since Princess Margaret's unfortunate performance in the annex, there'd been no whiff of a scandal, no news stories or press clippings to send Buck Place or Clarence House into a tizzy. Vera thought maybe the Press Office had possessed the clout to keep the story out of the papers. They hadn't, and there in black and white for everyone to read was the truth about Princess Margaret and Captain Townsend.

Each paragraph dripped with faux outrage and indignity that foreign papers were printing stories of Princess Margaret and Captain Townsend's romance. All the while, the piece gleefully repeated the rumors, making Captain Townsend's divorce as much a part of his identity as his distinguished war honors. It was a spreading of tales that would have made her mother and aunt Augusta proud.

The phone on Iris's desk rang, and everyone jumped. Iris eyed the phone as it if were a serpent; then, regaining the usual calm composure with which she regularly faced her duties, she answered it. "Miss Iris Peake, how may I help you?"

Captain Colville's raised voice could be heard clearly through the phone, and all Iris could do was stand there, getting in no more than a "yes, sir" or "no, sir" every once in a while.

Vera sidled up to Ruby. "What does the Queen Mother make of all this?"

"You don't think she's going to allow this to ruin the taste of her eggs, do you?"

"No."

"Nor will she. She'll leave it to her daughters and others to sort out."

"Has anyone been up to speak to the Princess about it?" Her Royal Highness didn't usually rise before eleven, and *The People* wasn't on the Clarence House subscription list.

Iris held her hand over the phone through which Captain Colville's voice continued to rise in volume and pointed to Vera. "You're elected."

No wonder they'd needed her here urgently. They didn't have the nerve to broach the subject with Princess Margaret, and Vera was drawing the short end of the stick. That's what Vera got for not having risen earlier that morning and seen the papers.

Vera tucked *The People* under one arm and headed upstairs, glad to escape the mausoleum for a while. However, the air outside the lady-in-waiting room wasn't any more cheerful. In the main hall, two maids stood whispering together. They jumped apart at the sight of Vera, scurrying off to the dining room to clean.

Everyone knows.

Vera passed the Queen Mother's room. The hallway was eerily devoid of footmen or maids and the chatter of the TV that usually emanated from behind the Queen Mother's door. The Queen Mother might not step in to deal with the matter, but the silence from her part of the house was telling.

Vera climbed the stairs to the first floor, rubbing at the paper until her fingertips were covered in ink. When she stopped at the Princess's door, she took a deep breath, raised her hand, and knocked.

"Come in."

Princess Margaret sat propped up in her wide bed, a tall glass of orange juice diluted by vodka clutched in one hand

and a cigarette and the *People* issue in the other. The breakfast tray, untouched except for some broken bits of toast, sat off to one side surrounded by a selection of rumpled and discarded newspapers and magazines.

"Good morning, Ma'am. I see you've read today's edition of *The People*?" Heaven only knew how she'd managed to get a copy. The woman was quite resourceful when she wanted to be.

Princess Margaret tapped the ash into the pewter tray on the cluttered bedside table and then settled against the pillows like a smug matron after a successful social coup. "Isn't it marvelous?"

She wouldn't think so if she saw the furor it was causing downstairs and down the Mall, but Vera didn't have the heart to tell her. Let her enjoy her triumph and happiness a little while longer. Someone else could crush her joy. "It's certainly an achievement."

"I told you I'd force it out into the open, and I did. They'll have to face it now, and with the entire country watching and judging them on how they choose to handle it." She raised the orange juice and took a victory sip, unaware that the same public would be watching and judging her too. "I must call Peter. He'll be thrilled to know that we'll soon be together for good."

Using a pencil so as not to chip her nails, she dialed his number on the white phone beside the bed.

"Vera, send Ruby up to dress me. I can't wait to meet the glorious day. Peter!" she exclaimed when he answered on the other end. "Have you seen it? You have? Isn't it marvelous?"

Her smile faded with whatever answer he gave her. "But, darling, don't you realize what this means for us? Of course they won't be happy . . . but, Peter."

Vera closed the door, glad someone had the temerity to tell her the truth. That it should come from Captain Townsend was probably for the best. If they were somehow allowed to marry, he'd enjoy a lifetime of delivering bad news, and she'd take it better from him than anyone else. Captain Townsend had been there for the Princess through her father's death, Queen Mary's passing, and the move to Clarence House. He would stand by her through this. Judging by what Vera had seen that morning, few other people would.

OVER THE NEXT few days, Vera and Iris fielded call after call from the palace as meetings between the Princess and Buck Place were arranged. The issue that Her Royal Highness had been asked to set aside for a while was front and center, and it was clear it would be dealt with quickly and, if the tone of the official calls were any indication, severely. With each irritated secretary of some minister that Vera spoke to, the reality that Her Royal Highness's world was about to come apart at the seams and she would be the last to realize it became all too apparent. If Vera could have done something to mitigate the impending pain she would have, but there was no tempering the reaction of Her Majesty's government and no swaying anyone important over to Princess Margaret and Captain Townsend's side. For all the prestige of Vera's position, when it really mattered, it was obvious that she held no sway or importance at all. No one in Clarence House did except the Queen Mother, and she wasn't doing a thing to help her daughter.

"How dare they, how dare they!" Princess Margaret's high voice carried from the dining room down the main hall.

Vera and Iris looked up from their work on travel arrangements for the upcoming Southern Rhodesia trip, the ones they struggled to deal with during the ongoing conundrum of the Princess and Captain Townsend's engagement. Without a word, they both rose and slipped quietly along the red wallpapered and curtained Horse Corridor with its paintings and statues of horses lining either side, avoiding the Lancaster Room, and stopping at the entrance to the main hallway to listen.

"My dear, you must see that, given the circumstances, it's for the best," came the Queen Mother's calm reply.

"But Peter arranged this entire trip. It's only right that he should go with us as planned."

"It isn't seemly, in light of recent events, for him to accompany us. He'll go with Lilibet and Philip to Ireland, and Lord Plunket will accompany us to Southern Rhodesia."

"If Peter doesn't go, then I won't go. You think I don't know what they're trying to do? They're trying to separate us. God only knows what those old men will plot while I'm away. The bastards." Princess Margaret stormed out of the dining room, her small feet pounding hard on the carpets and wood floors.

She jerked to a halt in the middle of the hallway at the sideboard with the porcelain figures arranged on top, snatched up a shepherd stealing a kiss from a shepherdess, and flung it against the opposite wall.

The Queen Mother appeared at the dining room door, glanced at the pile of figurine shards on the floor then at Princess Margaret with an air of indifference to make even Vera want to break something. "If you're going to throw things, at least throw that awful little clown figure with the beastly outfit. I've always disliked that piece."

Princess Margaret picked up the clown and smashed it to the floor.

"That's better, dear." The Queen Mother strolled back into the dining room as if the willful destruction of two figurines that were worth more than the yearly wages of the poor maid who'd have to clean them up made no difference to her.

"Cow!" Princess Margaret stormed upstairs, slamming the door to her room behind her.

Vera and Iris exchanged wary looks, both of them tensing to hear more shattering glass. Instead, the wailing voice of Ella Fitzgerald filled the house. For the moment, Princess Margaret would drown her sorrows in music and probably a heavy dose of whiskey and water.

"We'd better get back to work," Iris urged.

"Not before I make sure she's all right."

With a look that said "You're brave," Iris nodded her approval and returned to the office while Vera made her way upstairs. In the pause between the last song and the next, she knocked on the Princess's door. "It's Vera, Ma'am."

"Come in."

The calm inside the Princess's bedroom belied the chaos swirling throughout Clarence House and among the swarm of reporters waiting just beyond the wall. Vera turned down the volume on the record player when she passed it, dimming the singer's powerful voice. She expected a sharp reprimand for it, but there was nothing except the clink of ice in the Princess's glass as she took a drink.

"They're trying to separate us, Mrs. Lavish." Princess Margaret sat in the Thomas Sheraton chair, her legs tucked up under her, a whiskey in one hand, a cigarette in the other. There were no tears to mar her eyeliner or streak the royal cheek, but there was a sort of still about her, the kind that came from clinging to hope even while it was slipping away. "I begged Peter to resign, to get out from under their control, but he refused. He has no money of his own, and, as he was kind enough to remind me, his sons' schools aren't free."

"Perhaps while he has this employment he might find something else, Ma'am."

The Princess tilted her head to say she wasn't convinced, and neither was Vera. Captain Townsend had never demonstrated any real ambition, leaving his career to the whims of the Royal Family instead of pursuing positions and prominence the way most courtiers did. That he would suddenly develop some when it was needed the most was doubtful. "I thought the opinion of the people would be enough to sway all those old men, but even that won't soften their stony hearts." She waved her hand over the front of the newspaper on the floor, the results of a reader poll showing that the majority of people supported the match. The cigarette between her fingers wafted smoke over the crumpled newsprint spattered with small, wet circles. "Tomorrow's meeting isn't going to be pretty, is it, Mrs. Lavish?"

"No, Ma'am, I don't suppose it will be." Whatever was going to be discussed with the Queen and her ministers at Buck Place tomorrow wasn't going to be anything Princess Margaret wished to hear, but hear it she would; they would make damn certain of it. "But you've endured worse and come through it. You'll come through this too, no matter what happens."

"Thank you, Mrs. Lavish." She reached out and clasped Vera's hand, taking Vera by surprise. "I'm glad you'll be there tomorrow. It'll make it a great deal easier to bear."

"I'm glad I can be there too, Ma'am." Support was all Vera or anyone could offer. Not even the Princess's station and standing would be enough to shield her from the rough treatment that was about to come.

Chapter Fifteen

Vera sat in a chair along the wall beside Iris and a number of young, male secretaries, all of them silent while Princess Margaret, Her Majesty, Prime Minister Churchill, and Sir Lascelles faced one another across the Aubusson rug in the White Drawing Room. Vera wondered if they'd chosen this room deliberately because they knew what had happened behind the hidden door three years ago. Given the way the men faced Princess Margaret with stern, disapproving faces, Vera imagined they might be cruel enough to do such a thing.

"Where's Peter? You said he would be here. You promised me." Princess Margaret's small voice was nearly lost in the high ceiling and furnishings of the room. She sat across from these formidable men, not clutching a handkerchief and twisting it in her nervousness but radiating calm and cool, as if they were about to offer her a thrilling account of medieval calligraphy styles. Her royal training served her well. Vera couldn't say the same for herself, gripping her purse on her lap and finding it difficult to remain in her seat and not stand up and shout that they shouldn't be here, any of them and not for this reason, that they should be ashamed of themselves for bullying a young woman for nothing more than her desire to live a quiet life with the man she loves.

"Captain Townsend's position with the royal household has been terminated, effective immediately," Sir Lascelles announced with not one whiff of regret or apology or any effort to soften the blunt announcement, tugging at the top button of the waistcoat of his three-piece brown suit. "He is, at this moment, en route to Brussels to take up his new position as Air Attaché to the embassy there."

"Brussels?" The Princess's voice cracked. Vera opened her purse, ready to hand Her Royal Highness a handkerchief, but the Princess held back her tears, remaining stoic in the face of the hard-hearted men facing her. "You sent him away without telling me and before we could even say goodbye? What will the British people say when they hear about what you're doing to the two of us?"

"A matter of this magnitude that places the very morals of the monarchy in peril will not be guided or decided by the mob," Sir Lascelles all but spit at Her Royal Highness through his mustache, the lines on his square forehead furrowed with controlled anger, but Princess Margaret didn't back down, continuing to face him with a look to melt steel. "The Queen, as the head of the Church of England, cannot consent to the marriage of her sister, the third in line to the throne, to a divorced man. It flies in the very face of church teaching that nothing but death can dissolve a marriage." Sir Lascelles raised his hand, and the secretary seated beside Vera hopped forward to give him a typewritten piece of paper. Sir Lascelles held it out to Her Royal Highness, who didn't take it but eyed it as if it were a dead mouse. "Pursuant to the Regency Act of 1772, anyone in direct line of succession to the throne may not marry without the Queen's permission."

"I'm aware of this." Princess Margaret raised her chin in defiance. "I'm also aware that when I turn twenty-five, which is only two years from now, I can marry without my sister's permission, making this entire discussion moot." Princess Margaret began to rise and end this meeting when the crack of Mr. Churchill's cane against the floor and his booming voice made her sit back down.

"If you decide to marry Captain Townsend, even at twenty-five, you will be forced to forfeit your income from the Civil List. You will be forced to renounce not only your claim to the throne but those of your heirs. Your title will become forfeit, as will your place as a member of the Royal Family. You will no longer be known as Your Royal Highness but simply Miss Windsor. We did not fight for the sovereignty of Britain and the monarchy to have the Queen's sister tarnish it with a childish desire to marry an entirely unsuitable man."

Tears filled Princess Margaret's eyes, and she looked to her sister for help, encouragement, anything. Her Majesty remained silent, her hands folded tight over the skirt of her pale green checked suit, unable to meet her sister's pleading gaze.

Vera's heart sank for both of them as she realized how correct Lady Rankin had been. Whatever the Queen's personal opinion, she was bound by duty to follow the dictates of her government, no more able to overrule them in this matter than in the choice of the next Prime Minister. For all her exalted status, she was as powerless as her sister to follow her heart.

"Are you ready to give up this ridiculous notion of marrying Captain Townsend?" Mr. Churchill demanded from around the cigar tucked in the corner of his downturned mouth.

The bark of the formidable Prime Minister would have been enough to cow a lesser person into submission, but Princess Margaret sat straight-backed in her chair, giving as much venom with her look as she received. "How dare you try and bully the daughter of a king, the sister of a queen, a woman who outranks you in every way imaginable. You want your answer, Mr. Churchill? I'll give it to you when I'm good and ready and not a moment before."

With all the regal bearing of a woman descended from emperors, Princess Margaret rose, curtsied to her sister, and walked out of the room.

THE THREE DAYS of the Princess's sorrowful piano playing ended long enough for her to finally come downstairs and join the household for lunch. All the senior Clarence House staff ate together, the Queen Mother presiding over the table, but there was one notable absence—Captain Townsend. With no replacement yet, his chair sat empty across from the Princess's, a constant reminder of her loss. No wonder she'd skipped the past few meals.

"In Southern Rhodesia we are to dine with Major General Sir John Kennedy and his wife, Lady Kennedy," the Queen Mother said between sips of gin and Dubonnet, the drawn face of her daughter thoroughly ignored in her excitement over the upcoming trip.

"I don't care who we dine with," Princess Margaret grumbled into her barely touched salad.

"Of course you do, or at least you must pretend to. One must always put on their best face for the people, no matter where in the world they might be. I've ordered two more linen outfits because it will be quite warm there."

"You should've saved yourself the expense. Everything you wear always makes you look fat anyway." Without asking to be excused, Princess Margaret left the table, stomping up the stairs and along the upstairs hallway.

The Queen Mother smiled sweetly at the people around the table, but her fingering of the filigree on her fork gave her away. Princess Margaret's insult had hit its mark. "Well, one must do the best they can with what they have, mustn't they?"

Everyone muttered their agreement, eager to be done and return to the quiet of their work. Upstairs, the Princess resumed her piano playing. Vera studied the medallion and chandelier in the center of the ceiling. She pitied Her Royal Highness and sympathized with her, but she was sure she wasn't alone in wishing the piano wasn't so loud or that the Princess would pick some different songs. After three days, the constant sad concertos were beginning to wear.

Vera eyed the Queen Mother, who appeared as oblivious to the mournful melody as were the corgis lounging on the rug around her end of the table. The woman was a monument to never crumbling, and Vera wished she possessed a tenth of her fortitude. Perhaps she should start drinking gin and Dubonnet to build up her resolve.

The phone in the Princess's room rang, and the piano playing stopped. Vera heard more than one sigh of relief from somewhere across the table. No one had to ask who'd called. They all knew it was Captain Townsend, the English Channel now standing between him and Princess Margaret as much as Her Majesty's government.

By the end of lunch, the piano playing had been replaced by the wail of Ella Fitzgerald. Around teatime, when everyone had endured quite enough of the blues, Ruby poked her head into the lady-in-waiting office. "Vera, would you mind going up and checking on Her Royal Highness? I knocked and called through that if she's to be ready for the charity dinner by the time the car arrives at six, then I must be allowed in."

"Why don't you peek in? She's probably sleeping and must be woken up." It amazed Vera that not even Ruby would consider simply walking in to make sure the Princess was all right, but she hadn't, no doubt as afraid of the royal wrath as anyone. The entire house was on pins and needles because of the Princess and eagerly awaited her departure for Southern Rhodesia so they could finally breathe.

"And have my head bitten off for disturbing her? No thank you. She's more amenable to you and Miss Peake than any of the older staff. I thought you could rouse her."

"All right, I'll go up." As if she didn't have enough to do with coordinating travel for Imogene's Oxford wedding, which happened to be the day before the Southern Rhodesia trip. She was surprised Princess Margaret had agreed to attend at all given the present circumstances, but maybe being around her old friends and a change of scenery was exactly what she needed. Vera looked forward to it, especially since Dominic would be her date.

It'd taken all the planning skills she'd honed over the last three years to contrive time to see him almost every day during this crisis, and there were moments when she wondered if it was worth the effort. He was an almost unobtainable man, like Captain Townsend was for Princess Margaret, but like Her Royal Highness, Vera sometimes imagined it working out for them. Dominic had spent time in London once before for his work. It wasn't a fantasy to think he might do it again.

Thoughts of Dominic began to fade as the rich and sorrowful notes of Ella Fitzgerald's voice grew clearer and more intense the closer Vera drew to the Princess's bedroom. "Ma'am, it's Vera. May I come in?"

The music didn't stop or lower in volume, nor did Princess

Margaret entreat Vera to enter as she had the day before the awful meeting at Buck Place. Vera stood in the hallway waiting, wondering how the noise hadn't driven the Queen Mother out of her room, but it hadn't. She was probably sitting in her parlor watching the television as if this were any other day and her daughter's life and future were not collapsing around her. For a moment, Vera wondered what to do, especially when the second knock and announcement of her presence failed to provoke a reaction.

Vera, refusing to dither like Ruby, cracked open the door and peered inside. The curtains were drawn, cutting out the bright afternoon sun and keeping in the heavy air thick with music, cigarette smoke, and the distinct scent of whiskey. From the door, Vera could see the bed. It was empty; the coverlet and sheets were mussed, but little else seemed out of place.

"Ma'am?" Vera repeated with more conviction, determined to be heard over the record player. "Ma'am? Are you all right?"

A faint and garbled response came from the bathroom. Vera, not having been yelled at for venturing in where she wasn't invited, crept deeper into the room. "Ruby says it's time for you to dress for the charity dinner."

Again, another indistinct mumble came from the bathroom, but Vera could barely hear it over the music. Vera reached for the volume knob on the record player and then paused. She didn't want to have the Princess come flying out of the bathroom lobbing perfume bottles at her for daring to touch the royal record player. The Princess had been tolerant of her forwardness the other night, but Vera didn't wish to push her luck.

"Ma'am?" With cautious steps, Vera approached the bathroom door, careful not to barge in and startle the royal in who knew what condition. It was lighter in the bathroom, with the white tiles reflecting the muted sunlight coming in through the frosted-glass window over the tub.

On the floor beside the bathtub, Princess Margaret sat slumped against the white tile, her hair a mess, an empty pill bottle and a few scattered white pills on the floor around her.

"Ma'am!" Vera knelt beside her and dragged her limp body up to prop her against the side of the tub. Her head lolled on her shoulders, tilting back to reveal smudged lipstick and eyeliner among the tangle of dark curls.

"Ma'am, wake up, wake up!" Vera patted her face, trying to rouse her, but the Princess only groaned, her eyes half-mast against the creeping influence of the pills. "Ma'am, please wake up!"

Vera hugged her friend tight, her pulse pounding in her ears. *She can't die. She can't. Not like this.* It was all too ugly for someone who'd only wanted to be happy. *She won't die. I won't let her.*

Vera carefully laid the Princess on the tile floor and then ran for the bedroom door.

"Ruby, anyone, come quick," Vera called down the hall. "Princess Margaret has had an accident."

She knew very well that whatever foolish thing Her Royal Highness had done was no accident, but it didn't matter. She rushed to the Princess's white phone, knocking the needle off the record to stop the infernal music and making it scratch across the LP before it came to a stop, leaving nothing but static to hover in the air with Vera's panic. "Operator, operator, this is Miss Strathmore; summon Dr. Gilbert. The Princess is gravely ill. It's an emergency."

She set down the phone and hurried back into the bathroom, snatching one of the monogrammed towels off the rack next to the sink and folding it in half to lay it under the Princess's head. Princess Margaret continued to moan and mumble, and whenever she went quiet, Vera tapped her on the cheeks to keep her conscious, afraid that if the Princess fell asleep, she would never wake up. Vera had no idea what the pills were— the bottle lay beside the toilet and out of Vera's reach—but she could guess. She sat with Her Royal Highness on the bathroom floor for what felt like an eternity before Ruby and a number of other servants rushed into the bedroom.

"In the bathroom," Vera called out, glancing around at the pills scattered on the floor.

I should have cleaned up the mess, hidden the pills before the others came, she thought. It would have spared Princess Margaret some of the dignity she was trying to rob from herself along with her life. However, for the doctor to help her he would have to know, they would all have to know, what the

Princess had done. With any luck, the Princess would prove stronger than the pills.

"SHE'S VERY SORRY to miss the dinner. She was so looking forward to it, but this flu has really laid her up. Yes, I will pass on your best wishes for her quick recovery. Thank you." Vera hung up the phone and rubbed her eyes. It was the tenth phone call she'd made that day canceling Princess Margaret's engagements for the next week.

Thankfully, Princess Margaret hadn't taken enough sleeping pills to do more than make herself very groggy and to scare everyone in Clarence House and Buck Place. While the doctor had seen to her, a bevy of officials had convened to decide the official palace position on why she was suddenly too ill to attend public functions. The flu had been chosen, and Vera had her doubts about anyone believing it. There wasn't a person in Britain who didn't know about Princess Margaret and Captain Townsend and the formidable obstacles standing between them. There was also the unfortunate announcement in the papers about his new posting. Even the most dimwitted person could put two and two together to see that he'd been deliberately sent away, and it wouldn't take much for them to guess that she was "sick" because of it. She'd been conveniently sick a few times before during trips and when she had no desire to attend yet another ribbon cutting, especially after a late night. It was the involvement of the pills that had sent a shock through everyone in the house, including Vera.

"Miss Strathmore, Her Royal Highness would like to see you," Ruby said, still grave-faced after the events of the previous evening.

Vera reluctantly went upstairs, as hesitant to see the Princess as she'd been to barge in on her the night before. Everyone had expressed their gratitude to Vera afterward, including Queen Elizabeth, who'd rushed to be with her sister, comforting her instead of lecturing her until duty had called her away. Even the Queen Mother had stepped out of her rarified bubble of happiness to take Vera's hand and thank her for having found her daughter. Then she'd sighed in disbelief that Princess Margaret could be so unhappy.

Thankfully, the Queen Mother hadn't heard the whispers from a few of the elder staff, who doubted the Princess had ever really been in danger and that she'd pulled this stunt for no other reason than to garner attention.

"You're looking well this morning, Ma'am," Vera greeted when she entered the room, determined to be cheerful and positive despite the gloom hanging about Clarence House.

Princess Margaret sat up in her large bed, her hair down but clean and combed and her face free of makeup. She'd suffered no ill effects of her harrowing afternoon, except for the defeated expression darkening the circles beneath her eyes. She avoided looking at Vera, embarrassed by the unspoken reality of what had taken place here. Whatever she'd tried to do, she regretted it. That was clear.

"Would you like me to put on some music, Ma'am?" The

silence in the room was as oppressive as the music had been the day before. "Some Highland pipes, perhaps?"

"No." The Princess worried the edge of the sheet between her pink polished fingers, twisting it then releasing it over and over until Vera felt sure it would fray. Vera stood patiently at the foot of the bed, waiting while the Princess bit her bottom lip with her teeth, certain there was something she wished to say. Finally, the words came out in so soft a voice Vera had to lean forward to hear. "I can't give it up, not even for him."

"Give up what, Ma'am?"

Her eyes met Vera's at last. "My title, my place in the family. It's all I have. Without it, I'm nothing and of no consequence to anyone."

Vera came around the footboard and sat at her feet. Those words could have been hers. "That's not true, Ma'am."

"Of course it is, and they know it; that's why they said those awful things to me the other day. They knew where to strike me, and they did. The bastards." She slid the Cartier cigarette case off the nightstand, yanked one out, and tucked it between her chapped lips. With shaking fingers, she fumbled with the lighter while she struck the wheel, her unsteady hands making it difficult to touch the tip to the flame.

Vera raised her hands to help her then stopped. It wasn't the lingering effects of the pills making Her Royal Highness tremble but an anger Vera was all too familiar with. It was the hate and disgust at the world that had filled Vera when she'd given back the engagement ring, her hopes and dreams in ashes like half of Europe, and there'd been nothing she could do to change it.

"Foolish me, I almost let them win entirely, but I won't." Princess Margaret tossed the lighter on the table, and it clanked against the base of the lamp. "I will make them suffer for this. They want it over quickly, but I won't give them the satisfaction. I will drag this out for as long as possible. I'll rub their faces in it every chance I get and make it so they can't forget about it or shove it aside. I will force them to deal with it every single day until they come to rue their decision to meddle in my life like a bunch of old biddies. I will make those mustached old ministers suffer the way I have. They deserve it."

Chapter Sixteen

*I*mogene and her new husband, dressed in their traveling clothes, sprinted to their car beneath a hail of rose petals and rice thrown by the guests lined up on either side of Blenheim Palace's Ionic-columned front entrance. Princess Margaret stood with the Queen Mother at the head of the twelve hundred guests, her smile as stiff as the statues overlooking the drive from the top of the amber-colored stone façade. If the Queen Mother noticed her younger daughter's less-than-exuberant reaction to the wedding, she said nothing, patiently bearing her daughter's frowns as if they were nothing more concerning than one of her dogs barking.

Once the newlyweds were off, Vera and Dominic followed the rest of the guests back to the tents in the garden to enjoy more champagne, food, and dancing. The reception would continue on until the special railcars hired by the Duke of Marlborough were ready to take the revelers back to London in the late hours of the night.

"That was by far the most impressive wedding I've ever attended." Dominic plucked two flutes of champagne from a table laden with them and handed one to Vera. "It was almost as grand as the coronation."

"How do they do weddings in Arizona? Does the groom lasso his wife, throw her over his saddle, and haul her before the local magistrate?"

He leaned down close to her, his breath tickling her cheek. "Would you like to find out?"

Vera's hand tightened on the stem of her flute. With the sugary scent of wedding cake frosting drifting over the sharp smell of fresh-cut garden grass, the soft melody of the quartet playing over the clink of silverware against china, and the flutter of the canopy softening the brightness of the June sun, she could imagine finding out, and with him.

A male voice interrupted them. "Vera, there you are. I've been looking for you in this crush."

"Rupert!" Vera threw her arms around her cousin. It'd been three years since she'd last seen him, and he was softer about the waist and beneath his chin but with the same spry mischief in his eyes that had gotten them both in trouble so many times during country parties when they were younger. "I didn't think you'd make it."

"The drive down was dreadful." He stepped back and slid his arm around the waist of the petite redhead behind him, drawing her forward. "Allow me to introduce my wife. Mary, this is my cousin, the Honorable Vera Strathmore."

"The lady-in-waiting to Princess Margaret, how wonderful

to meet you," Mary gushed in her less-than-rarified American accent, making Vera stand up two inches taller in her Cuban heels. Even after all this time, she never tired of being recognized by strangers who weren't the press. "Rupert has told me all about you."

"And you were still willing to marry into the family?"

"How could I not marry someone so charming?" She fell against Rupert with an adoration to make Vera understand why Princess Margaret appeared so glum today. It was difficult at a wedding to forget that spinsterhood was walking with her like a shadow.

Rupert introduced Dominic, making Mary quite ecstatic to meet a fellow countryman this far from home.

"Where are my dear aunt and uncle?" Rupert asked.

"Over there with Alice and her husband." Vera tilted her flute to where her family stood at the edge of the tent, Vera's mother's pinched face as unwelcoming as Alice's smile was refreshing. Vera and her parents had enjoyed something of a truce over the past few months, especially after Vera had secured them tickets to an exclusive coronation viewing party at the Dorchester and to this wedding. Such trifles kept them in good spirits, and that alone was worth enduring their presence on a day like this.

"I see your sister is expecting again."

Alice's stomach was just beginning to show beneath her dress, allowing her to attend the wedding before her mother insisted she stay home because it wasn't decent to be at social events when one was in the family way. Her lanky husband with his blond hair stood with his arm around her, their other two children at home with his parents.

"In the autumn. It won't be long before you have some strapping sons of your own." Vera touched her thumb to her empty ring finger. That Rupert should have children long before she even had a chance rankled more than it should have. Despite her lofty position, some things hadn't changed.

"I have a duty to my line to produce heirs, and it's a great deal of fun trying." His wife's cheeks went red beside him, and Vera laughed, unable to think about anything but the cracks Caroline had once made about Rupert's inheritance. Vera would never look at her cousin the same way again.

"How is the British sports car market treating you?" Dominic asked.

"Very well, Doc. Americans love our cars. I have my new Austin-Healey outside. Come on and I'll show it to you and you can give me the Yank opinion on it."

"I'll do my best."

"I'll wait here while you do." Vera wasn't interested in traipsing too far in her shoes. "I need to make sure Her Royal Highness is all right."

"Can't you be off duty for once?" Dominic's pleasant smile went stiff about the corners.

Vera glanced at the Princess, who sat at the head table tapping her ash into her half-finished salmon with all the joy of a wake. "Like a doctor, I'm never off duty."

Dominic ground his jaw, less than impressed by her response.

"Do what you must, old girl. We won't be long," Rupert stepped in before urging Mary and Dominic to the cars.

At least someone understands. She wished it was Dominic instead of her cousin.

"Rather a common woman for Rupert to raise up to a viscountess, don't you think?" Vera's mother drawled, suddenly beside her.

"Uncle Reginald doesn't look as if he's going to die anytime soon." He appeared quite healthy while he laughed with Vera's father and Lord Glenconner.

"And what about this doctor of yours? What's he about?"

"Curing tuberculosis." The less her mother knew about Vera's personal life, the better.

"I hope you aren't foolish enough to consider marrying him. There isn't anything he can offer you in exchange for what you'd have to give up to become his wife in some flea-infested town in the American West."

"Arizona isn't full of outlaws and Indians, Mother."

"It isn't the Court of St. James either. You finally have something to be proud of. Don't throw it away like a common slut over some man who can offer you nothing but a dirty piece of land and clothes reeking of typhoid."

"Tuberculosis."

"It's the same thing." With that bit of maternal advice dispensed, Vera's mother returned to Alice to nag her about her pregnancy.

"Your mother being her usual peach of a self?" Sass linked her arm in Vera's.

"You just saved me from committing murder." More so because her mother was right and it was a truth Vera didn't want to face in the middle of a wedding reception.

"Imagine the headline if you did kill her. 'Princess Margaret's Lady-in-Waiting Murders Mother at Duke's Daughter's Wedding.' It would turn the old men at Buck Place white."

"It might be worth doing it for that reason alone."

"Speaking of scandals, how are you holding up?"

Sass was one of the few people outside of Buck Place or Clarence House who knew the full extent of what was happening, including the unfortunate incident in the royal bathroom.

"I'm not sure. At present, the grass is looking a great deal greener on your side of the fence."

"But you aren't ready to give it all up yet, are you?"

For the first time, Vera didn't have a quick or ready answer. The shock from the incident with the pills still hadn't worn off, and with everyone giving the royal a wide berth, she wondered if she was smart or stupid for heading straight toward her.

"I thought not," Sass said at her hesitation. "The devil you know and all that, heh?"

"Exactly, and she's my friend. You said it yourself: I have to take the good with the bad. I can't leave her to deal with this on her own."

"Neither of us can." Sass let go of Vera to sit down beside

Princess Margaret, and Vera took the empty seat on Her Royal Highness's other side. "How are you doing, Margo?"

"I'm simply smashing." Johnny Dalkeith and his blond wife strode by the table, neither of them sparing a glance for the Princess, too involved in each other to notice anyone else. The Princess watched them, the longing in her eyes heartbreaking. Vera wondered if she regretted having taken his flattery and attention for granted or for having toyed with him and the other men of the Set instead of trying to forge deeper relationships, ones that might have seen her married to one of them and happy today instead of sitting there alone. Vera doubted it. Admitting she was wrong was something Her Royal Highness did not do. "I never would have imagined Johnny would fall for a model. His aspiration always seemed much more refined. His ancestors must be turning in their graves to see so low a woman raised so high. And what a plain little mouse Sunny chose. *Tatler* declared her 'The Bride of the Autumn Roses,' which seems appropriate. Her bloom certainly faded fast. And poor Katharine, marrying a mere lieutenant colonel's son."

"Come off it, Margo." Sass rolled her eyes. "He's the grandson of the Earl of Rosslyn, a far grander background than some military men we know."

Vera stiffened, waiting for Sass to get the wrong end of a champagne flute for that thinly veiled reference to Captain Townsend, but her special immunity with the Princess remained, although it didn't spare her from a hard royal sideways glare.

"A lot of good it'll do either of them when she's living off nothing but his wages. I doubt her father or his *illustrious* grandfather will provide them with an annual allowance. Either way, it'll be one more wedding I'll have to suffer through this summer."

"At least you'll have Vera there to keep you company."

Vera wouldn't exactly call this a comfort for either of them. By July, Dominic would be gone, and Vera was no more looking forward to attending another wedding stag than the Princess.

The Princess, as unimpressed by the thought as Vera, listlessly plucked the old cigarette out of her holder and slipped the empty ivory between her lips. She glanced around the tent at the nearby gentlemen of the old Set, Peter, Johnny, and Sunny, waiting for one or more of them to rush to satisfy the royal whim for another smoke, but not a single man moved.

Darkness pooled in Princess Margaret's eyes. Vera sat back in her chair, wishing she'd gone to see Rupert's car instead of trying to keep Princess Margaret company. The royal temper was brewing, and who knew where it would strike.

Before the storm could break, Colin reached over the table and opened his cigarette case to her. "Allow me, Ma'am."

She selected one and set it in the end of her holder, then touched the tip to the lighter he held out for her. "Thank you, Colin."

"Always a pleasure, Ma'am." He raised her hand to his lips, bestowing on it a parting kiss before returning to where Lady Anne Coke, whom he'd been paying a great deal of attention to lately, stood with Laura and Katharine Smith and Lady Elizabeth Montagu Douglas Scott.

"At least someone here remembered me." Princess Margaret finished her champagne and motioned to a waiter to refill the glass. "And tomorrow the Palace is packing me off to Southern Rhodesia for two awful weeks in that hellhole. I can feel a migraine coming on just thinking about it."

Vera breathed a silent sigh of relief. With Iris serving as lady-in-waiting during the Southern Rhodesia trip, Vera could enjoy two weeks of freedom from herding a very uncooperative Princess through tedious public appearances and fielding Captain Colville's irritated calls concerning the news stories about the Captain and the Princess, the very ones he'd inadvertently encouraged because his tirades were proof that the Princess's plan to provoke Her Majesty's ministers was working. Already the scrapbook Her Royal Highness had ordered Vera to keep of the news stories concerning her and Captain Townsend, the ones the Princess usually fed to the press, was groaning under the strain, and it'd only been a week.

Across the tent, Dominic returned with Rupert and his wife from viewing the car. Vera glanced back and forth between him and the Princess, eager to be with him again. Princess Margaret, too involved in her own grief and misery, didn't notice, but Sass did.

"Go ahead, Vera. I'll stay with Margo."

Vera looked to the Princess. She couldn't leave until she

received royal permission. Princess Margaret continued to drink her champagne and smoke, taking her time in deciding whether to let Vera go.

"Yes, go to your doctor." She flicked the cigarette holder toward Dominic. "Enjoy yourself while you can. We both know it won't last."

No, it wouldn't. Going to Dominic was simply prolonging the pain, but still Vera went to him, irritated that Her Royal Highness, who of all people should sympathize with Vera, would be so snide about it.

Dominic took hold of Vera's hand and tugged her out from beneath the shade of the canopy. "Let's take a walk. I want to tell everyone back home what it's like to be in a duke's garden."

"It's like being in the Buck Place garden, only bigger."

"I haven't been there either."

"An oversight I may have to correct before you leave."

They slipped down the formal garden paths, passing a number of other couples searching for a place to be alone. It was some time and distance away from the reception before Dominic and Vera could find a hedge of their own.

In the shade of the boxwoods, Vera melded into his body, the shoulders of his gray morning suit made warm by the sun during their walk. With each flick of his tongue against hers, she anticipated the moment when they'd return to his room at the Savoy and do more of the things she'd dreamed about since Sass had told her he was coming back to England.

He broke from the kiss and pressed his forehead to hers. "You know, I never forgot you after I left last time."

She straightened the knot of his cravat. "Is that why you stopped writing to me?"

"You stopped writing to me. I thought you'd met some duke."

"I don't care much for titled men. A dance or two with those chaps is one thing, but they aren't known for their fidelity, and I have no desire to spend the rest of my life looking the other way."

"Good, because I don't know if I can leave you behind again." He tucked an errant strand of her hair behind her ear, leaving his hand to linger against her cheek.

Vera's fingers froze over the knot of his tie. "We promised not to talk about your leaving or the future when we're together."

"I want our futures to be the same." He covered her mouth with his. With the taste of him so potent, she imagined having everything she'd ever wanted, no matter how impossible it might be, including love.

But at what price?

She broke from his kiss, regretting it the moment they separated, for it shattered the spell of him and the day and the garden and dropped her into an awful reality she'd avoided since their first night together.

Realization spread across his face as he studied her. "I

thought, after three years, you'd have had your fun and be ready to move on."

"Are you ready to move on, to leave your clinic and come here?"

He let go of her, shocked at her suggestion. "What I do is important work that saves lives, not worrying about whether some pampered Princess never has to feel a moment of discomfort."

"That isn't fair." His words made her life seem so petty when it wasn't. Vera was important—both she and Her Royal Highness were—and he'd never been able to understand it.

"Isn't it? I've spent my entire professional career building the practice up beyond what my father ever imagined for it. I can't just leave it. Besides, what kind of life would we have if you jump every time the Princess snaps her fingers?"

"None." Every fantasy of them being together that she'd concocted during their nights out or when her mind wandered during her work wilted like the flower arrangements under the canopy. A future with him had always been nothing more than a dream, and she'd been a fool for believing it could ever come true.

He balled his fists at his sides before opening his fingers one by one. "Are you really willing to sacrifice your own happiness so she doesn't have to worry about who will hold her flowers or do her hair?"

"It's more than that. She's my friend, and I'm hers." Vera

touched her thumb to her empty ring finger. "And I'm nothing without this position."

"You could be so much more without it—a writer, a wife, a mother. Those are worthwhile things too and something she can never give you."

"You're asking me to leave my family, my friends, my position, and my country all because of the passion of a few weeks. What if it doesn't last? Then where will I be? In America with nothing. I've done that before in my own country; I won't cross the Atlantic to risk it again."

"There are no guarantees in life, Vera, not even with your Princess."

"But we've spent so little time together. We don't really know each other, do we?" It was a limp excuse, even to her ears.

"I thought we did, but apparently, I was wrong." The stoic doctor who faced the parents and spouses of dying loved ones stood before her instead of the laughing and passionate man from the Savoy. He was drawing away, and she wanted to pull him back, to change her mind and beg him to look at her the way he had when he'd held her in his arms, but she didn't. She couldn't.

The notes of a waltz drifted over them along with the laughter of some other couple farther up the garden.

"I guess this is goodbye then," he said at last, tightening the pain already squeezing her.

"I suppose it is." She scratched at her ring finger with the nail of her thumb, wanting to draw blood, but still she didn't change her mind. She'd worked too hard for what she had to let it go, even for him.

"Then I wish you luck and all the success in the world." He walked up the gravel path to the house, not once looking back.

Vera watched him go, hot tears burning her eyes, all the success in the world not seeming as grand as it had a short time ago.

Chapter Seventeen

"COME ON MARGARET! PLEASE MAKE UP YOUR MIND!"

Little do they know, Vera thought as she pasted the *Daily Mirror* headline and article into the new scrapbook. It was the eighth one she'd started in the last two years, and it'd probably be the last. After tonight, there wasn't likely to be a need for any more.

"It's the right thing to do, Margaret. This has already gone on far longer than either of us should have let it go." Captain Townsend's voice drifted in from the adjoining Garden Room where he sat with the Princess. The two of them used to take walks in the Clarence House garden when he'd sneak in during brief vacations home, but they couldn't tonight. Not even the autumn darkness was enough to shield them from the swarm of press and photographers perched outside the gates. How the bobbies were keeping the press from climbing the walls Vera didn't know, but it wouldn't surprise her if a wave of them broke through the gates and flooded in.

"I'm glad I did," the Princess insisted. "All those people who fought against us deserved to suffer."

"We're the ones who've suffered."

"And we shouldn't let them win. It isn't too late to call the BBC and pull back the statement. I'm twenty-five, outside the influence of the Regency Act. There must be a way."

"There isn't, Margaret."

"You're giving up, just like you did two years ago." The click of Princess Margaret's heels over the wooden floor punctuated her words. "If you'd stayed strong, resigned your position, and agreed to fight with me, we might have been together."

"But we didn't because neither of us was willing to make the sacrifices necessary for that to happen." Vera cocked her head, waiting to hear the smash of porcelain as Princess Margaret lobbed some antique at Captain Townsend's head for having been bold enough to place even a smidgen of their current miseries on her shoulders, but there was only the whisper of the breeze outside, and the occasional laugh of a newsman carrying over the wall. "It's over, and it's time for us both to move on."

The rustle of the leaves in the trees outside filled the quiet until the Princess spoke at last. "It's like the morning Mummy told me that Papa died. As if there's nothing to it, simply a fact, a truth one cannot escape but must deal with."

"I'm sorry, Margaret; if I'd been a different man or you a different woman, we might have been together, but we are who we are and we can't change it." The fading of Captain Townsend's voice drew Vera to the Garden Room. They were no longer there, standing together in the main hallway near the front door. Vera crept across the room and through the Lancaster one, careful to stay out of sight, unwilling to intrude on their final moment together.

"Goodbye, Margaret."

"Goodbye, Peter."

The front door clicked shut, and Vera ventured closer.

Princess Margaret stood alone beneath the Ramsay portrait of King George III, her white dress with the navy blue piping along the neckline and skirt the height of fashion, the clean lines betraying the sheer cost of it to her future and her happiness. She'd chosen all of this over him, and in a few minutes, the whole world would discover it.

The Queen Mother, as always, was in her room away from all the troubles, probably with a stiff gin and Dubonnet in her hand.

Throughout the house, the antique clocks began to chime the seven o'clock hour and from somewhere far off, in another room, a servant's perhaps, or a journalist's wireless outside the wall came the voice of the BBC announcer interrupting the evening program to read a special announcement from Clarence House.

I would like it to be known that I have decided not to marry Group Captain Peter Townsend.

Vera didn't hear the rest. She didn't need to. She'd been the one to type up the announcement before Princess Margaret had sent it to the BBC.

Princess Margaret finally faced Vera, defeat more than tears softening her blue eyes. It was the same look that had marred so many eyes in the days after Dunkirk, when it seemed as if, at any moment, the Luftwaffe would fly over England and crush their freedom and sovereignty. "I thought the end would be grander than this."

"It never is, Ma'am, not with loss." The yellowed telegram from the War Office in her dresser drawer proved it.

"I don't suppose it is."

Vera didn't hug her the way she had Alice all those many years ago when a boy she'd fallen in love with had gone off with another girl. She didn't offer the Princess useless platitudes about how she'd find someone else, because Vera wasn't sure she would. Almost every man of the Set had decided to pursue love and companionship with other women, a fact they were both keenly aware of.

"You understand why I didn't give it all up for him, don't you, Mrs. Lavish?"

"I do, Ma'am." It was for every reason she'd let Dominic go, returning to the reception as alone as she'd been when she'd first received the invitation.

"I knew you would." Princess Margaret climbed the stairs, pausing on the landing. "Please call Billy and ask if he'd like to accompany me to the ballet tomorrow night. He isn't with anyone at the moment, not that I know of."

"No, Ma'am, he isn't attached."

"Good. I don't want to stay home alone."

The Princess slowly climbed the stairs to her room, not slamming the door or putting on an Ella Fitzgerald record. Instead, there was nothing but quiet throughout Clarence House and the faint sounds of the city beyond.

Vera wandered down the Horse Corridor to the lady-in-waiting room and the scrapbook. The glue was dry, and she closed it and set it aside, revealing the American magazine, *Lady's Journal*, with the note attached to it on the desk beneath.

A friend of mine's parents own this magazine and they're dying for stories on English manners written by a real Englishwoman. Think it over and let me know.

Sass

P.S. Doc is engaged to be married to one of the nurses at his clinic. It's a damn shame it isn't you.

Tears blurred Vera's eyes and dropped down her cheeks to stain the note.

Yes, it was a bloody damn shame.

Chapter Eighteen

September 1959

No, it isn't right, nothing about it is right." Mr. Antony Armstrong-Jones leaned one slender elbow on the tripod of his camera and shook his head. "Change your dress; that one won't do at all."

"I like this dress," Princess Margaret hissed from where she sat perched on a piano stool near the gauzy curtains of her sitting room window.

"I don't care if you like it. Wear it to a ball but not in front of my camera. All those ruffles make you look like the top tier of a wedding cake."

Princess Margaret rose up to her full height, all five feet one inch of it, and pinned a hard glare on the impertinent photographer who was taller than her, but not by much. "Mr. Beaton would never address me this way."

"You didn't hire Mr. Beaton, you hired me, and I'll damn well give you the picture you want if you stop being difficult and do as you're told. Go change so we can get on with this. I'm sure neither of us wants to be here all day." He straightened the slim black tie sloppily knotted beneath the less-than-crisp collar of his white shirt paired with camel-colored trousers, not standing at attention or so much as humbled or left devoid of words by the royal outburst. Whoever Princess Margaret was outside these doors, in here with him in this makeshift studio it was clear that she was just another client. "Leave on the diamond necklace and earrings. I can work with those."

"Come, Ruby, and we'll see if we can find something up to Mr. Armstrong-Jones's exacting standards." Princess Margaret grabbed the sides of her dress and trounced off into her dressing room, Ruby nearly stumbling in surprise as she followed.

Vera stared in astonishment at the photographer with the blond hair while he adjusted lights and checked his camera again. The Leica stood on a tripod, ready to snap the Princess for her twenty-ninth birthday portrait once she was, in Mr. Armstrong-Jones's opinion, suitably attired. Vera guessed that given his brusque way of speaking this would be his first and last assignment photographing Her Royal Highness. Vera wondered why he was here at all. Cecil Beaton usually did all the official portraits, but Princess Margaret had specifically requested Mr. Armstrong-Jones after viewing the photographs he'd taken of Prince Charles and Princess Anne. There'd been something about Mr. Armstrong-Jones's compositions that she'd liked and she'd delayed the release of her birthday photograph by a month to allow her schedule and his to align. She wasn't so fond of his methods today.

"Her Royal Highness is to be addressed as Ma'am," Vera advised, hoping a little nod to the Princess's status might make the session run a great deal smoother.

"Is she?"

"She is."

"Well, lucky for her." He went on adjusting his lights.

Vera had to squelch a smile. Many officials and dignitaries, especially the wife of the French Ambassador who'd hosted Her Royal Highness the year before, would give their eyeteeth to be able to show this much disregard for the Princess's station. Some days Vera would too, especially when Her Royal Highness was refusing, yet again, to attend a scheduled engagement.

"Sit on the stool so I can adjust the lights." It wasn't a request but a command, the kind a man like him was used to throwing at assistants in his studio. Vera thought about refusing, but the readier his camera and lights were when Princess Margaret returned, the faster this photography session would end. She sat in the Princess's place. This wasn't the first time she'd stood in for the royal.

"Sorry, but you're taller than her." He stepped forward and held a light meter close to her cheek, his skin warm from his hurried motions about the room and the heat of the studio lights. He wore his blond hair parted to one side and combed off his forehead, and a few strands fell forward when he frowned at the reading. He raked his fingers through it, straightening it as he hunched behind the camera, observing Vera and oblivious to her all at the same time.

Watching him work, Vera could see why the Princess hadn't dismissed him yet for his arrogance. There was a certain something about him that Vera couldn't put her finger on. He wasn't attractive, at least not to her, for she didn't care for slender men, especially ones so close to her in height, but there was an unmistakable confidence around him that was rather appealing. If he weren't treating the Princess with little more respect than a nameless Parisian dress model, she might actually like him.

Princess Margaret huffed back into the room in a pale blue gown that would have made her eyes sparkle if it hadn't been for the irritation crystallizing them. "Is this more to your liking, *Mister* Armstrong-Jones?"

Vera gritted her teeth. Princess Margaret was pulling rank, and this never ended well for the other party.

"Yes, it is, Ma'am. Now sit down."

The *Ma'am* knocked the glare right out of the Princess's eyes, and with more poise than she'd walked in the room with, she sat on the stool.

Mr. Armstrong-Jones crossed his arms and raised his fist to his lips as he examined the scene. Vera hoped he wouldn't ask for another outfit change; she didn't wish to step between the snarling Princess and the arrogant photographer and risk catching the wrong end of one of Princess Margaret's barbs.

Instead, he dropped his hands to his hips. "Pull down the straps of the dress."

"I beg your pardon," Princess Margaret said with a gasp.

"Mr. Armstrong-Jones," Ruby remonstrated before one stern wave of his hand left her unusually silent.

"Your Highness, you have the most magnificent skin tone and a very pleasing shape to your shoulders. Draw the straps down and I promise this will be the most striking portrait of you that anyone has ever seen." His voice went from barking sharp to velvety smooth, each considered word delivered with the tenderness of a lover and all the sycophantic leanings of a practiced courtier. "You'll mesmerize the world with this portrait."

Temptation hung in the air between them, their eyes locked in a war of wills, and Vera waited to see who would win, placing her money on the Princess.

Then, Princess Margaret raised one red-nailed hand and slid down the right strap and the left, leaving the soft curve of her shoulders bare. The dress, without the support of the silk, dropped lower down the front of her breasts to reveal more of the full top of her décolletage. His gaze slipped with the fabric to admire the royal form, appreciation mixing with the smug certainty that, despite her protests and fits, he could make her do exactly what he wanted.

"Very good. But it needs one more thing." He came around behind her and, in what would have earned any other man a resounding slap, straightened a small section of the diamond necklace that had become twisted when she'd changed. His fingers brushed the back of her neck, the jewels beneath the bright lights sending a spray of rainbows over her luminous skin. He didn't touch her again but let his hand hover above her, daring her to defy his instructions and him. "That's better."

He stepped behind his camera.

"Turn your knees away from me. Look back at the camera over your shoulder. Chin down, eyes up. There. Don't move." Vera was surprised he didn't run his hands all over her to position her himself, but he remained behind his camera and, to Vera's great surprise, Princess Margaret did as she was told. She performed for him like a seasoned actress in the West End or Twickenham Studios, shifting when commanded while he snapped away.

Vera watched in amazement as the session continued. She'd never witnessed such synchronization between a photographer and the Princess before. Not even with Mr. Beaton during the numerous formal and birthday portraits that he'd shot over the years had there been this kind of chemistry. It was something Vera was sure would make every one of Mr. Armstrong-Jones's promises about this portrait come true.

"You have a very interesting professional manner, Mr. Armstrong-Jones," Vera complimented when the session was over and the Princess had left with Ruby to change her outfit. "Are you this direct with all your clients?"

"I am." He moved from light to light, switching them off. "They hire me to do a job and I do it, whether they're royalty of the stage or the kingdom. I assure you, she'll love my results. Everyone does."

"We'll see." How he'd become a celebrated society portrait photographer with those manners she couldn't guess, but it seemed, like the Princess, a great many high people were willing to be put in their places if it meant they'd look very good for posterity.

"CAN YOU BELIEVE the crap they print about me? What did I ever do to deserve this kind of press?" Princess Margaret held up an article from the *Daily Express* asking what the British people were paying Her Royal Highness for if she couldn't show up to official duties. The Princess sat at her dressing table in her pink silk robe and nightgown, brushing her short hair. The loss of her long locks in favor of this new style was still lamented by the Queen Mother, who'd endured a stream of insults from her daughter for daring to mention it at dinner the other night. "I suppose when you have the Virgin Queen on the throne, you have to have a black sheep somewhere. I could cure cancer and the newspapermen would still vilify me. At one time they loved me." Princess Margaret flung the newspaper on the floor to join the others scattered around her chair, then pushed aside the silver mirror resting on the glass top of her dressing table. Beneath it was tucked an old snapshot of the Princess, Her Majesty, and Captain Townsend perched together on a grassy bank while they watched a horse race. She traced the square corners of the photograph. "What changed?"

The answer to Her Royal Highness's question lay in the rumpled papers at her slippered feet, but Vera didn't dare point this out. The royal mood was collapsing, and if there was any hope of getting her out of her robe and into the dress Ruby had chosen for that day's ribbon-cutting ceremony, Vera must stop the old melancholy before it overtook her.

"The proofs for Mr. Armstrong-Jones's photos arrived for your approval, Ma'am." Vera slid the cardboard folder with the photos over the top of the old snapshot.

"Let's see if he kept his promise to make me look spectacular." The Princess untied the yellow ribbon holding the cardboard covers together and opened the folder.

Vera stood over her shoulder to view the photos with her while she turned the pages.

Princess Margaret gasped. "They're stunning."

"They are," Vera grudgingly agreed. She'd secretly hoped his work wouldn't live up to his overly developed sense of his talents, but his confidence was well deserved. The pictures were amazing.

The Princess reached the end of the selection and the note clipped to the last picture.

I saved the best for last.

Mr. Armstrong-Jones

It was the photograph of her with the straps of the gown out of frame and her body turned away from the camera to look back over her shoulder, the one he'd promised would be magnificent. It was like no other portrait of her taken before, not because it conveyed the elegance of her profile or position but because it was demure and titillating all at the same time.

"He's right, this is the best. Send him instructions to release this photograph to the papers at once." Princess Margaret snapped the folder closed and handed it to Vera.

"Are you sure, Ma'am?" The muscles in Vera's neck tightened just thinking about the calls she and Iris would receive from Buck Place when this became public. "Commander Colville won't be happy with your official birthday portrait being so . . . earthy."

"I hope it gives the old bastard a heart attack. If I could pose nude and send them out I would, but I suppose I have to maintain some modesty for Lilibet's sake." At least she recognized this fact. "What tiresome things do I have on the calendar this week?"

Vera, relieved to see the Princess taking the newspaper's advice to show more interest in her engagements, opened her calendar and read out the list of the Princess's scheduled engagements. "It's a fairly light week except for the opening of the nurses' school tomorrow and the presentation of debutantes at Buckingham Palace. You'll be sitting in for the Queen."

"No, I won't waste another afternoon watching all those jumped-up tarts curtseying before me as if they're the Duchess of Devonshire's daughters. Tell Buck Place to get Mummy to do it. She's a queen, and she has nothing better to do. What else?"

So much for taking her royal duties a touch more seriously.

"The Clarence House dinner on Thursday. Here's the guest list. I've attached brief biographies for everyone invited."

The Princess uncapped her Montblanc and read the list.

"I refuse to eat with Lady Gladwyn. She was an absolute witch to me when I stayed at the British embassy in France, all because I decided to have my hair done when I was sick. There's nothing wrong with looking good while one's eyes are puffy and their nose is red." She flicked an X over the offending name, creating yet another difficult phone call for Vera to make.

"Who should I list as her replacement?" Certain newspaper writers might condemn Her Royal Highness, but there were a great many other people who'd drop everything, perhaps even rise from their deathbeds, to hustle over to Clarence House because of a summons from Princess Margaret. It was the single power she wielded, and she didn't hesitate to use it.

The Princess capped the fountain pen and tossed it to one side. "Replace her with Mr. Armstrong-Jones."

Of all the names she could have suggested Vera would never have guessed that one. Most of the old Margaret Set had long since drifted away, too involved with families and the responsibilities of companies or ancestral homes to spend their nights fawning over Her Royal Highness, but they could still be counted on to return to Clarence House for dinner.

"Do you think he'll be comfortable, Ma'am?" With his manners, he was likely to irritate a number of the other guests who very much enjoyed their titles and all the honors accorded them.

"His mother is the Countess of Rosse." She tucked a cigarette into her holder and lit it.

"By her second husband, Ma'am."

"He isn't a chimney sweep, and there's no reason to look down on him. You, who are all fur coat and no knickers yourself, should know better than to do that."

Vera folded her hands in front of her, Caroline's old insult about Princess Margaret being a second-rate Princess coming to mind, but she wasn't about to say it out loud. It was best to remain silent and not take things too personally when the Princess was in one of these moods, but lately it was becoming harder and harder to do both.

"He was educated at Eton and Cambridge, and his father owns lands in Wales," Princess Margaret continued, using the crystal Fabergé bottle stopper to dab perfume behind her ears. The fact that Princess Margaret had called on her own resources to research his background was telling. She only ever did that when she was particularly intrigued by a person. What interest she could possibly have in a pompous photographer was anyone's guess. "Besides, he knows Colin. He photographed his wedding to Anne last spring. You were there; surely you remember him."

It'd been a memorable wedding in that Princess Margaret had not sat sullenly at a table making snide remarks about the bride or groom, but Vera couldn't remember the photographer any more than she could remember the servers during the reception. She doubted Princess Margaret did either. She could barely name the maids who moved through the halls on a regular basis, much less a photographer at a wedding six months ago. "I imagine he wasn't as brusque with Colin and Anne as he was with you, Ma'am."

"Yes, he was rather rough, wasn't he?" She touched the cigarette to her lips but didn't inhale, staring at something over the dressing table and contemplating what had happened that day. "Send him an invitation. The dinners here could do with a bit of fresh blood."

"ARE YOU SURE this is the right address, Miss Strathmore?" the driver asked as he parked the black Mercedes near the gray-door entrance to Mr. Armstrong-Jones's Pimlico Road studio.

"This is the one he gave us." That Mr. Armstrong-Jones had a stable of clients who were willing to travel to this part of London for a few snaps was telling of his talents.

"Do you want me to come in with you?"

She did, but it all seemed so silly. This was a photography studio, not a brothel, for heaven's sake. "No, I'll be fine."

The minute the stunning blonde showed Vera in through the front door decorated with a lion's-head knocker that was far too elegant for its surroundings, Vera's opinion about this not being a brothel changed. Mr. Armstrong-Jones liked his female assistants, especially young ones with a preference for the emerging fad of inappropriately short skirts. It was the first time Vera had been up close to what some magazines called

Mod. The grand dames of a decade earlier had been shocked by the New Look. They'd need their smelling salts if this style ever caught on.

"Thank you, Britt; now get those delivered." Mr. Armstrong-Jones swatted a passing brunette wearing hose that were too orange to be paired with a dress that red on the bottom. Her slender arms were loaded with envelopes for delivery.

"Right away, Tony." Britt spun around, nearly bumping into Vera before she slipped nimbly past her. "Pardon me."

Vera stepped deeper into the studio decorated in what her aunt Augusta would call bastard Regency, with classical antique tables and chairs that looked as if they were from a jumble sale filling the space. The accompanying tat was everywhere except for the official portrait area arranged in front of an aged brick wall covered with a selection of different colored and textured backdrops. The single male assistant in his tight jeans and an even tighter jumper moved a pair of plaster columns while the women flitted about him to organize peeling gilded chairs and tasseled velvet cushions into a kind of fantasy-court scene. Lights illuminated the space and heated up the studio, making a bead of sweat slip down Vera's back beneath her tailored navy blue wool suit coat and matching skirt. This outfit had always made her feel elegant. Today it felt frumpy in the presence of these agile women.

While they worked, Tony changed lenses on the camera, a cigarette dangling at an awkward angle from his bottom lip. One of the assistants giggled as she lobbed a pillow at her friend whose white shirtdress left little to the imagination. Vera wondered what images were in Mr. Armstrong-Jones's camera and what additional ones would join it once she and her very square presence took their leave.

"Miss Strathmore, what brings you to my neck of the woods?" Mr. Armstrong-Jones wore a collared shirt with no tie, the first few buttons open to reveal what Vera considered a somewhat weak chest. But then again, *strapping* was not a word she would use to describe a man she could practically see eye to eye with.

"I have the Princess's approved proofs and must review with you the proper distribution of the image. I also have an invitation for you to a dinner at Clarence House on Thursday." She handed him the portfolio with the stirring photograph and the smaller envelope with the invitation.

He turned the envelope over and admired his name in the fine calligraphy, compliments of Iris. "Are invitations usually hand delivered by ladies-in-waiting?"

"I needed to return the proofs, and it seemed easier to bring it with me."

"Then when you return, tell Her Royal Highness I'm happy to attend."

"The attire is black tie." A man with an Eton and Cambridge education should already know how to dress but, given his present surroundings, Vera had her doubts.

"I imagined it would be." He screwed the new lens into the camera body. "Tammy, darling, be a dear and pose for me."

"Sure thing, Tony." With a swing of her hips that were barely covered by her A-line dress, Tammy perched on the stool. She pressed her knees together and leaned toward the camera with a pout that would have put the ladies of Amsterdam's red-light district to shame. "Like this?"

"You always know what I like." Tony bent over to check the shot through the viewfinder.

"The instructions for distribution, Mr. Armstrong-Jones," Vera reminded him, afraid he might forget that she was here and start taking more adult pictures of a girl Vera was not certain was above the age of consent.

He leaned one elbow on the tripod and faced Vera. "Please, call me Tony."

She ignored his request, ready to be through with this errand and on her way home. With Princess Margaret packed off with Iris to a charity performance, Vera was free to do her own work tonight. She had another Lady Luella column for *Lady's Journal* to write and send to Sass, the only person who knew about her clandestine employment. Vera trilled her fingers on the cardboard portfolio cover, imagining the hell she'd catch if the Princess ever found out about this little side job. Her *Lady's Journal* column wasn't much—a monthly tutorial on proper British manners—and there was no logical reason why Her Royal Highness should object to it, but logic wasn't the Princess's strong point. "All the papers are to immediately receive a copy of the photo along with instructions that requests for additional copies should be directed to you. The only paper not to receive a copy is the *Daily Express*. Her Royal Highness detests that publication."

"They'll get a hold of it one way or another."

"Good, make them work for it."

He set the proofs down on a drafting table cluttered with pictures of women and society ladies all thrown together in a way they'd never be in real life. Looking quite out of place beside them were shots of two dancers in motion, the woman in her ball gown and diamonds sailing over her partner. It was obvious by the composition and energy that this type of portraiture was what Mr. Armstrong-Jones really longed to do. The snaps of pearl-bedecked debutantes simply paid the bills. "I'll see to it at once."

"Thank you, Mr. Armstrong-Jones." If it weren't for how much the picture would edify him as much as Princess Margaret, she wouldn't believe he'd allow business to interfere with this evening's shoot of passion. Let him have his moment of wild creativity. It was something Vera, after years spent at her typewriter at night, knew a little something about.

"Let me see you out."

Suddenly, the man had discovered his manners. "No, I don't want to interrupt any more of your work."

"I assure you, it's no interruption." He shifted past her to the front door, standing between it and her but not opening it to the street and the driver and the safety of the royal car beyond. "You know, we could do a lot for each other."

She could very well imagine what she might do for him,

given her contacts within society and the palace. What he thought he could offer her made her just curious enough to ask. "And what would you do for me?"

"With the proper portrait, I could make you a sensation in your own right, the way my picture will bring more acclaim to your already glorious Royal Highness."

"And you, by extension."

He shrugged. "One does what one must to climb the crag."

Didn't she know it. "No thank you, Mr. Armstrong-Jones. I prefer a more silent notoriety."

"The woman behind the women, heh?"

"Exactly."

"I'll keep that in mind." He tugged open the door, letting the damp evening air into the darkness of the studio. "Good evening, Miss Strathmore."

"Good evening, Mr. Armstrong-Jones."

Vera hurried to the car, hoping the Princess's interest in this man was nothing more than a passing whim. Mr. Armstrong-Jones was a kind of trouble that Princess Margaret didn't need. Things had long ago settled down at Clarence House. While it was far from the spirited place Maggie's Playroom at Buck Place had been ten years earlier, Iris, Vera, and Her Royal Highness got on with their daily business with some efficiency, each day blending into the next, the balls, dinners, ribbon cuttings, and the Princess's good and bad moods all fading one into another until Vera could barely tell them apart.

Vera climbed into the car, suddenly tired and eager to be

in her room and in front of her typewriter. As the Mercedes wound through the busy London streets, passing workers holding their bowler hats against the breeze, the photograph of the dancers remained with her. Tony, for all his crass oddities and distasteful behavior, had reminded her of what she'd given up when she'd abandoned Rose Lavish. She'd never willingly return to that miserable life, but more and more lately she regretted having been so quick to abandon her novel writing completely. Those old novels may have been silly, but they'd been hers.

The column is mine too. Lady Luella may not be the great Lady Penrose novel she'd once dreamed of writing, but if staying up late to type her little columns under a pseudonym meant reclaiming some of the old creativity, then so be it. She smiled to herself at the need to still be so secretive. Maybe someday she'd find a way to bring her work out into the open, but at present it was her private little pleasure and no one else's, and it would stay that way.

Chapter Nineteen

The official photograph of Princess Margaret was a smashing success, in that the outrage it caused among certain sections of society, especially Buck Place, had been larger than even Vera had predicted. The birthday photograph was labeled everything from breathtaking to obscene and elicited a chiding phone call to Princess Margaret from Her Majesty. From what Vera had overheard, the Queen had received an earful for her rebuke, the kind only a younger sister could give to an older one no matter how big a crown the latter wore. If that little bit of gossip had somehow become public knowledge, it would be circulating with all the whispers about the photo from the guests cluttering the Clarence House sitting room for before-dinner cocktails.

"It's about time she had someone besides Cecil doing her photos. He's so last century," Colin complained to Vera, their conversation keeping them from having to be bored by the invited dignitaries and officials who'd already cornered the

Queen Mother and the Princess. "Speaking of which, where is our esteemed photographer?"

"Probably in the arms of one or more of his models." Vera kept an eye on Princess Margaret while she spoke to the former Ambassador to Cuba. In another minute, Vera would have to rescue her and politely direct her into conversation with someone equally as tedious.

"I don't think Mr. Armstrong-Jones's tastes tend that way."

"If you'd see that harem of a studio he runs like a sultan, you wouldn't think so."

"Really?" Colin trilled his finger on his highball glass. "Maybe it's time I had a new portrait done."

Vera would warn Anne about her husband's intention if she wasn't already well aware that Anne was in danger of getting whiplash from doing so much looking the other way. Whatever understanding the two of them had in their marriage was no business of Vera's.

"Mr. Antony Armstrong-Jones," the butler announced.

"Speak of the devil." Apparently, Mr. Armstrong-Jones's assistants hadn't made him forget after all, and why should they? None of them could give him the one thing Vera sensed he wanted the most—status.

A hush fell over the Clarence House sitting room when Tony entered. He wore a black velvet suit and a multicolored scarf that resembled an ascot more than a proper tie. A couple of ill-concealed whispers told her exactly what a number of guests thought of his attire, but he ignored them, standing just over the threshold of the sitting room with all the arrogance he'd employed at the photo shoot, unashamed, bolstered even by the disapproval lobbed his way. His arrogance was further inflated when Princess Margaret abandoned the Ambassador without so much as a by-your-leave and made for the photographer as if he were the most important person in the room.

"Quite a warm welcome for the hired help," Colin whispered.

"Especially one with such unique taste in clothing." *So much for Eton and Cambridge having taught him how to dress.*

"All arty types dress like that nowadays. It won't be long before that ensemble is *très* chic."

"Heaven forbid." She couldn't imagine wearing the kind of outfits she'd seen on Mr. Armstrong-Jones's assistant. Red and orange weren't her colors.

"What in heaven's name is going on?" The Queen Mother rose from between the former Lord Chamberlain of London and a Right Reverend and, with more grace and decorum than Princess Margaret had shown to her Ambassador, left them to see what had caused the pause in conversation.

"It seems our last guest is finally here, Ma'am." Colin waved his hand toward the short blond man who looked over the room as if he owned the place. What Vera wouldn't give to possess such unearned confidence.

"And who is this gentleman keeping us all from our meal?"

"Mummy, may I introduce Mr. Antony Armstrong-Jones?"

It was the politest the Princess had been to Her Majesty in a long time.

"So you're the photographer responsible for that picture I've heard so much about." Vera and Colin exchanged looks, both of them expecting a royal dressing down, one Vera thought was well deserved by both Tony and Princess Margaret for having so openly flaunted convention. The Queen Mother disappointed them. "Good on you for tweaking a few noses in need of a solid tweaking."

"I aim to please, Your Majesty."

"And so you shall. With the flap your little picture has created, I'm tempted to have you take one of me. It's been a long time since anyone has been roiled up over my image."

"Name the date, and I'm at your command, Ma'am." He dropped into a low bow, sticking out one foot and flourishing his arm until it was almost to his knee, his position and his dark velvet coat giving him the look of a Tudor courtier instead of a Pimlico Road photographer with a dubious pedigree.

"Then I command you to escort me into the dining room. I'm tired of waiting for my dinner."

He proffered his arm, and the Queen Mother took it while everyone else lined up behind them according to precedent. A couple of guests grumbled about the newcomer sitting above the salt, but if the Queen Mother heard them, she ignored them, processing into the dining room on Mr. Armstrong-Jones's arm as if he were the King of Tonga.

"Sit beside me, Mr. Armstrong-Jones. I want to hear all

about your exciting work," the Queen Mother insisted, sending another wave of muttered complaints through the Clarence House dining room as everyone shifted down a seat to accommodate the young man. He sat between the Queen Mother and Princess Margaret, commanding their attention throughout the entire dinner and leaving it to Vera to settle the ruffled feathers of the MP on her right until the Queen Mother gave the signal to turn and Vera abandoned him to speak to Colin, who sat on her left.

The change in the direction of the conversation left Tony completely to the Princess, who was livelier and more animated with him than she had any reason to be. It wasn't so much Her Royal Highness's laughs that Vera noticed as much as her constantly leaning toward him to offer a generous view of the royal breasts well enhanced by the fitted halter-top gown. He wasn't sly or shy in admiring them, drinking in the sight of them like a rich brandy.

"If I didn't know better, I'd say he's caught her attention." Colin was no more thrilled by what he was seeing than Vera. "It's been years since she's been *that* accommodating to any dinner guest not named Peter Townsend."

"She can't be interested in him. This is only the second time they've met and he was quite unpleasant the first time." If someone at the photo shoot had told Vera that the same man who'd demanded that Princess Margaret pull down her dress straps would be eating dinner with her tonight she never would have believed it.

Mr. Armstrong-Jones's talent at dazzling his royal hosts continued during drinks after dinner, when, with the freedom to move about the room, he approached first one guest and then another, working them over as a barker did punters at a fair. It wasn't long before, with Princess Margaret fixed at his side, even the snubbed officials were smiling and laughing at his jokes, and the matron who'd tutted the loudest at his attire was requesting a photo session with him as soon as his schedule allowed.

"Isn't he marvelous?" Princess Margaret gushed to Vera and Colin in a rare moment when she'd willingly surrendered her place on Tony's arm to another female guest who couldn't have been a day below eighty.

"Absolutely amazing." His talent at charming was really something to watch.

"He knows ever so many people in the arts, more so than even you, Colin."

"He does get around, Ma'am."

"Of course he does. There's something about him one can't help but be drawn to."

Vera didn't think it was so much that others were drawn to him as he was to them, with all the eagerness of Edmund Hillary to climb Mount Everest.

"He should come with us to the ballet, Colin. It'll liven things up."

"I'll secure the tickets, Ma'am," Colin offered through a

wan smile, the prospect of sharing another evening with Mr. Armstrong-Jones not as enchanting to him as it was to the Princess.

"Sounds like a ripping night out, Ma'am," Mr. Armstrong-Jones said when the Princess pulled him into their group and mentioned it. He didn't look like a man for *Swan Lake*, but Vera sensed he would accompany them to the opening of an incineration plant if it meant spending more time in the royal presence.

The green hardstone clock on the mantle chimed eleven times, and a subtle signal from the Queen Mother set the footmen into action. They began collecting drinking glasses, going so far as to remove them straight from the guests' hands while handing those same guests their coats and wraps. It wasn't the first time that most of these people had been ushered out after a dinner, for it was standard Clarence House practice to make the end of an evening perfectly clear, and no one took offense except for Mr. Armstrong-Jones.

"What do you think you are doing? I'm not finished with that." Mr. Armstrong-Jones yanked his half-drunk gin and tonic out of the footman's reach.

Princess Margaret soothed him with a light hand on his shoulder while gently taking the glass and passing it to the footman. "Don't be upset. That's simply Mummy's way of making sure guests know the party is over. She doesn't wish for anyone to feel awkward or unsure about when they should leave."

"Interesting method, Ma'am. Maybe I should try it at my next party. I'd have a lot less people sleeping on my floor the next morning."

"Your parties must be very interesting if you can't get rid of your guests."

"Come see one for yourself. I'm having a little get-together at my Rotherhithe Street flat tomorrow night, a great many theatrical types and the like. I'd love it if you could join us, Ma'am."

"Ma'am, the Hussars Ball is tomorrow night," Vera reminded her.

"Skip it and come to my party instead," Mr. Armstrong-Jones all but ordered. "Bring your friends if you'd like. The more the merrier."

Vera waited for the Princess's answer, hoping for once that Her Royal Highness considered her responsibilities over her desire to be amused.

"I think I will attend."

Vera would give Iris the honor of making that phone call tomorrow.

"Good. Until tomorrow night, Ma'am." He slid his hand under her gloved one and raised it to his lips, his eyes, as ice blue as the Princess's, riveting in their intensity.

"Until tomorrow night, Mr. Armstrong-Jones."

"Call me Tony."

"Good night, Tony."

He lowered her hand and straightened, taking three respect-ful steps backward before turning and leaving.

The Princess watched the doorway where he'd disappeared for some time, oblivious to the many other people filing through it to take their leave.

"What is it?" Colin whispered to Vera. "What does she see in him, a mere tradesman, for heaven's sake? How gauche."

"I don't know." Perhaps he amused her like the actors and actresses Colin often included in his dinner parties, and she craved the same stimulation at a Clarence House dinner. It couldn't be more than that, could it?

Chapter Twenty

*A*n awkward silence settled over the gathering of long-haired and short-skirted women and goateed men in their tight, blue velvet suits when Princess Margaret, Vera, and Colin entered Tony's Rotherhithe Street flat. It was the same awkward silence that had greeted Princess Margaret backstage after the charity theatrical production Colin had talked her into producing years ago when Princess Margaret had made the mistake of asking Noël Coward what he'd thought of the performance. It was the first time the snippy man had ever been caught without a ready word in his perpetually sharp mouth.

The same reaction greeted them tonight, making Vera feel as if they were parents interrupting their teenage son's unauthorized party. There was no mistaking the difference in age between the majority of guests and the new arrivals. Nor was there any missing the contrast in attire. There was a cheapness to the younger guests' clothes, a sense of fleeting style with look supreme over the quality of the fabric, while the fine material and cut of Vera's and Princess Margaret's clothes, even

Colin's proper dark blue suit, looked stuffy and old-fashioned in comparison. Not until tonight had Vera ever felt how far into her thirties she really was. In Clarence House and Buck Place where only the maids and footmen were so much younger, and all the ministers were men of august years, Vera was always one of the youngest staff. Here, she was a veritable matron even if the Miss title still stubbornly clung to her.

"It's like Covent Garden exploded and all the rubble landed here," Colin drawled to Vera and Princess Margaret, nodding to the musicians, if one could call a guitarist and a reedy young man wailing away on a set of bongo drums tucked between his knobby knees musicians.

"I thought these were your kind of people." Vera was relieved to realize it wasn't just her who felt out of place.

"I cultivate legends of the stage, not this theatre flotsam."

"I think it's wonderful, and more vibrant than anything I would've seen at the ball tonight." Princess Margaret strode into the room with confidence, pausing here and there while she waited to be acknowledged by the guests, who did little but peer at her in question over the rims of their cocktail glasses before resuming their conversations.

"They have no idea who she is," Colin said to Vera as the Princess moved with less and less surety through the crowd, receiving none of the curtseys or *Ma'am*s she believed her birthright. Vera could already see the wall of defense rising up to cover Her Royal Highness as she passed men and women sitting cross-legged on velvet cushions and sidestepped a woman in a flowing patterned dress who twirled and hopped in time to the bongo drums.

It wouldn't be long before Her Royal Highness decided that it'd been a mistake to come here and then the three of them could leave.

"We'd better catch up with her before she lets them know exactly how she feels about that. I don't know about you, but I don't want this crowd turning on us," Vera warned. "They might get theatrical makeup on our clothes."

Colin snorted out a laugh and hurried with Vera to join Her Royal Highness, the two of them flanking her as they passed a clutch of older actors and actresses still garishly rouged up from their evening performance.

It wasn't until Tony noticed the Princess from where he lounged wearing a white coat with yet another paisley scarf playing the role of tie, his black patent riding boots thrown over the arms of a large wing-backed chair, that everything changed.

He rose and hurried to greet her as if the Queen had just entered the room, except Her Majesty, even when she was simply a Princess, would never have been caught dead in a place like this. Vera wondered what the Queen would think of her sister being here. Hopefully the papers wouldn't get wind of this and she'd never have to find out.

"It's wonderful to see you, Ma'am." Tony plucked the white cape with the black lining that complemented her white brocade cocktail dress off her shoulders and tossed it over the back of the chair. "We don't stand on ceremony here."

The abrupt removal of her cape startled the Princess, and Vera waited for her to snap at him for daring to touch her. Instead, his brusque handling seemed to set her at ease. "What do you and your type drink?"

Vera doubted Tony kept a ready supply of Famous Grouse whiskey and Malvern Water on hand.

"Let's find out." With a theatrical wave of his arm, Tony led them to a table covered with an assortment of cheap drinks and more expensive offerings, gifts, no doubt from clients and left untouched by most of the crowd, who favored the cheaper stuff, judging by the empty bottles on the floor.

"What can I get you, Tony?" a black-haired girl with far too much eyeliner asked from behind the bar.

"Gin for me, Tina."

Vera cringed, expecting Princess Margaret to remind them in her none-too-subtle way that she should be served first. Instead, she waited patiently to be served. The heads of a hundred country house hosts would burst if they saw this picture of deference, one she'd never, in all her years as a guest anywhere either in Britain or abroad, ever shown before.

Tina set the bottles aside and leaned on her hands, giving her customers a generous glimpse down the square neckline of her short sack dress to the black bra beneath. "Jimmy has some poppers if you really want to spice things up."

"A drink will do for now."

"And for your friend?" Tina eyed Princess Margaret with all the suspicion of a woman with a prior claim on the man showing this particular guest a little too much favor. "Well, what'll you have?"

Princess Margaret, finally remembering who she was amid all these nobodies, flashed the tart young woman an icy glare that should have set her back on her heels. "I'll have whatever he's having."

"Well, aren't you a posh one." Tina splashed the drink into a cheap glass and handed it to Her Royal Highness. "What are you? The understudy for Lady Macbeth at the Old Vic?"

"Tina, allow me introduce Her Royal Highness, Princess Margaret," Tony corrected, his Etonian air, the one he'd all but forgotten until that moment, descending over him. "This is her lady-in-waiting, the Honorable Vera Strathmore, and her friend, the Honorable Colin Tennant."

Tina threw back her long hair and laughed. "That's a good one, Tony."

"I'm very serious." He pointed to the picture of Princess Margaret hanging on the wall behind her, the one he'd taken and had released to the papers. It was mounted between portraits of other debutantes and society ladies, many of whom Vera recognized. Tina looked back and forth between it and Princess Margaret before the truth dawned on her.

"Well, I'll be gob-smacked." She slowly set down the bottle of rotgut and stared open-mouthed at Princess Margaret, Colin, and Vera, determined not to show an ounce of reverence to the royal guest and her companions. "Welcome to Rotherhithe, Your Highness. I think Tony has an old throne around here somewhere."

Vera wouldn't have been surprised if he did, given the eclectic collection of antiques and flea-market finds cluttering the tight quarters. The flat was stuffed in behind a small alley and an even tinier courtyard. Vera might almost call it charming if she didn't think there wasn't something contrived in all this bohemian chic, as if Tony had gone out of his way to make it look this odd simply to give himself some kind of Mod cache. He might play at being one of his guests, but it was clear from his fawning over the Princess and how easily he'd reverted to his Etonian roots that he had aspirations far beyond this alley bordering the Thames. How far up the social ladder his sights were set she wasn't sure, but seeing the way he flirted with the Princess made Vera wonder. That Her Royal Highness would even consider giving him a hand up was even more baffling.

"Thank you for the drinks, Tina." Tony took Princess Margaret by the elbow and led her across the room to where more photographs were pinned unceremoniously to the wall. These, unlike the regal photos behind Tina, were of common people at work or in the street in a part of London Vera didn't recognize.

"These are a study I did of the poor in the East End. What do you think, Ma'am?"

"They're marvelous," Princess Margaret offered with genuine enthusiasm. Even Vera had to admit that the photos were well done. He'd captured the essence of each individual despite their being some of the many nameless figures in London. Especially touching were his photographs of the disabled old soldiers in the park, the challenges of their troubles etched in the deep lines on their rough faces. For all his odd clothes, questionable manners, and strange tastes in décor, Tony was a talented photographer. "You really captured the truth of these people."

"How would she know?" Colin whispered in Vera's ear. "She's never ventured past Knightsbridge."

Vera nudged him in the ribs to silence him while squelching a laugh. She was glad she wasn't the only one who could see the humor and reality in this odd situation.

"For my next project, I'd like to do a perspective of orthopedic hospital patients," Mr. Armstrong-Jones explained. "What do you think, Ma'am?"

"I think that's a marvelous idea. I'm the patroness of the Princess Margaret Rose Orthopedic Hospital in Edinburgh and could secure your access to the wards whenever you wish."

"You own your own hospital? That's very benevolent of you."

"I don't own it. I lent them my name," she said with embarrassing seriousness, not catching his joke.

"I'll keep that in mind." He laid a hand on the small of her back, and rather than shake it off, she allowed him to start her toward the opposite wall, which was covered in black-and-white photos. "Let me show you some of my theatrical portraits."

"If you don't mind, I think I'll take a turn of the place," Colin said, having reached his limit of fawning over Tony's work.

"Make yourself at home."

A young woman in a jumper dress missing its underblouse, the sashes of which were the only thing maintaining her modesty, walked by and Colin followed her to chat her up.

"Care to join us?" Tony asked Vera, but, like Colin, she'd had enough of Tony for the moment. "I think I'll stay here and look at the rest of the portraits."

"Shall we, then?" His hand still firmly settled on Her Royal Highness, Tony guided her across the room. "I'd very much like to hear your thoughts on the portraits, you being a great lover of the theatre, Ma'am."

When they were gone, Vera sank into the old Victorian armchair beside the window to watch Tony show off his theatrical photographs. His presence near them attracted a number of the very subjects depicted. They crowded around Tony and the Princess, chatting and joking with her with a freedom not even the longtime Clarence House staff enjoyed. The Princess responded in kind, with no hint of the mask she usually wore when compelled to fulfill her royal duties or to hide the boredom that was the bane of many a dinner host's or hostess's—and Vera's—existence.

The Princess's enthusiasm for the party was like watching her in Monty's in the old days. Not even that odd club over the tobacconist shop had been as seedy or strange as this party, and Vera had never been as uncomfortable there as she was tonight. Vera peered out the small window overlooking the Thames. The river lapped against the wall beneath it, the high tide dark and murky like the sky with its thick cover of fall clouds. She was thirty-three and sitting in a beat-up chair in a run-down building watching an old actress with too much blue eye makeup and not enough fat beneath her wrinkled cheeks sway back and forth in time to bongo drums. This wasn't what Vera had imagined when she'd signed up for royal service, that after years of excitement and travel, of the prestige of her position and everything it had gained her, that she'd end up sitting in a questionable flat that stunk of polluted river water.

"Did you hear that god-awful upper-crust accent?" A voice caught Vera's attention. She turned to see some of the group who'd joined Tony and Princess Margaret to view the theatre pictures strolling on to their next amusement. The one who spoke was a gangly young man whose open white shirt and tight black pants made him look as if he should be swooning on stage as Hamlet, not haunting this party.

"She sounds like a mouse that's been stepped on. Squeak, squeak, squeak," his petite companion with a large necklace of paste stones and plastic flowers mimicked, her voice only an octave below Princess Margaret's in pitch.

"And those clothes. Have you ever seen someone so young dress more like your mother than your mother?" added their statuesque companion with straight hair and a somber black dress of synthetic fabric that clung to her legs with static while she walked, before the three of them melted into a larger crowd of people standing around discussing their latest performance.

"Any chance you can convince Her Royal Highness to call it a night?" Colin returned to Vera, having, for whatever reason, abandoned his more earthly pursuits. "As thrilling as this little bit of slumming is, I've had quite enough."

"Me too, but convincing her to leave will be difficult." Except this wasn't her party and no royal protocol had yet to be followed since they'd walked in through the narrow alley and side gate. Maybe a polite suggestion that they call it a night would be welcomed by Her Royal Highness for once. "Let's see what we can do."

Colin and Vera joined the Princess and Tony, who, much to their surprise, was already bidding Her Royal Highness adieu.

"I very much look forward to our tea to discuss plans for the Orthopedic Hospital shoot. It'll be a great project, Ma'am."

"I'm sure it will be. Good night, Tony."

"Good night, Ma'am." With some reluctance, Tony handed the Princess off to Colin to escort to the car.

It wasn't until Vera turned to thank him for an interesting evening that she noticed Tina watching them, her arms crossed over her chest, tapping her foot in impatience for Tony to see the stuffy royal out so she could have him alone. No wonder he'd encouraged the Princess to leave well before the party was over. Princess Margaret's willingness to do so stunned Vera, as did the nagging thought that Colin had been right and there was something brewing between the blond photographer and the Princess. That the Princess should lose her head over this nobody of no means and very slender connections when there were still one or two very respectable and unmarried sons of the nobility available, or at least a rich banker or two, boggled her as much as the continued playing of the bongo drums.

"What a marvelous party." Princess Margaret threw out her arms to the few stars visible in the courtyard above the ragged brick and stone tops of the surrounding building. "I've always loved theatre people, more so tonight when they all behaved as if I was one of them."

Vera was tempted to tell her about the snide remarks of the actors and that at no time had they considered her one of them, but she didn't wish to crush the Princess's elation. There'd been precious few instances of it in the past few years.

"You could have been one of them, Ma'am," Colin said with far more conviction than Vera could have mustered. "A famous opera singer, perhaps, or a star of the stage, even a concert pianist."

"Yes, I could have been, if so many things had been different." She tucked her arms around her against the chill night, her steps a touch heavier through the alley toward the parked car waiting for them. "Imagine the freedom I would've had if Uncle David hadn't abdicated."

Four years ago Her Royal Highness had been offered that very freedom, but she hadn't possessed the courage to let go of all her privileges to seize it any more than Vera had been able to give up hers. What might Vera have become if she had?

The image of Dominic standing across from her in the garden at Blenheim Palace wavered in the shadows around her. *You could be so much more without it—a writer, a wife, a mother. Those are worthwhile things too and something she can never give you.*

"I am more. I'm a lady-in-waiting to Her Royal Highness," she whispered to herself, shoving aside the wisp of regret clinging to her like the night mist. The urge to go home to her typewriter hit her as hard tonight as it had after the visit to Tony's studio, although to what end she didn't know. She kicked a rusty bottle cap, sending it bouncing off the brick alley wall. This was the only life that'd ever given her anything of real value, and she must remember this even if tonight, with the stink of the Thames permeating the air, her position didn't feel like the illustrious honor it'd once been.

They left the confines of the alley, and the music of the party was replaced by the gentle lap of the Thames against its banks and the puttering of a boat's engine.

They were almost to the car when the Princess jerked to a halt. "My cloak. I must have left it inside. Vera, run back and fetch it."

Not a request but an order. For the first time in a long time, Vera was tempted to refuse, but she knew better. "Yes, Ma'am."

Vera walked back down the alley to the flat. She didn't knock this time and wait for someone to answer the door but slipped inside, eager to fetch the cloak and get out of this artistic opium den as fast as she could. She spied the black-and-white cape lying over the armchair where Tony had tossed it. After years spent keeping track of Her Royal Highness's discarded outerwear, she'd honed her ability to remember where they'd been tossed. It was the most useless of the many skills she'd gained in this position. She draped it over her arm, ready to go, when Tina's voice from somewhere nearby stopped her.

"What the devil are you doing with the likes of her? It's one thing for you to chase after all those toffee-nosed girls who flock to your studio for society shots, but her? She isn't in your league."

"Careful, Tina, people will think you're jealous." Tony cornered the lithe beauty behind a cutout screen, a drink in one hand, his arm stretched past her young face to rest on the wall. With his back to Vera, he didn't notice her and she didn't move, clutching the cape tight against her while she listened.

"Do I have a reason to be jealous?" Tina pouted.

"Not at all."

Vera didn't wait to see them kiss. It wasn't any of her business what he got up to in his spare time. After what she'd seen of the two of them this evening, they deserved each other.

Tomorrow morning, after the cheap gin wore off, Princess Margaret would have very different memories and opinions about tonight. Even if these were the sort of people the Princess wanted to mingle with, it wouldn't be long before they revealed their true opinion of her and put an end to her ambitions. The Princess would rage about their lack of manners, but at least the three of them wouldn't have to visit this part of London again. It was how often Tony intended to haunt the Princess's circle, and how much further into it Her Royal Highness planned to invite him, that Vera wondered about.

"YOUR ROYAL HIGHNESS, the performance has already begun." The young usher stepped between Princess Margaret and the entrance to the royal box, as respectful and deferential as he could be while coming between the Princess and what she wanted.

Vera stood behind her with Iris, Colin, Tony, and Judy Montagu, another recent addition to what the press at one time had called the Margaret Set, back when they'd been more tolerant of royal antics than they were today. Recently, their news stories simply listed them all as friends when they didn't come up with more colorful names.

"I'm well aware that the performance has started," Princess Margaret huffed. "We were late to dinner and now we're late for here, but if you think I'm going to miss any more of it by waiting until the intermission, you are quite mistaken."

"But taking seats after the performance begins disturbs the dancers, Your Royal Highness," the man continued with admirable courage in the face of the royal fury.

"If they're well trained, and they should be, then nothing will disturb them." She stepped around him, leaving him to watch as the others filed in behind her while twisting his hands in front of him, caught between not offending the royal and enforcing the theatre rules.

Vera offered him an apologetic smile, embarrassed for the Princess, who'd long ago lost the ability to feel that particular emotion.

They took their seats as quietly as they could, but there was no mistaking the disturbance the Princess's arrival sent rippling through the audience, and, to judge by more than one performer's turned head, onstage.

"What utter tripe that man spouted. Everyone can plainly see I did not interrupt anyone," Princess Margaret said to Judy, settling herself in her seat, oblivious to the many people who watched her instead of the dancers and the faint whisper of astonishment that carried beneath the music of the orchestra.

"She certainly likes her way, doesn't she?" Tony chuckled.

He sat beside Vera, deliberately placed there so no one would make the connection between him and Her Royal Highness. The press may not fawn over her like they used to, but they still enjoyed making a great deal out of her male friendships, especially new ones. They'd have her engaged to any man brave enough to sit beside her at a royal outing. At twenty-nine years old, far past when most people thought she should have been married, who the Princess might finally settle down with was practically something one could bet on in East End bookie offices.

"Her Royal Highness is very particular about what she wants," Vera tactfully answered, hoping he'd take the hint to be more respectful where Princess Margaret and her titles were concerned. Vera wasn't sure why she bothered. Besides

Sass, he was the one person Princess Margaret wasn't willing to pull rank on. She should. The arrogant man deserved a good comeuppance.

"The debutantes who come to my studio are like that with their snobbish airs. All it takes is a strong man to put them in their place. They may not act like it, but they want a little discipline."

She didn't dare ask what kind of discipline he meant, but she could guess.

"That's a very nice tuxedo," Vera complimented, guiding the subject away from his command of social sitters. His sedate formal attire was a shocking change from his usual avant-garde suits and jumpers and not wholly unexpected, especially with him becoming a regular member of the Princess's social circle over the last couple of weeks. Rebellion was interesting, but it could carry a person only so far.

"Denman and Goddard." He flattened the crease in his lapel. "They're very talented."

"And expensive." She could see the fine weave of the wool even in the dim lights of the ballet.

"Having certain friends does open doors, doesn't it?"

"Yes, it does." Given the wardrobe at home full of things she'd received from behind many luxury doors, she couldn't hold his choice of tailors against him. "What other doors are you hoping to open?"

"As many as I can." His smug smile was the same one her aunt Augusta always wore whenever she threw a turkey-jowl arm around Vera's shoulders and introduced her to all her friends as *My favorite niece, the one who is Princess Margaret's lady-in-waiting.* Tony's arms might be a great deal slimmer, but there was no missing that desire for importance by association. "I plan to show my mother that the son she abandoned for her Irish earl and her precious heir by him will rise higher than she ever imagined or dared to do herself."

Vera fanned herself with her program, his words touching a bit too close to home. "Your mother and mine sound like they could be friends."

He tilted so close that she could smell the spicy scent of his Turkish cigarettes on his breath. "We aren't so different then, are we, Vera?"

In many ways they weren't, but she refused to admit it to herself, much less to him. "Some of us have earned our place in the royal circle. Others, not so much."

He sat straighter, his eyes as hard as Princess Margaret's could be when she was perturbed. "I assure you, I've earned my place everywhere I've ever been. I earned the ability to walk out of that Liverpool infirmary instead of dying of polio in it. I earned my reputation as a photographer, and I've earned the right to visit your precious Princess."

His vehemence didn't rattle Vera. He was mincemeat compared to dealing with Her Royal Highness. "Then let me give you a word of advice. Keep the success you've earned, and don't yearn for anything else. Then you won't have to look around someday and realize your entire life depends upon it, and it isn't even your own."

"I'll keep that in mind." He smirked, not having heard a word of Vera's warning. All he could see was the shimmering glamour and fame, not the pills, the tantrums, and the constant constraints. If he chose this path, he would have to learn about its pitfalls and traps the hard way, as Vera had.

"Are you still bringing Her Royal Highness to Rotherhithe Street tomorrow night?" He leaned past Vera, catching the inviting glance Princess Margaret threw his way.

"If that's her wish, then it's my command." Neither Vera's life nor her achievements had been her own for a very long time. Everything she had came from the Princess, except Vera had earned her place in the Princess's life through genuine care and not greed. They were friends, and sometimes they were the only people who understood each other. It was something she often forgot but needed to remember, especially at moments like this.

"Do you two mind? Some of us are here to see the performance," Colin hissed from Vera's other side. "At least what's left of it."

"Sorry, old chap." Tony fell silent, watching the ballet for a while before something more engaging caught his notice.

Down the row, Princess Margaret shifted forward to look at him again. Aware of her watching him, Tony leaned past Vera to wiggle his eyebrows at Princess Margaret. She suppressed a smile behind the back of her hand before trailing her fingers slowly down the curve of her ruby-and-pearl necklace to where it hung between her breasts just above the line of her red-tulle-and-satin strapless gown. From beside her, Vera heard Tony's breath catch when he leaned back in his chair, his hand tight on the armrest between them.

Vera sat as still as the stage scenery, horrified by this little performance and that anyone in the audience might have seen it. Her Royal Highness was mad to consider Tony for more than another dance partner or a ready supply of drinks and cigarettes during nights out. The photographer was no Sunny Blandford, whose discretion was all but assured, but a very large unknown with a taste for upward mobility. A scandal with Princess Margaret might give him the push he needed to reach the next level of notoriety, but it would do nothing for her. There'd been no admonishing phone calls from Her Majesty recently, but something like this would set the white telephone in Princess Margaret's room ringing and burn up the papers with more unflattering press. Surely Princess Margaret, who'd always been so careful with her choice of acquaintances, was smart enough to realize this, but Vera wasn't sure. Deferential men like those from the old Set hadn't exactly made Her Royal Highness savvy when dealing with the opposite sex.

And there's nothing you can do about it if she does decide to chase after him. The Princess wasn't one to listen to reason or caution. Let her and Tony enjoy each other for a little while. As Rupert had said that night at the Dorchester, the Princess was a difficult rose to cultivate, and Vera doubted Tony was really up for the challenge. That alone might be enough to knock him out of the Princess's circle long before he caused any real problems for either of them.

PRINCESS MARGARET STOOD at the Clarence House door to see off a weary Judy, Iris, and Colin. They, like Vera and the staff forced to stay up until this ungodly hour, were relieved that the Princess had finally decided to call their after-ballet cocktails quits.

Tony was the last to leave, lingering at the door while the butler collected the discarded glasses in the Garden Room and trudged off to the kitchen. Vera picked up her coat, pausing as Tony's words drifted in from the hall.

"Some old friends of mine are having a dinner party next week. I'd like you to come with me, Ma'am."

"A party like the one in Rotherhithe Street?" Princess Margaret asked with a touch too much enthusiasm.

Vera tugged on her jacket with a sigh, already thinking of ways to avoid enduring another evening near the Thames.

"No, these are respectable people. Jeremy Fry and his wife. He's heir to the Fry Chocolate fortune, Ma'am."

"Not a stuffy gathering of old men, I hope."

"No, Ma'am, I assure you, they're anything but stuffy, like me."

Silence followed this last proclamation, the quiet of a parting kiss that was more than a peck on the cheek. Then the opening and closing of the front door and whispered goodbyes before the Princess floated into the Garden Room.

"Isn't he marvelous?" The Princess leaned against the door-jamb. "There's something raw about him, and gentle at the same time."

"But is he really the right man to encourage, Ma'am?" Vera asked, regretting it the moment the words left her lips.

The Princess snapped out of her reverie to eye Vera as if she'd informed Her Royal Highness that one of the diamonds had fallen out of her Rose of York brooch. "Of course he is. Why shouldn't he be?"

"Because he isn't accustomed to all of this." She opened her arms to the room. "And the restrictions and discretion it demands."

"Good, I'm glad he's not a part of all this; I don't want him to be. There are days when I don't want to be a part of it." She sank into a Chippendale chair, her bliss from the goodnight kiss fading. "Sometimes I think I should've given it all up for Peter."

"You couldn't have left your family, Ma'am."

"No, I couldn't have." Princess Margaret picked the photo of Queen Elizabeth, Prince Philip, Prince Charles, and Princess Anne off the side table and studied it. She'd taken it at Balmoral, a family snap instead of a formal portrait, with everyone smiling and happy in the chilly Scottish air. "But if I had, I'd be a mother by now, with my own household and all the joy Lilibet has when she's with the children. Not having that is the hardest sometimes."

"I know." Vera touched her thumb to her ring finger, trying not to remember the Blenheim Palace garden and Dominic walking away. "Every time my sister and her children come down from Oxford, I have to hear about it from my mother after they leave."

"Sometimes I think it'll never happen and I'll end up rotting here like old Prince Arthur did, with everyone waiting for me to die and make way for someone else who wants to live in this awful house." Princess Margaret set the picture back on the table, the corner of it clinking against Tony's empty whiskey glass. Her Royal Highness touched the rim of it and the faint imprint of Tony's lips on the crystal. "I won't be forgotten or ignored like that, especially not when there's someone who cares about me."

She couldn't possibly mean Tony.

"No one is better than the wrong person, Ma'am," Vera dared, unwilling to watch her friend suffer more heartache than she'd already endured by setting her sights on another unsuitable man. "That's what you said to me after Billy Wallace, wasn't it?"

"It was." The memory of that brief disaster of an engagement four years earlier drew down her shoulders. "But I'm no longer sure that's true."

"Of course it is, Ma'am. I've seen Colin and Anne, and others. So have you."

She picked up the glass and cradled it in her palm. "I'm not them."

"No, Ma'am. They're allowed to suffer in private. You'd have to endure it all in the press."

"I'm tired of my love life being everyone's business." Princess Margaret jumped to her feet, making Vera shrink back into the sofa, surprised at the outburst, especially when Her Royal Highness chucked the empty tumbler on the floor. It bounced off the thick rug, not breaking before coming to rest against the curtains. "It isn't. It never should have been, and it won't be now."

Princess Margaret stormed out of the room and upstairs, leaving Vera to pick up the thrown glass with an exhausted sigh. The Princess had never been one to listen to reason, but her stubborn insistence on Tony irked Vera as much as the tired ache in her back.

It isn't your job to question her life, no matter how involved you are in it.

There could be a great deal less involvement in it if she didn't remember that. Her Lady Luella column wasn't going to keep her in the prestige to which she'd become accustomed, and there was hardly anything more glamorous or noteworthy than her lady-in-waiting position waiting in the wings to take its place. At present, it was Clarence House or nothing, the way it'd always been, a sobering fact that haunted Vera far too much lately.

Chapter Twenty-One

"*Y*es, Mayor Cartwright, Her Royal Highness is sorry to miss tomorrow's tea. She was very much looking forward to it. I'll be sure to pass on your wishes for her speedy recovery. Thank you." Vera hung up the phone and leaned back in her chair. With the Princess being so "ill" as of late, it was a wonder there weren't stories in the papers suspecting she might have cancer. What she had was a terrible case of Rotherhithe fever, one Vera and Iris worked hard to keep from the press and Buck Place. Given the frequency with which Princess Margaret's bedroom telephone rang lately, Vera guessed Her Majesty suspected something more than debilitating headaches was laying her sister up. Vera was glad she didn't have to handle those calls. It was one thing to lie to mayors and quite another to lie to an anointed Queen.

She glanced at the electric typewriter on her desk, tempted to slip a piece of paper in it and write a few lines of her next column while waiting for the Princess to come down, but she wasn't foolish enough to work here and risk anyone from the Princess to a maid seeing it and discovering her side employment. Not that Her Royal Highness was likely to notice a Lady Luella column even if Vera was careless enough to leave one lying about. The Princess never took an interest in any of the secretarial aspects of Clarence House outside of the personal letters Vera and Iris sorted and left on her dressing table each morning.

Vera's discretion proved justified when Princess Margaret entered the room as healthy as a horse, dressed in a simple tweed skirt and a plain rust-colored jumper and carrying a long scarf. "Are you ready?"

Vera closed the appointment book on her blotter. "Yes. Your schedule for tomorrow is clear."

"Good, because I intend to be out all night again." The Princess flipped the scarf up over her hair and tied it under her chin. "You don't know how wonderful it is to be with him, just the two of us and no one else, not Buck Place or Clarence House or all the press." She tugged the scarf a little lower over her forehead to further hide her features. "He cooks for me, spaghetti with cheap wine and crusty bread. Do you know what he calls me? Love."

Behind her back Vera wouldn't be surprised if he called her a sucker. If he didn't, then those catty artistic friends of his certainly did. She'd overheard enough of their snide comments at the many other get-togethers she'd been dragged to in the last few weeks to know. "That's very romantic, Ma'am."

Vera hadn't been anything but outwardly supportive of the relationship since the night of the ballet. She had no choice. The Princess had set her heart on him, and nothing else mattered. The most Vera could do was help mitigate the potential damage to the Princess and the Royal Family. It was a tiring, difficult, and narrow path to walk.

They strolled out of the house toward the side entrance of Clarence House where a nondescript black car waited.

"Tony is so talented, and I don't mean with his camera." Her Royal Highness took a second scarf out of her purse and tied it over Vera's hair, her fingers trembling with her anticipation. "Not even Peter could do the things Tony does to me, and it's heavenly."

This was far more about their relationship than Vera wished to know.

"As long as you're careful, Ma'am." That was a conundrum she wanted no part of and one she wouldn't put past Tony to land the Princess in if he thought it might benefit him.

"I'm careful, but if I were to completely forget myself, it would be with him." She bit her bottom lip, leaving a stain of lipstick on her white teeth.

They climbed into the car. Vera sat by the window while the Princess crouched on the floorboard, her knees drawn up under her chin. The car rolled through the gates of Clarence House and past the few pressmen mingling on the pavement outside. They grabbed their cameras, ready to snap a shot, but lowered them when they saw it was only a lady-in-waiting.

The ruse had worked again. Their discretion, along with Tony's surprising ability to keep a secret of this magnitude, kept the papers, society, and the court unaware of what was going on. Whatever excuses Princess Margaret gave Her Majesty for missing engagements during their phone calls or dinners probably weren't even close to the truth, keeping Her Majesty in the dark as much as everyone else. Those who did hear the rumors probably dismissed them as a gag. Few could imagine Princess Margaret being infatuated with a photographer when, at one point, she could have had the pick of almost all the sons of the nobility. Little did they know.

They rode like this for some time until they were well past any part of London that might recognize the vehicle or its passengers.

"You can come up now, Ma'am."

She hauled herself off the floor and sat beside Vera, brushing specks of dirt off her tweed skirt. "I can't believe we did it again. The press are such fools."

"They'll catch on eventually, Ma'am." Either a maid or a cook or one of Tony's friends would inform them, and then these clandestine trips to Rotherhithe would end and the real headaches would begin for everyone.

"Not if I can help it. For the first time ever I have something that's mine, not the world's or Buck Place's but mine. If I have to ride in the boot all over London to keep it that way, I will."

Vera couldn't argue with that, because it was the whole reason she'd sent off yet another Lady Luella article to Sass that morning.

The car parked in the alley leading to the flat. Vera would see Her Royal Highness into Tony's place and then, when they felt it was safe for Vera to leave, she'd return to the car and be ferried home.

The two of them hurried through the small courtyard and misty air to the flat. Princess Margaret rapped on the door, and a moment later Tony opened it. He wore his usual tight pants but with a white rolled-neck jumper that hugged his slender frame, his Denman & Goddard suits neatly tucked away.

"Tony, darling." Princess Margaret rushed into his arms, leaving it to Vera to close the door.

He took her hands from around his neck and held her out, scowling at her outfit. "What in the world are you wearing? You look like a Scottish heifer in that tweed."

"I wear this at Balmoral. And you're awful to say such a thing. You don't think I'm fat, do you?"

She didn't sound so sure, and neither did Vera, for he was awfully caustic for a man so much in love.

"Maybe a little less pasta tonight, and great deal more exercise afterward." He nuzzled her neck, making her smile return, but there was no mistaking that it wasn't as wide or sure as it had been before his nasty comment.

Vera cleared her throat to remind them that she was still

here before Tony decided to try to get Her Royal Highness out of that skirt.

"Vera, thank you for bringing her to me." He didn't take his arm out from around the Princess's waist, and she leaned into his chest. Even with his limited stature it wasn't difficult for him to be taller than Her Royal Highness. "Tell the driver he doesn't have to return for her in the morning."

"But, Tony . . ." Princess Margaret began to protest, but he laid a silencing finger on her lips.

"I'll take you home on my motorcycle. With your hair covered, and in that dreadful ensemble, no one will guess it's you on the back. They'll think you're some floozy housemaid."

She turned in his arms to press her body against his, taking hold of his shirt and pulling his face down to hers. "You can get me out of this outfit if you hate it so much."

"Oh, don't worry, I will." He gave her a long, lingering kiss before breaking from it to slide Vera a sideways frown. "You can go now, Vera."

She was about to tell him that she took her marching orders from the Princess and not him, but the way Her Royal Highness rested her head on his shoulder and allowed the command to stand told her there was no point in making a row. He was dominating Her Royal Highness like he did his socialite clients, and it was clear she wanted more of it.

Vera left the flat, struggling not to slam the door behind her in frustration. Princess Margaret had sacked footmen for forgetting to curtsey to her, but she allowed Tony's insults and commanding behavior as if he were lord of the castle. He must be great in bed for Her Royal Highness to put up with his attitude, but his sexual prowess wouldn't help him with Her Majesty's government.

It was the one bit of venom Vera delighted in as she stepped into the car. Her Majesty's government had objected to an upstanding man like Captain Townsend on the grounds of his divorce. The powers that be would howl at the idea of a man viewed by many as no better than the hired help being allowed to rest his head on a princess's pillow, and the Queen wasn't likely to intercede this time any more than she had the last. Vera didn't wish to see the Princess endure the kind of circus she'd faced with Captain Townsend, but Her Royal Highness was the one willingly going to Tony and refusing to hear any word of caution against it. She was making this bed, and she must lie in it.

At least she has someone else's bed to lie in. It was more than Vera could say.

"HAVE YOU SEEN the latest *Tatler*?" Vera's mother held up the paper the moment Vera stepped into the sitting room. Alice, with her ever-increasing family, came down from Oxford less and less frequently, leaving it to Vera to keep her parents company. She would've let a flat of her own ages ago if her position with the Royal Family didn't demand that she live a life above reproach by remaining under her parents' roof. "That Katharine Smith friend of yours is finally engaged to be married."

"I know. The wedding will be in the spring." Then there'd be one less spinster in Princess Margaret's circle of friends, and it wouldn't be Vera.

"You'd think with all the sons of lords and ministers of state your position throws in your path you'd have landed at least an MP by now."

Her mother might be much thinner and her hair grayer, but she hadn't lost her knack for finding Vera's weak spot and driving her claws straight through it. "If I married, I'd have to resign my lady-in-waiting position."

This made her mother think twice about the subject of matrimony. "At least you have that."

"At least I have that." Except tonight it seemed as petty a position as Dominic had suggested six years earlier. "If you'll excuse me, I'm going to bed."

She trudged upstairs to her chilly room and dropped her purse on the bed. She removed her earrings and slipped out of her tweed ensemble, wondering if it made her look fat too. Unlike the Princess, there was no one here to hang it up for her or to see that it was freshly laundered and returned to her wardrobe. It was up to her to put everything away, and she did, undressing and preparing for bed until she was in her nightgown and robe, clean-faced and ready to meet another night, alone.

Vera sat down at her desk, the Remington, brought out of retirement for her Lady Luella articles, before her. She rolled a clean piece of paper in the typewriter and flexed her fingers over the keys, ready to begin her next column. The work would give her something to think about other than the irritation of tonight, and fill the long hours between now and when she decided to go to sleep, but manners and how to properly steep tea didn't interest her. Ideas for the wayward countess, Lady Penrose, did.

I'd be banished from court if I published that.

If it ever saw the business side of a bookstore, almost every scene in the story could be traced back to her time with the Princess. It would, like Crawfie's tome about the Princess's childhood, make Vera dead to Princess Margaret and the entire Royal Family. It wasn't a future she wished to contemplate, except nothing else came to her tonight, not even one of the old ridiculous plots from a Rose Lavish novel. It was Lady Penrose's story and nothing else that demanded to be written.

It never has to be published. I could write it for myself, a little fun to bring back the passion, perhaps see what else it shakes loose. The rest of the world might be oblivious to it, but she'd know it existed and that she still had something of the old dreams and talent, the ones she'd let wither over the last nine years.

Setting her fingers to the keys, she began to type, the story of Lady Penrose flowing out of her until sometime after midnight, when, her back cramped from hunching over her work, she turned off the light and crawled between the covers. Lying in bed, she stared up at the plaster ceiling turned orange by the streetlight outside her window and smiled to herself. Yes, she still had the talent. Even if no one ever saw it, it was good to know it was still there in case, God forbid, she ever had to rely on it again.

Chapter Twenty-Two

A plump young maid held up an ashtray for Princess Margaret, moving it back and forth in quick jerks to try to follow the waving royal cigarette holder before the Princess cracked it against the crystal to knock off the ash. The maid was only half-successful in her efforts to catch the ash, and more gray dust flittered down to further sully the Persian rug of Jeremy and Camilla Fry's London town house.

If the young host and hostess minded that their royal guest was ruining their furnishings or frazzling the poor maid, they never said anything or appeared to notice. The two of them stood in near rapture in front of Princess Margaret while she spoke about how much she adored Bath and how she would positively love to visit their estate, Widcombe Manor, when her schedule allowed.

Vera leaned against the fireplace mantle watching the acrobatic show, glad it was the maid and not her dancing around with the ashtray. She wasn't as taken with Jeremy and Camilla

Fry as Princess Margaret and Tony. This was the first time she'd had the honor of meeting them, Iris having accompanied the Princess here the last time. The entirely too attractive couple had served an admirable enough dinner with all the required graces, but the refinement had ended at the dining room door. The after-dinner cocktails could have given Tony's Rotherhithe Street party a run for its money. Vera had already turned down two different offers for pills and had discarded her drink, afraid someone might slip something in it and leave her with a little too vivid an impression of tonight. Despite their questionable pedigrees and money, they were incredibly common people, a phrase Vera never would have imagined herself thinking, but there was no way around it. They were common.

"Smile, Vera; it's a party, not a funeral," Tony said encouragingly, slipping away from his friends and Princess Margaret to speak to Vera.

"I'm sorry, it's been a long last few nights." Lady Penrose had dominated all of her free time as of late. The countess and her story might never see the light of day, but pouring her frustrations into the spoiled heiress's tale helped Vera sleep better after depositing Her Royal Highness at Rotherhithe Street at night.

"Yes, it has." He rubbed his chin lasciviously as he admired the Princess's derriere beneath her white satin sheath gown. Did the man have no sense of decorum? "I understand Her Royal Highness is traveling with the Royal Family to Balmoral soon. I've never been to Scotland. I'd like to see it."

"I wouldn't order your stalking clothes yet. The guest list isn't up to Her Royal Highness or me. Her Majesty and the Queen Mother decide it."

"Then it's a good thing the Queen Mother likes me." Princess Margaret laughed at something Jeremy said, her white silk evening gown cut tight to her figure moving with her chest. Tony shifted closer to Vera, his arrogance sliding for a moment to reveal a humbler man. "You know, I do genuinely care for her."

If he didn't care for himself more, this would be a real comfort to Vera. "I'm happy to hear it."

"I'm glad she has someone like you to watch out for her."

If Vera had the clout to really watch out for her, then they wouldn't even be here, but the sneaking suspicion he already knew this, and hence his false gratitude, was hard to ignore.

"Why don't we join her?" Tony suggested.

"Why don't we?" It was better than standing here alone.

"Can I get you another, Tony?" Jeremy motioned to Tony's empty drink when he and Vera entered the circle of conversation.

Tony rattled the ice in his glass. "No, I need to pace myself."

"Bollocks. Have another. We can always have your usual room made up for you."

"We left it just the way you like it," Camilla purred, her blond hair done in tight curls pinned to her head that didn't move as she hung on her husband's arm, eyeing Tony as if he was one of the chocolates her husband's family produced.

"Go ahead, Tony, I don't mind," Princess Margaret encouraged.

"All right, then." Tony handed the empty glass to Jeremy, who was quick to see it filled. Vera wondered if Tony could keep up with Her Royal Highness's thirst or if they'd have to leave him behind in the care of his dear old friends and finally go home. It was near midnight, and Vera had enjoyed enough fun for one evening.

"Speaking of my favorite room, you should see it, Ma'am," Tony urged. "There's a four-post bed in there that belonged to Anne Boleyn."

"Or so the family lore says." Jeremy laughed.

"It's the most heavenly bed you can imagine too, isn't it, Tony?" Camilla lowered her pointed chin and looked at Tony through her lashes.

"Yes, it is." Tony smirked into his drink, making Vera want to stomp on his foot.

"Then let's see it," Princess Margaret suggested, either not noticing this little performance between Camilla and Tony or too blinded by her infatuation for Tony to realize what it meant. Vera guessed the latter. She could tell the Princess that Tony had just committed murder and show her his bloody hands and the knife, and it wouldn't make a bit of difference.

"You come too, Vera," Tony suggested.

Vera hoped it was because he wanted to maintain some sense of decency and decorum where Princess Margaret was concerned and not because he hoped for a ménage à trois. If it was, then he was about to be sorely disappointed.

Vera reluctantly followed Princess Margaret and Tony up the staircase to the first-floor bedroom she'd already heard too much about. It was unremarkable in that it looked like every other aristocrat's guest room in London, but Vera grudgingly had to admit the bed was impressive. With its tall posts carved with flowers and birds and the square headboard with the same matching detail, she could believe it had been owned by the notorious queen.

"It's said that Anne Boleyn conceived Queen Elizabeth I in this very bed, before she and Henry were married." Tony grasped one post and swung around to the other side, not spilling a drop of his drink.

Princess Margaret set her glass on the side table and sat down on the edge of the bed. She rested back on her hands, making her full breasts in her white satin gown stand out. Then she lowered one shoulder and the thin satin strap of her evening gown slid down to hang over her arm. "I can imagine a monarch being conceived here."

Tony stretched out across the bed as much as a man of his short stature could to lie on his side next to the Princess. "So can I."

Tony slid his arms around Her Royal Highness and gently laid her back on the embroidered cover, leaning over her to kiss the royal mouth.

Vera stared in horror at the intertwined couple in front of her, wanting to bolt but hesitating. The many nights she and Her Royal Highness had spent sneaking out of Clarence House, of Vera sitting beside Tony at the opera and ballet, would all be for nothing if Vera appeared downstairs alone. It wouldn't take much for anyone who'd been paying attention to realize what was going on up here and let it slip to the press. Except there was nothing Vera could do but leave. If she dared to interrupt them by suggesting caution, they'd turn on her like a couple of rabid wolves.

Unwilling to have her head bitten off or to remain here and learn a great deal more about the royal than she already knew, she slipped out of the room. In the hallway, the music and conversation from the sitting room filtered up the stairs while Vera stood in the semidarkness, reluctant to go down. However, she couldn't sit up here for who knew how long while Her Royal Highness and Tony messed up those carefully made bedsheets.

Making her way slowly down the stairs, Vera worked to concoct a convincing lie to explain where the Princess and Tony had gone off to. By the time she reached the bottom she wondered why she was even bothering. No matter what Vera did to try to help the Princess, Her Royal Highness either ignored it or undermined it. She was determined to have her way, no matter what the cost, and there was nothing Vera could do about it. She couldn't help her friend when she didn't wish to be helped.

"Don't be so upset about Tony and Her Royal Highness, Miss Strathmore." Jeremy staggered out of the drawing room, coming to lean against the bottom banister and much too close to Vera. "There are plenty of other people here to keep you company."

He ran his fingers down her arm, and she knocked his hand away and pushed past him. Without a thank-you to the hostess, for heaven knew which room Camilla had wandered off to and with whom, Vera collected her purse and coat and left. Her Royal Highness was occupied with a man who wasn't shy about seeing her home in the mornings. There was no reason for Vera to stay.

Outside, she rushed down the pavement toward the nearest Underground station. In this part of London, she wasn't afraid to walk alone, and she slowed her steps, thinking what a sight she'd be on the Tube in her fur coat and pearls. This hadn't exactly been on her mind when she'd chosen her attire for the evening, but she didn't hail a taxi. The bracing night air helped dissipate some of the seediness of the Frys'. It did nothing to ease the lingering doubts trailing her.

She stopped at a crossing, tucked her hand into her coat pocket, and traced her ring finger with her thumb. Her position had once been so dazzling and glamorous and, even during the difficult moments, something she was proud of. With Tony continuing to hang on, she wasn't certain when or if it ever would be again or how much lower Tony might drag the Princess and Vera before this all finally ended. She wasn't certain she wished to remain at Clarence House long enough to discover the answer.

The traffic passed, and Vera yanked her hand out of her pocket and hurried across the street toward the neon lights of the station entrance. Of course she wanted to stay and see it through. Iris wasn't fleeing, so there was no reason for Vera to abandon the Princess either. When things with Tony ended—and they would, given the temptations available in his studio—the Princess would need her friends as she had in the weeks after parting from Captain Townsend, and in time things would return to normal. It was the single comforting thought she could muster as she descended the long flight of stairs to the Underground platform.

Chapter Twenty-Three

"Tony, darling, you won't believe what I have to tell you." Princess Margaret threw open the blue Pimlico studio door, leaving Vera to close it behind her. It was past ten at night, the Princess having ended her appearance at a charity ballet performance far earlier than the organizers would have preferred, eager to be with Tony. "Mummy and Lilibet are inviting you to Balmoral. You'll simply love it."

Princess Margaret jerked to a halt, and Vera nearly ran into her before she stopped too. Across the room, Tony stood over Tina, who sat on the stool in front of a backdrop. His hand was on her shoulder, and he was bent over her as if the two of them either had been kissing or were about to. Tina's wide eyes dropped to the floor, and she pulled the loose cloak tighter around her shoulders.

Tony straightened and patted Tina on the shoulder as if he were nothing more than an indulgent headmaster and she a beloved student. "Thank you, Tina, for your help tonight. See you tomorrow."

The young woman slipped off the stool and, without a word, snatched her coat off a hook next to the door and fled into the damp night.

Tony threw out his arms to the Princess, coming forward to embrace her. "Love, I didn't expect you here this early."

"Obviously." She crossed her arms and tapped her small foot. "What the hell was that slut doing here at this time of night?"

"Tina is my assistant," he said through clenched teeth. "She isn't a slut."

The Princess glared at him. "And what exactly does she assist you with?"

"My work. Remember, I have to work for a living. I don't have the people's tax money to support me."

The Princess dropped her arms to her sides, her stony look fading to one of hurt. "I have responsibilities too."

"Yes, all those champagne bottles won't break themselves against the hulls of ships, will they?"

The Princess balled her fingers into fists at her sides. "How dare you."

"How dare you come into my studio and question me," he roared, making the Princess and Vera flinch. "I don't barge into Clarence House and ask what you've been doing all day."

"I didn't barge in; I was invited, and I'm sorry I came."

"Then leave." Tony marched up to her and raised a warning finger in front of her face. Vera waited for her to smack it to one side, but the Princess stood there, allowing him to tower over her in a rage she had only ever given and never been on the receiving end of before tonight. "If you can't have faith in me and how much I adore you, then I don't need you around."

He turned his back on her, hunching over a table littered with negative proofs to examine them through a loop.

The whir of a small fan running in the corner filled the stillness while the Princess and Vera waited for him to turn around and admit his mistake, to beg for forgiveness and to not be cast out of the royal favor. He did none of those things, continuing to work instead, his stiff shoulders the only nod to the fact that they were still here.

Finally, having endured enough of this common treatment, Princess Margaret stormed out of the studio. Vera followed, wanting to congratulate the Princess for at last displaying some royal dignity where Tony was concerned. They hurried to the car, the night darkening the black of the paint and dulling the chrome trim. The driver opened the door for the Princess, and Vera was eager for both of them to bid goodbye to this street and that photographer, but the Princess didn't get in. She looked at the flat, her lips pressed tight together in worry and, if Vera was not mistaken, regret.

"Ma'am, don't go back in there," Vera cautioned. "Don't let him treat you like this."

The Princess twisted the strap of her purse, making the leather creak. "He's sorry, I know he is; he always is after one of our rows, and so tender and gentle. You have no idea what it's like to be in his arms, to hear him tell you that you're the most important person in the world and that nothing, not your title or wealth or station, matters to him, only you."

Vera doubted very much that her title and station meant as little to him as he claimed. "You saw yourself what was going on, Ma'am."

"Nothing was going on. They were simply working together."

"This late at night?" She couldn't be this blind or in love with him to accept that paltry excuse.

"That tart means nothing to him, but I do, and she can't keep Tony happy the way I can or give him what I can give him."

"Which is far more than he deserves for behaving like this."

"How dare you talk about him like that." The Princess turned on Vera with a fury that should have been lobbed at Tony. "You have no right."

"I'm trying to help you."

"It isn't your place to help me or tell me what to do," the Princess screeched, stepping toe to toe with Vera, who looked down on her. She couldn't avoid it. She was taller than Her Royal Highness, but the ice in the woman's eyes made Vera cower. The Princess glared at her as if she were nothing more than an impertinent maid and not a friend who cared about her. "I'll decide what's best for me, Miss Strathmore, not you. Do you understand?"

"Y-yes, Ma'am."

"Good, because I don't need this kind of impertinence in my life." Princess Margaret settled her shoulders and, with an imperious raise of her chin, turned on her heel and marched across the street, away from Vera and back into the arms of her cheating lover.

Vera sagged against the car, struggling to calm the tremors racing through her. She'd overstepped her place and she shouldn't have, even if it'd been done with the best intentions.

"Miss Strathmore?" The driver approached, having had the tact to wander off to the hood during her and Princess Margaret's heated discussion.

"I'm fine; please take me home." She dropped onto the back seat, grateful when he closed the door, but the solitude of the dark car wasn't deep enough. She wanted to be in her bedroom where the tears of fear and frustration stinging her eyes could fall without anyone, especially her mother, seeing them. She refused to be humiliated like that, not when a greater humiliation might be waiting for her tomorrow.

Vera tugged a handkerchief out of her purse and dabbed her eyes. Heaven only knew what she'd find when she arrived at Clarence House in the morning. It could be her things packed up and waiting for her on the front stoop. If Her Royal Highness decided to cast her out like she had Caroline, Vera would have nothing because the last nine years of her life had been nothing but the Princess's, a mistake Sass and even Dominic had warned her about making. She hadn't listened to them any more than the Princess had Vera's cautions about Tony. Vera twisted the linen between her fingers, winding it tight. Not since her first days with the Set had she been this nervous and unsure of her place with the Princess and her future. She wasn't ready to quit Clarence House, but the fear she could be invited to leave long before she was ready to do so was, for the first time ever, too threatening to ignore. Tonight, the Princess had chosen that philandering liar over her friend. It wasn't difficult to imagine that she might do it again.

"WHAT DO YOU think of the story?" Vera sat across from Rupert over tea at Harrods. He was the only person besides Sass she trusted enough to send a copy of the manuscript to for an opinion. After the incident in Pimlico Road, burying the story in the back of her wardrobe seemed as big a folly as having waited this long to write it.

"It's quite a tale you've penned, and you've certainly given Her Royal Highness, I mean Lady Penrose, a happier ending than she's likely to write for herself."

"We'll see what sort of ending the Princess gets." It was the ending Vera needed to craft for herself that had consumed her over the last two weeks. Things with Her Royal Highness had returned to normal since her outburst in Pimlico Road, but there was no mistaking the tension lingering in every encounter with the Princess, forcing Vera to walk on eggshells more with Her Royal Highness than she'd ever had to do with her mother. One would think a woman so in love would be a great deal happier.

"Lily not as gilded as it used to be?"

"Quite tarnished as of late." The Princess was spending the

weekend at Widcombe Manor, Jeremy and Camilla Fry's estate near Bath. Tony had assured Her Royal Highness that the staff there could be trusted to keep a secret. Not that it might matter, for the trip to Balmoral was fast approaching. So far, the press hadn't gotten wind of the extra visitor and why he'd been invited. With any luck, it'd stay that way and everyone, including Vera, could enjoy the Scottish holiday in peace.

"Then publish the book and see what happens. With your résumé, publishers will fall all over themselves to get a hold of this. That alone could make it and you a success."

"And if it isn't, then what? I won't go back to being the spinster daughter of an inconsequential lord, banished to her room to peck out a meager living on her typewriter." It was the argument that had been going around and around in her head for the past two weeks. She couldn't throw away everything she'd gained as a lady-in-waiting on something as unlikely and uncertain as literary success. It seemed as foolish an idea as Princess Margaret thinking her love life wasn't fodder for the entire world or that her relationship with Tony wouldn't end in disaster. However, if Vera continued to mind her tongue in the royal presence, perhaps the lingering unease from the other night would pass and with it the doubts about her future that'd driven her to mail Rupert the manuscript and to this tea today.

"Don't be so hard on yourself, old girl; you have more strength and resources than you give yourself credit for. You must have, to have endured Her Royal Highness for this long, and if this manuscript is any measure of your talent, you're a damn fine writer. Maybe it's time to show the world a little of that and finally get out from under the royal thumb."

He slid the manuscript across the table to her, and she stared at the white pages and the black typewritten title on the front. It seemed such a small thing to hang her entire future on. There was too much of her experiences with the Princess in the story, and even though Vera had hidden the reality behind a fictional façade that no one outside of royal service or circles was likely to recognize, the Princess would see it if she ever read it. Her Royal Highness would realize at once that the friendship and faith she'd placed in Vera for all these years had been betrayed, even if Vera was no longer sure how much friendship and faith Princess Margaret still placed in her.

Chapter Twenty-Four

Balmoral, Scotland

$\mathcal{I}$ can't believe the Royal Family allowed that one here," Ruby said from beside Vera. They stood at the window in Balmoral Castle's tartan-embellished drawing room, watching Tony stroll about the grounds, taking pictures of the countryside and the old castle.

The rest of the men had set off for their morning stalking, but Tony's inability to pull himself out of bed before ten o'clock meant he'd been left behind. He and Princess Margaret had made a late night of it, with her slipping back to her room long before the maid had arrived with the breakfast tray.

"At least he had the sense to dress properly." His pristine stalking suit must have kept Denman & Goddard busy.

"The clothes I'll probably have to see to the laundering of if he ever deigns to get them dirty. He's so high and mighty with the servants, you'd think it was him who was married to the Earl of Rosse and not his mother," Ruby sniffed before looking around to make sure they were alone. "A friend of mine who works for those Fry friends of his told me there are rumors that Mrs. Fry's daughter isn't her husband's but Mr. Armstrong-Jones's."

"Judging from what I've seen of those two and Tony, I wouldn't be surprised."

"I'd tell the Queen Mother that little bit of gossip if I thought it would make a difference, but it won't. She's as smitten with that man as her daughter. If Princess Margaret hadn't pulled him away last night, the Queen Mother would have danced with him until he dropped."

"Which would be sooner rather than later, given his weak build."

Ruby threw back her head and laughed, wiping tears from her eyes before she sobered. "Well, I can't stand here all day gabbing. I've got to attend to Her Royal Highness's things before *he* returns to the house and has me scraping mud off his boots."

"And I have the Princess's schedule to review before she rises."

Vera strolled through the arched hall of the old Scottish castle, climbing the curving staircase with its plush red rug and gray stone walls. At the top, a long row of mounted stag antlers hung above the level of the doors, adding to the symmetry of the hall. The chill in the air was more pervasive here than in any of the other royal residences. Thankfully there was an electric heater in the Princess's sitting room or Vera's fingers would turn to ice trying to respond to Her Royal Highness's correspondence.

It wasn't warmth that greeted Vera when she opened the sitting room door but Princess Margaret, standing at the window with the view of the front lawn.

"Good morning, Ma'am?" Vera greeted as brightly as she could through her apprehension. It wasn't like the Princess to be up and dressed before eleven.

"He's engaged to be married," the Princess replied in a soft voice thick with tears.

"Who, Ma'am?" God willing it was Tony and the man would be packed off at once.

She turned and held up the letter she had clenched in her hand. "Peter. He's marrying some Belgian tart who's ten years younger than me. He wished to tell me about it before it appeared in the newspapers, to spare me the difficulty of reading about it." She threw the letter on the floor and stomped it with the heel of her riding boot. "He'll go to the altar ahead of me, and the whole world will know he can catch a wife at near fifty while I'm still a spinster at almost thirty, and that he no longer loves me."

Princess Margaret slouched on the sofa, and fat tears rolled down her cheeks.

"I'm so sorry, Ma'am." Vera sat beside her and placed her arm around the Princess's shaking shoulders, allowing her to cry into her thick wool jumper.

"He loved me, Vera, he did," the Princess said, gasping between sobs.

"He did, Ma'am. He did."

"He said he always would."

"And he will, Ma'am, in his own way, like you will."

The Princess jerked away from Vera, facing her with red-rimmed eyes. "Then how can he marry someone else?"

Vera said nothing while Her Royal Highness blotted the tears from her cheeks. They both knew the answer.

Outside, the crack of gunfire in the distance echoed across the countryside and through the room.

Princess Margaret leaned back against the sofa and pressed her palms to her forehead. "The press will eat this up when they hear about it."

"They will, Ma'am." Vera could already picture them outside Clarence House, stalking everyone who went in and out, especially the Princess, giving her no peace to deal with it as she deserved.

Princess Margaret rose and went to the bar cart beside the fireplace. She poured herself a stiff glass of whiskey, forgoing her Malvern Water. "I can't let him show me up in front of the entire world."

"He isn't showing you up, Ma'am, but moving on, as you have."

"I have, haven't I?" She drained the glass and then poured herself some more, not drinking it but carrying it with her to the window to stare out at the leafless trees and brown hills surrounding the castle.

Vera came to stand beside her, the scenery still except for the lone figure of Tony moving across the grounds, pausing here and there to raise the camera up to his eye and take a picture. The Princess watched him while she sipped her drink.

"I won't allow anyone to pity me because Captain Townsend is getting married before I am." She drank down the whiskey and clutched the empty glass against her chest. "I'll prove to Peter and everyone that I'm as over him as he's over me and that I can get married too."

"Ma'am?" Vera glanced back and forth between Tony and the Princess, the same icy dread that had filled her when Princess Margaret had vowed to force the issue of Captain Townsend washing over her again.

"Ask Tony to come see me."

Vera shifted in her shoes. "Ma'am, you've had a great shock; perhaps it's best to be alone and give yourself some time to take in what's happened."

"I've waited long enough, and look what it's gotten me. I won't wait any longer. Go fetch Tony."

Vera could barely breathe as she remained where she was. "I can't, Ma'am."

The Princess turned to her, her eyes narrowed. "What did you say?"

Vera opened and closed her hands at her sides. She should

do what she was told. It wasn't any of her business who the Princess saw or didn't see, except she knew why she was summoning him, what she intended, and Vera couldn't let it happen. "You can't marry him, Ma'am."

The Princess's glare turned to acid. "Who are you to tell me what I can and cannot do?"

Everything in Vera warned her to stop and keep her reservations to herself, but she couldn't. She hadn't picked the Princess off the bathroom floor to watch her throw her life away on a two-bit photographer. "I'm your friend, and I care about you, Ma'am. I've seen the way he treats you, and he isn't faithful. You saw him with that Tina woman; we both did."

"I told you that was nothing." She turned the glass in her hands. "You don't know him. Once we're married, he'll be faithful."

"A wedding ceremony won't curb Tony's appetites. It didn't curb Colin's or Lord Beaufort's."

"Tony isn't like them." She stalked to the bar cart and snatched the crystal stopper off the decanter of whiskey and tipped another two fingers full in, her hand shaking so hard she spilled more than she poured.

"He's worse. There are rumors that Camilla Fry's daughter isn't her husband's but Tony's."

"That's a vicious rumor spread by people who are jealous of him and his talent."

"But what if it's true?"

"You want them to be true because you hate him." Princess

Margaret slammed the stopper in the decanter so hard a chip broke off and plinked against the tabletop. "You've always hated him and tried to make me stop loving him despite how much he loves me."

"He loves what you can give him, and it isn't your heart but this." She threw her arms out to the castle and the antiques filling the room. "He's a social climber, and he's using you to climb as high as he can."

"It isn't like that." She marched up to Vera, who held her ground in the face of the royal fury, unwilling to be goaded into losing her temper or raising her voice.

"It is, Ma'am, and if you marry him, someday he'll humiliate you in more public ways than Captain Townsend's marriage ever could."

"I won't end up a spinster like you," she hissed, with enough venom to wound Vera, but Vera refused to back down. She couldn't, not this time.

"Better a spinster than a miserable, ignored, and humiliated wife."

The Princess hauled back her hand and cracked her palm against Vera's cheek. "I'm not asking your permission to marry him. I'm telling you I will."

Vera staggered back, clutching her stinging face.

"Go fetch him like I ordered!" the Princess yelled.

Tears of pain and shock blurred Vera's eyes as she backed away from the Princess. She hit the cool and smooth wood door and reached behind her for the knob, her fingers shaking while she turned it. She all but fell into the hallway when it swung open, the cold air biting her smarting cheek.

Her legs barely supported her as she rushed down the hall toward her room, praying she wouldn't run into a footman or butler or, heaven forbid, Her Majesty. She didn't want to explain to anyone the red handprint on her face or the tears spilling from her eyes. Thankfully, there was no one about, and she locked herself in her room, wetted a handkerchief, and pressed it to her face. She could see the outline of the Princess's fingers on her skin before more tears blurred her reflection and she sank down onto the floor, her fist in her mouth to muffle the sobs.

THE SUN FADED from the room, draining the green and red out of the tartan rugs and pillowcases and turning the heavy, dark-stained furniture a deeper shade of brown. Vera lay on the old bed curled on her side, the tears having faded hours ago but not the ball of worry hollowing out her insides.

At the chest of drawers, the footman packed up the last of her things, carefully folding each item of clothing in tissue paper before he set it neatly in Vera's suitcase. At least they weren't throwing her wardrobe out on the lawn for her to collect. It was the single thing to be grateful for.

"I booked you a sleeper berth on the overnight train to London, and Perkins has called the car to take you to the station," Iris said from the foot of the bed, the butler standing watch over them by the door to ensure Vera didn't make off with some Scottish souvenir besides the welt on her cheek. "I'll see to it your personal things at Clarence House are packed up and returned to you."

Vera hauled herself off the bed, trying to conjure up her shattered dignity. She'd need it when she donned her coat and walked to the car. By now the story must have flown through the house, and even if the servants and staff weren't standing at the door when she left, they'd be watching from the windows. "Thank you, Iris."

"I'm so sorry, Vera." Iris enveloped her in a hug that threatened to start the tears she'd worked so hard to stop.

"I don't suppose she'll see me?"

Iris shook her head. They both knew that wouldn't happen. After nearly ten years of service, she was being dismissed like a gardener or a scullery maid. All that was left to do was to tell everyone—her friends, her parents, the entire world—that she was no one again.

THE DARK OUTSIDE the train windows obscured everything except the lights of villages and cars and stations the train passed as Scotland slipped farther and farther behind her. Vera said nothing when the porter came to unlock her bed, leaving the white sheets and taut blanket undisturbed, unable to rise from her seat at the window and the darkness beyond.

Vera dozed off sometime after the sky began to turn a pale shade of gray blue, jerking awake when the train pulled into King's Cross station.

She stood outside the station, her smaller bags stacked beside her, the larger ones on a wheeled cart where the porter had left them while he hailed a cab. All around her, a mass of people rushed to catch trains and taxis or walk to work. Vera had nowhere to go but home.

"Miss Strathmore?" Lady Riverdowne approached, followed by a porter with a cartful of the lady's monogrammed luggage. She wore a traveling suit of gray wool, her smile much too fawning for Vera to endure this morning. "I'm so glad I ran into you. We must have the Princess at the Museum Ball. She's the biggest draw."

"You'll have to contact Miss Peake about the Princess's schedule. I'm no longer with Her Royal Highness." There wasn't a lie Vera could tell about why that would cover the crack in her voice or the circles under her eyes or make Lady Riverdowne not guess that the separation hadn't been voluntary.

"I see." Lady Riverdowne's smile vanished, as did the supplicant bend in her back. She stood up straight, the slight twitch of a gloating smile drawing up the corners of her lips. "Well, then, I'll contact Miss Peake."

With a flick of her fingers to the porter, she left to catch her train, having no further need for Vera.

VERA STOOD ON the pavement in front of her parents' Mayfair town house, staring up at the stony front of it turned black by decades of coal dust. She didn't remember it being anything but dark and sooty, like the rest of the block. Behind her the cabbie unloaded her suitcases from the boot of the cab.

No one rushed out of the house to greet Vera, but the flick of a curtain at her mother's window told her she was watching and wondering why Vera was back so soon. Her not coming to the door to find out made it clear she'd guessed why as easily as Lady Riverdowne had, as everyone would once they called Clarence House. If they didn't, then the notice in the *Court Circular* that Vera was no longer assisting the Princess would leave them in no doubt of Vera's changed status. It'd make for a great deal of whispering at Lady Mattlemore's annual Christmas ball and every other family and social event between now and the New Year.

The cabbie slammed the boot closed, startling Vera. "The fare, please?"

Vera looked at his wide outstretched hand with the deep lines and then back at the cold house. Her chest tightened, and she wanted to sit down on her suitcase and cry. This was everything she'd worked so hard to escape, and yet here she was, with nothing more to look forward to than her typewriter and whatever dreams she could concoct to carry her through this misery. "I can't go inside."

"Do what you like, luv, but pay me so I can get on with me day."

There isn't anywhere else to go.

She still couldn't reach for her wallet or do more than stand on the pavement, as lost as she'd been the day the soldier had handed her the telegram about Henry.

What am I going to do?

There was little to do but go inside. In the quiet of her room, she could decide how to face everyone, including her mother. She took out her wallet, turning to pay the cabbie, when her toe hit the edge of one of the suitcases surrounding her. They were full of dresses, clothes, everything she'd needed for Balmoral.

Everything she'd need to live anywhere but here.

"Miss?" the cabbie urged, nodding at the money clasped in her fingers.

I don't have to go inside. Rupert was right; she had resources and connections, friends who'd gladly give her the time she needed to get back on her feet, but to what end? She'd done nothing for the past nine years except what was required of her at Clarence House. It left her fit for no other position than that of private secretary, indebted to yet another person for her place and her worth. She had nothing of her own.

Except my writing. And New York.

The idea crept over her like the morning sun rising above the tops of the roofs across the street. With her savings, she could go to New York. Sass was there, and she could help her. She even had a copy of the manuscript, and Alice could be counted on to send Vera the rest of her things. There was nothing stopping her from going and no reason to stay here and endure the nasty remarks and humiliation. There was no reason to be that Vera Strathmore again.

She pressed the money into the cabbie's hand, picked up her two smallest bags, and climbed into the back seat, settling herself in despite the cabbie's astonishment. "Take me back to the station."

She'd book passage on the next ship to New York and a new life, whatever that might be.

Chapter Twenty-Five

May 6, 1960

"I can turn this one off, if you want." Sass reached for the knob on the television set, one of three arranged in various places in her New York apartment living room for her royal wedding viewing party.

"No, leave it on." Vera sat on Sass's white sofa, watching Princess Margaret come down the aisle of Westminster Abbey on Prince Philip's arm. Sass sat beside Vera as the camera caught a glimpse of Iris's face in the crowd when the Princess passed the pews full of guests. "I'd be sitting there if things had been different."

"Instead you're here with your books in stores and gobs of adoring fans." Sass waved her hand at the room behind them and the revelers, most of whom had also been at the party Sass had thrown last month to celebrate the release of Vera's Lady Penrose novel. Some of the people Vera worked with at *Lady's Journal*, where she wrote a weekly, syndicated Lady Luella column. Others were from Vera's publisher's office; the rest were Sass's New York friends, a circle that had widened to include Vera since her arrival seven months earlier.

"Thanks to you." Vera tilted her glass of champagne at her friend. Sass had shown the Lady Penrose novel to a publisher friend before Vera had even disembarked in New York. He'd snapped it up, rushing the book into print once the Princess's engagement was announced, eager to capitalize on royal wedding fever. The book had been an instant hit.

"It looks like you aren't the only one not wild about Tony and the Princess." Sass pointed to the TV and the cutaway to Queen Elizabeth. She sat in the front row of Westminster Abbey, the disapproving line of her lips a sharp contrast to the bright turquoise of her taffeta dress. It was a rare moment of unguarded expression from a woman renowned for her discretion. "If she doesn't like him, why didn't she put a stop to it?"

"She couldn't, not after last time." Apparently, the Buck Place officials hadn't insisted Princess Margaret give Tony up either. Maybe they hoped Princess Margaret's marriage to someone, anyone, might settle her down and make their lives and that of the Monarch's easier. Prince Philip gave the bride's hand to Tony, who wore a black morning suit and seemed to tower over the royal, who, even while wearing the high Poltimore tiara, wasn't very tall. She must be in flats for Tony to appear so tall, the first of what Vera imagined would be many concessions to his ego but it couldn't last. She wasn't likely to ever forget that she was royal or allow him to forget it for too long. What Vera wouldn't give to be there when they finally had that conversation.

"Do you miss it?" Sass asked.

"Not anymore." She raised her champagne glass to clink it against Sass's. "Here's to my new life."

"To your new life," a familiar male voice offered from behind them, leaning over to add his flute to theirs.

Vera turned and gripped the back of the sofa hard. Dominic stood over her, a dark blue suit covering his still impressive frame. The accents and music surrounding them had changed, but he hadn't, except for the slight lines at the corners of his eyes that deepened with his smile. It was the same amused one she'd noticed at the Dorchester all those nights ago, and to her shame, it made her heart flutter.

She picked at a loose thread on the cushion, surprised he'd bothered to approach her. She hadn't exactly left him with a reason to think well of her six years ago.

What's he even doing here? She wondered why Sass had bothered to invite him since he was married. Princess Margaret might flirt with other women's husbands, but Vera didn't.

"Come and join us, Doc." Sass slid over on the sofa and patted the cushion between her and Vera.

He didn't mumble any excuses about needing to be somewhere else but took the offered seat, settling in between the two women with an ease Vera admired.

"What are you doing here in the slums of New York instead

of the wide-open spaces of Arizona?" Vera asked, tracing the etching on the crystal flute with her finger.

"Despite my better judgment, a colleague of mine talked me into accepting a year teaching tenure at Columbia University Medical School."

"Is your wife enjoying New York?" *I never should have turned him down.* Three years in royal service should have been enough, but she'd been greedy, and she'd paid the price. He was married, and in the end, all her sacrifices for the Princess hadn't been worth it.

He held up his bare ring finger. "We divorced two years ago. She was more in love with the idea of being a doctor's wife than she was in love with me."

Vera glanced over his shoulder at Sass, who smiled like the devil. This was a bit of gossip Sass had failed to tell her.

"I'm very sorry to hear that," Vera offered, far more excited than she should be.

"Are you?" he pressed, with a roguish smile that turned Vera quite serious.

"I am. I know what it's like to be disappointed by someone you care about who you thought cared about you."

He nodded, then leaned over and picked a copy of the Lady Penrose novel off the coffee table. "A little revenge, then?"

"A little something of my own that isn't anyone else's." For the first time in ten years, her life was her own. It was hers when she went home alone at night to her Fifth Avenue apartment, one loaned to her by a friend of Sass's who'd been dazzled by the tenuous royal connection. It was hers when she wrote her columns or attended an art opening or the theatre without having to trail behind a petulant Princess or carry flowers. It was hers when people's eyes lit up on learning that she'd once worked for royalty and they gushed over her when they discovered she'd written their new favorite novel.

"And what does your husband think of it all?"

"I'm not married." She held up her left hand with the bare ring finger, thinking Sass had been quite lax with her gossip lately.

"I'm glad to hear it."

"Are you?" After her rejection she was surprised he wanted anything to do with her at all.

"It means there's no one to object to my asking you to dinner." He shifted closer to her, his knee touching hers.

Vera tilted closer and rested her elbow on the back of the sofa, the warm scent of him as heady as the champagne and his tempting smile. "No one at all."

Epilogue

January 2002

Vera leaned against the horse gate in her old jeans and plaid shirt, watching John, her grandson, on the back of the brown American Quarter Horse. He rode while Dominic held the tether, calling out riding instructions to the boy, who listened and obeyed with the seriousness of his father, a natural-born rider.

"Mom." Vera's daughter Susan joined her at the horse fence, careful not to lean on it and get her dress dirty. She wasn't at all like her brother or elder sister. "There's some woman on the phone with an accent like yours who says she's calling from Clarence House. I thought it was Julia pulling my leg, but I think she's for real, and she wants to speak to you."

Vera's hands tightened on the rough metal of the corral. She hadn't heard anything from anyone royal in almost forty years. She hadn't even received a Christmas card or a thank-you for the cards of congratulations she'd sent for the birth of

Princess Margaret's two children. After that day at Balmoral, it was as if Vera had never existed or been a part of Her Royal Highness's life, but she'd very much been a part of Vera's, one she'd never forgotten.

"I'm sure it's real. Keep an eye on your son and make sure your father doesn't have him jumping fences. He isn't ready yet." Vera strolled toward the one-story ranch built on the rise above green fields set against the backdrop of the red hills. It was where Dominic and Vera had raised their three children and Vera had written her numerous books about Lady Penrose and her family and the foibles of the British upper class, ones that had led her to be dubbed the American Nancy Mitford. It'd been a long time since her last release, the quiet rhythm of her day-to-day life more of a draw than fame or stories of a long-dead world.

She went to the phone in her office, the covers of her novels framed on the walls between the windows. Out of them was a view of the horse lake at the bottom of the rise where the grass gave way to low scrub and large rocks. She hesitated a moment before she set the receiver against her ear to hear a little something of the old life at Clarence House.

THE LONDON SKY was as gray and cold as it had been fifteen years earlier at her mother's funeral. Alice and her children had been there, as had Vera and her children, and the sisters had shared stories of growing up in Parkston Hall and the town house in Mayfair. Both houses had been sold shortly after her father's passing in 1972. Vera had even taken the children around London and introduced them to Colin and a few of her other titled friends from the old Set who were still here. Later, she'd enjoyed a quiet tea with Colin, Caroline, Sunny, and Imogene, all of them reminiscing about their days in the Margaret Set, when the Princess had been at the height of her popularity before the scandals of infidelity and divorce had marred her.

Vera entered the redbrick front of King Edward VII's Hospital with the same hesitation and anxiety she'd carried with her into the Savoy in 1949. She'd longed so much to be a part of the Princess's Set and she had been, and now Her Royal Highness, after years of silence, had called her back. The old desire to be liked and accepted filled her as she followed the nurse down the neon-lit hall to the private room. She wished she could call Sass and get her take on this long-delayed summons, but Sass had passed from cancer in 1996. There wasn't a day that went by that Vera didn't miss her spunk and spirit.

"Ma'am, there's a Mrs. Vera Reynolds to see you," the nurse cheerily announced as she led Vera into the room.

"So, you finally married your doctor, Mrs. Lavish," Princess Margaret greeted in a high but weak voice, the old cut-glass accent roughened by thousands of cigarettes and the aftereffects of her stroke. She sat up in bed, her dark hair gray, her face thin and gaunt, the left side of it sagging and a sharp contrast to the right. The white pillows and sheets almost engulfed her, along with the machines and tubes sustaining her. The sight brought a mist of tears to Vera's eyes, but she refused to cry. The Princess needed cheer, not Vera wailing over her.

"I did, Ma'am." Vera stepped up to the foot of the bed, easily falling into the old posture of the obedient and respectful lady-in-waiting.

"And did he cheat on you with a bunch of floozies the way mine did?"

Vera smiled. Her Royal Highness's sense of humor hadn't faded with her health. "No, Ma'am, he didn't."

She didn't congratulate Vera on her marital success but frowned. "They say I've had a stroke and if I have another it'll be the end of me. I think they're hoping for it, to finally get me off the Civil List. I'm surprised they even remember I'm still alive and drawing my income."

"They've never been able to ignore you, Ma'am."

"I made damn sure they couldn't. I never let them or anyone tell me what to do, except where Peter was concerned." She sighed, her weak chest rising and falling beneath the teal hospital gown. "I'd trade my diamonds for a cigarette."

Vera reached into her purse and pulled out a package of Gigantes she'd purchased at a tobacconist shop on the way to the hospital. She removed the cellophane wrapper and handed it to the Princess, the ability to anticipate Her Royal Highness's needs never having left her, even after all these years.

The Princess didn't thank her, but the delight in her blue eyes when she put one in the good side of her mouth and allowed Vera to light it was thanks enough. The Princess struggled to close her lips around the base, revealing the depths of her weakness but also her strength. She refused to be denied her pleasure, even if it took some time to bring her lips together enough to inhale. Pure bliss came over her when she did before she exhaled. "I don't suppose you brought anything to drink?"

"As a matter of fact, I did." Vera took the small bottle of whiskey she'd been given on the plane and held it up. "It isn't Famous Grouse, I'm afraid."

"I don't care what it is." She snatched the plastic cup from off the bedside table and held it up. "Pour."

Vera twisted off the cap and drained the small bottle into the cup. The Princess held it up, whiskey in one hand, the cigarette in the other, and nodded to Vera. "Cheers."

She drank with a rapture equal to the one she'd shown with the cigarette, sinking back into the pillows to enjoy the forbidden luxuries. "It reminds me of when we used to get drinks at the 400 Club after a Royal Command Film Performance or some other dry event. Nothing ever tasted as good as that first whiskey after all the hot air of those stuffy officials."

"We could work up quite a thirst, couldn't we, Ma'am?"

"We sure could." She enjoyed the cigarette, letting out the smoke slowly to savor it before offering Vera a lopsided smile. "We had fun back then, didn't we, Mrs. Lavish?"

"We did, Ma'am."

"I was more popular than Princess Diana before she got herself killed in Paris."

"You were the darling of the press, Ma'am." Vera's voice cracked to see Her Royal Highness so old and frail now.

The Princess took a deep pull of whiskey, working hard to drink it so it didn't dribble down her chin. "I read that book of yours."

"What did you think, Ma'am?"

"You did a fine job capturing all those marvelous times." The Princess peered wistfully off somewhere over Vera's shoulder before coming back to the room to finish the drink and tap off the ash into the empty cup. Then her faded and tired blue eyes met Vera's. "You were one of my best friends, Mrs. Lavish, one of the only true ones I ever had."

Vera swallowed hard past the knot in her throat. "I did my best, Ma'am."

"Yes, you did." The Princess finished the cigarette and then crushed it out, hiding it, the cup of ashes, and the package beneath the sheets before the chubby nurse in the sensible shoes entered the room.

The nurse's nose twitched at the lingering smoke aroma, and she smothered a mischievous smile but said nothing as she approached Her Royal Highness. "Viscount Linley and Lady Sarah are here to see you, Ma'am."

"I'll go so your children can visit with you, Ma'am." Her

Royal Highness needed to spend time with them more than she did with Vera.

"Thank you for coming, Mrs. Lavish, and for everything."

"It was my pleasure, Ma'am."

Vera hesitated. This would likely be the last time she'd see Her Royal Highness. There were no words she could think of to tell her, no proper goodbye that she could offer. Simply a respectful curtsey, three steps back, and then out the door.

In the hallway, she passed Viscount Linley and Lady Sarah, echoes of their parents stamped on their features. They smiled and nodded at Vera, and she wondered if Princess Margaret would tell them who she was or if they already knew. It didn't matter. Vera was no more a part of their lives than the Princess was her children's, simply a story to tell after dinner or during long car rides, a life that had ended long ago and had given her everything she had today.

About the author

About the book

Insights,
Interviews
& More . . .

Meet Georgie Blalock

Courtesy of the author

GEORGIE BLALOCK is an amateur historian and movie buff who loves combining her different passions through historical fiction and a healthy dose of period films. When not writing, she can be found prowling the nonfiction history section of the library or the British film listings on Netflix. Blalock writes historical romance under the name Georgie Lee.

Behind the Book

Vera Strathmore, and her position
as Princess Margaret's second lady-in-
waiting, is a creation of my imagination.
Vera was a way for me to enter into and
explore the life of Princess Margaret, a
woman many people refer to as a tragic
princess. I did a great deal of research
into the real Princess Margaret in order
to create my fictionalized version of her,
and through it I came to think of her not
as tragic but as someone whose life was
forever marred by her status as second
best. It was a position that was foisted on
her when her uncle, King Edward VIII,
abdicated, changing her from the adored
younger daughter of the Duke of York
to the spare princess with no clear place
or role in life and with very few options
for gaining one. It was an impossible
situation to rise above, one filled with
both frustration and privilege. Much
of her outlandish behavior was a desire
to escape the confines of her restrictive
life, but at the same time, a sense
of respect for the monarchy and the
Royal Family left her beholden to it.
In addition to these challenges, many
of her struggles to define herself and
her place in the world played out in the
public eye. ▶

Behind the Book *(continued)*

Princess Margaret was the Princess Diana of her era, and the public wanted to know all about her. That made it difficult for Princess Margaret to find friends and confidants who could be trusted to resist the temptation to profit from their royal connection. One person who failed to do this was the Princess's childhood governess Marion "Crawfie" Crawford. After leaving royal service because of her own marriage, Crawfie published a glowing account of Princess Margaret's and Queen Elizabeth's childhood. Despite her favorable depiction of the royal children, the sense of betrayal was enough to see her written off by the Royal Family. Lesser people close to the Princess would also write tell-all novels, including a footman and a driver. There was money to be gained by giving the world an intimate look at the Princess's private life, and Princess Margaret could never be sure who would avoid the temptation and who wouldn't. Even Captain Townsend would write about her in his autobiography, published in 1978. However, during her later years, the Princess was not above feeding stories to the press about herself in an effort to remain in the limelight.

The events portrayed in this novel are based on real ones that took place in Princess Margaret's life. However, timelines and certain situations that lasted for months or years, such as her relationship with Captain Townsend, were changed or condensed for the sake of the narrative. Despite taking liberties with Princess Margaret's life and a number of her personal relationships, I did my best to remain true to the reality on which they were based. Many of the characters in the novel are real people, but in some cases I created characters, such as Imogene Spencer-Churchill, or changed relationships, such as Princess Margaret's falling-out with Caroline Thynne, to fit the needs of the story. In reality, the Princess and Caroline remained close friends for many years, as did the Princess and most of the old Margaret Set.

Vera's involvement with Princess Margaret ends around the time of the Princess's engagement to Antony Armstrong-Jones. While he was courting the Princess, he was also dating two other women, whom he broke up with after his engagement to the Princess. It is also true that Tony enjoyed a relationship with ▶

Behind the Book *(continued)*

Camilla Fry and fathered a child by her. Despite these indiscretions, Princess Margaret and Tony were happy for a number of years after their marriage. Tony was made the Earl of Snowdon in 1961, two months before the birth of their first child, Lord David. A daughter, Lady Sarah, arrived three years later. Despite all of Princess Margaret's scandalous behavior, the Princess proved to be a devoted mother. Her children went on to lead normal lives out of the limelight and free from scandal. I believe that her success as a mother was one of her greatest achievements and a source of intense happiness and pride.

When Tony married the Princess, he entered a very circumscribed life that eventually frustrated him as much as it did Princess Margaret. Like his wife, Tony never truly found a purpose or place within the Royal Family, and he would struggle for years to cultivate an identity as more than Princess Margaret's husband. Also like Princess Margaret, he had a very strong personality, and when the passion that had drawn them together cooled, there was nothing left but animosity. They did their best to hide the rift in their marriage from the public, but over time stories of their deep loathing for each other leaked out. Both Tony and Princess Margaret indulged in extramarital affairs, but Tony proved more discreet with his. Princess Margaret's affair with a young singer in the mid-1970s became a shocking public scandal and led to an even more shocking divorce in 1978. Despite the divorce, Tony remained on good terms with the Royal Family and continued to serve as a royal photographer, snapping some of the most iconic images of Prince Charles, Princess Diana, Prince William, Prince Harry, and even Queen Elizabeth II. He passed away in 2017.

Princess Margaret would never find the love that she'd sought with Captain Townsend or the passion she'd enjoyed in her early days with Tony. Captain Townsend did marry a young Belgian woman almost twenty years his junior, who bore a striking resemblance to Princess Margaret. They remained married until his death in 1995. Princess Margaret would meet Captain Townsend one last time in 1993, but they never were what they had been to each other in the early 1950s. The Princess's ▶

drinking, chain-smoking, and scandalous behavior eventually took their toll, and after years of failing health, she passed away on February 9, 2002.

One of the challenges in writing this story was navigating the often complex and confusing titles of the British aristocracy. Dukes are at the top of the hereditary hierarchy beneath the Royal Family. Beneath dukes are marquesses, earls, viscounts, and barons. The four highest titles—duke, marquess, earl, and viscount—usually hold additional lesser titles. The first sons of these aristocrats use one of their father's lesser titles, if available, until he inherits. In this novel, Johnny Dalkeith is called Lord Dalkeith because he was the heir to the Duke of Buccleuch and used his father's lesser title, Earl of Dalkeith. Younger sons of dukes, marquesses, and earls are styled "lord," while younger sons of viscounts and barons use "honorable." The daughters of dukes, marquesses, earls, and viscounts are given the title "lady." Barons' daughters use the term "honorable." All of a baron's children, including the heir, use the title "honorable," as seen with Vera and Colin Tennant.

Princess Margaret's life spanned a time of great change. During the first four decades of the twentieth century, the last of the old royalty and nobility, and the honors accorded to them, were greatly weakened by World Wars I and II. The many mid-century social changes ended them for good, but it was the old world that Princess Margaret had been raised to inhabit, and that was gone by the time she reached adulthood. I enjoyed researching and exploring this changing time through Princess Margaret and Vera and the conflicts it created for both of them. The touch of glamour that the early 1950s imbued was fun to re-create, as was the life of this very complex and conflicted Princess. ∾

Reading Group Guide

1. What do you think attracted Vera to Princess Margaret and her Set? To what extent do you think Princess Margaret truly liked Vera? In what ways was Vera perhaps just a new "bauble" to toy with?

2. How do you view Princess Margaret? In what ways is she perhaps a tragic figure? In what ways was she her own worst enemy?

3. If Princess Margaret had actually married Peter Townsend, do you feel they would have been happy together? Why or why not?

4. The author chose to tell the story of Princess Margaret through the eyes of one of her friends. Why do you think the author made this creative choice?

5. Princess Margaret was as glamorous and fascinating in her day as Princess Diana was in hers. Are there ways in which you think their lives were similar or different? Who, if anyone, do you think is the current Margaret in the British Royal Family?

6. Why do you think Vera chose to stay with Princess Margaret for so long?

7. Vera dreams of going to America. What do you imagine America means to someone like Vera, who had to live through the deprivations and bombings of World War II?

8. Princess Margaret once said, "I have always had a dread of becoming a passenger in life." Do you think she succeeded in not becoming a passenger in life?

9. Antony Armstrong-Jones seemed to make Princess Margaret happy for a time. Who do you think was at fault for the failure of their marriage? Or was it possible that it was never meant to survive?

10. Ultimately, Vera makes the right choice for the direction her life will take. Did Princess Margaret ever make these right choices? How do you think her life could have been different if she'd made different choices, or was she a product of her times? ∾

Discover great authors, exclusive offers, and more at hc.com.